PRO1
4th Aug

It was just before midnight that the carriage screeched to a halt at the dockside. The door was flung open, and the newborn baby was wrenched from the arms of the screaming wet nurse, and quickly taken on board the waiting ship, which quickly vanished into the darkness.

Less than five minutes later a volley of shots rang out. There would be no witnesses.

CHAPTER 1
Friday 11th September 2009

'Alix I'm so sorry to hear about your mum,' Tony Edwards stood up in the crowded bar that was the usual Friday evening scrimmage in the Rose and Crown in Ely in Cambridgeshire England.
'Well, I can't say I'm sorry, as dementia is a terrible thing, and mother had been in a home for too long, not a cheap exercise either' said with a grimace, 'so at least that is over.'
Tony looked at Alix, 'Is the Head going to give you some time off?'
'Absolutely no chance, I wouldn't ask, and he probably doesn't even know.' After a moments pause Alix added 'No History class tomorrow', so get the pints in!'

Moments later the two of them were sat in the corner, and Alix having swallowed a good mouthful of his beer, continued the conversation. 'You do know that mother and I haven't seen eye to eye for years, really ever since Helen went away and didn't come back. At which point Alix looked a bit wistful, and slightly hesitant. 'You must remember Helen, the love of my life, looking straight at Tony.' You did me a favour in one respect by setting up our original date, then after she left, mother then tried to bag me off with some absolute horrors and she never quite forgave me for dumping them.'

At which point Tony giggled, 'God that was a lifetime ago, so what were their names again?'

'God knows'
'Well,' Tony said, 'I can tell you, there was Sheila, preceded by Morag, preceded by Anna as I remember.'
'My God I don't know where my mother found them, they were awful, but I'll always wonder what happened to Helen.' Alix said.
'And with respect you should know, as you arranged the blind date with the two of them, and at least you ended up marrying Jane.'
'Yes, and look how that ended', said Tony, shaking his head sadly then downing most of his pint.
'Tony let me get you another drink,' returning moments later with two full pint glasses and two large whiskies.
That was close to the last thing Alix remembered as his lawyer friend absolutely ensured he drank enough to drown any sorrow he felt.

CHAPTER 2

Saturday morning arrived to find Alix very much the worse for wear, sitting in the kitchen of his mother's house which he had never managed to leave, as he had never fallen in love again, or even got close after losing Helen.

His head hurt, even a black coffee and two Alka-Seltzer fizzing away in the glass of water wasn't much help, when the noise of the radio playing quietly in the background was overwhelmed by the ringtones of the doorbell.

'I'll kill Tony' was Alix's thought as he tied up his dressing gown and staggered to the door, to unexpectedly be confronted by a large grey haired man in a heavy blue overcoat, holding out what seemed to be a small business card in his hand
'Good morning I am sorry to trouble you so early, but my name is Willem Barentsz,'.......
'Sorry I don't see salesmen' Alix moved to close the door.
'No no, I am a lawyer,' raising his hand, 'I represent the legal firm Johann Duyck from Ypres, and now your mother has died I have come to see you on behalf of your late grandmother.'
The astonished frown on Alix's face must have shown that in his slightly befuddled state he wasn't really taking anything too much in.

Mr. Barentsz took a small step forward, 'look I have some information your Belgian granny wants you to have, so may I come in?'

'Belgian granny?'

'Yes, your granny is Belgian, but possibly, quite obviously in fact you didn't know that.'

'No, I definitely didn't, is this some kind of a con or a wind up?'

'Absolutely not, please take my card, and you can ring the number on it, if you need more proof.'

'Yes of course, I'm sorry I just wasn't expecting anyone, I'm normally teaching, but one of my friends decided I should drown my sorrows, and I've no class to teach this morning so here I am,' he added somewhat ruefully, 'hungover.'

'Of course I understand,' and suddenly Alix realised the accent was definitely not English, which as he said to himself was logical, but why Ypres?'

'Please wait a minute.' With that Alix closed the door and went back into the kitchen, opened his laptop and found Duyck's website in Ypres, to see a photograph of the man standing at his front door standing next to Johann Duyck himself.

Returning to the front door, Alix apologised to his unexpected visitor for keeping him waiting.

'I'm sorry, one has to be careful in this day and age, please come in.'

His visitor smiled, 'you can't be too careful so no doubt you have just checked me out!'
Alix led the lawyer into the kitchen, gestured to a seat at the table, thinking I'm not sure about this, so I really don't know I want him to be here long, but good manners are necessary as I am always telling my boys.
'Sorry again, I am being very rude, you've obviously come a long way. Would you like a coffee, or even some breakfast?'
'No, it's fine thank you, a coffee, black, two sugars would be great', and with that the lawyer put his briefcase which Alix hadn't noticed before on the table, unclipped the two locks, and brought out a folder.
'Before I can give you any information from your Belgian granny I need to see some identification proving you are in fact Alix McBride'
'Yes of course' and Alix went across opened a drawer and brought out his passport, which he handed over.
The Belgian Lawyer looking at his telephone added, 'just to confirm, your telephone number ends in 206?'
'Yes, that's correct.'
'I think you've passed the security,' the lawyer smiled as he handed the folder to Alix.
  'Would you like me to leave whilst you read this?'

Alix looked at him, eyebrows raised.
'Do you mean you want me to read it now?'
Shuffling in his chair Alix continued slightly aggressively. 'Anyway, what is this all about?'
The lawyer replied, 'I think if you read it you will understand. As I said it is information your Belgian granny needs you to have, and obviously she can't be here as she has been dead for some time.'
 He then added 'You need to read this, for that is my explicit instructions from Herr Dyuck. There are some other things as well that you need to see, and some legal stuff to sign. I think you need to read this now, and perhaps you might want to ask some questions afterwards,' adding.
'Oh, thank you', as Alix handed over the coffee, 'In fact, it would be sensible if you had a lawyer here as well.
Alix sat down with a thump, not really having paid attention.
'Why?
That question became irrelevant as he looked at the envelope which had a wax seal, something Alix hadn't seen before, which made him go the drawer and use a sharp kitchen knife to leave the seal intact.
The paper was heavy with two folds, and Alix opened it very tentatively, noticing immediately the spidery yet beautiful writing, and the signature at

the bottom was that of Granny Dubré, whom he couldn't remember ever meeting.

His first thought strangely enough was 'I wish I could write like that, and his second thought was my semi-literate sixth form could take a lesson here.'

His next thought was who on earth is this Dubré woman, who this man is telling me, is my granny? Slowly he began to read the document, because that was what it felt like, much more than a letter.

My Dearest Alix,
I am only sorry we didn't have the opportunity to get to know each other. I am your Granny Maria, and I love you very much. I am sure you are very like your grandfather Willie, and he would have wanted you to know who you are and where you came from.
Firstly, I have to tell you the house you have lived in with your mother in Ely is in fact owned by you, and I know this will come as a surprise, but I originally bought it for your parents so they would have a safe place for you to be brought up in.
Secondly, Chateau Hugend which I think you know as the large house overlooking the military cemetery where your grandfather lies buried. I can tell you it is our property, as is the 170 or so hectares of land we still own. In fact, you have owned it since your father died but it has been held in trust by our lawyers Frederick Dyuck in Ypres until the death of your mother. As this has now happened, there are some other things you I need to tell you.
Their representative who should be sitting on the other side of a table as you read this will also get you to sign some documents allowing you to access various bank accounts, which you as the owner of the chateau now have control over, although the expertise of Dyuck's will help you with all of this until you have found your feet.
There is also money in stocks and shares I have been able to accumulate over the years, and also some money in the Bank of Ireland . Dyuck's hold my last will and testament, which leaves all my financial affairs to you

You obviously will be anxious to find out what all of this means and how it has come about. It is now that my letter to you becomes more difficult for me to write.

It is imperative that you understand, your father who had been an extremely brave man during the Second World War was murdered but reported as having taken his own life.

Also, I must tell you that my beloved Willie didn't die a soldier's death in the War, but he was murdered by one of the young estate workers and his friends. The reason being jealousy because your grandfather had chosen me, and so they stabbed my poor darling Willie to death.

It is important that you take legal advice before doing anything or signing any documents.

I must however ask you to do one thing for our family. Please visit a village in Ireland in a place called Blacksmills just outside Cork. You need to go to the church and ask the priest for the gravestone of a McBride.

All my love
Granny Dubré

Alix read the letter again, without really making much sense of it.

Looking at the lawyer, and saying in a voice that was almost a whisper, 'am I just being dull, or for reasons I don't understand, have I just inherited a house here in Ely, a chateau in Ypres, plus about 500 acres if my conversion from hectares is correct?'

The lawyer nodded and re-opened the briefcase which had magically returned from the floor to his lap.

'There is more you need to know and sign for.. here' handing over a brown envelope to Alix,'

Your Granny's last will and testament which you must read.'
'I'll get my lawyer.'
'Yes of course, that would be very sensible.' As he said that the lawyer nodded towards the table. 'There are some documents here you need to sign, the transfer of ownership, the bank accounts, and a few other details to be confirmed, although you have already confirmed your identity.' He smiled, 'after all we'd all hate this to fall into the hands of an imposter.'
'I'm glad you said that because I'd want my solicitor here to make sure all this is above board, so if you don't mind, I'll just see if I can catch him…' knowing bloody fine his idle and probably hungover friend would still be sound asleep.

CHAPTER 3

During the thirty minutes it took a startled Tony to arrive, Alix had been handed a photograph which Granny Dubré had included with the documents. It was a group of very young-looking soldiers dated 25th May 1916, and underneath the words 4th Platoon 8th Battalion The Royal Munster Fusiliers Although faded, the names of the lads were quite easily discernible, including 'Fusilier W. McBride'.

Alix had never seen a photo of his grandfather, and so young as well, but he must have only been about seventeen, eighteen at most having been born on the 6th of June 1898.
 As he was studying the photograph, the doorbell rang again. Standing in the porch was a decidedly rough looking Tony. No greetings, just, 'what the fuck is this all about.'
Ten minutes later, and a steaming black coffee with four spoonsful of sugar, Tony slowly began to be a lawyer again.

Documents were soon studied by him, the contents of which made Tony whistle.
'Alix I assume you have read your grandmother's will.'
'Yes.'
'So you understand that she has left everything to you?'

'Yes'

Tony shook his head, 'Have you any idea how much money you have been left, never mind the share value?'

'No'

'Well, the shares alone must be worth 150 million, never mind the 150,000 euros in her bank account.'

'You are joking, I didn't see that. It isn't possible' said Alix who had gone very white in the face, and immediately leant on the nearest chair

'No Alix I am not.'

Tony turned to the lawyer and said, 'Do you know where all this money has come from, because there is no way it is from the chateau and the farmland.'

'I believe at one point it has come from something called the Chaesar Estate, but all that was long before my time or even Herr Duyck's time. So, I am sorry I cannot be of much help on that, but we will enquire when I get back home.'

At this point the lawyer stood up to leave. 'Thank you for your courtesy, and I will expect to welcome you both to our offices in Ypres soon, and we will arrange the various transfers to England.'

As the Belgian lawyer was shown out and Alix closed the door he turned, walked back into the kitchen and said 'Bloody hell that's unbelievable. Have I imagined all that?'

'No, you haven't' Tony said with a grimace', the only question now is, will you carry on teaching, because by any standards you are an unbelievably wealthy man, and a landowner to boot!!'
'Yes, but what about all of this business about my father, and Granny's letter. I can't just ignore that, don't you think I should go to that place in Ireland?'

As the fullness of everything he had just read and heard began to hit him, Alix sat down somewhat heavily onto the dining room chair.
 'Tony, you're my best mate, just tell me what you think I should do, I am totally hungover….'
'Me too' Tony responded, 'but I tell you what, father would be a good person to ask, because I think he had some dealings with your granny,' looking at his watch, Tony added,' shit, I must go, I'm supposed to be helping father move some furniture.' As he got to his feet Tony saw at the same moment as Alix, a brown envelope the lawyer seemed to have left behind.

Alix picked it up, and it was open, he tilted it up and the contents slid out. A slightly torn and very aged photograph, and another envelope.
Alix picked up the photograph, seeing immediately the same young man as in the other photograph.

'God that's my grandfather, and that must be granny.'
As Alix said that, at the same time he was opening the envelope, and unfolding the slightly scruffy and well-worn sheet of paper, whilst peering over his glasses at the writing.

'What on earth is that gibberish in the envelope? Here', as he handed it over the Tony who had sat down again.
Tony frowned, 'well it isn't dated, that's a bit odd, and then read it out loud.

My Darling Will,
Yellow and red roses from you all bunched together just serve to remind me of the countless wonderful times we spent together, my darling. Now you leave me heartbroken as I am here all alone, so why did you have to take your love and go.
Yesterday we were together and now you are gone, everything is lost please can I be with you for eternity.
Yes it does hurt so much, just hellishly every minute of every day. There will never be another you, so I cherish every single wonderful moment we were together as the best time in my life and I will love you forever. '

'No idea at all, it's obviously a love letter written by your granny, because that is her handwriting, and I can sort of understand why she kept it. It's quite scary in one way to think'…….Tony hesitated for a second, 'well it makes no sense, it's almost as if she wrote it after your grandfather died. The flowers makes no sense at all.'

'It isn't signed' Alix said. Tony continued 'We actually have no proof at all apart from her letter to you in the same handwriting, that it is your granny who wrote it.'

'I suppose he could have given her the flowers just before he was killed' was Alix's immediate response.'

Stuffing the letter and the photograph back in the envelope, Alix asked Tony again, 'what the hell do you think I should do, go to this place in Ireland, or….'

Tony cut in, 'I do need to go, give me a couple of hours and then come over and see dad, and I'm sure although his short-term memory is poor, he is phenomenal when it comes to remembering completely irrelevant facts from long ago. The history questions on University Challenge, for example, he consistently will get the right answer even when the highly intelligent team can't!'

Also he'll know about this Chaesar thing, and his advice will still be relevant and good.' As he walked towards the door Tony said over his shoulder, 'I'll give you a call in a few minutes just to confirm when to come round, and we'll take a longer look at exactly what all this means for you.'

With that Tony left leaving Alix stunned to the point of numbness, just sitting at the table staring into space.

 Twenty minutes later the phone rang, 'Mother has lost a crown off a front tooth and isn't keen to be seen by you or anyone else for that matter, but how about you come for Sunday lunch tomorrow, and hopefully whoever is the emergency dentist will have sorted her out.
Mum and Dad are looking forward to seeing you, because it's been ages, and they've not been back from Kyrenia long.'
'Yes of course I understand, I don't think I'd be too keen to see anyone with a front tooth missing either. As he put the phone down Alix muttered 'Shit'
Patience wasn't one of his best attributes, and he wanted answers, if there were answers, and now if not sooner.
 Alix couldn't wait until tomorrow, so he opened his laptop and using the map software he located Blacksmills, just outside Cork, and looking at his watch, he literally ran to his car, not for one second thinking about booking the flight.
By some miracle, not only did he get a seat on the flight but also on the one returning mid evening to Stansted.

CHAPTER 4

On arrival in Cork, it was raining and Alix in his rush hadn't thought to bring a coat. Fortunately, the car rental office and pick up were all in the same building, and within about thirty minutes he pulled up in front of quite a considerable church for such a small village.

Alix got out, noticing that the rain had stopped to be replaced by warm sunshine, so he removed his jacket, slung it over his arm and walked into a wonderfully cool church and straight into a man he assumed, by the fact he was wearing a dog collar, to be the village priest.

He was not what Alix had imagined a priest to look like in an old Irish village, virtually untouched by the 21st century. He was young, with receding auburn hair, freckles and an infectious smile.

'Welcome,' he said with a pleasing Irish lilt. 'I am Father O'Connor and how can I be of assistance to you on this fine day?'

'My name is Alix McBride and I think I'm looking for a grave with the name McBride on it, but to be honest I'm only here because of a letter I've received this morning.'

'You'll not be the first or the last to be looking for an ancestor, and you're hoping I'll have the records that the Four Courts can't supply you with.'

It was more a statement than a question, but it seemed to deserve an answer.

'What name did you say again?'

'Willie McBride.'

'Yes, I think we do have a McBride in the churchyard. Would it help if I showed you where it is? McBride isn't a common name around here; this might be because a lot of the families in this village left and emigrated to the United States.'

As he talked, he gently ushered Alix out from the coolness of the church into the warm daylight.

They walked into an old churchyard, surrounded by oak trees, their leaves just beginning to turn, the grass a beautiful green and immaculately cut between the old headstones, some of which leaned at various angles, some toppled right over, and others full of inscriptions. They stopped in front of a small tablet set into the ground. The inscription read:

WILLIE MCBRIDE
SON OF JAMES AND HELEN MCBRIDE
4TH AUGUST 1898–30TH NOVEMBER 1898
HE RESTS WITH GOD

Alix was totally shocked and looked again, as if he couldn't believe his eyes. He even got his glasses out of the top pocket of his shirt and looked for a third time. He took his diary out of his pocket, and flicked through the pages until he found what he was looking for. There could be no mistake at all.

The priest looked on anxiously.

'Are you alright?'
Alix looked at him, his heart pounding.
'Yes, I think so, but somewhat shocked, as my grandfather Willie McBride was born on the same date as is on this headstone but was killed at Ypres in 1917. I've been to his grave, so this is very odd – very strange indeed.'
There must have been a full two minutes of silence as neither man spoke or moved after Alix's shocked comment.

'Are there any other McBride gravestones to see – the parents, for example?'
'Actually, come to think of it, there isn't. McBride isn't a name from this village, really, and there are none to the best of my knowledge who live here now. I'll check the parish rolls and registers, to see if there is anything that relates to that time, but I have a feeling you're going to be unlucky.'
The two of them retreated into the coolness of the church, but not before Alix had taken a couple of photographs of the headstone, still confused at what he had just seen.
The priest, who had disappeared leaving Alix to his thoughts, returned after what seemed no more than a couple of minutes.
'You're in luck. I have a baptism of William McBride here,' he announced as he brandished a heavy dust-covered book, 'with the address as Beech

Farm Cottages, with his father James McBride described as a farm labourer.'

At least that was progress and might in time help him to get to the bottom of this mystery.

Suddenly the priest exclaimed, 'There is something else, just hang on,' and he almost ran towards the church altar. He reappeared bearing a large chalice.

The priest held it out towards Alix. It most certainly wasn't light as Alix took it into his hands, and he put it down quite quickly on a chair nearby.

'The chalice is the cup used to hold the Blood of Christ in the liturgy of the Eucharist, and it should be made of fourteen-carat gold, but poor churches like ours normally only have gold plate, sometimes even brass.'

Alix and the priest leant forward to read the inscription, which was as clear as the day it was new.

The priest broke the silence. 'The McBride family must have had a lot of money for a farm labourer, because a gold-plated chalice like that would not have been cheap.'

Alix looked more closely at the chalice and realised that he was looking at a gold hallmark, so no wonder it was so heavy. He shook his head in disbelief. 'I hope you have this insured, it's certainly not brass, or gold plate, this is solid gold, and you ought to be keeping it somewhere safe, like a strongbox.'

'You're joking' then with some hesitation, the priest said, 'well no, it just sits out, and is used by the congregation every week, and no-one has ever commented before. I assume it must be marked in some way or another.'

Yes, and the marks on this show an anchor indicating it was tested and found to be pure in Birmingham, the number 18 meaning 18 carat gold, so very high quality. I'm not sure what year the date letter indicates, but my guess is 'x' is around 1897-98.'

'How do you know that?'

The date young Willie died, because we must assume whoever had it made, had it made for the parents of the child, but they must have been wealthy for there is a lot of gold in that chalice.'

'Alix took out his pen and wrote down the marks on the chalice on an envelope.

'Would you mind if I took a photograph?'

He took a photo of the chalice and the hallmark with his mobile phone.

'How on earth could the McBride's afford something as beautiful and as expensive as this on a farm labourer's wage?' Alix muttered, more to himself but loud enough for the priest to hear.

'God moves in mysterious ways,' said Father O'Connor with twinkling eyes, 'but if you give me a couple of hours, I may be able to find out how it came about from the church records.'

'I'd be very grateful if it's not too much trouble, but in the meantime could you direct me to Beech Farm Cottages, assuming they still exist?'

'Oh, they are there alright. If you just take the road opposite the church' – the priest pointed over Alix's head – 'go for about half a mile, and on the right-hand side next to the road, there's a row of three cottages. Go on another four hundred yards and that will take you to the driveway up to Beech House itself. My advice, for what it's worth, is to go straight to the house. Major Nesbitt will be there, and I think you'll find him very approachable. The Nesbitt family are very large landowners and have been here forever, it seems. They also farm all the land, and Beech Farm Cottages is where their employees have always lived. If you want information about your great-grandparents, then the major will know exactly where to look, and I'd go now because I'm certain he'll be there.'

Alix headed for the door, talking over his shoulder.

'Thank you, Father. Can I pop back later and see if you've had any joy over the chalice?'

'Yes, of course, my son. If I'm not here, I'll be over the road.'

CHAPTER 5

Alix got back in the car, and within a couple of minutes had arrived in front of an imposing Georgian building with two Adam style pillars on either side of the large front door. The gravel crunched beneath his feet before he mounted the four stone steps up to the door, on which a highly polished brass knocker hung from a lion's mouth. Before he could knock, the door was opened and an elderly gentleman spoke in an accent more English than Irish, albeit with a lilt.

'Hello. You must be Mr McBride. My name is James Nesbitt. Please come in.'

Alix realised that the priest must have phoned, telling him to expect a visitor.

As Alix followed Major Nesbitt through the large entrance hall with staircases rising on either side to meet on a landing, he could tell from the large portraits of what must be ancestors on the walls that the Nisbett's were – despite the trace of an upper-class English accent in his host – a very well-established family in this part of County Cork. When they entered a small, book-lined room off the hall, James Nesbitt turned to face his guest.

'Can I get you a drink?' Seeing Alix's hesitation, he laughed. 'I usually have a glass of stout about this time – will you join me?'

A slightly startled Alix had thought that the elderly, tall, clean-shaven military gentleman who stood before him, slightly stooped from age, would have been more likely to offer him a pink gin, but he was nevertheless quick to say, 'Thank you – that would be very nice. You have a lovely house and grounds. Has it been in your family a long time?'

He realised his host had already disappeared out of the door.

After a few moments, Alix was drinking out of an antique silver tankard bearing a crest, already glistening and wet from the coldness of the beer fresh from the fridge. As he finished a quick mouthful of his beer, Nesbitt replied to the question Alix thought he hadn't heard, 'About three hundred and fifty years'.

'You don't have much of an Irish accent,' Alix observed.

'Perhaps because I went to Eton and then Oxford, then I was commissioned into the Micks – sorry, the Irish Guards to you – and then I stayed in the army until the early seventies, whereupon I became a stockbroker until my father died a few years ago, and now I'm here.' He gestured towards an armchair. 'For goodness' sake, take a pew.'

Alix sat down, but before he had the chance to open a conversation, James Nesbitt chipped in, 'I gather you had an ancestor who worked on the estate?'

Alix quickly gulped another mouthful of what was a truly extraordinary beer.

'Yes, my great-grandfather, James McBride, and his wife Helen lived in the farm cottages down the hill, and my grandfather William was born here in 1898. Well, I say that, but I know he died at Ypres serving with the Royal Munster Fusiliers. The only problem I have is that there is a grave down the road with his name and the date he died, showing he died here in infancy.'

'That's more than a little odd,' putting down his tankard and wiping his top lip, without quite managing to remove all the creamy head of the beer. 'So how can I be of help, because it sounds as if you might need it?'

'To be honest, I'm not sure,' Alix replied. 'You've been very hospitable already, and I hesitate to ask, but would the estate have any records from the early 1890s that might relate to my great-grandfather?'

Major Nesbitt waved towards all four walls.

'That is exactly what we have here. There are records relating to every aspect of the estate going back to the beginning, when my family first arrived. I could tell you how many beef cattle we had in 1695 and how much milk we produced in 1750. Not only that, but we also have records of the men who worked the land for us, where they lived, what rent they paid, who they married, details of their children, and what they died of. In addition, some of my ancestors kept diaries, and the entries in these are a fascinating social history of their times. When did your ancestor live here?' he ended, gesturing around the property with his right hand.

'Well, Willie was born in June 1898, and died in November that year.'

Major Nesbitt stood up, and went over to the wall opposite the windows, opened a glass door, and extracted a large, fat, leather-bound book, and 13 small ones that looked like the kind of notebooks which Alix surmised were probably the diaries. His host then placed them on the desk.

'The large book contains things like rent payments and wages from 1890 until about 1904, and the smaller ones are my grandmother's diaries, covering about the same dates. Please feel free to check through them. I think we might have some photographs from that time, too, so if you'll excuse me, I'll see if I can find them.'

Alix went immediately to the diaries, and to August 1898, almost immediately finding entries relating to his great-grandparents. He tried to reassure himself they were his family but was finding it increasingly difficult from the knowledge he had gained. Nevertheless, coincidences did happen, so he felt he mustn't leave any stones unturned. An entry in Major Nesbitt's grandmother's diary dated 10th of August stated:

The McBride's baby boy doesn't seem well. Prayed for him.

Another entry on 15th of September read:

I don't think little Willie McBride is to live, he's such a lovely baby but so poorly. I visited today and brought them some fresh cow's cream of the milk. I prayed for all of them tonight.

The next entry mentioning the McBride's was for 2nd of December 1898:

Poor Willie is in heaven. How sad and I cried for a long time and prayed for them all.

Despite the century that had passed, and even allowing for the fact that this Willie McBride couldn't possibly be his ancestor, Alix felt quite emotional after reading a diary that the writer would never have expected to be seen by anyone, never mind a total stranger. These excerpts and the whole content that Alix had read was a wonderful and tragic picture of life and death in Victorian Ireland.

Major Nesbitt re-emerged through the door, carrying several pictures.

'I think we may have your great-grandparents here, and perhaps even your grandfather. From about 1895 my grandfather began to use the most modern technology. He was one of the first in Cork to have photos taken of his family, and from the writing underneath, this photo seems to show Lady Nesbitt, my grandmother, with her two servants, Mary and Helen. Looking at the picture of the estate workforce and their wives and children in eighteen-ninety-eight, the same Helen is holding a tiny baby, and is sitting next to a man. Whilst there are some forty people in the photo, this must be your great-grandmother, holding your grandfather, and' – Nesbitt pointed at the man next to her – 'that must be your great-grandfather.' He smiled and said, 'Can't see much family resemblance there, mind you!'

Significantly, the 1899 picture showed only Mr. and Mrs. McBride, as did those from 1900 and 1901, but in the 1902 photo there was another baby. The 1904 picture, the last that Major Nesbitt had brought in, contained no Helen McBride, or for that matter the child or great-grandfather James.

For some reason Alix continued to search through the diaries, and after reading many pages with no mention at all, he finally found on 24 th October 1902:

A very well-dressed man arrived at the house in a very smart horse and trap, which excited the servants. Very posh English voice and he asked for the McBride household.

The entry dated 3rd February 1903 said:

Helen asked to give her notice. She said they were going to emigrate to America, and they had booked their passage. She wore smart clothes, from where I don't know.

The final entry was for 4th March 1903:

The McBride's left today in a large horse and trap. I think it was the same one we saw before. They weren't sad, but I was, and I cried, and prayed to God they would all be well.

Alix put down the diary and sank back into the chair. He had undoubtedly solved one part of the mystery. A stranger had entered James and Helen's lives, and as a result the McBride's, plus one offspring, had suddenly become better off financially, and as a result had upped sticks and taken off for the United States.

Whilst Alix was ruminating over this turn of events, the major had been studying the larger book containing all the farming and accounts details.

'This is a bit odd,' he announced. 'I've got as far as 1903, and James McBride has continued to be paid, and then it stops suddenly in the first week in March. The entry here says that he has left and asked that his week's wages be divided amongst the farm workers, to include his laying money.'

Alix looked up from his chair. 'What's laying money?'

'Back in those days, when a man started work his first week's wages weren't paid at the time. It was known as a 'week's laying money' and it was left 'laying' until the worker left, probably so he had wages to tide him over until he could get another job.'

Alix looked at his watch. 'Oh, I really need to go. I'm on the eight o'clock flight from Dublin to Stansted, and I've got to see the priest again before I go.'

The major smiled. 'Oh, young Father O'Connor; he's a lovely man. You would have guessed that he rang to tell me you were on your way here.'

Alix continued as if he hadn't heard.

'Thank you so much for all this information. It's just amazing, but I must assume that James came into some money, which enabled him to change his life and emigrate. That news is fantastic, but it doesn't help me except that in a way he is excluded as the source of the wealth. I didn't tell you when I arrived, but I have inherited a huge amount of money from somewhere, and James McBride seems to have more money than a labourer's wages, but I can't see where he fits into my past. His son Willie is obviously not my grandfather, as he died in infancy, so the man buried at Ypres and who appears to be my grandfather seems to be a man with no past. It's all very mysterious, and you have been a huge help. Thank you for the stout – it was quite superb.'

'My pleasure,' said the major. 'If I can be of any more help, then please call.' At which point he went into his jacket pocket. 'Here's my card,' with that he shook Alix's hand and escorted him back to the front door. Within moments Alix was back in the car, and at the door of the church.

Alix entered having half-expecting to find the door locked, but in fact the priest was inside standing by the pulpit and almost seemed to be waiting for him.
'Hello again, Mr McBride. I've got some information for you. Did you find your visit to the big house helpful?'
'Very, and thank you for opening the door for me, so to speak. I appreciate that. The Major was a very nice man, but what have you managed to find out?'
The priest smiled.
'Well, the chalice seems to have been presented on behalf of the McBride's, from a firm or shop called Mappin and Webb in London in March 1903. I can't tell you any more than what the parish records say, which is that it was delivered here as a gift from James and Helen McBride, who had apparently left for the United States to start a new life.'
Alix realised that there was little more he could do in Blacksmills, so he wished the priest good day and thanked him for his efforts. Conscious that many churches were short of funds, he also slipped a 20-euro note into the offertory box on his way out, but then realised for perhaps the first time that, given his new-found wealth, he should have donated more.

CHAPTER 6

On the journey back to the airport, Alix's mind was in a turmoil.

How could two people with the same name Willie McBride, with the same date of birth, but one buried in a churchyard in Ireland as a small child, and the other in a military grave in Ypres, having been murdered be a coincidence. That was just about possible, because the names whilst not as common as Smith or Jones are nevertheless not uncommon in Ireland.

No that isn't the point, he told himself, and that is where it goes far beyond coincidence.

How on earth could a woman telling him she was his granny in a letter brought to him by a lawyer from Belgium, recommend he visited a grave in Ireland where he found all of this out?

A woman that he had to the best of his knowledge no real memory of. All of this at the same time as discovering he had inherited serious wealth including a chateau and all the land that went with it. His brain was working overtime with all these thoughts.

Alix spent the time in the car trying to prioritise what he should do next. Both frustrated and excited by what was turning into a hunt for clues about his family almost like something out of a crime novel –

or, as he thought ruefully, even a murder story – he resolved to do three things.

First, he had to find out what happened to James and Helen McBride; even though they seemed no longer to be family, he felt some kind of affinity towards them, especially after reading the Nesbitt diary.

Second, he would see if Mappin & Webb had any trace of the chalice in their records.

Thirdly he needed to find out about the Chaesar Estate and who they were and how they fitted into everything else, although they seemed almost on the fringe.

The flight back to Stansted left on time, and arrived on time, and Alix spent the flight with his brain in turmoil.

When Alix got into his car to drive home from the airport, he opened his mobile phone which had been surprisingly quiet, and found he had accidentally switched it off, although in his hungover state he had no idea when.

Immediately it rang, and there were four messages, all somewhat inevitably from Tony, and Alix could hear the frustration in his voice.

'Where the hell are you? Mum and dad are really looking forward to seeing you, so I need to know that you will be coming to lunch tomorrow.

Alix was about to respond to the 121 messages when his phone rang and not unexpectedly it was Tony.

'Where the hell have you been?'
'In Blacksmills in Ireland, but I'll tell you about it when I see you, the traffic here is horrendous, so I need to concentrate.'
'OK, Mum and Dad are looking forward to seeing you, and Dad tells me he can answer some of your questions because the firm had some dealings with your granny. So, see you about 12 tomorrow'. With that the phone clicked.
Alix made no attempt to reconnect as his mind was still reeling at what he had seen and heard over the previous few hours. There are coincidences in life, but this could not be a coincidence.
What on earth did it all mean?

When Alix finally got home it was close to midnight but, with the bit firmly between his teeth he went and signed up to Ancestry.com. He then looked for information on people emigrating from Ireland in 1903. It would be after 4am when he got to bed, but he was excited at what he had found out.
James and Helen McBride had sailed from Cork on 1st of June 1903 on the RMS Saxonia.
Launched in 1899, the Saxonia was a Cunard liner with a huge single chimney stack that took thousands of emigrants across the Atlantic from Liverpool to Boston via Cork. Alix discovered that the passenger accommodation had space for 164 in first class, 200 in second class and 1,600 in third

class or steerage. Most if not all the Irish emigrants – along with many continental Europeans seeking their fortune – travelled in steerage, but Alix wasn't entirely surprised to discover that the McBride's had travelled first class.

He went to bed with his head still whirling. Where had the money come from? How do you go from earning a few pounds a month to being able to afford that kind of luxury? These remained the unanswered questions that just wouldn't go away, and despite the lateness of the hour sleep was nigh on impossible.

At shortly before 12 noon on the Sunday Alix was tentatively walking toward Tony's house when he came upon Tony walking towards him.

'I was just coming to make sure you were out of bed McBride.'

Just stop being an old Etonian snob you know perfectly well I have a first name, adding 'I know you think all Old Stoics are some kind of inferior species…….' At this point his voice trailed off as he could see Tony laughing at him, 'it never fails'….

'What never fails?'

'The wind up, I've been doing the same thing for well over twenty years now with the McBride thing, and you never fail to rise to the bait.'

'Anyway', ignoring Tony's last remark Willie added, 'how is your mother by the way, I've just realised I didn't ask how she was?'

Tony smiled. 'Oh, mother fusses over me as if I was still sixteen, and most days father who is now eighty-eight years old wants to come into the office to check I'm running the place properly. You know what they say about old lawyers – they don't die, they just lose their briefs!'

Tony paused for a second, still smiling at his lousy joke. 'We're almost home, so you can see for yourself,' adding, 'but tell me what you found in Ireland.'

'I will, just let's get into the house first before the rain starts.'

The house looked exactly as Alix remembered it from his student days. Many were the times that Mrs Edwards cooked mountains of bacon and eggs to feed several hungry students, himself included, and Alix used to love going there because it was always full of people. Tony had two brothers and a sister, so it was a real family home, and Alix had a sudden memory of how quiet his own home was by comparison, which was one of the reasons he had been a frequent visitor to the Edwards's house.

Tony flung open the front door and called out, 'Mum, Dad, Alix is here.'

Mrs Edwards came out of the kitchen, apron on, drying her hands. Apart from the fact that she looked somewhat older, it was a scene from Alix's past. The number of times he had seen her wearing an apron, walking towards him, about to ask him and the gang of friends if they were hungry, was beyond count.

'Alix – how lovely to see you looking so well. It's been such a long time.' She kissed him full on the mouth. 'We were so sorry to hear about your mother,' added as an afterthought, 'but you do look thin – are you eating enough?'

'Thank you – you look terrific Mrs Edwards! I'm sorry I haven't been to see you.'

Tony's father emerged from the sitting room, glass in hand – another familiar sight.

'Hello, Alix, you look well. Still trying to control those awful King's louts, I suspect.'

Mr Edwards was looking his age, but he still had the twinkle in his eye that Alix remembered. 'Sorry about your mother. You're not eating enough – too thin by far.'

Alix's stomach reminded him that he hadn't eaten since the previous day. Since his mother had gone into care, he had relied upon school catering for his main meals, but the weekends and his lack of cooking skills put paid to that.

'We've got the briefcase,' continued Mr Edwards, 'so come into the study, and I'll get us a drink – and then you can open it up and see what's inside.'

'What briefcase?'

'Didn't Tony tell you we found a briefcase along with Grannie Dubré's files?'

'No, he certainly did not,' looking daggers at Tony. 'Well dad I could hardly tell Alix about something I didn't know about myself, and you've obviously been rummaging around in the basement at the office,' Tony added angrily, 'and I'm fed up telling you, that you are retired, I'm in charge, not you!'

The quite hostile atmosphere was saved by the arrival of Mrs. Edwards out of the kitchen with a tray carrying three bottles of beer and glasses, a bowl of crisps and another of peanuts. It's incredible, thought Alix, how parents whose children are in their forties still assume they like beer, crisps and peanuts, and by and large are usually correct – although at that moment he could do with a stiff whisky.

Alix dismissed these uncharitable thoughts, as his nostrils were filled with the aroma of garlic and roasting meat, and he remembered just how hospitable the Edwards were, and how once again they were drawing him into the bosom of their family.

Calm again, the three men settled comfortably into the well-worn leather armchairs, Tony looked at his father who had the briefcase on his lap.

'So, what's with the briefcase?'

At this point Mr. Edwards interjected,

'Alix please tell me what you found out in Ireland.'

Mr. Edwards didn't appear to hear Tony who repeated in a louder voice. 'The briefcase what's in it?
'His father quickly responded. 'Shouldn't we leave Alix on his own to check it out?'
Alix looked at Tony who was slowly shaking his head.
'Well, I might as well open the briefcase now, I'm sure there's nothing incriminating….' at which point Mr. Edwards cut in, 'please put us out of our misery and tell us what you found in Ireland, Tony told me you went to see a grave.

Alix half joked, 'Are you sitting comfortably, then I'll begin,' to which Tony replied with a slight grin, 'Come on McBride, it's time to sing for your lunch' which Alix totally ignored.
He began his tale with a short description of the flight, the hire car, the church and the priest. 'It was quite unbelievable, there in the churchyard was the grave of a baby 'Willie McBride with exactly the same date of birth as my grandfather, only he was just a baby when he died.' As he said that he clicked on his phone and let the two of them see the photo he took. You could have cut the atmosphere with a knife, and just a moments silence, followed by Tony 'Well what happened next?'
The priest found the record of the birth and where the parents lived which was on the local estate. I

went up there and the landowner a very nice ex Guards officer dug out the farm details and his great aunt's diary which described a very sick McBride baby, and its tragic death.'

'How very sad.' His two companions spoke in unison, followed by Mr. Edwards commenting, 'then what happened next?'

'Well, this is where the plot thickens because apparently a very well-dressed man turned up and took them away in a smart horse and trap, and the father left his wages to the farm hands……'

'That's very odd'

'Well, it gets odder still, because I should have said the parents presented a communion chalice to the church in memory of young Willie,'

'That wasn't totally unexpected, was it?'

'It was only solid gold made by Mappin and Webb'

'Bloody Hell' said Tony, Alix continued, 'and then last night I found they had emigrated to the USA on the RMS Saxonia, travelling First Class.'

'It just makes no sense at all, I'm sure you'll agree with that, but I'd be happy to have your take on it.

Mr. Edwards was the first to speak, 'I agree, but perhaps the briefcase might shed some light on this mystery, so I suggest you open it now.'

CHAPTER 7

As Alix leant forward to pick it up Mr. Edwards said, 'I'm even more intrigued after all you've just told us, and as far as I can remember it has been in the vaults since your grandmother died, so that must be over 40 years ago. I might be able to help with the contents, that is if you don't mind me staying.'
With that he stood up and handed Alix the briefcase, and along with Tony turned to make for the door.
'Don't be so daft, sit down, I'm sure there can't be anything that is so family confidential I wouldn't want anyone to see. You are after all my lawyer as well as old friends, and now we all know about my grandfather, I'm also sure you are as intrigued as I am.' Nodding to Mr. Edwards, 'also you might be able to help me with whatever is inside.'
Tony and his father both sat down again and leaned forward in anticipation as Alix took the briefcase and sat it lengthwise on his knee.
The catch easily fell open to display two sections within. One contained some faded photographs, which Alix took out, before closing the case again.
'Can I do this at the desk, it'll be a lot easier for us all to look at it.'
'No problem.'
Alix sat down at the desk and the two Edwards men stood looking over his shoulder.

At this point the shrill tones of Mrs. Edwards rang out seeking help in the kitchen, and Mr Edwards left with a 'Just carry on I'll be back in a minute.'

Alix pulled out a picture of Intake 131, 8th Battalion Royal Munster Fusiliers; in what was obviously professionally done, complete with mount, and listed there on the mount, in the second row at the far left, was Fusilier W. McBride.
The next photograph was of a family group: a woman Alix immediately recognised as his mother, holding a baby, and alongside her an older woman.
'Do you think that is Grannie Dubré?' At which point Mr. Edwards, who had silently re-entered the room nodded as if to confirm that was the case, but he remained silent almost as if he didn't want to break the considerable tension that was now in the room.
Next there was another, almost identical, photograph of a baby with its mother, and a younger looking woman compared to the last picture who must be Grannie Dubré. This photograph left Alix somewhat confused. Who was this baby? Did he have an older brother or sister about whom he knew nothing? Perhaps his mother had been godmother to a friend's child, and this was just a family photograph. But if that was the case, why was his grandmother in the picture?
'Just who the bloody hell is that?'

Tony shook his head 'God knows.'

'Let's see what else there is, it might shed some light.'

He re-opened the briefcase and took out the remaining bundle of slightly torn and creased papers. As he began to open them out in the middle hidden away there was a small picture of what quite obviously was his grandfather, resplendent in his soldier's uniform. What a fine-looking young man Willie McBride was.

Alix whispered, 'Bloody hell.'

He was shocked at the emotion he felt, but also angry at his mother – you would have thought she would have wanted her son to see his family, and to know a little bit about them. He then remembered that the briefcase had been left by his grandmother to him directly, or to his heirs, which was a little odd.

Alix moved the photos to one side and Tony continued to study them in silence.

Putting these thoughts aside, he now concentrated on the certificates.

What he had pulled out were folded, faded, slightly torn pieces of stiff paper which Alix quickly realised were his family's birth, marriage and some death certificates.

He delicately unfolded them, and there they were. He held in his hand his father's original death certificate, grandmother Dubré's death certificate and his parents' marriage certificate – in fact, at first glance everything he needed to begin to find out more about his family. They were quickly placed down on the desk, and just as quickly picked up by Mr. Edwards.

Grannie Dubré must have kept them all together, but the question that continued to go round and round in Alix's head was why I have had to wait until now to see this. Then he remembered they were in his grandmother's briefcase, which had been specifically left to him, and obviously as with the letter, he wasn't to be allowed to see all these things until his mother died, but why? What had his mother done that was so bad her mother-in-law had essentially cut her out?

Alix had been so immersed in reading and taking what he was seeing on board, that he had failed to notice that Tony had silently left the room.

One certificate gave Alix his second shock of the day. It was the birth certificate of a child called William McBride, showing the address as 43 Downham Road, Ely and the date of birth as 26 April 1943. The father's name was William McBride and the mother's Gillian McBride, maiden name Fitzgerald. She was listed as a student and his father as a civil servant.

How could he have an older brother, born in this house, who he never even knew existed. His mother had never spoken about him, not even a mention, not once.

Next on the table lay his parents' marriage certificate – a very interesting document, as it showed the date as 1 November 1942. Alix was no mathematician, but he realised almost immediately that his brother's date of birth and his parents' wedding date were less than nine months apart. His mother, Gillian, must have been pregnant when she got married. In fact, using his fingers to count, his mother must have been around four months pregnant, probably not enough to show. The mother's age was given as 18, the father's as 24. The marriage had taken place in the Register Office in Market Street, Ely. The informant was given as Marie McBride, Alix's grandmother, listed as 'groom's mother'.

This looked very much like a very quiet affair, with possibly just Alix's grandmother present. It was probably done in a hurry, and he wondered if any of his mother's family had even been there. It was also interesting that his grandmother was named McBride and not Dubré; perhaps Willie did marry her, after all.

Was William put up for adoption? Was he simply forgotten about? Did he go away? Where is he now? These were the thoughts that rushed through Alix's brain. He picked up the small pile of certificates again, desperate for any clue, and suddenly there it was.

The death certificate for his brother, William.
He had died in 1945, on 31 March. Not even two years old, Alix thought sadly. The cause of death was given as internal bleeding. The informant was, once again, Marie McBride, listed as 'grandmother'. The place of death was the RAF Hospital at Ely.
Alix realised it was no wonder that he wasn't born until 16 years later – such a shattering event must have changed his parents' lives forever. But it still didn't explain why his mother had never told him about William – not even a photograph. And then he realised the significance of the photo of his mother with Granny Dubré and the baby, where Granny looked younger than in the other photo. That must have been William, possibly at his christening, and the only photograph of him that existed.
He had just picked up his father's death certificate when the kitchen door reopened, and Tony reappeared.
'Crisis over, slight delay for lunch, the Aga is going out again, so we've had to transfer the lamb to the electric cooker.'
'I wondered where you'd gone,' said Alix looking at Tony.
'Sorry, it was all obviously personal, and you were totally in another world, so I just left. I'm not surprised you didn't notice.'
At which point he walked towards the table,

'Alix Are you OK? You look as if you've seen a ghost right now.

Alix grimaced.

'Perhaps I have. Would you like to look? I've just found something interesting – in fact it's knocked me sideways, as you can see.'

It's my father's death certificate from 1962

Under Cause of Death, it states Pulmonary Embolism.

A visibly upset Alix then pushed a photo towards Tony, saying 'but it's not only that, and Granny's letter kind of prepared me for that, but it's this.'

'That's a very good-looking man – who is he?'

'That's my grandfather, the murdered Willie McBride,'

'Good Lord!'

'It gets better – or worse, depending on your point of view.' Alix handed Tony the two photos of the babies and his father, mother and grandmother. 'See anyone you recognise?'

'No how could I,' handing the photos onto his father Mr. Edwards dropped his spectacles onto the bridge of his nose and peered intently at the pictures.

'Well, that's Gill and her mother-in-law, Mrs Dubré.'

'Say that again! Did I hear you say 'Mrs Dubré'?' Alix interjected.

'Sorry, I forgot – it was 'Madame Dubré', how silly of me.'

'Not Mrs McBride?'
Mr. Edwards looked at Alix quizzically.
'What do you know about your grandmother?'
Alix thought for a moment.
'Virtually nothing– but now with you calling her 'Madame Dubré', I'm a bit confused as I thought she would be 'Mrs McBride.'
'She was, but what you probably don't know is that she used to tutor A-Level candidates in French, and Dubré was more marketable than 'McBride', so when it suited her, she used her Belgian name. When she made appointments to see me, she always used that name.'
'So, Mr Edwards, how well did you know her?'
Tony's father thought for a moment before responding.
'Well, firstly I met her through my father which was long before I graduated. He always maintained she was one of our best clients and he used to give her advice about her investments. I didn't see her that often, but just followed my father's instructions when he retired. As I remember they did quite well.'
Tony smiled. 'I'd say very well – and I'm sure Alix is very happy about that, aren't you?' he added, nodding in the latter's direction.
Mr Edwards added as an afterthought, 'We also did the conveyancing for her houses in Cambridge and Ely'.

This took Alix by surprise. 'My house in Ely was bought by my grandmother?' Sorry I'm being stupid, it was in her letter to me, I'm just a bit shattered by all of this.'

'Don't worry, it's perfectly natural' Tony smiled, 'it's not every day you become a millionaire.'

'Yes, that was her second house. If my memory serves me right, she originally bought 103 Hills Road, Cambridge, when your father went up to the university, which I think was sometime before the war, so he had somewhere to live, and she lived there. I think she bought the Ely house a few years later – probably, although I'm not sure, about the time your brother William was born. It's so long ago I can't be sure of dates, but I'm fairly certain it was because of the embarrassment of the birth so soon after the wedding, and it got your parents out of Cambridge for a while and silenced the scandal. You shouldn't forget that a child born early, after a shotgun marriage, was considered to be almost a bastard in those days.

'I think your parents moved back to Cambridge and into the same house after William died, and that's where you spent a bit of your childhood. You were certainly born there and then, sometime after your father died; your mother moved back to Ely to be with her mother-in-law at forty-three Downham Road. Your Granny Dubré died there, and you continued to live there until now. The house in

Cambridge was sold around the time your father died, I believe.'

Alix was dumfounded and confused.

'Where did all that money come from, though? As far as I can deduce, Marie, my grandmother, left Ypres in a hurry, and for some reason ended up in Cambridge. You could think she was almost cast out by her mother. My grandfather Willie, her son was born, but I haven't a clue where. He was a private soldier in the army, so he couldn't have had any money, and yet here I am, inheriting a mansion and a huge amount of land, and I don't really understand why. What I haven't a clue about is who or what on earth Chaesar is, and where do they fit into all of this. Add to this the fact that I now discover from birth and death certificates and a photograph that I had an elder brother who died before I was born!'

Mr Edwards looked at Alix, and then at Tony.

He was about to say something else, but Alix interrupted.

'Why did my mother not ever tell me about my brother?'

Mr Edwards pursed his lips and looked out of the window for a second as if seeking inspiration.

'I have no idea. The briefcase as we already know was nothing to do with your mother, I'm fairly certain she didn't ever know it existed. The briefcase was left with me by your grandmother about the time your father died, with strict instructions – and she was fond of those,' he smiled at the memory, 'that you were to be given it only,' and he re-emphasised, 'only after your mother died, and under no circumstances was your mother to be told about it. If you had died first, then it was to be given to any male child that you might have produced.'

'From that letter,' pointing to the envelope, 'it was as if she wanted me to use it to find out about my family'.

'It does look like that, doesn't it, especially the fact that William, your brother, was never mentioned to you by your mother.' Tony interrupted 'Dad, do you remember William, and what happened to him?'

Mr Edwards thought for a few seconds. 'Not personally, but I think I remember being in dad's office once or twice when they came in. I'd have been a law student then doing odd jobs around the place in the holidays, because both mum and dad were there at work.'

He continued, and it all seemed to come out in a rush.

'It was a long time ago, around the end of the war, as I vaguely remember. William wasn't a particularly well child, and he seemed to bruise easily. In fact, today social services would have been called in on suspicion of your parents harming him. I saw an example of how easily he bruised once, when he came to the office with his mother and grandmother. All babies learning to walk fall over or walk into things, and William banged his head, and within seconds a huge bruise appeared, and a bump came up. Your mother took him to the doctor, and I never really saw him again. Then I think he fell down the stairs and that killed him. It was all very sad, and I know your mother was anxious that you would never know, so she kind of hushed it all up, and probably that's why she never told you.

The bruising could have been a hereditary thing, from what I remember being told, and I think she worried you might pass it on to any children you had, even if you didn't have it yourself, although your father didn't have any similar problems because I do remember asking her at the time. Therefore, I think – and I can only guess – that was why you have never married. Unless I'm mistaken, she put all your girlfriends right off.'

Alix quickly retorted. 'On the contrary she spent a lot of time trying to marry me off to some extremely unattractive girls as Tony here would confirm,' nodding towards Tony who grinned back at him.

Alix then sat in silence, until Mr Edwards broke into his thoughts.

'Alix, I was fairly junior when I first had dealings with your grandmother, and although I can't be certain I'm pretty sure it was my father who took her on as a client. Somewhere we must still have files because Mrs, sorry, Madame, Dubré' – he raised his eyebrows in exaggerated apology,' nodding at Tony,

'Father, your grandfather Tommy, asked me to look after her when he retired. Tony, I'm sure if you were to go to the back of the cellar in the office you stand a good chance of finding out about Chaesar.'

As he finished speaking, Mrs Edwards popped her head round the door and announced lunch was ready, so the three men trooped through to the kitchen, which was exactly as Alix had remembered it.

CHAPTER 8

'So, what was so important you had to hide yourselves away?' Mrs Edwards enquired.
'Betty, dear, do you remember old Madame Dubré, Alix's grandmother?' Mr Edwards said as he poured out some red wine.
'Of course I do.'
'Well, young Alix here –'
Alix interrupted with, 'I like the young bit!'
'Alix,' Mr Edwards continued, 'is trying to find out a bit more about his grandmother. He now knows she taught French to struggling students, and as you know tutors didn't make a great deal of money, but his grandmother has left him a lot of money, Alix interrupted, 'a serious amount, millions,' which raised Mrs. Edwards eyebrows, 'and he wants to find out where it came from.'
She looked at her husband with a sweet, sympathetic smile and spoke in the kind of voice that mothers and wives reserve for the men in their lives when they think they are blithering idiots.
'Simon, darling, surely you can't have forgotten, because I remember witnessing a document transferring funds, or something like that, when I was your secretary and Madame Dubré came to the office. Surely you must remember – I can still see the look of amazement on your face, because it was about seven hundred and fifty thousand pounds,

which is a huge amount of money even now, but then it meant that she was a very wealthy woman indeed.' She turned to Alix and smiled as she continued, 'It might even have been some kind of trust for Bill, your father. I'm not sure of that bit, but it could well have been.' She stopped for a second, as if recalling a distant memory. 'We also acted for her in a house purchase, it could even have been two, and definitely a sale as well. If you' – nodding at her husband – 'and I didn't do it individually, then we as a firm did, and I vaguely remember seeing it in her files.'

She stopped and then added, pointing around the table 'Now just help yourselves.'

'Can I just say thank you for lunch, and I apologise that I haven't been to see you more often,' Alix quickly and anxiously added, 'is there really a chance you still have those documents?'

Tony turned to his father, who looked helplessly at his wife, and it was she who spoke first.

'Well, I placed all the historical documents in our vaults in the cellar, but Tony you'll have to answer as to their whereabouts nowadays.' She smiled at her husband. 'I retired when he' – pointing at Tony – 'was ten, if you remember!'

Tony retorted, 'Oh no you didn't, you were still in the office when I was well into my teens,' then added almost defensively, 'You know perfectly well, Mother, that our old historical records have all been microfiched, and our records since the mid-1990s are all computerised. We keep all the originals in the cellar.'

Turning towards Alix, he continued, 'So you needn't worry– the records of everything we have ever done for the Dubré family will be there, and the cellar is a locked fireproof vault.'

'What my dear son means,' said Mrs. Edwards, 'is that he will dig out any relevant documents tomorrow.'

'As if I've nothing better to do!'

Alix addressed both of Tony's parents.

'I can remember nothing of my father as I was a baby when he died, and I'm quite surprised there are no photographs of him anywhere. Can you tell me about him?'

They looked at each other, and there was a slight hesitation before Simon Edwards spoke.

'Alix, your father was a very private man, and I don't think anyone ever had a decent conversation with him because he never ever talked about himself. It used to be said he was either painfully shy or hiding from someone, or something. Oddly I heard on good authority he didn't like having his photograph taken.'

'Are you saying he was odd?'

'Perhaps, but in fairness he did no uniformed war service, as I understand, because he was in a reserved occupation; the rumour was he worked for

MI6, or something secret like that. Quite a lot of those people weren't allowed to be photographed, I believe.'

'Didn't you read he was a civil servant on the certificate we've just looked at?' interjected Tony.

Mr. Edwards came in very quickly, 'during the war that could cover a multitude of jobs from being a spy, or in SOE in Europe, to working at Bletchley Park. Does it really matter?'

With that the subject seemed closed and the rest of the meal was spent talking about the gold chalice, and Mrs. Edwards suggested Alix wrote to Mappin and Webb to see if they had any details about who had paid for it. Once again with the traumas of the last 48 hours or so, Alix had totally forgotten that was one of the three tasks he had set himself.

After thanking the Edwards again, Alix left to walk home on his own. When he had been back in the house for about half an hour, he naturally had returned to his computer which was showing the records of the Royal Munster Fusiliers when the phone rang. Not unexpectedly, it was Tony.

'Alix, can you come to the office at about five o'clock tomorrow? I should have dug out all the relevant documents and microfiches relating to your grandmother by then. Mum and Dad were so pleased to see you today, but I didn't want to suggest you came into the office in front of Dad, because he'd only want to come along as well, and goodness – the

trouble I've had stopping him from interfering since he retired! The funny thing is, I remember him telling me he couldn't keep his father away, and doubtless when my son John succeeds me the same thing will happen again.'
Alix was quick to respond as Tony paused.
'Thanks, Tony – and thank you for taking me to see your parents. I feel very guilty now. It was amazing how clear their memories are about my grandmother.'
'We'll see tomorrow how good they really are!' Tony chuckled, and the phone clicked and went dead.
Whisky once again helped Alix to get a good night's sleep, although it wasn't exactly dream free, he kept having pictures in his head of the two graves, which just wouldn't go away.

Morning arrived eventually, and his 6th Form A Level History class and a double period immediately after assembly, was the last thing Alix needed. Quickly he set them an essay on 'Was Wellington a Lucky General' which he felt should keep them occupied for at least half the lesson, which enabled him to email Mappin and Webb with the photograph of the chalice, where it was, the inscription, and a request for the details of who ordered it.

He just had to hope that this would be forthcoming, as privacy laws might prevent them from releasing details but as it was over 100 years ago and with all the genealogy enquiries that are being made in the present day, he just had to be optimistic

He couldn't get Chateau Hugend out of his head. He knew it well, having taken what seemed like generations of boys to the military cemetery over the road as part of their A Level history, but the thought that he was now the owner was impossible to comprehend.

Alix knew his grandfather was buried in the part of the military cemetery just over the road from the chateau. That's fine, but not fine because he was his grandfather and not just one of the millions who died in that terrible conflict. That isn't the point right now he told himself. Willie had been a private soldier and had obviously been in a relationship with Grannie Dubré who must then have been a young girl.

Why-why-why, just kept running through his head, why did she leave everything to me?

Why did she own the chateau in the first place? Surely, she had brothers who would have inherited. She must have been extremely wealthy to have owned houses here in England as well.

The whole thing was just in the back of his mind all day, and obviously other teachers noticed at lunch with comments like 'Are you sure you are OK

Alix', even one or two of his pupils commented 'Sir, is everything OK?' Others had obviously heard about his mother, so he was also hearing sympathetic comments, which obviously explained his apparent distant look.

How on earth could he ever explain that millionaire status had been conferred on him and he didn't really know why?

Some days go fast, and others slow, and the day Alix spent waiting to see Tony, he mostly spent clock-watching. Fortunately, as it was early in the term Alix had schoolwork to prepare, and there was a meeting of the history staff at the school to discuss GCSE and A-Level curriculums and candidates, but the rest of the time hung heavy.

As 5pm loomed he ambled through Ely, peering into shop windows and greeting pupils, former pupils, other teachers, parents, parents of past students – Alix realised just how well known he was in the town. At last, and on time, Alix walked into the offices of Dawkins & Edwards and was ushered straight into Tony's office.

Tony rose to greet him, with a questioning, slightly amused look on his face.

'Have we got some interesting stuff for you, McBride?'

'Well, get on with it, Tony. Don't keep me hanging on and will you stop calling me McBride' Alix responded, slightly irritated; it had been a long, tedious day waiting for this moment. 'What have you found?'

'Mother was right insofar as she said she witnessed a document involving seven hundred and fifty thousand pounds in the 1950's and giving us permission to invest it on your grandmother's behalf. It also says where the money was sitting, which was in the Bank of Ireland on deposit. Unfortunately, it doesn't tell us where it came from before that.'

Tony paused as if there was more to come, as he handed over a single sheet of paper.

'You might remember my parents saying that Madame Dubré was handed on to them as a client by my grandfather, probably as he was winding down, and whilst I can't find anything relating to that transfer, I do have some very interesting documents that are older, relating to my grandfather's dealings with your grandmother.'

As Tony handed the first one over, he continued with certainty, 'You'll be very interested in this gem. It is the original will, drawn up by your grandfather, leaving everything to your grandmother. It is signed, and witnessed by a James Edmundson, a major in the 8th Battalion, Royal Munster Fusiliers, and it is dated the twenty-fifth of August 1917.'

'That's amazing,' Alix interrupted, leaning forward he continued, 'I just don't believe that. How can an army private have the money to leave a will? Add to that –'

Tony cut back in.

'Wait till you hear this, then. The devil, as always, is in the detail, and there are two hugely significant sentences. Your grandmother is to have 'restricted' access to accounts at Georges Blumeur PrivatBank, as a trustee, but that any single withdrawal will be limited to a total of ten thousand pounds sterling and limited to £100,000 annually. It goes on to state, 'Complete access will be permitted only to my heir on proof of identity and production of account details and password'.

Alix interrupted again.

'What on earth does that mean?'

'God alone knows' would be my initial response, but with my lawyer's hat on I'd say that there was a very significant amount of money stashed away at Georges Blumeur, which is I think in Zurich, because there is the line about total access being restricted to his heir.

I wonder if that means Willie was titled and has lands, or enough of an inheritance to justify a Swiss bank account.'

Tony scratched his thinning hair for a moment, as if contemplating what he had just said before continuing. 'You are quite right, just what is an Irish private soldier doing with a Swiss bank account, and that kind of money?'

At this point Alix fished out his mobile phone, keyed something in, and in a shocked voice said 'Today we are talking about the equivalent of well over three million pounds a year. Come on Tony that is ridiculous, totally unbelievable, nobody has that kind of money to throw around.

There was no immediate response from Tony, who hesitated for a second, then picked up another sheet of paper and started off again.

'There is another document here, in fact a letter from the Bank of Mayo to Madame Marie Dubré, which gives her name and account number and confirms a deposit of seven hundred and fifty thousand pounds on the second of July 1918 in her account, which is in the name of Mme Marie Dubré.' After a moment's pause, he continued, 'Now I have made some quick enquiries and they show that the Bank of Mayo was absorbed into, in other words taken over by, the Bank of Ireland in the early 1930s. I'm assuming they will still have records of historical transactions, especially if the sums of money are this large.'

As Tony handed over the letter, two thoughts crossed Alix's mind. First there were no details of where the money had come from. He could only assume that Grandmother Dubré had been in possession of them, and they had been lost. Secondly, he needed to speak to someone at the Bank of Ireland.

'With the total lack of detail about the source of the money, shouldn't I try to get as much information as I can from the Bank of Ireland?'

'You may struggle on the telephone, but an initial phone enquiry might throw up enough to make a trip to Dublin worthwhile, at least that's my opinion. As for your grandfather Willie McBride, I think he deserves some in-depth investigation. What with Swiss bank accounts, you might just find you are the long-lost heir to a massive estate in Switzerland as well as the one you have just inherited in Belgium.

Alix laughed, despite some misgivings.

'Tony don't be ridiculous! But trying to find out more about Grandpapa Willie and the source of the money is a great idea. I assume you've made copies of all the documents we've discussed?'

'Yes, here they are.' As Tony handed them over, he added, 'You will keep me posted, won't you? I'm absolutely intrigued by all of this and be assured your secret is safe with me – lawyer–client confidentiality and all that! … Seriously though, Alix, I wouldn't be telling too many people about your good fortune, or where it came from – at least not yet anyway.

He then added, there are still several legal formalities to sort out and fortunately we are in touch with Ypres, and you have signed all the relevant documents so it should only be a few days, and then we need to sit down and have a serious chat.'

As Alix rose, he suddenly said, 'Hang on, there has been no mention nor have we seen mother's will, or for that matter granny's will. What is the proof of all of this?' He then added, all I have got is granny's letter, and that wouldn't stand up in court if someone contested it.'

Tony responded. 'You have been the owner of everything that you have heard and seen in the past two days. There is no will needed, and I am certain the lawyers in Ypres can show you that again. That is what he came about yesterday. Insofar as your mother is concerned, she effectively only owned what she had in the bank which I now realise hasn't been mentioned, what with everything else. In fact,' at this point Tony almost looked embarrassed as he said it, 'she has left all her money to the Battersea Dogs Home!'

'What!!!, she didn't even like dogs.'

'Yes, Battersea Dogs Home. She obviously knew you stood to inherit a considerable amount of money, and all I can add to that is she did receive some kind of monthly payment from the Bank of Ireland, but that has obviously ceased.' At this point Tony stood up which indicated the meeting was at an end, they shook hands and seconds later Alix found himself outside walking down the street, feeling as if he had been hit with a pick-axe handle. His mind was exploding with questions.

'Who the hell was Willie McBride? 'Followed a few seconds later after a bit of mental head scratching.

'Who were Willie McBride's parents, what did they do, and where did they live?'

It is obvious they weren't the couple who emigrated to the USA but I'm going to try to trace the family anyway more out of curiosity than anything, but you never know.

Once he'd started this thought process it wouldn't stop and his thoughts just came tumbling out, like a river in spate.

'Where did all the money come from?'

'OK I can see the chateau and the land, but not the money from Chaesar, who are they?' That seemed to him the real question, because whilst he could hardly understand why he was the owner of the chateau, being the grandson of Marie and Willie, which had some logic. Chaesar is something different altogether with the sheer scale of the money involved.

'Where did my mother have an income from because I never remember her going out to work. My father died so long ago I assume she had his pension, but that couldn't have been worth much.'

'How come Willie was well enough educated as an ordinary soldier to be able to write and sign a will?'

'How come he had a Swiss bank account?'

Suddenly Alix realised he had been talking out loud and he looked around anxiously, but thankfully the street was deserted.

There was little doubt now in Alix's mind that he desperately needed information and lots of it.

In what seemed like no time at all, Alix found himself unlocking the door to his house. As he poured himself a large whisky, the thought uppermost in his mind was that a story like this was stranger than fiction. Nobody gets left several million pounds without knowing where it came from.

He remembered a fellow student at Cambridge once saying that the only people who knew anything about their great-grandparents were those who had been left, or were heir to, a lot of money or land because of them. When that was the case, you knew all about your ancestors.

'That's all baloney', Alix thought to himself. Most people knew some if not all their grandparents, even if no money was involved. But he had a huge sum of money coming to him, and not a clue about its origins.

Alix muttered out loud to himself, 'I actually don't know what to do next.' At this point he felt he deserved another whisky, and that meant the television came on, and it was a pre-cooked meal in the microwave.

CHAPTER 9

Half an hour later, just as Alix was about to eat supper his mobile phone rang.

He didn't recognise the number, and a very cultured English voice spoke.

'Am I speaking to Alix McBride?'

'Yes, you are, who am I speaking to?'

'My name is John Peterson, Colonel John Peterson, and no doubt you are aware that I am your tenant at Chateau Hugend.' By way of explanation, 'my lawyers have just been in touch.'

'Yes, I am Alix McBride, and I have just found this out as well, and as I sure you understand it's all a bit confusing, to put it mildly.'

John Peterson's response was very warm and friendly. 'Look it would make sense for us to meet, and for you to check us out so to speak. I'm sure your lawyers here in Ypres probably want to tie up a few things with you as well, so when can you come and see us? You'll be very interested in your room……'

Alix interrupted, 'my room?'

'Yes, there is a special room, the best room, which we reserve for very senior visitors, generals, government ministers, that sort of thing, the best room in the house, you'll love it, so when will you come so we can meet, and you can find out what you now own?'

Alix thought for a moment, 'I'll have to get back to you,' thinking quickly that he needed to go to Dublin to see the bank, and actually that is my priority, 'look I need to organise my teaching, because I do have a weekend coming up when I have no class on a Friday or Saturday. Without checking my teaching diary, I can't be precise when that will be, and also, it's not worth it unless I can meet with the lawyers as well.'

'I understand, well you have my number on your phone now, so I'll wait to hear from you.' With that there was a click, and the line went dead.

This reminded Alix that he hadn't checked the contents of the envelope Tony had given to him. It was lying on the dining room table, and inside was his mother's death certificate, her will indicating she was leaving everything to the dog's home, which made Alix smile. There was a copy of the of the original will, drawn up by his grandfather, leaving everything to his grandmother dated the twenty-fifth of August 1917.'

He was reminded his grandmother is to have 'restricted' access to accounts at Georges Blumeur PrivatBank, the total amount available to be limited to a total of one hundred thousand pounds sterling annually. It goes on to state, 'Complete access will be permitted only to his grandfather's heir on proof of identity and production of account details and password'.

The letter from the Bank of Mayo to Madame Marie Dubré, which gives her name and account number and confirms a deposit of seven hundred and fifty thousand pounds on the 2nd July 1918 in her account, which is in the name of Mme Marie Dubré.

There were two further documents inside the envelope because it was all very well to have been told he had inherited all this wealth, but legally he had to prove it.

The first was a copy of his father's will which was very short and to the point. All it stated was that everything was to be left to his son, and in the event he did not outlive him, then any son he might have. There was absolutely nothing specific in terms of what the everything was, which was a bit odd.

The second was his Grandmother's will, which he noted had been written in 1962, after his father's death. Again it was quite brief but what it stated was the Chateau, the land, the bank accounts, in fact everything was to go to Alix McBride, and if he was no longer alive to an eldest son, but only on the death of Mrs. McBride his mother. Until such time there was also a note added by the Ypres lawyers Dyuck which stated that they would in the meantime act as agents for Alix McBride or any heirs until such time. There was a letter signed by her and the lawyers written a few days after the will stating that Alix McBride had been gifted everything that was in the earlier will, stating she now would only take an income not exceeding £50,000 a year from the Hugend Estate. He just assumed this would in time remove any risk of death duties as he assumed the law in Belgium was similar to the UK. Perhaps he mused it might also keep any tax burden on him when she died to a minimum.

As he read it Alix had the idle thought that suppose there were no children, and he had none, at least so far, what was to happen next?

That thought was very much to the forefront as he slid the contents back into the envelope. He then had the belated thought, how did Colonel Peterson have his telephone number, realising almost immediately that he would have got it from the lawyer. That was all very well, but how did the lawyer know what it was as he suddenly remembered their first meeting.

This whole business seemed to be getting more and more mysterious, and his supper had gone cold. By this time his appetite had vanished, so out came the whisky bottle, on went the television, and it was on one of the antique programmes, which Alix was about to change the channel when he heard the name Mappin and Webb mentioned.

His ears pricked up, he put the volume up as the presenter described the lovely silver rose bowl which had apparently come from Brazil in the 1930's as a presentation gift from the St Andrews Society of Sao Paulo. Isn't life strange Alix thought, only 24 hours after sending his email to them, that they should be on Television.

He then had the thought that he could possibly use the Ancestry website to find out more about Willie's military career.

What Alix discovered helped him a lot. The documents he downloaded and printed from the National Archives confirmed Willie McBride's birth on 4th August 1898 in the village of Blacksmills, but that was all.

Alix was more than a little frustrated until he remembered that Willie had joined the Royal Munster Fusiliers, and he read intensely from the historical records from the Royal Munster Fusiliers and the 16th Irish Division.

Willie had joined the army in the city of Limerick, where he was enlisted with the service number 5/6814 into the 5th (Extra Reserve) Battalion of the Royal Munster Fusiliers, and he went on to Curragh Camp, County Kildare. The role of the reserve battalions was to take over garrison duties from the regular battalions and to train replacement drafts for the battalions who were in the field. The reserve battalions never left Ireland.

Willie was sent with a replacement draft to join the 8th (Service) Battalion, Royal Munster Fusiliers in the middle of August 1916, landing at Étaples, and was then sent to the Somme sector with his draft to join the service battalion. The 8th was part of the

16th Irish Division that captured Guillemont, but the 8th failed to take Ginchy, suffering heavy casualties when attacking the town for a second time with only 200 men. Other battalions of the 16th Division completed the capture. All this took place over the period 3–9 September 1916.

The 8th was then moved as part of the 16th Division to Ypres, where it rotated in and out of the trenches until 8 November when, with only 21 officers and 446 other ranks remaining, the battalion was disbanded and the remnants, including Willie, were drafted into the 1st (Regular) Battalion, which had just returned from Gallipoli. It had been reduced to just five officers and 305 other ranks at this point.

By 1 December 1916 the 1st Battalion consisted of 48 officers and 1,069 men. The men spent Christmas in the trenches and were rotated in and out with 'light casualties' (two officers and 20 men killed) until the middle of March, when they were withdrawn for training. They took part in the battle of Messines, which began on 7 June 1917 with the detonation of 19 huge mines. The 16th Irish Division took all its objectives, including the village of Wytschaete (Wijtschate), and over two miles of ground was gained with minimal casualties. Following this, the 1st was relieved and returned to the Ypres Salient in late August.

At this point Alix sat back in his chair, trying to imagine what it must have been like to be a child, and then at only 18 or 19 being on the Somme, at Ginchy, on the Messines Ridge or at the Ypres Salient.

At King's School he taught boys who were almost Willie's age when he was killed, and the word 'murdered' didn't seem a natural or easy expression to use. Alix just couldn't imagine how people coped with the death and destruction, when at some stages only one man in five survived, not considering the wounded.

At least Alix now knew exactly how Willie came to be at Château Hugend in early September 1917.

A quick look on the screen showed Alix it was close on midnight and time for bed, although once again he knew that sleep would not come easy. He left a note for himself to ring the Irish bank in the morning, probably at mid-morning break.

CHAPTER 10

A phone call to the Bank of Ireland at 11.15 had got Alix nowhere, save that he had the name of an Alan O'Farrell, who had agreed to see him but insisted that physical proof of the relationships between Alix, his mother and Willie McBride would be required before any financial information could possibly be divulged.

This meant a trip to Dublin, and a call to O'Farrell's secretary got Alix an appointment for noon on the Friday, so he booked a flight to Dublin for 7.00am that morning, having explained the situation to the headmaster, who somewhat reluctantly gave him the day off, with the words 'Alix don't make a habit of this'.

After an uneventful flight and a taxi ride into Dublin, Alix alighted outside the Bank of Ireland's headquarters in Baggot Street Upper. He was in plenty of time for his appointment. At noon Alix was ushered into a modern, brightly lit office on the seventh floor of the Bank of Ireland building. A smiling secretary offered him a coffee which he had accepted, remembering the times when he had been interviewed by his bank managers in the past, always without coffee!

A surprisingly young man in an open neck checked shirt and chinos came out to greet Alix, introducing himself as Alan O'Farrell.

After both men sat down in a lounge-like area with three or four comfortable armchairs and a low coffee table in the middle arranged with cups and saucers and biscuits, Alix quickly realised that the man unlikely as it seemed on first sight was a senior official in the bank.

Opening the conversation with the usual small talk about where Alix had flown from, whether it was a good flight and what he did for a living, the banker moved to a direct question.

'You want to know about the banking arrangements your grandmother made with the bank, I understand, and your grandfather was a Willie McBride?'

'Yes, absolutely, and before we go any further, can I just show you photocopies of some documents? I have the originals but, as you will realise, they are important enough to be in my lawyer's vaults at his office in Ely.'

O'Farrell nodded, and Alix continued, pushing the documents across the table as he spoke.

'Firstly, here is my grandfather's will from 1917 stating that my grandmother, Madame Dubré, is to have access to accounts at Georges Blumeur PrivatBank as a trustee, but that any single withdrawal will be limited to a total of ten thousand pounds sterling, and limited to £100,000 annually.

Complete access is to be restricted only to Willie's heir, on proof of identity, and production of account details plus password.'

Alix handed O'Farrell the second document. 'Here is a letter relating to the Bank of Mayo, an account number, the name Mme M Dubré, and a deposit of seven hundred and fifty thousand pounds on the second of July 1918. I have made some enquiries and they show that you took over the Bank of Mayo in the early 1930s. For some odd reason, there is no name of the account holder who initiated the transfer, but I'm assuming you will still have records from that period. Nor is there any mention anywhere of further transfers to my grandmother. Can I assume you will have such records and that I can see them? Was there a continuing inflow of funds, perhaps from the Swiss bank account.'

'Mr McBride,' said O'Farrell matter-of-factly, 'all this is fascinating, but so far you haven't shown me documents proving you have the right to see any information at all.'

'Oh, don't worry, I have these here,' said Alix, smiling as he pointed to another envelope on the table and handed over a third document to the banker. 'This is a document involving seven hundred and fifty thousand pounds and giving the legal firm I still use permission to invest it on my grandmother's behalf. It also says where the money was sitting, which is on deposit.'

Another document left Alix's hands, leaving the first envelope empty.

He then slipped over the other envelope. 'In here you'll find my mother's birth certificate, and her death certificate, also my father's will, and Granny Dubré's letter, and her will. I think that's conclusive, don't you?'

O'Farrell nodded, but said with a degree of finality, 'Pretty conclusive, yes, but I'm afraid I'll need to see the originals, and the letter isn't a will, although I do see her will as well. That is a different thing to the details of the bank account. Everything is to do with the chateau and all their banking details will be with a Belgian bank, what you want has to do with my bank and the old bank of Mayo. As I said two completely different things I am afraid.' He then continued without smiling, 'as things stand I can't give you any information without sight of the original documents.'

'Oh, for goodness' sake, can't you speak directly with Tony Edwards, my lawyer? He will confirm he has the originals safely in a vault.'

'Yes, I can, but he should have told you that I would need the originals, in much the same way photocopies of birth certificates are no good for passport applications, and I repeat I have no banking information about the chateau.'

'Shit!' Alix made to get up. 'Can I please have these copies back? I don't want them getting into the wrong hands. And please maintain total confidentiality about this.'

Alan O'Farrell opened his hands, raising them slightly, almost in a gesture of apology and surrender.

'Look, I know you're annoyed, and I sympathise, but please understand that I am bound by some stringent rules and regulations. You probably feel this is a wasted journey, but I am prepared to tell you that we do still have the details you seek, and you will find the records helpful. So,' O'Farrell continued whilst standing and ushering Alix towards the door as he handed back his pile of papers, 'shall we say you'll give my office a call when you have the originals, and we'll meet again. I'm sorry I've not been more help.'

With that he ushered Alix out of the door to the outer office.

'Anne, looking towards his personal assistant, 'Mr McBride is leaving but I need to see him again. Make sure he can have an appointment when it's convenient for him.'

Looking at Alix, he said, 'sorry again. That's the most I could do, so I'll bid you goodbye for now.'

Before Alix could reply he had closed the door with a click, and after a few brief words with the business-like Anne and a couple of moments checking that the documents were all there, that he placed them in the right envelopes, and he replaced the envelopes into his bag. Then he caught the lift down to the street and set off back to the airport.

As he was waiting at the airport Alix rang Tony, and the conversation was short and to the point, regarding original documents being necessary. Tony was unrepentant saying simply that the bank manager was totally wrong, but accepting of the fact that Irish banks possibly have their own, as he put it, antiquated rules.

Tony offered to drop the documents off early the next day on the Saturday if that would help, and a phone call to the bank was put through to Alan O'Farrell, who laughed when Alix asked if senior management worked on a Saturday, responding,

'Yes, unlike our English cousins, sometimes all-day Saturday.'

'When you know roughly when you are going to arrive just phone my secretary and I'll make time to see you.'

When Alix finally got home it was close to midnight, but sleep was nigh impossible. He had got himself on a morning flight to Dublin, and a return flight later in the day, but that just added to the many thoughts running through his head.

Alix was showered, shaved and dressed, when at 9.00am prompt Tony rang the doorbell. He cautioned Alix to guard the documents carefully and to ensure they always stayed in sight. In return Alix promised to tell Tony what he had found out. He then rang Alan O'Farrell's secretary, drove to Stansted to catch the noon flight to Dublin and arrived at the bank, for a meeting with the banker at 2.00pm.

O'Farrell was prompt and polite, as before. Alix showed him all the original documents, and the banker visibly relaxed.

'Mr O'Farrell,' he said with a smile, 'here is the information you are looking for, I think.'

O'Farrell then handed over a summary bank statement showing ten equal payments into his grandmother's account at the Bank of Mayo of £50,000 each, made every year on 2nd August from 1918 until 1927. The payments were made from an account named 'Chaesar Estate'.

'Can you tell me who the Chaesar Estate account belonged to?' Alix asked, already knowing what the answer would be.

'No, I'm afraid not,' admitted O'Farrell, without a smile.

'Why not?'

'I'm afraid that's not information I have bearing in mind how many years have passed. '

Alix felt that reply wasn't exactly honest, and when he posed his next question about account numbers and names at the Georges Blumeur PrivatBank, this too was met with a negative response.

'Mr McBride, I'm sorry I'm not in a position to tell you, and you must realise I have to take account of the bank's responsibilities in terms of confidentiality.'

In his heart of hearts, Alix hadn't really expected much information to be forthcoming, so he thought he might just as well cut his losses and leave.

'Mr O'Farrell, I'm obviously wasting my time here, as the questions I need answers to are ones you are obviously not willing to help me with. I understand the confidentiality issue, but for goodness' sake, all the people involved are dead, and some a long time since.'

As Alix got up to leave, O'Farrell began scribbling on a slip of paper. Then he handed Alix the account summary of the annual transactions and the note he had just written.

'I'm sorry you feel that way, but the name Chaesar gives you something to go on. I'm also giving you the account transactions up until your grandmother left for England, and you will see withdrawals where I assume she made investments, and the dividends coming into the account. I think she must have been well advised throughout this time, and you will also be able to see the cheques she wrote.'

He handed the bundle to Alix.

'I'll bid you good day', said O'Farrell, offering his hand to shake, but Alix didn't respond.

He was quickly out of the door and down the corridor, every bit as angry as he had been after the first meeting with the Bank of Ireland man. It wasn't until he was seated jammed into his tiny seat on the Ryanair flight back to Stansted that he remembered the hastily written note.

As he read it, Alix thought his eyes were playing tricks. O'Farrell had been very clear that no more information would be forthcoming, and yet this note nonetheless seemed helpful.

No details of the Swiss bank available, sorry, but £750,000 deposited by them in the Bank of Mayo account on15th Nov 1918. If you need to talk some more, best ring me out of office hours on +353 [0]85 624 1986

Alix pocketed the slip of paper quickly and closed his eyes – as much as anything to avoid talking to his neighbour, who was obviously itching for a conversation. It also gave him time to mull over the new information he had been given in a way that made him think that, despite Alan O'Farrell's apparently uncooperative attitude, he really did want to help.

Although Alix wasn't any closer to finding out about the source of his wealth, he felt progress had been made, and with that thought he quickly fell asleep despite the uncomfortable seat.

Alix arrived back at Stansted just after 5pm and he rang Tony Edwards and arranged to meet him in the Black Bull in Market Street at 8.00pm.

CHAPTER 11

As Alix ducked under the top of the doorway between the public and lounge bars, on which he'd often bruised himself over the years (a sign above the door warned 'duck or grouse'), he found Tony with two pints of Adnams ale in front of him.

'Hello' and 'Cheers' were the only words exchanged until half the contents of the glasses had been drunk.

'There's nothing like a pint at the end of the day,' Tony said with a smile. 'So, tell me your news.'

For 20 minutes Alix recounted his story to a silent Tony.

'Hmm,' he mused. 'I think it might be worthwhile checking out the McBride's in the States, because they might be able to tell you where the funds came from.'

This was followed by a slight hesitation to let his thought processes catch up. 'And you obviously need to look into the Chaesar Estate, to see who owns it now, as they may be willing to help.'

He paused for a sip at his beer. 'The next point is that your grandmother must have used a stockbroker of some sort, so it might be worth your while investigating that angle. They will probably be in Dublin, but their name should appear somewhere on a bank statement.'

Tony shrugged his shoulders and shook his head slowly as he continued.

'I think you are going to struggle to find out much about the first payment to your granny from the Swiss bank Blumeur, but you never know. It does seem a long time ago when the payments started, and it would be terrific if you could find that out. Plus, the chalice from Mappin and Webb – that might be another interesting route to go down …'

Alix was on his way to the bar as Tony was still pontificating. When he returned with a couple of fresh pints, he quipped, 'did I miss anything important?'

'You shouldn't walk away when your elders and betters are speaking,' Tony shot back with a smile. 'As I've already said, you should check out the American McBride's and see if you can find out some more about what happened to them. You should be able to do that fairly easily online. Then there is the Chaesar Estate, and you might just drop them a line, or …' Tony's voice faded slightly, then returned as if he had given some more thought to the matter. 'Look, just call them and explain who you are and what you are looking for and see if they can help.'

Tony finished his beer before continuing.

'Then you might write to Blumeur, and also Mappin and Webb, not that I hold out any hope that either will be able or want to help.'

Alix was getting the distinct impression that Tony had consumed at least a couple of pints before he had arrived, as his speech was now slightly indistinct, and he was beginning to repeat himself.

'I've already writte……' as Tony stood up, picking up his scarf and bowler hat, and obviously not listening.

'I'll be late for supper with Mum and Dad and that won't do, so I must be off, McBride. Thanks for the drink, and I'm getting really intrigued about the McBride family fortune. No doubt you'll keep me informed…… if there's anything the office can do for you, just yell.'

He headed for the door and Alix heard 'shit!' as he forgot to duck. Alix thought if he had a pound for every time he had caught his own head on that doorframe or seen even regulars like Tony do it, he'd be worth a fortune. Then he had to remind himself that he was already worth a fortune. And the bump proved that Tony had indeed sunk a few beers! To Alix's surprise, Tony popped his head back through the doorway.

'Alix, the other thing I meant to say was that my father thinks your father, William, may well have done something in the later stages of the war he didn't talk about. Apparently, he was a fluent French speaker, with a Belgian accent thanks to his mother. It's possible he may have been with the SOE – you know, who parachuted agents into enemy territory. It's possibly nothing, just a thought, really.'

With a cheery wave, Tony vanished again, leaving a very thoughtful Alix. Perhaps this might explain the almost total lack of any kind of information about his father.

He went back home and during the evening he wrote to Blumeur PrivatBank in Zurich, explaining some of the background and asking for an account number relating to his grandfather.

Finally, following some online research about the Special Operations Executive, he wrote a brief letter to the headquarters of the Secret Intelligence Service at Vauxhall Cross, the logical successor, he thought, to the SOE.

'Dear Sirs,
I am trying to discover whether my father William McBride, born in February 1918, worked at any time during the war or immediately afterwards for the SIS or SOE, or its equivalent.
Yours faithfully,
Alix McBride'

Alix posted the letters by first class mail the next morning on his way to school.

The first reply two days later was from Blumeurs saying they were unable to help due, of course, to the bank's rules on customer confidentiality and data protection. They missed out Health and Safety, Alix thought as he read the letter.

The following week an email arrived from Mappin & Webb, apologising for the delay and explaining that all the firm's old records were held away from head office, and it had taken a little time to dig them out. The chalice had been made under instruction from a Mr William Edmundson from the Chaesar Estate in Ireland, who had collected it himself. The letter also said that the chalice was 'one of eight requested by William or James Edmundson in the period between 1900 and 1911.'

Alix was amazed. He nearly missed his first school lesson as he phoned Mappin & Webb and waited for the call to be answered. When it was, the man who signed the letter said he would be very happy to send the details of the other seven chalices.

The email arrived almost immediately listing all eight chalices, all made to the same design and with virtually identical inscriptions, to children who had obviously died in infancy. There were, however, no details of where these children had been born or where they died. The letter also stated that each chalice was invoiced at £200 – a considerable sum at the beginning of the 20th century, Alix noted – and paid for in cash. His only thought was, were the chalices paid and collected or paid and sent.

Alix was glad he was sitting down as he read the email, which he printed off immediately. The words 'can of worms' came to mind, and his thoughts were only interrupted by the sound of the doorbell. He realised that he might be late for his first lesson of the day, and that the doorbell would be Margaret, his cleaner.

'Good morning, Margaret,' he said as he opened the door. 'I'm late, as usual. Just ignore the papers on the dining table, you don't need to tidy them away. I'll get you a key cut, to save you needing me to open the door for you every time.'

She had been recommended to him several months ago, in fact not long after his mother had gone into care; she had excellent references, one of which he checked, and everything in it was confirmed. She was new to the town, with a friendly smile, and kept the house absolutely spick and span; she even polished his shoes. Alix realised how lucky he was to have employed her.

Grabbing his jacket Alix set off at speed for the school. As he closed the door, he called over his shoulder, 'Just put the snib on the door when you go'.

His mind was in overdrive, so much so that he almost walked under a car on the main Downham Road. He waved an apology, but he just couldn't stop thinking about all the chalices.

It was then the penny dropped, and he realised what was troubling him. One of the chalices was for two brothers called O'Dwyer, namely Sean and Fergus. These names stood out because he had once taught a boy called Sean O'Dwyer, who was a history genius and had gone up to Oxford, where he got a first-class honours degree, and was now climbing fast in the Foreign Office. He grimaced slightly as he thought about this, noting that Sean was his only Oxbridge first class honours degree success.

What was more to the point, he remembered there had been two lads named O'Dwyer in the photograph of the Royal Munster Fusiliers. A second car screeched to halt just inches from Alix as he once again stepped off the curb lost in his thoughts. This time he didn't even acknowledge the driver, because a slow-dawning realisation had suddenly quickened to full daybreak.

'What if the other soldiers in Willie's company were all the same?' he said out loud – in fact so loud that the people walking past looked at him as if he was drunk. Alix didn't care; his mind was in turmoil. There's something very strange going on here was all he could think.

Alix looked up and realised he had reached the History Department, and his lower sixth class were all filing in through the door, a few stepping back to allow him in. Choruses of 'Morning, Sir' and 'Morning, Mr McBride' greeted him. Normally Alix would respond but this morning he was far too deep in thought.

As he entered the classroom, he realised that the day's study topic was 'The Great War (World War I) and its Implications for the Social Structure of

Great Britain'. What was even better, as far as Alix was concerned, was that this topic had been given to the group of 17-year-olds to prepare a week before, and he knew that, as reasonably enthusiastic A-Level candidates, the 40-minute period would almost run itself.

The discussions inevitably centred on the great battles of the Somme and the three battles of Ypres, which still had a lasting and deep imprint in many English minds, the youngsters under his guidance being no exception. Indeed, he was due to take this very class to Ypres at the autumn half-term – a trip arranged months before that now struck him for the first time as a remarkable coincidence given his own new connection with the place.

Alix didn't need to be much more than a referee, allowing debating points to be made, shutting up the loquacious and encouraging the less vociferous. He was impressed by the youngsters' knowledge and amazed at their understanding of the significance of the casualty figures, particularly the high proportion of officer deaths. They were able to quote statistics such as the case of a battalion of 50 officers and 1,000 men reduced to six officers and 150 men during a couple of days.

As the discussion, sometimes quite heated, went on, Alix suddenly remembered the O'Dwyer boys and wondered how many of the lads in the first photograph, then all in the same company of the Munster Fusiliers had survived.

Less than two hours later he was able to escape back home for his hour-long lunch break. With a cup of instant soup and a plate of baked beans on toast next to him on the dining-room table, it took him a few minutes to get his hands on the photos, and not for the first time wished he was tidier. His eyes scanned first the photo of Willie in Intake 131, 8th Battalion Royal Munster Fusiliers and his mates, and then, with the aid of a magnifying glass, 'A Coy, 8th Bn Royal Munster Fusiliers'. It took but a few seconds to notice that all 18 lads were in both pictures.

He then took the email he had printed out from Mappin & Webb, which didn't come immediately to hand because he must have moved it whilst searching for the photographs. He realised that the dead children to whose parents the eight chalices had been given not only had the same surnames as men in the photo but also, and very significantly, the Christian names of which the first letter matched the soldiers' initials.

Not for the first time that day, Alix spoke out loud to himself.

'Bloody Hell!' he exclaimed, wondering what on earth to do next.

It didn't take long for him to realise that he could confirm what he thought a certainty, but as yet was still supposition, by checking the churchyards in the parishes where the infants were buried. The only problem was that he had no idea where that was, and the fact that Irish family history was very difficult to confirm because so many records had been destroyed in the Four Courts Fire in Dublin in 1922. Needles and haystacks to Alix seemed an appropriate thought.

Nevertheless, remembering where he had obtained Willie's army details, he went back to the resources of the National Archives and Ancestry.com.

Looking at the records of the Royal Munster Fusiliers it took him less than an hour to realise that every youngster in the photograph had joined the army from the same place, called Termoncarragh House

In the morning, he rang Mappin and Webb again to ask if they retained any details of where the other seven chalices were delivered to, because he thought in unlikely they were delivered by hand from England.

Less than two days later he received the information he was looking for, and he began to list all the young soldiers by name, and cross referenced them with the seven chalices.

The next seven days passed in a blur as he rushed home between lessons at school to use his laptop, and also sat up long into the night until he found the details of all of the young men in the company photograph. A combination of ringing churches and speaking to parish priests who were extremely helpful, and searching through births and deaths in parish registers until eventually he had the details of every young man who had enlisted with Willie.

In addition, he was able to get the names of the parents of all the young men, but most importantly he now knew where they were all from

He made a list and underlined the other six names which matched the information from Mappin & Webb.

1. <u>Willie McBride</u> 2nd August 1898 Blacksmills Co. Cork, to James & Helen McBride

2. <u>Sean O'Dwyer</u> 21st April 1890 Shillelagh, Co. Wicklow, to Mick & Sheila O'Dwyer

3. <u>Fergus O'Dwyer</u> 21st April 1890 Shillelagh, Co. Wicklow, to Mick & Sheila O'Dwyer

4. <u>Al Molloy</u> 3rd May 1891 Doonbeg, Kilrush, Co. Clare, to Seamus & Ann Molloy

5. <u>Mick Moroney</u> 16th February 1889 Collooney, Co. Sligo, to Harry & Moira Moroney

6. <u>Patrick Coghlan</u> 10th December 1891 Creagh, Co. Galway, to Patrick & Annie Coghlan

7. <u>Eamonn O'Connell</u> 3rd March 1894 Drumcliff, Co. Clare, to Tom & Nancy O'Connell

8. Sean Stringer 31st August 1893 Kilshanchoe, Co. Kildare, to Sean & Mary Stringer

9.   <u>Colme Fitzgerald</u> 10th May 1892 Lorrha, Co. Tipperary, to Sean & Mary Fitzgerald
10.   Pat Hayes 16th June 1895 Kinlough, Co. Leitrim, to Mick & Kathleen Hayes
11.   Donal Lenihan 31st March 1889 Boyle, Co. Roscommon, to Conor & Rose Hayes
12.   Phil Kyle 8th September 1895 Lismore, Co. Waterford, to Eoin & Mary Kyle
13.   <u>Peter Patrick</u> 17th December 1891 Hacketstown, Co. Carlow, to Liam & Aileen Patrick
14.   Alan Smith 22nd July 1896 Dunamaggan, Co. Kilkenny, to John & Ciara Smith
15.   John Smith 6th May 1895 Graiguenamanagh, Co. Kilkenny, to John & Ciara Smith
16.   Frank Clinch 7th February 1891 Kenmare, Co. Kerry, to Eoin & Lauren Clinch
17.   James Clinch 17th April 1892 Kenmare, Co. Kerry, to Eoin & Lauren Clinch
18.   Jack Mahony 14th July 1893 Abbeyleix, Co. Laois, to Sean & Emma Mahony

He wasn't sure how he felt about this list he had discovered, but it seemed to him that for some reason, no-one would have easily been able to find all this information out. What the bloody hell was going on here was Alix's first second and third thoughts.

Eight children apparently dead in infancy, remembered by seven very expensive gold chalices, just didn't seem possible, and certainly not a coincidence.

He now knew the remaining children who had grown up to become the young men in the photographs were all orphans. There could be little doubt that if he could find out what had happened well over a hundred years ago, then perhaps he would find the answer to where his inheritance came from.

One answer of course was from the chateau and its land but that still brought him no closer to finding out about the Chaesar Estate. In fact the more he thought about it the Chateau was something totally separate. There was no way the estate which was by no means small could ever have generated that kind of income.

Apart from anything else the will of his grandfather Willie mentioned a large amount of money that his grandmother could access every year, and the £50,000 deposit into the Bank of Mayo rather brought into sharp focus the Chaesar estate and Blumeur's Bank in Zurich.

The tall and the short of it must be that Blumeur's Bank and Chaesar are inextricably involved. Whilst it was obvious that Termoncarragh House was a common factor, and he wondered if it was an orphanage. If that was the case, why were some of the children not children anymore, but men according to their dates of birth when they left to volunteer to fight in the war.

It was once again very late into the evening when Alix finally abandoned what seemed like a puzzle, and he collapsed into his bed, but sleep just didn't come easily.

CHAPTER 12

When Alix went home from school at lunch time the next day his phone was ringing as he came in the front door, and after a moment's thought he let it ring until the ansaphone cut in. When he had once complained to his tutor at Cambridge about people not answering their telephone, he had been told that the person who makes the call is in control. Thereafter, Alix would let the phone ring until the message service clicked on and the caller revealed his or her name before he decided whether to speak. Now he stood where he was and listened to the disembodied voice.

'Alix? Hello, it's John Peterson from Château Hugend. Look, I'm still waiting for the documents I must sign for the new lease. I hope everything is OK at your end. Can you call me back, please?'

The call, although pleasant in tone, had a slight touch of a senior officer addressing one of his subordinates, and Alix, not much taken by that, muttered, 'You can wait'.

It was now decision time. Alix was fairly certain what he wanted to do next but felt slightly guilty about pestering Tony again. He was beginning to feel both insecure and not a little scared; apprehensive might be a better word. Confidentiality seemed important, as he had inherited a lot of money through the actions of people he didn't know anything about, and then after much deliberation he decided instead to speak to the school chaplain, whom he had known for well over half his life.

The Reverend David Hughes was of an indefinable age, almost certainly 20 years beyond normal retirement, and he was wise even beyond that! Alix just felt in a way that he almost needed a confessional type of chat, although he hadn't done anything wrong, but he needed the absolute certainty of confidentiality.

It was about 8pm when Alix called David, but the phone rang out without response. He didn't leave a message, due more to indecision than bloody-mindedness. However, almost immediately his phone rang.

'This is David Hughes. You just rang me?'

'David, it's Alix McBride. Could I possibly come and see you? I need your help.'

'Of course, would you like to come now?'

'If it wouldn't be an imposition.'

'Come on over. I'll put the kettle on – or perhaps you'd like something stronger?'

'I'm on my way – thanks.'

Alix gathered his notes and certificates and set out on foot. Ely may be described as a city because it has a cathedral, but it's very small, and most places can be easily reached in ten minutes on foot, unless you must climb up the steep hill, which Alix didn't on this occasion.

Alix was soon sitting opposite David in a comfy old armchair with a cup of tea. He noticed David had his chapel face on, something that staff and pupils used to giggle about. The expression signified that David was about to deliver a Christian homily, and not one of his more entertaining and amusing sermons, which, although they always had a point; it was normally a moral one as opposed to a religious one. Recognising this, Alix jumped in first.

'This isn't about mother, so don't worry. She had run her course and I'm sad, but not sorry. Having said that, there is something which involves mother that I need advice about, and I need it to be confidential, which is why I'm here.'

The chaplain smiled.

'She was a good Christian woman. But what is it you're worried about? I'm assuming, of course, you haven't got some kind of STD!'

His smile became a giggle, then a laugh. Alix smiled too when he remembered David's sermon on STD, which he and several older members of staff had first thought stood for Subscriber Trunk Dialling.

'No, it's about my grandfather, Willie McBride, who I've only just found out died at Ypres in 1917. But there's a problem …'

'Go on.'

'It's all slightly complicated, you see I have just found out since mother died that I have inherited a huge amount of money, and I haven't a clue how this has happened.'

David leant forward in his chair and nodded his head.

'I like a good mystery, so don't stop, I'm very interested to hear more.'

'It's a bit complicated and even far-fetched.'

'Go on I'm all ears.' Smiling as he said it.

'Look, since my mother died, I found out I have inherited a lot, and I mean a lot of money, and a chateau in Ypres in Belgium. Somehow or other it is all tied up with my grandfather Willie McBride who was murdered during the Great War.'

'Murdered?'

'Yes, but not like Field Marshall Haig had them murdered. No, he was killed by a bunch of farmhands for getting my grandmother pregnant in the middle of the battle of Ypres.'

'That doesn't seem possible.'

'Well, I can assure you it happened, but crazy as that sounds, it gets even odder.'

'Go on, how did you find this out?'

There was a letter from my Belgian grandmother Mmme Dubré brought to me the morning after mother died by a lawyer from Ypres. Basically, it told me about my inheritance, so I whistled up a very hungover, 'smiling as he said it, 'Tony Edwards to ensure I was doing the right thing.'

'Of course, very wise.'

'The letter also asked me to visit a McBride grave in Castlemills outside Cork, and so I flew there the next day. There I found a grave of a baby boy with exactly the same name and date of birth as my grandfather.'

David interrupted 'That's a big coincidence.'

'It gets better or worse depending on your point of view.'

'What exactly do you mean?'

'There's a photo of the lads in Willie's platoon, or company or whatever, and …… sorry I should have said; that the church where Willie McBride was buried received a solid gold chalice from the parents who were only poor farm labourers, so there is no way they could have afforded that.'

'Absolutely.'

'So, I asked Mappin and Webb who made the chalice, about the circumstances, and they told me there were in fact ten chalices made and eight delivered.

After researching all the lads in the army group online, not one of them are who they appear to be. I have found that all of them appear to have died as babies and have graves in their local churchyard. There were however seven chalices were presented by the grieving parents to that church, to commemorate their children. I'm not sure what happened to the others whose parents didn't get chalices for their church.'

Alix briefly drew breath before continuing with the words tumbling out.

'Incidentally Willie's parents then emigrated to the USA travelling first class by ship, and I suspect the same will hold true for the other parents who presented chalices.'

'Wow, that is some mystery.'

'Yes, and I'm really worried I've accidentally stumbled onto something that I'm not sure I want to know about, but I feel I must get to the bottom of it.

David – whose looks belied his age, for he must have been a good eighty-five years old but was very popular with the boys and girls of the school – had sat, apart from the odd interjection, impassively until Alix finished. He thought for a moment, hands together in a prayer-like attitude with the index fingers resting on his mouth.

'Alix, as you now know your father killed himself, but what you almost certainly don't know is that quite possibly he tried to kill you too at the same time when you were a small baby. Your mother told me he put his head in the gas oven after taking an overdose of tablets, but thankfully she arrived in time to rescue you.

'What……!!' David held up his hand to stop Alix.

'Are you telling me you didn't know that?'

'No-no way. I've got his death certificate at home, and I'm certain it states 'pulmonary embolism'.
Alix then just sat staring into space, slowly shaking his head.
'You're telling me your mother never talked to you about it?'
'No never….' Alix thought for a moment. 'On second thoughts she did, and just said he was a coward, that he had committed suicide and ruined her life, and I was never to mention his name again, but that was a long time ago as I remember.
I thought suicide or something that means that had to be put on the death certificate. You don't think my mother could have been lying, do you?'
'Sometimes parents can be less than honest with their children, often just to protect them.
'But she never told you about your escape?'
'Definitely not.'
David looked up and Alix was crying silent tears.

As if from nowhere, David handed Alix a glass, poured a substantial measure of whisky, with the comment. 'This might help, so get it down, and don't be embarrassed. What you've just found out would be very emotionally traumatic to anyone no matter how long ago. I think you're very resilient.'
Alix looked at David accusingly. 'If you've known about this all that time, and we've been colleagues

and friends for well over 20 years, why have you never said anything?'
'It's not the kind of thing you bring up, and I obviously thought you must have known, and you never at any time said anything……..'till now,'

David continued, 'There was a rumour at that time that he had possibly accidentally killed your older brother by pushing him or throwing him down the stairs, but the postmortem said accidental death from a fall.'
Alix said accusingly, 'so you've known about my brother all this time, and I have only just found out, why didn't you ever tell me?'
'Don't get angry, I felt some things were best left unsaid, and possibly that was wrong, but it is what it is, and I'm sorry.'
Alix nodded, 'that's OK I'm just a bit raw.'
David continued, 'you will have a copy of your father's death certificate, I think it was a home office pathologist who stated the cause of death was a pulmonary embolism if my memory serves me right. I do also believe he had tried to hang himself before, but your mother stopped him.'
'How can you be so sure; it was a very long time ago, and why a home office pathologist?'
'It's not something you easily forget especially when it is a family you know quite well, and I don't know the answer, but get that whisky inside of you.'

Alix then followed the chaplain's instructions to the letter, downed the whisky, blew his nose, and wiped the tears away, as David continued.

'Look Alix, I don't know why it was a pathologist from the home office, but there has obviously been something very odd going on, what with the murder of your grandfather and the 18 soldiers who weren't who they appeared to be, and all that followed by your father's suicide.'

Once again Alix tried to interrupt to no avail as David almost rushing his words so no interruption would be possible continued.

'Perhaps there's something you need to know, but I don't want to make things any worse than they are. A long time ago I was a curate in Cambridge, in the Jesus College Chapel. You were a baby at the time and, although you are probably not aware of it, I baptised you. Around that time your father came to see me, quite convinced his house had been the subject of a break-in, although nothing was taken. He felt whoever had been in the house was looking for something. When I suggested your father went to the police, he wouldn't. I just felt that he wasn't being entirely straight with me, because there had to be a very good reason, he didn't want to get the police involved. Whatever it was he was clam like about it. This might sound a bit odd, but whilst I knew your father, I didn't know him if you get my drift.'

With a slight shake of the head, Alix cut in.' That's a bit creepy because old Mr. Edwards described him as a man who may have done some secret work during the war, and of course I don't even have a photo of him.'

David said, 'Look that doesn't surprise me, he always struck me as a man who spent his life looking over his shoulder, almost as if he was checking he wasn't being followed.' He then continued gently, 'Now, after your father's death your mother moved here to Ely to live with your grandmother, and quite coincidentally I was sent here too, and it was nice to have a parishioner I knew. You were still a youngster, when the same sort of thing happened again. Your grandmother was made of stern stuff and, although she'd had double locks fitted, there was never any sign of a break-in, but it must have happened four or five times. She, like your father, knew that whoever it was, was looking for something specific, because nothing was ever taken.'

Alix looked surprised.

'I didn't know my mother and my grandmother lived together.'

'Well, they did, but' – David sucked air in through his teeth – 'I had the distinct impression that your grandmother wasn't over-fond of her daughter-in-law, but then that's not an uncommon state of affairs!' As he finished, he chuckled quietly to himself.

'Did she go to the police?' Alix asked softly. 'Perhaps I should go down to the police station and see what records they've got.'

'No, I don't think she did.'

Alix more or less dried up at this point. The thought of his father's suicide was a lot to take on board, plus the idea of strangers entering his home both in Ely and in Cambridge. Then Alix remembered arriving home only a few days ago, and how the house seemed different. At the time he had put it down to the simple fact that although she hadn't been there for some time, things didn't seem to be in quite the same place.

He then spoke, 'David, I remember a few days ago there was something different in the house when I came home. You know what it's like when you can't find something because you had moved it but didn't remember. Well, that was what it was like, but nothing I could lay my finger on. Now you've brought it up I think someone had been in the house, but I can't be sure.'

He resolved to ensure that, henceforth, every time he went out the window were always locked and the alarm on, the double locks on and Yale locks deadlocked. Alix remembered thinking how like Fort Knox the house was with alarms, plus double locks and now he realised why.

'Anyway, David I've taken enough of your time. But what would your advice be?'

'Most importantly are you alright. All this must be a huge shock.'

'And some, but you know it's all ancient history now, it's just I need answers, a lot of answers. What would you do if you were me?'

'You mean apart from going home and pouring a large Scotch,' eyes twinkling, 'I'd take a few days as soon as you can and go to all the parishes on your list and see what you can find out about the boys and their parents.'

With that Alix thanked David, left and walked home in the dark.

When he got to the gate, he felt it looked slightly menacing in the darkness, and resolved to have outside security lights installed.

He just couldn't wait until the holidays to find out about the Irish children, but he wondered if it was feasible to hire a car at Dublin airport early on Saturday morning, for two days maximum, and visit 17 parishes spread across Ireland in that time. He quickly decided he had to try.

CHAPTER 13

On the Sunday evening when he was back in England, and more worried than ever, Alix consulted all the notes he had made on his lightning visit to Ireland.

In two churchyards he found the graves of two of the children's parents, one couple killed when their horse and trap ran out of control, and another in a house fire. This eliminated the parents of Alan and John Smith and Phil Kyle, but still left eight unaccounted for, and Alix was now convinced that the children in whose names the chalices were given had been those of the parents who had gone to the USA, and he was certain they would all have been travelling first class.

This was confirmed after several days of in-depth research on his computer. In all, eight had travelled to the US between 1901 and 1905: the Coghlan's, Fitzgerald's, Patrick's, Mahony's, O'Dwyer's , Molloy's, the O'Connell's and McBride's.

The big surprise came when he found the Molloys and the O'Connells had sailed on the ill fated maiden voyage of the Titanic in 1912, but were listed as dead.

After extensive searching through emigration lists for not only the USA but also Canada, Australia, New Zealand and South Africa, he was able to account for all the others. They had left shortly after their children had died, even before the families named on the chalices, and all these emigrants had gone to Australia. That eliminated the Moroney's, the Hayes, and the Lenihan's.

He couldn't help but wonder why only eight chalices, when these other parents went abroad as well. He then realised that it was obvious James Edmundson had not needed to bribe them to go, as they all had travelled steerage. Alix surmised that in their grief they just wanted to start a new life.

The Clinches and, of course, the Stringers, were both dead anyway.

Something else Alix noticed was that all the children on the list were older than Willie, so presumably whoever replaced them must have been older too.

It did look very much as if this man Edmundson had wanted them all out of the way – and a long way out of the way, so far that they were unlikely to return.

Alix had by now worked out that there had been some kind of substitution. It was obvious that the odds of this substitution being discovered were remote because the children all came from quite widely dispersed towns and villages, so none of them could possibly have been known to each other. Alix then wondered what would have happened if these children had grown up and become famous. It was a passing thought but one that wouldn't go away; however, he pushed it to the back of his mind because suddenly he wanted to know what had happened to the McBride family in the USA.

One of the great things about the US Immigration Service is the comprehensive records that it keeps. It didn't take Alix long to discover that the family had landed in Boston, Massachusetts in late May 1903. They were taken out to Illinois, where James McBride began as manager of a 10,000-acre ranch called Felmersdale near the small township of Airs in Champaign County, about 120 miles south of Chicago. Further enquiries eventually showed that some of the family settled in Chicago, and finally Alix was able to discover a James McBride, aged 61, grandson of the one born in 1898.

Email is a wonderful tool, and James McBride was delighted to make a family connection from old Ireland. He was able to supply Alix with family photographs of himself, his father and his grandfather, who he remembered well. He also added a helpful description which was that all had copious red hair, which, he assured Alix, his grandfather had told him that all McBride men had. But Willie McBride's hair according to the black and white photograph had been fair, which really confirmed the absence of a link.

Alix was anxious to know from James McBride the financial position of his grandfather when he arrived in the United States. He was able to tell the McBride in Chicago that his grandfather had been a farm labourer, who suddenly had enough money to buy a solid gold chalice for his church and travel to America first class on the Saxonia.

James said that one of his brothers now owned and ran the farm at St John's Valley, which extended to 50,000 acres, part-arable, part-beef. As far as he could remember, his grandfather was able to buy the farm and ranch in the late 1920s or early 1930s at the time of the Great Depression for something like ten cents an acre. He promised to try and find out who the vendor had been.

The next email from James, a few days later, said that without any doubt his grandfather had bought out a company called Chaesar Farms, which owned the land.

'Whew!' Alix whistled aloud.

Although he didn't need to, Alix spent the next week doggedly tracking down the other five sets of parents who went to the USA first class. Without exception, all began as farm managers and then became owners, all had been employed by Chaesar Farms, and all had been able to buy Chaesar out at about the same time – but each was far enough away from the rest not to know the others existed.

Alix now had a much clearer picture in his mind of what had happened, and after much thought he concluded that for some reason 18 dead children in Ireland had been replaced by 18 others in the last few years of the 19th century. Most of the parents emigrated on their own , but eight couples were bribed to emigrate by the Chaesar Estate, with very good farm-manager jobs in the USA and Canada. Four sets of parents were dead by the end of 1912, either in Ireland or drowned at sea.

 Chaesar was heavily involved in some early financial transactions with the Blumeur bank relating to Alix's grandfather and grandmother. The Chaesar Estate appeared to have gone under in the Great Depression, and six Irish farmers had been able to buy up the land they farmed and became seriously wealthy.

Seventeen children had joined up with Willie, who was barely 18, and were drafted to the 8th Battalion, Royal Munster Fusiliers in 1916. They fought together until Ypres when Willie died – or, rather, was murdered.

Alix could see that the Chaesar Estate was the key to everything, as it was emerging as a common denominator or at least was heavily involved in all of this. The men who took on the identity of the dead children might well remain a mystery forever, but the Chaesar Estate had to be the place to look to find out more. The answer he needed to find out was just where did Willie McBride fit into all this?

 There was obviously something very odd going on, and as an avid fan of the movie The Day of the Jackal, Alix was well versed in the use of a dead infant's details to obtain a false passport. All of what he had discovered so far led him to think that it was uncannily similar, in that there had been some kind of substitution.

Nevertheless, there still had to be a logical explanation, and the first thing to do was find out as much as he could about the Chaesar Estate.

Once again, the Internet was to give him the answers, and Alix was to spend many hours in front of his laptop hunting down all the information he could find about Chaesar.

A Google search for 'Chaesar' proved fruitless, even when combined with 'Blacksmills'. Then Alix tried County Cork, still nothing. Following that he tried Chaesar with Munster, and then at the point of almost giving up, Alix began to try all the provinces of Ireland, and he hit gold dust with County Mayo.

Not only did the word Chaesar appear, but also a place called Belmullet and with it the names of O'Donnell, Edmundson, and Termoncarragh House. Opening one page led to others, and the history of a family called O'Donnell appeared. It was fascinating reading for Alix, a real insight into the tragic history of 19th-century Ireland.

The O'Donnell's initially went to County Mayo from Ulster in the late 17th century. By the middle of the next century, thanks mainly to illegal activities like smuggling, they were well enough off to buy the lease of the Burrishoole barony, on the coast in the west of the county. From the small town of Newport and covering all of Achill Island, they became the main landowners. They also owned 30,000 acres in the neighbouring barony of Erris, which included Belmullet off the north-west coast. Indeed, the O'Donnells were at one point the only landowners from Blacksod to Erris Head. However, it seemed that from around 1840 they were in considerable financial difficulties, and by the middle of the 19th century they had sold out to a family from England called Edmundson.

In real terms what this meant was that the Edmundson family owned most of the north-west corner of County Mayo. More enquiries showed that the Edmundson family originally came from Surrey, and were a family of adventurers and soldiers who had amassed a fortune from tea and tobacco, from both the Far East and America, during the 18th and early 19th centuries. The low cost of land in Ireland due to the potato famines meant they could afford to buy it up in large quantities, although quite what they hoped to gain from owning so much land in Ireland was the subject of guesswork. The land was purchased through the Encumbered Estates Court in 1849. The only other interesting fact that Alix was able to glean was that the Edmundson estates in Ireland were sold immediately after the First World War. From the information Alix had obtained, he guessed, or at least surmised, that the same family had by that time bought huge tracts of land in the

USA, which was where the parents of the dead children were effectively bribed to go to become farm managers.

This detective work was beginning to get Alix down. Sure, he had found out a great deal about life in Ireland in the mid- and late 19th century. He even believed he had stumbled accidentally upon a massive fiddle, perhaps even a conspiracy. Most importantly, though, he was no further forward in discovering who his grandfather was.

CHAPTER 14

Fate took a hand, in the form of toothache. Alix wasn't by any means a regular visitor at his local dental practice. There were two problems. The first was that, on a schoolteacher's salary, he couldn't afford private fees, and the second was that the only National Health Service dentist, where the fees were affordable due to government subsidy, was a chap called Chris Heron – an old friend of Alix's from school.

Alix went only when he had to, because he had seen Chris in action socially far too often and, whilst his services had a very high reputation in the town, Alix didn't feel comfortable in his care. It had become almost a joke, and now 18 months had passed since his last examination and Alix's penchant for Polo mints had caused a tooth to break. The pain alone was bad enough, but in addition the rough edge was tearing his tongue to pieces.

When he called the surgery, he could hear Chris's peals of laughter when the receptionist asked if Mr McBride could have an emergency appointment. The next afternoon he found himself flat on his back, mouth open and with a bright shining light in his eyes, experiencing the exquisite agony of the injection in the back of his mouth. Chris was still giggling, and Alix thought he hadn't probably stopped since the previous day.

'So, apart from eating mints, what else have you been doing recently?'

Alix could already feel the numbness spreading, and the pain from the tooth receding.

'I'm trying to trace my grandfather in Ireland.'

'That's interesting, because I've been doing my family tree, and in fact met my second cousin, my grandfather's brother's grandson, in Bristol a few weeks ago. I was staggered because he turned out to be a dentist, just like me.'

Fighting the increasing numbness and sounding as if he was the worse for drink, Alix asked, 'How did you manage that?'

Chris smiled, partly because of the way Alix was slurring his words.

'Census returns show everyone who was living in a house. You can now get the returns up to 1901. They happen every ten years, by the way, and I found out not only who the whole family were, but also where they came from. I thought we all came from Bristol, but the censuses showed that we originated in a small village in Lincolnshire.'

A metaphorical light bulb came on as, for the first time in years, Alix was happy to be at the dentist's, thanks to this pointer. Half an hour later he left, tooth repaired, and new knowledge acquired.

Census returns are easy to access online, and the only real problem was where to begin the search. Alix chose Belmullet for his initial search of the

1901 census, if only because that was where his father had been born. He used 'Termoncarragh House' as a keyword and, hey presto! up it came after only a couple of hours search late into the evening.

Termoncarragh House in Belmullet was described as an orphanage and – lo and behold – there were all 18 of the lads, ranging in ages from the three-year-old Willie McBride up to the 11-year-old Mick Moroney. The adults living in the house were Mr Chris Glanville, whose age was given as 45, born in Blacksmills, and Mrs Helen Glanville, aged 45, born in nearby Binghamstown.

Whilst this wasn't yet job done, it seemed like a major triumph to Alix, who had to resist the temptation to ring Tony there and then, almost forgetting it was past midnight.

It seemed obvious to Alix that what he had to do next was to go to Belmullet and Termoncarragh House. Before leaving for school in the morning Alix once again booked himself on a flight to Ireland on the next Saturday, but this time to Shannon airport, where he hired a self-drive hire car.

Getting a return flight later was easy, but it was still with some trepidation he pulled out of Shannon for the 140-mile drive to the Mullet Peninsula, and the village of Belmullet where with luck he might find out about Termoncarragh House. He really felt he was getting much closer to the answers he sought, although whether he was going to like what he heard was a different matter altogether.

The nearer he got to his destination; the more Alix realised how much he was travelling into the back of beyond. By the time he reached the outskirts of the small town – more a large village – of Belmullet, he felt on the edge of the world. After fruitlessly driving round for half an hour, Alix realised he was getting nowhere. He asked one or two locals where Termoncarragh House was and no one had even heard of it. The last person he spoke to suggested he went to the Civic Centre. The lack of yellow lines made parking easy, and as Alix pushed open the large glass doors he found himself in front of desk piled high with books.

'Hello and how can I help you today.' The delightful Irish accent and the welcoming smile reminded Alix of days long gone in the UK.

'My name is Alix McBride, and I'm trying to find out about a Chaesar House at Termoncarragh, and I hoped you might be able to help me,' said with a shrug of the shoulders, 'I'm kind of lost.'

'Don't worry, most folk who come in here are lost so we're accustomed to it. I'm Kathy Gibson, librarian, tour guide, in fact I'm supposed to be the fount of all knowledge around here, which isn't quite true, but I have a good computer, and if I don't know the answer, and the computer doesn't then I probably know someone who does.'

She put her pink rimmed glasses on, 'Ah that's better, I can see you now. What on earth makes you want to go to Termoncarragh?'

'Well slightly more specifically an orphanage called Chaesar House. In fact Termoncarragh House and Chaesar House I think may possibly be one and the same thing. I've found entries in the 1901 census return if that is helpful'

'It's seriously desolate out there. Just give me a moment,' and with that she crossed the room, and a computer whirred into life. 'There we are, I'm now looking at the census returns for 1851 for Termoncarragh,' at which point Alix interrupted.

'Sorry to interrupt you but I thought most of the Census Returns were destroyed in the Four Courts fire.'

Kathy just smiled and said, 'well now they can say what they want but we do still have a few records here, and this is one of them, which shows a hundred and thirty-three persons in twenty-six houses. Today I can tell you for certain, as I am also the local postmisteress, there is absolutely no one living there permanently.' She looked up from the desk to Alix. 'It was the terrible potato famine, and emigration. There's a big graveyard out there you should look at later.'

The mouse moved again, and she pointed at the screen. 'Just confirming what you said. In 1901 the number living in Termoncarragh House has risen to twenty in just one property, but it was now called Chaesar Orphanage.'

Alix chipped in, 'and that's where my grandfather was.' He grimaced, 'is it not still there?'

'There aren't any houses – just a few barns and sheds, plus a couple of holiday homes. It's a great place for birdwatchers.'

At that moment a tiny elderly Irish lady – almost a perfect caricature of what you would expect one to look like – popped her head round a bookcase only a few feet from where Alix was leaning. She spoke in a delightful soft Irish brogue.

'I couldn't help but overhear you telling the gentleman about Termoncarragh House. Whilst it's none of my business, I can tell you for sure, it burnt down sometime in the 1920s. It became Cheasar Orphanage and then Chaesar House.'

She stopped to draw breath, and Alix got a better look at her. She must have been 90 if she was a day, and tiny, probably no more than four feet six inches tall, dressed in a tweed suit with a stained woollen jersey and a knitted hat with a bow at the front, which had seen better days.

'It was an orphanage, you know,' the woman continued, 'and it was so sad, because my mother told me all the boys went to the British army in the war, and not one of them returned. Only the Major survived, it was a terrible thing. People said he and his wife set the house on fire and killed themselves from the sorrow.'

'Mary, you are a scandalous old rumour monger,' said Kathy with a smile. Then, to Alix, 'this is Mary O'Hara. What she doesn't know about this area isn't worth a candle, and I was about to suggest you paid her a visit, because she can tell you far more than I can. Mary, this is Mr Alix McBride.'

'Hello,' said Alix. 'My grandfather, Willie McBride, was in the orphanage and was killed in 1917 at Ypres.'

He felt it inadvisable to use the word 'murdered', especially as Mary O'Hara was giving a good impression of being the local gossip.

The woman nodded.

'You're talking to the right person. Kathy,' she said, smiling sweetly, 'check the Mayo Advertiser for 1922, and I think you'll find all the details.'

Kathy excused herself, and old Mary continued almost in a whisper. Alix wasn't sure if it was the fact they were in a library, or she just didn't want to be overheard.

'So, your grandfather was in Chaesar House, was he?' Without waiting for an answer, she continued, 'A very secretive place, you know. They apparently kept themselves very much to themselves.' She suddenly went off at a tangent. 'I'm ninety-one, you know. I was born in 1918, and my mother used to do their laundry before I was born. If you'd like to come to my house, I can show you a photograph of my mother and grandmother outside the house. She took in the cleaning until the war came and her 'boys', as she called them, went away. My grandmother did the laundry before my mother.'

'You called it Chaesar House, but wasn't it Termoncarragh House?

The old lady smiled, 'Well that depended on who you were. The locals such as we were always called it Termoncarragh, but somehow or other it was also became known as Chaesar House, having originally been the Chaesar Orphanage in Termoncarragh House.'

Alix was fascinated at how he had come to this out-of-the-way place to find out more about Chaesar House, thinking logically it would still be there. The fact that it wasn't called that, but it had been known as Termoncarragh House shouldn't have surprised him, but then to have this chance encounter with an old lady whose family had taken in the laundry was amazing.

'I'd like that very much, if you're sure it would be OK,' as Kathy returned with a dusty large folder.

'Here's the first two months of 1922, and I have found the story on the front page of the twenty-sixth of February.'

The headline read: 'Two Dead in Mystery Fire at Termoncarragh'. Underneath was a picture of the smoking ruin of a large building with what seemed to be a fire engine and several firemen. The text read: 'The bodies of two people, presumed to be the owners, Major James and Mrs. Mary Glanville, have been found in the burnt-out ruins of Chaesar House, the former orphanage. It is believed, although Chief Superintendent Murphy would neither confirm nor deny it, that a pistol was found next to the bodies, both of which had gunshot wounds to the head.

Friends who did not wish to be named said the Glanville's had been very depressed since the end of the War, when it was finally confirmed that all their beloved orphans had perished during the four years of fighting.

It was felt by those who knew them best that this may have been a suicide, although the police have refused to rule out foul play. '

Kathy showed Alix a further edition of the newspaper from a week later, which said that, after extensive police investigation and the result of a post-mortem plus close examination of the pistol, it was concluded that Major and Mrs Glanville had ended their lives by gunshot wounds to the head whilst the balance of their minds was disturbed. It also announced that the funeral would take place on Thursday 10 March at Belmullet Roman Catholic Church, with the interment at Termoncarragh graveyard afterwards.

Alix asked if there was a newspaper for Friday 11 March, and sure enough the entry was there.
'The funeral of Major James and Mrs Mary Glanville took place on Thursday 10th March at Belmullet RCC. Fr. Andrew O'Malley officiated at the Service, and Colonel James Edmundson gave the funeral oration.
Major James Glanville, DSO MC , was the first son of the late Major Christopher and Mrs Helen Glanville. He was educated at Belvedere College in Dublin and as a very young officer served with great distinction in the Boer War, where he was present with Baden-Powell at the Siege of Mafeking and distinguished himself in the field. During the Great War he served in the 1st and 8th Battalions of the Royal Munster Fusiliers, where he won medals for gallantry at the Battle of Messines in 1916. He married Mary Peterson, from Surrey in England, in 1911 and took over running the Chaesar Orphanage at Termoncarragh at that time from his father and mother. He took all 18 of his gallant orphans to France and Belgium with the Fusiliers, where all were tragically killed in the defence of freedom.
It is thought that the strain of his loss, and the lack of any children from the marriage, caused the balance of his mind to be disturbed and resulted in the death of himself and his good lady, and the destruction of the house.

At the interment a volley of shots was fired over the grave by soldiers of the Royal Munster Fusiliers.
Family mourners included David Glanville (uncle) and Mrs. Glanville, John Glanville (cousin), Major John and Mrs. Freya Peterson, Colonel James and Mrs. Sheila Edmundson, Miss Ann Peterson, Mr. John Peterson and Major and Mrs. James Tucker. Sympathisers included representatives from the Royal Munster Fusiliers and many others.'

Alix tried to look as unemotional as he could, but this information had come as a shock to him. Was Colonel Peterson at the chateau related to this John Peterson? He assumed Colonel Edmundson was the same officer who witnessed Willie's last will and testament on the battlefield but had survived the war and been promoted to colonel. The coincidences struck him as odd, although his face remained impassive.

'Kathy, is there any chance of a photocopy of all these interesting accounts you've so kindly produced?' Alix asked. 'And how much do I owe you?'

'Oh, nothing, it's such a pleasure to be of help, to be sure,' Kathy said over her shoulder as she disappeared again.

When she returned with the photocopies Alix thanked her and left the building with old Mary O'Hara, who insisted he take tea with her.

Mary lived in a small, terraced house not far from the Civic Centre, and very hospitably made Alix a cup of tea before bringing him some old but still quite clear photographs.

The first showed a forbidding large house, with what seemed like a high wall in the background, and a young woman at the front door.

'That's my mother in front of the orphanage,' said Mary as she handed over a second, almost identical photo, with an older woman, 'and that's my grandmother.'

A third photograph showed the grandmother holding a small child.

As Alix was thinking that could be my grandfather, and how truly remarkable this all was, Mary interrupted his train of thought.

'I can remember my mother saying how private they were. She and her mother were never allowed into the house and the laundry was always brought to the door, so I'm not sure how this photograph with the small child came about. Mother always felt they were all a bit backward, because in the summer when the windows were open, she could hear what sounded like elocution classes, as if they were being taught how to speak. The children rarely left the orphanage to go to the big house, and they went by horse and trap.'

'How on earth do you know all this, when you weren't even born?'

'I can tell you this my mother told me tales and stories about our family going back to her great grandmother, it's how we store knowledge, and I've just always done it too. I can tell you stories about Great Grannie Annie away back in the 1840's.'

Alix smiled, remembering an old boy who came back to the school, 30 or so years ago, who was able to talk about the Crimean War and the Thin Red Line as if he had been there, just because his great grandfather had.

'OK that makes sense, but what do you mean by 'the big house'?' asked Alix, frowning,

'Well, the Edmundson's were the big landowners, and they lived not so far away at Edmundson Grange outside Binghamstown, and the children used to visit. I think it was Mr William Edmundson who had the house. There was also an occasion of great excitement when the children all went down to Scotchport for a boat trip, and that must have been around 1910. What was quite peculiar was they seemed different after that – not that mother and granny got to speak to them – but before that the little boy in the photo seemed to be able to run around without any restrictions at all, then after that boat trip time he always seemed to be looked after by the older boys. I'm only going on what my mother told me, you know, but I remember a lot of what she said, because she always felt there was something not quite right about Termoncarragh

House and the Chaesar Orphanage, although they paid very well. It was their secrecy, like they were a secret society or something like that.'

Alix sat in silence, trying to picture the events that must have taken place almost a hundred years before, but was still struggling to see them as real. Feeling the conversation had gone as far as it could, he thanked Mary profusely for the tea and showing him the photographs. He left his name and address with a 20-euro note and asked the very willing Mary if she could get copies of the photos made and sent to him.

Alix had gone out into the street when he remembered the one question he had meant to ask. He knocked again on the door.

When Mary answered, and before Alix could speak, she said: 'You meant to ask me a question, didn't you? Well, the answer, young man, is yes – Edmundson Grange outside Binghamstown is still occupied, and by the descendants of the Edmundsons. The house used to be called Binghamstown Grange.' She smiled sweetly and said, 'Goodbye, I must go,' before closing the door in Alix's face.

A somewhat surprised Alix turned to walk down the road, but as he did so the door opened again and Mary spoke once more.

'Oh, I forgot – it's a couple of miles down the road out of Belmullet, follow the R 313 south-west. Go through Binghamstown, which is signposted, and it's on your left after the crossroads.'

With that the door closed again. Alix smiled broadly, continued to his car and drove off.

The visit to Edmundson Grange proved somewhat unproductive. The elderly lady who answered the door said that her great-great-grandfather had owned the house, and it had been passed down, but the family name was no longer Edmundson. She wasn't forthcoming about her surname, and in truth she was less than friendly. In fairness, however, Alix left with an address she had given him to visit in Doolough, where, he was assured, he would find a Glanville still resident.

Back up to Belmullet and then south, Alix didn't take long to cover the ten miles to Doolough and Doolough Grange. Again he rang the doorbell, not sure what to expect, but this time the door was literally thrown open by a jolly woman, probably in her late fifties.

'Hello, and what can I be doing for you?' she enquired breezily. This brought a smile to Alix's face, and the lady smiled as well.

'My name is Alix McBride, and I'm here doing some research into my family tree. I was told you are a descendant of the Glanvilles, who had the orphanage at Termoncarragh. My grandfather lived there as a child, I believe, and I wondered if you might be able to help me find out more.'

'To be sure,' said the woman. 'I'm Annie Glanville, and my late husband's grandfather was the cousin of Chris Glanville, who founded the orphanage, and he was always called 'Uncle' by the poor sad James, who died by his own hand in the burning in 1922. Please, will you come in?'

Annie stepped aside, and Alix walked into the kind of hall beautifully furnished with antiques, that you would expect to find in a house named The Grange. The woman continued where she had left off.

'Oddly enough, my husband always referred to him as 'Uncle James'. You don't mind the kitchen, I hope. You look like you could do with a cup of coffee and a bit of homemade cake.'

'Thank you, that's very kind,' said Alix, stopping opposite an oil painting of a beautiful Georgian house.

Seeing him stop, Annie said, 'that's Termoncarragh – or was, I should say. What a waste, what a tragedy.'

'Well, it was the most beautiful house, and my grandfather can count himself lucky to have lived there.'

Alix sat down in the large old kitchen, with what he imagined were some of the original fittings and beams still in place. A large Aga stood in what must once have been the fireplace with a kettle on top, and its permanently hot water ensured that coffee was produced quickly and without fuss. Alix was left to add milk and sugar as his hostess produced a homemade fruit cake.

'Exactly what is it you feel I can help you with?' asked Annie, looking at him quizzically.

'I was hoping you might have some old records of the orphanage – in fact anything at all to throw some light on what it was like.'

Annie replied. 'Unfortunately, in fact it was more than that, it was a tragedy that all the records were destroyed in the fire. There had been some talk of a memorial for the boys, I believe, just after the war, but the family were very opposed to it, although no one was sure how James felt, and then suddenly he and his wife Mary were both dead. Local people felt that it was no accident, you know!'

Annie said this last in the tone of voice that doesn't allow disagreement, but Alix had the feeling the incident had been the subject of some arguments down through the years.

Then she quickly added before Alix had a chance to say anything. 'There were some who said that his wife Mary was responsible, because she wore the trousers in the marriage, which was why they had no children of their own.'.

'Can you tell me a bit more about the history of the Glanville's?' Alix broke in. 'You know, where they came from, what they were like – anything at all, really.'

'I wish I could but, to be honest, there is no one left from that part of the family, so anything I tell you is very much second-, third-, even fourth-hand. There was a rumour, and no more, that James Glanville, who won the DSO and the MC in the First World War, had rushed into a marriage that was never that happy. There was always a feeling that somehow or other the parents, Chris and Helen Glanville, who started the orphanage, had told son James there were no prospects for him in Mayo, and he ended up going off to South Africa. Whether it was to emigrate is unknown, but I believe he was at the Siege of Mafeking with the man who founded the Scouts – Baden-Powell, I think.'

As she hesitated, Alix nodded in affirmation, and at that moment made the decision to pay someone to research the Edmundson family tree to find out more about them and the Glanville's, perhaps even the Petersons.

Alix needed to get back to the library in Belmullet, although a quick look at his watch showed that this would have to be another day. The archives might well show a report of a prominent young man like James Glanville going off to war, and even more so a triumphal return. Added to that, his engagement would probably have been reported and his marriage must surely have found its way into the local paper.

He also wanted to see Termoncarragh, as it was a major priority to find out a lot more about the

Edmundson's and the Glanville's, because both families seemed to have a degree of involvement in what was rapidly becoming the Willie McBride mystery.

Annie's voice interrupted his thoughts.

'So he must have fought in the Boer War, because there was a photograph of him I once saw in uniform, and how glamorous and handsome he looked. Anyway, when James came back Mary made a huge play for him, what with all the glamour of the uniform, and some said she was pregnant when they married, but as far as I know they never had any children.'

How Alix wished he had a tape recorder, because the information he had heard just in one day had completely changed his outlook on his research to date. Although he wasn't any closer to discovering more about who his grandfather was, he felt he was getting a more complete picture of where Willie had come from.

Alix knew he had to go to Termoncarragh before returning to Ely. After all, that was where his grandfather must have spent the first 17 years of his life and, although the house was gone, he felt very drawn to the place.

After thanking Annie for her help, he drove back to Belmullet and then headed off north-west to Termoncarragh. The sun was shining in through the driver's window of his BMW and the lush green landscape was attractive but there wasn't a lot to see when he reached what he assumed, from the map in the car, to be the place his grandfather was brought up. It was to the right of the road past what he took to be cattle barns, but Alix was able to conclude from what was left of a once-imposing wall and the rubble of two pillars that this must have been the orphanage.

Whilst it was a pleasant afternoon and agreeably warm, Alix nevertheless felt a strange chill as he got out of the car and walked about. It was a remote spot, and he could see and almost smell the sea, off to the west. Of the house there was little left, other than moss-covered stones scattered randomly around, although the outline made it obvious that there had been a substantial house here. How difficult to imagine the laughter of children and life in this desolate place! As he looked around all four quarters of the compass, Alix could see the signs of stones where other houses must have stood. He remembered the 1851 census showing that more than 120 people had lived here and then virtually everyone had left by the end of the nineteenth century. Why on earth the Glanville family chose to locate their orphanage here?

Then again, he thought the village that had once been here would have had a large house, a Lord-of-the-Manor-type of place, and he would have expected it to be called Termoncarragh House. The

name Chaesar just seemed to crop up without any explanations. With little else to do, he walked beyond the house and through a gate into the surprisingly large cemetery. Without consciously looking, Alix soon came upon an impressive brick lined vault, around the obelisk at the top was the inscription:
THE GLANVILLES OF TERMONCARRAGH HOUSE AND CHAESAR ORPHANAGE
This was obviously the family grave. The lettering below, whilst worn, didn't look sufficiently weathered to be almost 100 years old. It contained the inscription:
COLONEL CHRISTOPHER GLANVILLE
BORN 12TH DECEMBER 1856
DIED 1ST JULY 1913
TASK ACCOMPLISHED
Underneath this, Alix read:
HELEN EDMUNDSON
BELOVED WIFE OF CHRISTOPHER
BORN 14TH AUGUST 1858
DIED 10TH AUGUST 1913
LOVING MOTHER TO 18 ORPHANS
On the west-facing surface of the obelisk, Alix saw:
MAJOR JAMES GLANVILLE DSO MC
BORN 8TH MAY 1878
DIED 25TH FEBRUARY 1922
INTERRED WITH HIS BELOVED WIFE
MARY PETERSON

BORN 22ND JULY 1880
DIED 25TH FEBRUARY 1922
THEY FULFILLED THEIR EXPECTATIONS

Alix whistled to himself, and not for the first time caught himself talking out loud.

'Why does the name Peterson keep cropping up, it must be a coincidence.'

He checked his watch and realised it was later than he thought. With a plane to catch, he quickly photographed several views of the obelisk, got back into his car and drove back to the airport.

All the way back to Shannon, something was really bugging Alix. He was at the rental company's return point handing back the BMW when it came out of his subconscious and right to the front of his mind.

He clearly remembered Annie telling him earlier in the afternoon that she couldn't tell him much about that part of the Glanville family because they had died out with the death of James and Mary in the fire of 1922.

In that case, who paid for the obelisk above the graves?

CHAPTER 15

That was only one of the questions Alix needed answers to, and on the flight from Shannon to Stansted he began to make a list.

First and foremost, he could see a connection between Glanville and Peterson, and Edmundson, but where did Willie fit in, if at all? That could mean a lot of investigative work to discover how the two families fitted together, which confirmed Alix's earlier decision to pay someone to research these family trees.

Second, when did Termoncarragh become Chaesar, and what did 'Chaesar' mean? Alix thought it must be a Gaelic word.

Mind you he could see the house remaining Termoncarragh but the orphanage being Chaesar, and then eventually the house being called Chaesar because it was simpler.

By the time Alix got home, he had a clear plan in his head as he walked up the path to his house.

The ansaphone was pinging as he opened the door, and pressing the play button it was Colonel Peterson again. He sounded somewhat aggrieved that not only had Alix not bothered to call him back, but it was imperative he did now, and a meeting needed to be arranged to discuss what was to happen.

Alix swore under his breath, but to be fair Colonel Peterson had a point, and under the circumstanceS he would be the same.

Somewhat annoyingly when he rang the number the phone was answered by a woman.

'Hello this is Chateau Hugend, Mary speaking.'

'Oh hello I was expecting Colonel Peterson, ——'

'I'm sorry he's out with his guests, can I take a message.'

'Yes, my name is Alix McBride, and the Colonel rang to arrange a meeting, and that's the reason for my call.'

'Yes of course, we have been expecting you. I'm Mary and I run things here for the Colonel, and I know how anxious he is to meet with you.'

'I'd like to come next Saturday if that is OK, and perhaps stay for two nights.'

'Oh that's marvellous, the Colonel will be so pleased to meet you, can you give me any idea of what time you will get here.'

'Hopefully late afternoon.'

'That's fine we'll have your room ready.'

'Thank you, I look forward to meeting you then. Goodbye.'

What should have been a clock watching week in fact passed quickly. Alix rang Tony because he was desperate to tell him what had happened, but Tony according to his father was somewhere in the Outer

Hebrides and completely out of contact as there apparently was no phone signal.

Alix became more excited as the week wore on, firstly to turn what still seemed like a dream he hadn't even begun to get used to, into the reality of being the owner of the Chateau. Colonel Peterson had rung when he was out, leaving a message to say the lawyers had a document ready to sign, and this reminded Alix to call and book an appointment with them.

To be fair there was very little more to discover as he had been very close to the chateau on numerous occasions when visiting the battlefields with his sixth form history group. They always visited the Tyne Cot cemetery although their school's sad connection was at the Hooge, another of the cemeteries that dotted the landscape.

Alix had found most of what he was looking for at Booking.com and TripAdvisor where the Hotel Château Hugend – positioned close to the centre of much of the fighting in the Ypres Salient of 1917 got very good reviews.

How on earth had this come about, and why did he not know anything about it was uppermost in his mind and the main reason that he found it hard to sleep. His grandmother must have hated his mother, her daughter in law. Of course, this kind of thing was not uncommon, and he had seen enough family strife in his years at the school.

Alix had wondered at the lack of surprise in the Ypres lawyer at the sums of money involved., but perhaps that was more a question of his hangover on that Saturday morning.

On the other hand, why did all this have to wait until his mother died?

That was the real question that wouldn't go away.

Added to that was the realisation, almost for the first time was his lack of family. He was now well and truly an orphan in that he had never known his father, or at the very least didn't remember him at all.

His mother had always been very dismissive when he had asked about his father, saying she didn't want to talk about it, that he had committed suicide and ruined her life. Her opinion was that he was a coward. That was very much that, no matter how hard Alix had tried, until eventually he just gave up. It was only now that he had found out that a Home Office pathologist had declared the cause of death was a pulmonary embolism. Why? He asked himself did there need to be a Home Office pathologist, what was wrong with a local doctor or pathologist.

He had never got to know his grandparents on his mother's side, because they had been killed in a car accident, and had only a vague recollection of his father's mother, Granny McBride, as he had been just a small child when she died. He was, in every sense of the word, an only child, and as far as he was aware there were no cousins. This had never struck him as odd; indeed, he had never really given it a thought until now.

As Alix drove across the flat countryside of northern France and Belgium, and the closer he got to Ypres and the Chateau, the more evidence there was of a conflict that, although it had ended over 90 years before, was still very much in people's minds. Military cemeteries were dotted here and there around the countryside, all signposted, and whilst the post-war industrialisation of the area would have hidden landmarks known to the men who fought and died there, it was still a very emotive place in British and German history.

Every time Alix had been to Ypres, he had become upset, especially during the evening ceremony at the Menin Gate, to which he always took the children from school as an important part of the trip. It wasn't only the fact his grandfather died here, but it was the 54,896 officers and men who were killed in the Ypres Salient with no known grave and whose names were inscribed on the Menin Gate Memorial to the Missing that always got to him.

The seemingly endless lists of names adorned the Portland-stone panels on the inside of the memorial and even on the staircases and the inside of the loggias to the north and south sides of the building. Alix had always felt drawn to this small part of

Belgium, but now he was perhaps about to find out why it was more than his grandfather.

As he drove, he was again very much reminded of the fens around Ely, and he began to think anew about his grandmother's will, his mind wandering once more to his immediate family.

In addition to not knowing his father, how odd it was that the chateau had never been mentioned, or the fact that he obviously had a Belgian grandmother – and odder still that she had left the chateau in trust to him. Why him and not his mother?

The more he thought about it, the more Alix realised how much of an only child he had been. Never mind not knowing about his grandparents, he realised there were no cousins on his father's side of the family, and he didn't remember any relatives at all on his mother's side – she was also an only child as far as he was aware. He knew that his mother had been brought up by an aged aunt she couldn't stand. Until now Alix had never given it a second thought; he just thought they were an ordinary family. Suddenly seeing a road sign for 'Leper' brought back to him where he was going, and that he had been there before, and these thoughts were pushed to the back of his mind.

His car's Satnav took him to Dehaernesstraat and the offices of Frederick Dyuck, just after 12 noon. Formal greetings over with Frederick himself, who spoke perfect English, with a welcoming cup of coffee in front of him, Alix asked the question.

'Exactly what do I now own?'

Herr Dyuck smiled, and said 'how long have we got?'

'Just tell me in words of one syllable, and also what I need to do with it please. I am still quite confused, and it has obviously all come as a shock.'

'As you are already aware the chateau and the land have been in trust to you, and obviously you are now the owner. In addition you are inheriting over five million Euros scattered around three or four bank accounts, plus some real gilt edge stocks and shares valued at around three million Euros.'

Alix swallowed, 'OK, and I assume you have been handling all of this for some years now.'

'Yes, for a very long time because you may not be aware that during the battles around here in the Great War, your great grandparents were killed by a German shell which hit the chateau and your grandmother was the only survivor, which meant she inherited everything. She was not here at the time, and so the instruction in the will was that we were to take over all matters relating to the estate. My grandfather who set up this company, and whose photograph is behind me did just that, and so that is what we have been doing, especially as your granny decided to spend a lot of her time in England.'

Alix nodded and asked, can I assume that meant investments, and day to day banking as well?'

'Yes of course, and this has been a big undertaking for us, so we have a member of staff, who, under my supervision does just that.'

'I assume that explains the very healthy financial position I seem to have inherited.'

'Yes of course.'

Alix dug around in his pocket and brought out a sheet of folded paper. 'Hopefully you will know something about Blumeur's bank and the Chaesar estate, because they seem to be tied up with my family.'

Herr Dyuck quickly consulted the computer screen in front of him, clicked on the keyboard, and shook his head, 'I don't see anything,' shaking his head, 'in what context.'

Alix went back into his pocket and brought out a typewritten sheet, reading out loud.

'Mme Dubré, who is obviously my grandmother, is to have 'restricted' access to accounts at Georges Blumeur PrivatBank, the total amount available to be limited to a total of one hundred thousand pounds sterling annually. Complete access will be permitted only to my heir on proof of identity and production of account details and password'.

Again, a shaking of the head from the lawyer, Alix continued.

'Then my grandfather's will from 1917 stating that my grandmother, Madame Dubré, is to have access to accounts at Georges Blumeur PrivatBank, but that any single withdrawal will be limited to a total of ten thousand pounds sterling. Complete access is to be restricted only to Willie's heir, on proof of identity, and production of account details plus password.'

Alix continued, 'There is a letter relating to the Bank of Mayo, an account number, the name Mme M Dubré, and a deposit of seven hundred and fifty thousand pounds on the second of July 1918 by Blumeurs. The Bank of Ireland took over the Bank of Mayo in the early 1930s. For some odd reason, there is no name of the account holder who initiated the transfer. Nor is there any mention anywhere of further transfers to my grandmother, who was entitled to receive up to sterling.

There was £500,000 deposited by Blumeur in the Bank of Mayo account of Chaesar, 15 Nov 1909, but that is something separate altogether I think.

The Chaesar Estate appeared to have gone under in the Great Depression.'

Having read all this out Alix sat back in his seat and waited for a response.

After a few moments silence, the lawyer said, 'None of that makes sense to me. If we still had all the documents going back to the Great War then I might be able to give you more information, but quite a lot of stuff was, how shall I put it, another victim of the war, adding as an afterthought, 'these offices are not the original ones, they were just across the street, but were flattened by an RAF bomb in 1943.

He continued, 'Have you checked your mother's banking arrangements, because that might through some light onto things.'

'Come to think of it, with everything that has been going on I haven't.'

Alix made a mental note to continue his clearing up of his mother's things when he got home, directed especially towards the boxes in the cellar.

He still knew very little about the Chaesar Estate and its finances apart from the one fact they went out of business in the USA at the time of the Great Depression.

Alix was pulled out of the reverie by the lawyer. 'There's very little to sign, just the one document which simply continues the agreement your grandmother had with us, and also entitles you to draw funds from the savings account, any time you want which as you see is very well funded.'

Alix opened the folder on the desk which had been lying there in front of him with his name embossed on the front. There were the details of the current value of various stocks and shares, plus the savings account which contained well over a quarter of a million euros.

Alix only asked two questions the first being 'Can I read all of this and come back to you later?'
'Of course, and the second question?'
'How is the savings account financed?'
That is financed by the very profitable estate, the monthly rental from Colonel Peterson, and the bar profits, which are not inconsiderable' he said with a grin, adding 'don't forget all the land has no mortgage as it is owned outright by you.'
Seeing the look of shock on Alix's face he then said. 'Whenever we have threequarters of a million euros we then invest into stocks and shares, so as you can see you are now in a very strong financial position.'
Alex responded quickly 'Thank you very much, I'm sure we'll talk again soon, very soon, after I have got my head around all of this.' He then added, 'I want you to continue as things have been, and obviously I am more than happy to continue to pay whatever.'

The lawyer then pressed a bell on the desk and the young lady who had seen Alix into the office entered, 'Janice will witness both our signatures, and so long as you know I am almost always available on the phone,' handing over his card, 'and the second number is my brother's.'

Alix signed and took the original document. 'Look I'm perfectly happy to continue to be what I am, which is a schoolmaster, and I'm certain everything will continue as before, although I might want to sell the house in Ely and move, so I imagine all I need to do then is to….'

'Yes of course that wouldn't be a problem,' the lawyer interrupted.

Polite goodbyes were exchanged, and a shake of the hands and Alix having opened the door, turned around and said, 'Thank you again, we'll chat soon and then he was back out in the street.

In all it had taken no more than 30 minutes for Alix to be confirmed as a multi-millionaire, which he reflected was ludicrous, but he was perfectly happy at the outcome which only really meant that nothing would change because he wasn't really interested in the Chateau or the money. Not he thought, I'd give it all away, but I have no-one to leave it to.

He then got into his car and set off for Chateau Hugend.

CHAPTER 16

As a schoolmaster teaching history to teenagers, Alix was very familiar with the First World War, and he had visited battlefields at both the Somme and Ypres several times. Knowing exactly where Château Hugend was didn't lessen his slight degree of anxiousness because this visit was going to be totally different to anything that had come before. He still couldn't believe he was now the owner, and so didn't quite know what to expect when he arrived and introduced himself.

At last, the chateau came into sight, and Alix was struck by how big it seemed in the evening sunshine – far larger than he had remembered when passing it. Of course, when he had been here before, there had been no reason to study the chateau, but today was different.

Standing on a slight slope, the two-storey building had 16 windows to the front and was at least three windows deep, standing in quite considerable tree-lined grounds. In short, it was impressive.

As Alix drove through the gates, his car's tyres crunched on the gravel within a walled garden and, although the parking area wasn't entirely full, it was difficult to manoeuvre his car into a parking spot because of an obstruction in the middle. At first glance this looked like a sawn-off tree trunk surrounded by circle of grass edged with bricks some two feet higher than the driveway. On closer inspection the tree was obviously dead; indeed, it resembled the shattered trees in the Ypres Salient during the war that Alix had seen in photographs, smashed by shell and high explosive. This tree looked as if it had been treated with preservative, and three vertical cast-iron supports held it up. It was still taller than a man and a good four feet in diameter, so it must have been a decent-sized tree in its day, and Alix assumed it was in its own way 'a casualty of the Great War'.

The front door was open, and there was no-one in reception, so Alix put his overnight bag down, and hearing a voice he walked slowly and a bit tentatively down a short corridor towards it. The walls of the corridor were literally covered in photographs, and not wishing to disturb what sounded like a lecture he stopped to look at them. Some were views of Ypres during the battles taken from the air as well as from the ground, and others were obviously army regimental groups. His eyes were particularly drawn to a frame enclosing what Alix recognised as the white, purple and white ribbon of the military cross with the medal underneath. The citation read to '2nd Lt John Peterson for gallantry in active operations.'

Alix thought to himself that somehow it was logical to see Colonel Peterson's photograph but not the medal citation. Then his eye caught sight of another army group photo, with rows of men and in the middle was one Major John Peterson Company Commander Queen's Company 1st Bn Irish Guards. Alix continued down the corridor passing what seemed to be the bar on the way and straight into the back of a sizeable, traditionally decorated room with two windows on each of two walls, through which the sun still shone brightly. Through the windows could be seen the green leaves of trees in the garden, with rows of headstones in the military cemetery in the distance.

Several comfy-looking cushioned armchairs were drawn up theatre-style, and an attentive audience of almost 20 people were listening closely to a tall man with fair hair streaked with grey and half-moon glasses. He wore cavalry twills, a double-breasted blazer complete with four buttons on the cuffs, a checked viyella shirt, waistcoat with a pocket-watch chain snaking down into the pocket, and a striped dark-maroon-and-dark-blue regimental tie.

Without a shadow of doubt, this had to be Colonel Peterson, and his audience was presumably one of his tour parties. He was almost a caricature of what you would imagine a British army officer to look and sound like; Alix put him in his early sixties, perhaps even late fifties.

The group was, in the main, middle-aged couples, some of whom looked to be military types, and behind the colonel stood a large screen showing a map.

'So tomorrow it will be an early start,' he was saying. 'I want us all in position A by 0530 hours so we can follow what happened to the 1st Battalion the Cambridgeshire Regiment on this day over ninety odd years ago.'

The colonel then placed what looked like an army cane on the table and added, 'that is the debrief from today over and the briefing for tomorrow complete. In your rooms, you'll find all the maps and photographs you'll need in the morning to help you to chart what happened. It's going to be another tiring and emotional day for some of you, so not too many late-night parties in the bar, please – you'll need to be fit and raring to go. Dinner will be served in half an hour and breakfast, for those who want it, will be served out on the battlefield. Thank you.' All said in a voice used to giving commands.

As the Colonel walked through his audience exchanging pleasantries, Alix hovered in the background feeling sure he would realise there was someone different in the room. Eventually he started to walk past where Alix was standing, stopped, and said in a typically English way, 'I don't think we've met?'

'No, we haven't. My name is Alix McBride. Can I assume you are Colonel Peterson?' Alix smiled. 'I think you are expecting me. I'm sorry I couldn't speak to you personally, and I can see you are somewhat busy!'

Colonel Peterson smiled. 'Yes, more than somewhat,' followed by, 'please call me John'.

Although Alix was certain he was the last thing Colonel Peterson needed at that moment as he had clients to satisfy, his manners made him every inch the English gentleman, as he shook Alix's hand.

'My friends call me Alix.'

Introductions effected, John said quizzically, 'so, you're the new owner of Château Hugend?'

'Very much so. Didn't my solicitor tell you?'

'Yes, but somehow, I just assumed your name would be Dubré, as that is your grandmother's name, and the name that goes back several generations. The family name Dubré has always been on the title deeds, as far as I'm aware.'

After an awkward silence of a few seconds, the Colonel then cleared his throat. 'Look, I've got some things to attend to, but please you must join me for dinner. Can you excuse me for one minute?' With that Colonel Peterson turned on his heel and walked off returning a few seconds later with a very attractive middle-aged lady.

'Alix this is Mary who runs everything here in the chateau for me, Mary this is Mr. McBride our new owner,' followed by, 'could you organise his bags and show him to his room, please?'

With that John was tapped on the shoulder by a small gentleman with a beard, and he disappeared into the crowd, with a last over the shoulder remark almost issued like an army order.

'Eight o'clock here in the bar, don't be late!!'

As Alix followed Mary up the long straight wide wooden staircase, thickly carpeted with lovely polished mahogany banisters he was very surprised at the effect it was having on him. The hairs on the back of his neck were doing a war dance, and competing with the goose bumps, yet he didn't quite know why.

After reaching the top of the stairs it was turn right down a short wood panelled corridor and in through the heavily carved door at the end. Alix marvelled at the beautiful, fitted carpet that felt soft and giving under his feet, and the discrete lighting that almost gave a feel that the place was lit by candles and not light bulbs. The whole impression was one of 19th century grandeur, and if this was intended it had certainly worked. As Mary opened the door to allow Alix to enter, he half expected his grandmother to greet him, but what he became aware of was a large bedroom, similarly dimly lit, with a large four poster bed in the middle of one wall, and the room very expensively furnished. Mary having laid his case out on the bed turned to Alix and said,

'Mr McBride, may I welcome you to Chateau Hugend, this was Madame Dubré's room, and it is seldom used, because we reserve it for only the most important of guests. I'm very pleased indeed to be of help to our new owner, so if there is anything you want just call,' pointing to the telephone by the bed.

'Thank you Mary, I assume the bathroom is behind the door in the corner.'

'Yes Mr. McBride, would you mind if I went back to the guests, we are very busy as I think you could see?'

At 8 o'clock prompt, changed and showered Alix re-emerged from his room, came down the large ornate staircase and walked into a crowded bar. Colonel Peterson broke away from the small group he was chatting to, came across, and as he shook Alix's hand said in that affable way that English gentleman have.

' Settled OK?' and before Alix had the chance to reply,

'That's good' followed by 'what can I get you to drink?'

Armed with a glass of red wine, and the Colonel carrying the bottle, the two of them headed off towards the busy dining room, then out into a kind of conservatory where a solitary table was laid for two.

'I hope you don't mind the isolation, but I felt you might want some peace and undisturbed quiet whilst we talk about things over dinner.'

Alix felt a little uncomfortable at Colonel Peterson's directness. He realised the two of them needed to sort a few things out, but he just felt it might be better left until the morning. It would have been uncharitable to say no, so he just nodded in acquiescence.

'That's fine by me.' As they sat down at the table Alix looked out of the window and was very aware of the military cemetery which seemed only yards away, so he nodded in that direction. 'I expect you get used to the view.'

'Yes, but never to the point of being casual about the huge number of headstones. It's a daily reminder of pointless sacrifice.'

'So you don't subscribe to the sacrifice for our freedom notion?'

'No I don't, my grandfather lies out there, and for what?'

Thankfully at this point the waitress came towards them to take an order.

'Well I must say the menu looks lovely; your reputation precedes you. I have passed your door many times but never felt I could afford to come in on my salary. I have often suffered the hunger pangs that go with your lovely kitchen aromas, and all I had was the promise of a dry cheese roll and a bottle of water with my boys!'

The Colonel smiled, 'What do you mean with your boys,' then after a moment's hesitation, 'of course, how stupid of me, I should have remembered you are a schoolmaster and an historian.' Alix winced, 'Yes in a manner of speaking, and two of the school's old boys lie over there both killed in the first battle of Ypres in 1917. However right now, food is uppermost in my mind.' Alix looked at the waitress I'll have the ham soup, followed by a steak medium rare and a green salad, and no potatoes, please.'

Colonel Peterson's choice was identical except the steak was ordered rare, 'So a good Vet could resuscitate it', followed by enough of a laugh from him and a sympathetic giggle from the waitress whom Alix reckoned had to suffer the same line every night of the week she was working in the dining room, from the way she raised her eyebrows out of the Colonel's line of vision.

In polite society the point is never arrived at immediately and it was to be late in the proceedings after the delicious puddings had been cleared away, the cheese, biscuits and coffee consumed, that the small talk finished.

By this time Alix had discovered that the Peterson's were a military family through and through. His father, and grandfather, back to Great, Great, Great Grandfather before him had served Queens, Kings, and country with some distinction. In fact his ancestors had fought at Waterloo, and were in the Charge of the Light Brigade in the Crimean War.

Colonel Peterson, and his father had served with the Irish Guards, and his grandfather served with the Royal Munster Fusiliers. As Alix had found out very quickly, John's grandfather had been killed at Ypres, and indeed lay in the very cemetery they overlooked, being killed shortly before the war ended. Very sadly an uncle and another distant relative also lay over the road, both killed in the Ypres salient. Alix was reminded by the Colonel that one of the tragedies of the 1st World War, which was to be the War to end all Wars, was the way that recruitment was initially done in villages, streets, and factories. Friends volunteered with friends all ending up in the same battalion of the same regiment. When a battalion went into action and suffered heavy casualties, because of the recruiting policy, it meant that whole streets, factories, even football teams, sometimes came close to being wiped out, and this was one of the main reasons the Great War had such a catastrophic effect on huge parts of English life.

All of this was of course small talk, and Alix suddenly realised that phase of the evening was over. He had learned over the years of dealing with parents to see the warning signs that a conversation is about to get serious. There is normally a clearing of the throat, or a sneeze into a handkerchief, or a wiping of the jowls at the end of a meal. Colonel Peterson didn't disappoint, because he went for all three!!

Before he could begin, Alix said very quickly, 'Look I don't want to change the arrangement you've had with my family over the past years, so please don't worry about that. I'll never live here, my life is in England, I'm English, but I do already feel like I belong here, and so I'd like to be able to come and stay now and again.'

The Colonel nodded, flushed slightly and said a very simple and quick 'Thank you............................,' and after clearing his throat somewhat nervously again.

'I must confess it has been worrying me quite a lot, and quite honestly I didn't know quite what to expect from my new landlord, and that has set my mind at rest, but that wasn't the only reason I wanted this chat.'

He shuffled around on his seat, almost as if he was composing himself.

'Look, what do you know about your grandfather?'

'I know absolutely nothing at all, except a letter written by my grandmother Marie, and she said he was murdered because they fell in love so the village boys murdered him as some kind of revenge.'

'You've never tried to find out more, done your family tree, or anything like that?' The Colonel quickly responded in a voice that indicated his astonishment.

'I only found out a short time ago, and …..' Alix was about to start to tell the Colonel about the graves and the orphanage, but he felt this wasn't the time.

Sensing Alix's hesitation the Colonel started talking.

'Well, there is a lot you should know, and some of it might shock or even disappoint you.'

Alix didn't really expect that, 'What do you mean shock or disappoint?'

'Firstly, as you know, your grandfather Willie McBride is buried right out there' he said pointing over his shoulder at the headstones.

'How did he die, do you know?' Alix could hear the tremor in his own voice, but the response from John Peterson almost knocked him flat on his back.

The Colonel looked at Alix rather sadly through his half-moon glasses, nervously smoothing his silvery blond hair back over his head, and said 'Are you sure, really sure you want to hear this?'

'Of course, for it was a long time ago, and whilst obviously it could be upsetting, I think I need to know, to start to find out where and what I've come from.'

That drew a very old-fashioned look from the Colonel, and he pulled out a lovely gold hunter watch from his waistcoat pocket, suspended on a heavy gold chain, which Alix thought was trying to slightly less than politely say it was late, and it was time to go off to bed.

'I know it's late, but I need to know, you can't leave it like this, how was he murdered?'

'Just give me five minutes to check that everyone's gone to bed, and the staff has locked up and I'll tell you all I know.'

The five minutes seemed like eternity. Alix sat alone in the conservatory asking himself the same question repeatedly, did his grandfather's murder have anything at all to do with the huge amount of money he had just inherited?

Looking at his watch as he waited Alix realised it well after eleven o' clock and they'd been chatting already for over three hours. He wondered how long the Colonel had waited to tell this story.

Perhaps it was going to be so terrible, in fact terrible enough to be the reason that Chateau Hugend had never even been mentioned in the family, never mind visited. In fact it was almost as if it never existed.

Alix's thoughts were interrupted by the chink of glasses, two heavy Edinburgh crystal tumblers to be precise, a bottle of Jameson's Irish Whiskey, and an ice bucket.

'I hope you'll join me, because we could be here chatting for a while.'

'Just a small one and some ice would be great.'

Drinks in hand, the Colonel began his story.

'Do you mind if I just fire away, and then when I get to the end, there'll be questions which I'll happily answer.'

'Absolutely'

The Colonel took a large swig of his whiskey, followed by a deep breath and plunged into his tale.

'It appears that Willie McBride originated from a small village in County Cork, and he joined the Royal Munster Fusiliers with a load of his mates in the early part of 1916 after the Battle of Loos.

I believe about 17 friends joined but by the time he was murdered they were down to around 10.'

The 8th Service Battalion of the Royal Munster Fusiliers after the battle of Loos needed its numbers replenished, and the 9th Battalion was disbanded, because of the huge losses they suffered, and the 8th casualties were replaced by 12 officers and 200 men from the 9th.

It was at this point that Willie and his mates joined the 8th Battalion, and indeed went into A Company, and number 4 Platoon.'

'Chateau Hugend, right where we are now was badly damaged by the fighting during the middle part of 1917, although it found itself a mile or so behind the front line at the time we are interested in. The Dubré family who had built, and lived in the Chateau since the eighteenth century, and their servants, plus the families who worked the fields, at that time they owned some 150 hectares all took shelter in the cellars, and I'll show you just how large they are tomorrow.'

Colonel Peterson took another swig of his whiskey, crunched on the ice, and went on.

'Battalions were moved in and out of the front line, and you may not realise this but infantrymen such as your grandfather probably spent not much more than seven days every month in the trenches, if the mud holes at Passchendaele could be called trenches. The rest of the time they were either in reserve or resting. For that reason, Willie and his mates probably visited Chateau Hugend several times over a period of about eight weeks. It appears that young Willie who after all was only a boy of about eighteen rather fell for the daughter and only child of the Dubré's. Her name was

Marie, and she must have been no more than sixteen, and as you will see, very beautiful. By all accounts the feeling was mutual...................'

'Excuse me interrupting it is through her I have inherited the chateau!!'

'Yes, yes, I know all that, please don't interrupt; you'll ruin my train of thought.'

'Sorry' and the Colonel refilled both glasses and continued where he had left off.

'It would appear that young Willie and Marie got carried away, and she became pregnant.

It must have been becoming apparent on Willie's last visit to Chateau Hugend, that Marie was going to have his baby.

To say that was a disgrace is putting it mildly, very mildly indeed, in a good Catholic family, it was probably regarded as the very worst kind of sin, and shortly afterwards, she was sent away, as far as I'm aware to England.

I don't know if a wedding was ever envisaged, what I can tell you is that terrible revenge was taken.

It seems that someone, or a group of people took Willie, tied him to the remains of a tree. In fact, the tree you probably nearly hit in the car park, and literally chopped him to bits.

Before you ask why they weren't brought to justice, you must realise that the night they took Willie, his battalion were moved out to fight. Shortly after that the Germans retook the Chateau, and it was to be fought over for several months, during which time several of the members of the household were killed including your great grandfather and his only two sons. Consequently, the murder of Willie faded into insignificance in the context of the wholesale slaughter of the 3rd Battle of Ypres.

In short, I can only assume that he was cut down from the tree, possibly hidden behind the wall, or somewhere, then when the battle returned to the Chateau, and his body was discovered he was just another battle casualty.

The tree still stands because your great grandmother refused to allow it to be cut down, and although you wouldn't know, it became almost a shrine for her, and never a day went past without her standing in silence often in tears in front of it. She had the stone wall built around the tree to protect it after a delivery lorry almost flattened it.

I can still see her running out of the house yelling at the driver as he reversed straight towards the tree.'

'How do you know all this?'

'I've been in business here since I left the army over thirty years ago, and Grand Madame Dubré, your great grandmother, who can't have been a day under 90, told me about it in bits and pieces which I've been able to piece together, and what I'm telling you now is the whole story insofar as I know it.'

'Assuming that it was my grandfather that Marie was pregnant by, what happened next?'

Without a moment's hesitation Colonel John retorted,

'Yes of course it was your grandfather, and as far as I can be certain she came to England, had the baby, which was then brought up in England. Your grandmother then spent most of her life in England although she did visit frequently over the years, to keep an eye on the estate.

I believe initially she returned here after the baby was born, but without him, and as far as everyone was concerned, she had been suffering from

Consumption, had gone away to be treated, and in fact didn't reappear until after the war was over.

I know your father was called Willie McBride as well, for obvious reasons. He grew up met your mother, married, and that's why you are here now, although I know very little more than that.

I don't think there's much more to tell really, and obviously you know where he is buried.' Colonel Peterson looked at his watch, 'I must get to bed; I've an early start as you must have heard when you arrived.'

I wish you good night, perhaps we can chat tomorrow, and I'll try and answer any more questions you come up with.'

Colonel John stood up, as did Alix. 'Thank you, I've learned more about my family tonight than in the past 30 years. One question before you go. Does the name Chaesar mean anything to you?'

The Colonel pursed his lips, and after a few seconds slowly shaking his head, said 'No that's not a name that means anything to me.'

He then smiled put his hand out to shake Alix's.

'I'm glad to have been able to fill you in on a few details, and if there is anything else, anything at all

I can do just call, remember you must treat this place as your home, which of course technically speaking it is. Madame Dubré's room will always be available for you.'

With that the Colonel wandered out of the room leaving Alix alone with his thoughts.

Alix stood in silence for a few minutes, then moved away from the table, and headed for the door, where the catch slipped open easily, and he stepped outside. It was a lovely moonlit night, a clear sky, so light it was almost like day, and Alix wandered out into the car park, convincing himself he needed to check his car was locked, but totally drawn to the tree trunk where his grandfather perished so horribly all those years ago.

Like many others of a more mature age Alix had never supported the masses of flowers that appear at the roadside after an accident today, but he felt so moved by the whole scene that he picked a single red rose off the proliferating beautifully perfumed climbing English roses on the wall of the car park and went to place it by the tree.

As Alix approached, he was astonished to see a small bouquet of garden flowers, obviously picked during the day, and held together by ribbon, lying on the ground at the foot of the tree.

Someone else obviously knew the story, knew he was here, and that was enough to make him cry silently for a man he had never known. His grandfather, he had never even seen a photograph of until a few days ago. The almost unbelievable thing was somehow or other Willie had left him not only a huge amount of money but also the chateau. The chateau part he could just about understand, but he was no closer to finding out about where Chaesar or the Swiss bank came into all this This made him even more determined to find out the whole story about the 17 young men who also had two graves.

CHAPTER 17

The emotion of what he had heard and seen left Alix mentally exhausted, so that after his brief visit to the tree, he returned to his bedroom via the whiskey which he sank in one gulp, went to bed and fell immediately into a deep and surprisingly dreamless sleep. He only woke in the morning when there was a knock on the door, and a voice saying
'It's Mary, I've brought you some tea.'
'Come in'
As Mary laid the tray down with the cup and saucer plus the teapot, Alix realised what a nice matronly woman she was, with a lovely smile, and he guessed probably about his age, but it was difficult to be precise.
'Thank you Mary, that's kind of you, but I thought you were in management here, so tell me first of all, why are you bringing me the tea, and second tell me how long have you worked here at the Chateau?'
She smiled, 'firstly you are the most important occupier of this room since Madame Dubré, and I say occupier because you aren't a guest this is your home, and so the Colonel, who is out on the battlefield felt it right I should be the one to bring you up a tray.' She then added.

'As to the other, over 35years, and if I may say so it is a privilege to serve such a close relative of Madame Dubré'

For the first time Alix noticed there were a couple of portraits on the wall, faded by the sunlight.

'So Mary, you tell me you've been here for over thirty years, so I guess you must have known my grandmother.'

'Yes................... 'She was struggling to know how to address Alix, that much was obvious, but she was strangely hesitant.

'Please call me Alix; I'm not big on Sir, or Mr. McBride, I have enough of that at school!!'

She blushed 'Thank you.'

'Mary, can you tell me about the pictures on the wall?'

The room itself being in the corner of the house not facing the cemetery wasn't to strike Alix as significant initially. He hadn't really noticed it last night, and of course when he came to bed it was dark, the room only being lit by a bedside lamp.

'Let's start with the picture closest to the door shall we, it looks older than the other one, so who is that?'

'That is Madame Dubré, your great grandmother of course, who lived to a ripe old age, but that was painted about 1900.'

The picture was beautifully painted, and although Alix knew less than nothing about art, it looked like a water colour, quite magnificently framed. She must have been a very beautiful woman.

'Can I assume the other is my granny?' Although he could never remember seeing Madame Dubré, and he had no memory of his father, and although he must have seen her, but he was very young when she died.

There was a long silence, and whilst it seemed like that it was probably one that lasted for only a few seconds, but long enough to notice. Mary was suddenly very quiet, and Alix realised of course that she could well have known her

Alix broke the silence, 'How many years did you work for Madame Dubré?'

Alix offered her his red spotted handkerchief and she blew her nose before replying.

'I didn't, and you know she lived to be 103, but she still was the grand madame of the house even although it had become what it is today. We had lots of chats and she told me so much about the history of the place. I just adored her, and such a strong lady after all her suffering, and so nice to me.'

'Look I need to get up, have some breakfast and then pay my respects to my grandfather over the road, so I'd better shower and make myself presentable.'

With that Mary excused herself and left.

This allowed him to get up and try out the plumbing. The shower whilst it was a magnificent thing to look at, all highly polished copper and brass fittings, it really was as antiquated as it looked, and either threw out scalding heat or ice-cold water. Its brass fittings belonged to another era as did the bath which was large enough to accommodate a complete family of four. Alix continued to have the feeling that he was surrounded by ghosts of his past, and he felt somewhat uncomfortable about it.

Logically Alix had no reason for feeling that way, but perhaps it was the emotion of the past twelve hours that were making him imagine things that weren't there.

All he could really think about was how his ancestors, the Dubré's must have slept in that room, used the bath and the ancient plumbing.

Alix knew he had to visit his grandfather's grave, and that was where he was going but he badly needed some sustenance, so breakfast was a priority.

It was served in the Conservatory, and once again despite it being at the civilised hour of eight thirty, a time when hotel dining rooms are packed, Alix was in splendid isolation, as everyone else was out walking the battlefields. A cup of coffee, a couple of croissants, one of them full of dark Belgian chocolate and he felt ready to go outside and find his grandfather.

As Alix stood up to leave, and it was another glorious day in the making, so there was no need for an overcoat, he realised that Mary had appeared to his right, quite silently, not to startle him, but somehow it did.

She was carrying a small posy of flowers and she smiled gently and said, 'You might like to take these with you.'

Alix could see by the sympathetic look in her eyes, this was a scenario that must have been played out a lot, when guests at the Chateau went out to pay respects to their long dead relatives.

'Remember it's Section B Row 336, and almost at the far end, pretty well opposite the gate from the garden. You'll find a gate to the cemetery exactly opposite on the other side of the road, but be careful, there's a bend to your right, and cars can come at you suddenly and at some speed. I think you will only have to go about five rows down, and then it is straight along.' Mary then hesitated and in a soft voice said, 'Would you like me to come with you?'

'No, I'll be fine thank you.' As he said that Alix felt it was strange that she knew exactly where his grandfather's grave was. He knew where it was of course, only he hadn't entered the military cemetery from the chateau side before, but the last thing he expected was for Mary to know. Mind you he thought, she probably made it her business to know as he was now the owner and technically her boss, but what a strange thought!

Walking outside, and over the small road to the cemetery left Alix as totally awed as he had ever been, and it didn't matter how often he had visited this military cemetery it never failed to move him, but today was different.

As Alix walked past the headstones on the beautifully maintained grass slope, he noticed many of the graves had small flowers even a touch of heather growing at their base. All very neat and tidy everywhere and so he began reading the headstones. It was the age of the men, not men really; many of them still teenagers, boys in fact, which made the lump in his throat grow even bigger than it was when he started out. The other thing was the huge number of Regimental names on the graves, something he had never given much thought to before.

The most emotional part of the walk every time he visited with his pupils, were the short messages on the headstones

'He was the light of my life', 'Much loved Son', 'He died for freedom.'

Alix was just thinking that everyone responsible for these messages were themselves now dead when all of a sudden he was there, the words:

'6814 Fusilier Willie McBride, 1^{sth} Battalion Royal Munster Fusiliers, killed 3rd September 1917 aged 19

4/8/98-3/9/17'.

It was different because there was no inscription on the bottom of the stone, and once again and for the second time within 12 hours someone had been there before him, and this time they left a single red rose. This struck Alix as very strange after the posy of flowers at the tree in the car park, and the fact that he had left a red rose there only a few hours ago. Alix got down on his knees to place the flowers, swallowing and gulping rapidly to control his emotions.

After getting back to his feet Alix slowly picked his way back through the headstones to go back to the Chateau, it was hard for him to believe that this oasis of calm was once the scene of one of the bloodiest battles of the 1st World War, or any war for that matter.

He saw to his left, just in front of the Cross of Sacrifice an elderly man cutting the grass sitting on a power mower that looked almost as old as him. As Alix came towards him, he switched off the very noisy machine, and the conversation began in the way that many English people with a poor knowledge of languages do abroad.

'Do you speak English?'

He nodded 'Yes of course, can I help you?' In what sounded almost Home Counties English with a faint French accent.

'My name is Alix McBride, and my grandfather is buried here, and I wondered if you could tell me what exactly happened in this immediate area during the First World War. Although I am a history teacher and I bring my pupils here every year, I'm especially familiar with the 3rd Battle, but not as it related to the chateau.' Alix then apologised, 'I'm sorry we've never met, my name is Alix McBride, I'm sure you must know a great deal of what actually happened here next to the chateau.'

'Of course you are now the owner of the Chateau.' Alix said, 'May I ask your name?'

'Alain Nallen at votre service.' Doffing his well used sweaty looking beret to reveal a completely bald head polished and glistening in the sun. He then began to speak quite rapidly. 'How sad for the family Dubré, as there was no-one left, at least no man to take on the running of the Chateau when peace came in 1918, and then no-one here to run the Chateau in the old way when Madame Dubré died.'

Alix immediately concluded that this elderly gentleman didn't really approve of the Chateau being run as a hotel, but for the moment he kept that to himself.

'I worked for a while on the estate, and your great grandmother ran it, but she was a very sad old lady, having lost her husband, and sons to a shell, and then of course there was the incident over the daughter and the unwanted baby, and the young man who was then also killed by the Boche. You know I don't think she ever got over the deaths, and she wore black all the time as far as I remember.'

'Well Willie McBride, the young man who was killed was my grandfather.'

'Have you just visited your grandfather's grave?' he asked.

'Yes, but what I really wanted to know about is about the fighting round here.'

Alain took Alix over to a small grey bricked building to the side of the cemetery, and pointed to some very large unframed, board mounted photographs on the walls.

They were all panoramic pictures of the immediate area with a clear view of the chateau on the slope, the trees, the road, and the date above was 1915. The same picture in early 1917 shows quite severe damage to the chateau, shredding of the trees, and shell holes, plus an outline in blue of where the

German front line was. This photo appeared to have been taken from an aeroplane, or perhaps an observation balloon.

The next photo later in 1917 was taken from the chateau away from what is now the cemetery and again some devastation, but the German front line looks a good mile away.

The final photo in the series, was another aerial view, which shows the chateau almost totally destroyed, the trees are stumps, the German front line is once again almost in line with the chateau and the landscape is one of mud and what looked like large puddles, which as he pointed out are in fact shell holes. It looked like a vision from hell, and the surface of the moon combined.

On the wall to the left was a larger photograph obviously taken close to the present day with cemetery and the chateau close by, again taken from the air.

'Can I please just ask you something, you said Great Grandmother Dubré was a very sad old lady, and I can understand that what with the wreckage of the Chateau, the loss of her husband and two sons to the Boche, but to lose contact with her daughter as well must have been terrible. Did her daughter my grandmother not come back at the end of the war?'

He thought for a moment, lifted his beret and scratched his head.

'Mm – I believe she did come back, but she never lived here again, and in all the time I have worked here or there,' pointing to the Chateau, 'I can recall only seeing her on a few occasions.'
'OK, do you mind me asking how old you are?'
Alain Nallen chuckled to himself, 'I am 82.'
Alix was totally amazed, at worst I'd have said late sixties, 'So you must have been born in the 1920's?'
'Absolument ... 1926 in fact,'
It was rather nice almost eccentric how Alain occasionally mixed his French up with his English, and before Alix could reply he added, 'and I worked at the Chateau from when I was 14 years old, first bringing in wood, and making the fires, then cutting the grass, and generally doing odd jobs. In 1950 I joined the War Graves Commission and I've been here ever since, still cutting grass!!'
He then added 'I've been around the Chateau since I was a child, my parents were there during the Great War, so there isn't much I can't remember from when I was very small.'
'Obviously then you must know Mary?'
'She is my niece.'
There was more than a little logic in that, but somehow Alix was still a little surprised.
'Look I must get back, thank you for chatting to me, can I come and see you again, when I come back?'

'Of course – au revoir'
Alix was about to walk off, but he stopped 'Alain do you mind if I ask you one more question?', then without waiting for a reply 'You don't really like the Chateau being used as a hotel do you?'
'It is a necessity, and we must live with the twenty first century, and be grateful we have survived.'
The old man bowed in farewell as he said that, leaving Alix feeling he was also a diplomat as well as an obviously highly skilled gardener.

CHAPTER 18

Alix was now quite confused, although bewildered might be closer to the way he felt as he walked back to the chateau.

He understood why he had inherited the chateau, but not why he hadn't been told until his mother died. His grandfather and his granny were obviously in love, and because there was no male heir to the chateau after the Dubré men in the family died in the Great War it had fallen to his grandmother to inherit. After his father's untimely death Granny Dubré had passed the chateau to him in trust without telling his mother, that in itself is a bit weird.

Why had his father tried to kill himself more than once, and why on earth was the home office pathologist involved. Everything he had heard and seen did make Alix want to know more.

One of the oddest things was Blumeur's Bank and their links to the Chaesar estate somehow involving his grandmother and grandfather.

Finally, the name Peterson is somehow involved, and is there some kind of tie up there?

All these things kept rushing around in his brain as he made his way through the cemetery, back towards the chateau.

For the first time in his life Alix realised he needed to investigate where his family came from, particularly his grandfather Willie McBride, because he obviously did not come from Castlemills, but how on earth could he find out where he came from, never mind the other young men who were brought up in the orphanage and then went to war together.

He also knew there were places to go and look, thanks to television programmes about ancestry research, and there were online sources, and that was what he had to do next.

By the time Alix had thought this all out, he was back at Madame Dubré's room in the Chateau. He spent a good few minutes looking at the paintings of his grandmother, and his great grandmother.

'I wish you could talk to me', escaped his lips almost by accident, as the door opened behind him, and Mary came appeared.

'Oh, I'm so sorry, I thought you were at the grave, and I've just come in to check the cleaner has done her job, and I thought you would still be there.'

'That's OK, you just took me a bit by surprise,' Alix grinned a bit self-consciously, 'I must be going crackers, because I've just been asking the paintings to talk to me!!'

She smiled, 'More's the pity they can't.'

Mary then noticed the suitcase open on the bed, 'You're not leaving already are you?'

'Yes, I need to get back to school, the headmaster isn't too pleased with me at the amount of time I've had off recently since mother died. I think it's probably sensible to try to find out more about where I come from.

It's silly really, getting to my age and knowing nothing at all about my family.'

Mary smiled, almost as if she was hoping that was what Alix was going to say, and as she left the room saying. 'I'll say au revoir then, because you'll be back soon.'

'Thank you Mary and goodbye for now.'

The door closed and immediately re-opened, 'What would you like me to say to the Colonel?'

'Just give him my apologies for leaving without saying goodbye but tell him I'll be writing to him formalising our arrangement.'

With that Alix picked up his bag, and left, just spending a moment or two staring at the tree stump, before getting into his car, and once again narrowly missing it as he left, not so much bad driving, more because the pent up emotion of the past few days and the enormity of the task in front of him had blurred his vision and tears were not far away.

The drive back through Belgium and Northern France passed in a blur. Alix only just remembered to take the turning to the Channel Tunnel, but he was very grateful he had chosen that route because the weather had deteriorated considerably since leaving Ypres, the wind had got up, and had Alix chosen the ferry he could have been very sick indeed.

The tunnel gave Alix the chance to sit and relax a bit, and to put his thoughts in order. He was very conscious of the fact that he was the end of the family line. He had no children, no brothers or sisters, and in fact his family name and line would die with him.

He was born on the 27th of March 1961 in Ely, which made him forty-eight years old and never married, never even close. Every girl he brought home was treated so shabbily they never came back, and there must have been at least three 'suitable' girls his mother arranged for him to go out with, none of whom he fancied in the slightest. Alix reckoned to himself that he probably had been in three serious relationships, all but one of which were put off by his mother who didn't approve and made it obvious too. He smiled as he remembered the first 'love of his life' Anna, when he was in his first year at Cambridge University. She was some girl, passionate, funny, and just wonderful to be with, with lovely auburn hair, and freckles that came out with the sun. Mother approved of her, he recollected. Sadly, she didn't return for a second year and she had rejected every attempt Alix made to contact her, and had he available funds, at the time, and not the poor student he was, he would have pursued her to the wilds of Western Ireland, but it never happened.

Alix had always lived at home, feeling the responsible child as his mother aged, with his father dead when he was a baby, and he had always told himself mother couldn't really fend for herself. He had the grim thought that perhaps she had been so selfish she had put on this act of helplessness just to keep him at home.

To some extent he'd thrown his life away, in terms of marriage and children, to care for an ever-demanding parent, who had destroyed any chance that he had of happiness. Also, bachelor teachers are viewed with some suspicion in a society that feels any man who is in his forties and unmarried is a paedophile, gay, or both. This made promotion at King's School Ely where he had taught for over twenty years difficult, although he was now head of the history department. What he had really wanted was to be a housemaster as well, but as a bachelor this was never going to happen.

However, there is no point in being bitter and twisted Alix told himself, as he forced his mind back to his mother, who had always made him feel very special when he was in his twenties, then for some reason a degree of bitterness seemed to overwhelm her, until they didn't really get on at all. In fact, so special Alix could still quite clearly hear her say that he was more special than she could put into words. His mother also said she had yet to meet anyone who was right for him, except the lovely girls she had found for him. Alix suddenly realised that he never quite knew where some of these unattractive girls had been found by his mother, because he never saw them before they were foisted upon him, and he never saw them again afterwards.

All of that time in his life seemed suddenly unimportant. It was all water under the bridge, gone, and probably best forgotten. The events of the past few days had changed everything, but foremost in his mind was Chaesar, Blumeur, and the Bank of Ireland and how they were involved in his grandparents life, and now his.

Also it did seem to be a coincidence that the name Peterson was on the obelisk, and the same name as the Colonel in the chateau.

Alix also began to realise that he had other responsibilities as the owner of a chateau and land plus all the money he had inherited, and of course no-one to leave it all to. He laughed inwardly to himself that, as with his mother, Battersea dogs' home might do quite well at point future!

By the time Alix had got home, there was a clear plan in his mind, and he put it into action almost immediately.

One of his fellow teachers Ray Jones, a soft-spoken ex rugby playing Welshman who taught modern

languages was also an amateur genealogist, although Alix knew he also advertised online, had a website, and made a bit of money on the side by doing searches for individuals.
On the Monday at lunch Alix buttonholed Ray in the staff common room. After a brief chat about the School XV's prospects for the coming season, as Ray was the rugby coach, Alix asked him about his genealogy business.
'Would you do some research for me in terms of a family tree, only it's not mine ....I'm happy to pay the going rate.... no favours for friends or anything like that?'
Ray looked at Alix, 'Do you want to explain a bit more, and then perhaps we could meet after school, and I'll give you an idea of costs.'
'That's fine,' Alix took a sip of his coffee and continued. 'I want to know about a family called Edmundson who settled in County Mayo sometime in the last century.' Ray was about to interrupt; he had held up his hand, but Alix continued, 'I know what you're going to say, and that is research into Irish Ancestry is almost impossible because of the Four Courts fire in the 1920's.'
Ray finally managed to interject, 'Just what I was about to say myself!'
Alix undaunted continued anyway,' The family are or were major landowners in northwest Mayo around Belmullet, and if you want to come round

this evening, I'll show you what I have, and that should get you back to the middle of the 19th century anyway. Just give me an idea of costs.'
Ray grinned, 'to you £1000 an hour, for anyone else a flat fee of .... 'he left it hanging, and got up from his chair, with a final comment over his shoulder as he walked out of the door. 'I'll be round about seven, remember I can't stand lager,' with that nasal Welsh pronunciation of the word, making lager into laager.
By the time Ray arrived at seven o'clock Alix had himself organised. Beers on the kitchen table, shepherd's pie in the oven, just in case it took longer than Alix thought, and he knew that the recently divorced Welshman may appreciate some food.
The doorbell rang, and the two of them were soon seated, beers in hand.
Ray opened the conversation with a question.
'You've really intrigued me Alix, because I can't remember ever being asked to trace someone else's family, so why?'
'It's quite a long story, Alix replied, 'but I'll try to keep it simple.'
He went on to explain his grandfather was brought up in an orphanage in Mayo but left out the as yet unsourced riches bit. Additionally, he didn't tell Ray about the seventeen other orphans. Alix also didn't explain how his grandfather had died, or

even his name, because he felt it might distract Ray from his search.

What he did tell him about was the Orphanage Fire, the Glanville's, the Petersons, the obelisk with both their names. Edmundson House, the names of the family mourners at the Glanville's funeral .

He re-emphasised the name Edmundson, because Alix was beginning to think that he was the common ancestor of all the other names mentioned. Ray remained silent throughout the explanation, and when Alix had finished just asked one question.

'How much detail do you want?'

'If possible, I'd like everything from the Edmundson who bought the land in Mayo, his children, down to the present day. I'm not really interested in surnames apart from the three I've mentioned.'

Ray looked at him rubbing his hands in anticipation. 'This'll cost and cost you good. I think a case of Glenmorangie, should about do!!'

Alix who had done some homework on the cost of professionally researched genealogy research projects was mightily relieved. 'That's more than OK, so how long will that take?'

'You'll need to give about a month, because I've got to take A level French to Paris, and the 1st XV to Wales.'

'Cash on delivery or do you want a deposit?' said over his shoulder, as Alix was opening his drinks cupboard, hidden in a Georgian mahogany corner cabinet.

'A small gesture of goodwill does nicely – cheers.' As two fingers of amber liquid disappeared down Ray's throat in one swallow.

Three hours later Ray staggered out the door, muttering about whether he was to consider the whisky as a deposit or just a goodwill gesture, and Alix went to bed.

Sleep proved impossible as over and over Alix tossed and turned again and again as he kept wondering about the 17 other children who had appeared at the orphanage. It seemed logical they had appeared between the time Willie was born and the census return in 1901, because they were certainly at Termoncarragh in 1901. On the other hand, could they have arrived prior to Willie's appearance?

The next unanswered question was had they all arrived altogether or in ones and twos throughout the previous few years. The last thought he had before falling asleep was to check on the 1891 census.

The sleep lasted for all of twenty minutes, resulting in the quick donning of dressing gown and slippers, and once again onto the computer.

The 1891 Census showed Termoncarragh House only occupied by Christopher Glanville and Helen Glanville, as parents, and young James Glanville aged 13.

Alix realised from the list that only Donal Lenihan, Mick Moroney, Fergus and Sean O'Dwyer could possibly have been there in 1891, the rest having been born later, and of course it was still Termoncarragh House at that point.

That was very much a non-starter, and Alix also realised that the children who had taken on the identities of the dead children didn't have to be born on the same dates, just approximately.

He also surmised that it was unlikely that this had been done piecemeal, in other words the chances were, the children in the orphanage were there because their parents were killed in one accident. This reasoning was based on the simple thought that someone would have to go to an awful lot of trouble to find 18 children of the right age and then give them false names and a false identity one after the other.

Again, that line of thought was probably wrong. From everything he had heard in Belmullet, it seemed that Willie was a child apart. He was the one that everything and everyone seemed to revolve around in the orphanage, and by all accounts he was the youngest. In which case, Alix was looking for 17 children not 18, not that this made his task any easier.

He realised that to try to find deaths of two parents leaving just one child as an orphan, in Ireland at the end of the nineteenth century, and the child being of the right age would be like looking for a needle in a haystack. Apart from the lack of records because of the Four Courts fire in 1922, there was also the difficulty of finding families where there no brothers and sisters, or relatives to look after the recently orphaned child.

Alix then had the horrible thought that perhaps it wasn't an unfortunate accident, but one that had been carefully arranged.

This more and more looked like a carefully planned job. Someone had invested a huge amount of time and effort in placing the children at Termoncarragh, and he had to assume for a very good reason. He began to wonder if there had been several murders by design, or perhaps just one mass murder. Curiosity aroused, and now totally wide awake, Alix did a 'Google' Search to see if there were any accidents involving adults that could have left 17 children orphaned but had no success at all.

The more he thought about it, the more Alix became convinced that to become orphans both parents had to have died and the children rescued. It seemed very unlikely that such an event could ever happen, and it wouldn't just have been children rescued, only the boys. That then becomes deliberate mass murder, and Alix couldn't see anyway that the murderers would get away with that.

At which point Alix had one final attempt, and that was to try to see if the Times had archives where he could search. Sure enough, there was a website where a comprehensive search could be mounted. If his guess was correct Alix felt the orphanage would have been occupied sometime between 1897 and late 1900, because all the children were in the 1901 census return. Using a two year window and having taken a subscription to the Times online for one month, enabling him to extract full articles, Alix began searching the archives. He looked specifically for 'Major Disasters', for 1897, and 1900, and found nothing appropriate at all, although there were two ships that sank with loss of life, one in Lake Michigan, where thirty people drowned and the other in the Atlantic, but there were only 16 deaths and therefore nothing to fit his search. There was also a pleasure disaster near St Petersburg in Russia, but everyone on board perished including the children, effectively ruling that one out.

1898 and 1899 was equally unhelpful, with only one sinking, but no possibility of children being orphaned as a consequence. The problem with everything he had found so far was the total unpredictability of the disaster. He also searched under 'Rail Disasters, and again found nothing that was in any way predictable. Earthquakes, and Disease also proved equally unproductive, even the Irish Potato Famine, and by the time Alix had gone through every eventuality he had spent most of his free time for nearly a week, and was becoming very frustrated, when suddenly it came to him that he had perhaps been looking in the wrong place.

The question that needed answering was this. Why did the children have to survive the disaster? The logical answer is because if they didn't survive there would have been no children to use as replacements.

Supposing the children did not die, but were reported as dead after some great accident, surely that would suffice.

The answer to that must be that the bodies of the adults would be recovered but not the children, so people, such as relatives and the press would know they had disappeared and would be suspicious.

Supposing there were no relatives to come and see the bodies, and whoever planned this whole thing had set it up, so it would be this way.

For that to have been planned and executed would have to mean a terrible accident a long way from home, so the bodies could not be returned, and no relatives would be close by to identify and count bodies.

With this awful thought Alix went back to his original search parameters and soon came back to the pleasure boat disaster near St Petersburg. It had taken place in late September 1897 and 144 people, in fact all the passengers drowned in this tragedy. The article in the Times was quite limited, but it did say 117 adults and 27 children. This seemed to rule this out as well, until Alix realised that all the families were from Vladivostock, which is about as far away from St Petersburg as you could get.

The brief story told of a trip of a lifetime for around 56 Russian families, some of whom brought their children, as reward for splendid service to Tsar Nicholas 2nd. They had travelled by special train to Moscow, followed by a six day boat trip down the Volga River to St Petersburg where they were to be presented to the Tsar himself.

The trip ended tragically when the boat appeared to go badly off course sailing into Lake Ladoga, where it vanished. There was only one survivor, and he died shortly after coming ashore to report the tragedy.

Amongst the victims were the following families with children and he wrote their names down with their ages in brackets.

Sadyrin, [5]Cherchesov, [4] Borodyuk, [8][3] [ ]Onopko, [10] Beschastnykh, [8] Mostovoi, [8] [6] Yachvilli, [3] Salenko, [6] Romantsev, [7]

Ignatyev, [8] [9] Byshovets, [4]Yartsev, [11] Sychev, [10] Pavlyuchenko[3], [4] Pogrebnyak, [8] [7] Zyryanov, [10] [11] Berezutski, [6] Ozil, [1] Nevski, [3] Domski [9] [9]

As he read the list Alix realised it didn't give the sex or name of the 27 children who drowned along with their parents, only the ages.

Alix then hunted around the shambles that had been a well ordered room and pulled out his list of the boys who lived in the orphanage, or at least the names he had been given.

1. Willie McBride * 2/8/98 Castlemills Co Cork to James & Helen McBride
2. Sean O'Dwyer * 21st April 1890 Shillelagh Co Wicklow to Mick & Sheila O'Dwyer
3. Fergus O'Dwyer * 21st April 1890 Shillelagh Co Wicklow to Mick & Sheila O'Dwyer
4. **Al Molloy** 3rd May 1891 Doonbeg, Kilrush Co Clare to Seamus & Ann Molloy
5. Mick Moroney 16th February 1889 Collooney Co Sligo to Harry & Moira Moroney
6. **Patrick Coglan** 10th December 1894 Creagh Galway to Patrick & Annie Coglan
7. **Eamonn O'Connell** 3rd March 1891 Drumcliffe Co Clare to Tom & Nancy O'Connell
8. Sean Stringer 31st August 1893 Kilshanroe Co Kildare to Sean[deceased] & Mary Stringer[deceased]
9. **Colme Fitzgerald** 10th May 1892 Lorrha Co Tipperaray to Sean & Mary Fitzgerald
10. Pat Hayes 16th June 1895 Kinlough Co Leitrim to Mick & Kathleen Hayes
11. Donal Lenihan 31st March 1889 Boyle Co Roscommon to Conor & Rose Hayes

12. Phil Kyle 8th September 1895 Lismore Co Waterford to Eoin & Mary Kyle
13. **Peter Patrick** 17th December 1891 Hackettstown Co Carlow to Liam & Aileen Patrick
14. Alan Smith 22nd July 1896 Dunamaggan Co Kilkenny to John & Ciara Smith
15. John Smith 6th May 1895 Graiguenamanagh Co Kilkenny to John & Ciara Smith
16. Frank Clinch 7th February 1891 Kenmare Co Kerry to Eoin & Lauren Clinch
17. James Clinch 17th April 1892 Kenmare Co Kerry to Eoin & Lauren Clinch
18. **Jack Mahony** 14th July 1893 Abbeyleix Co Laois to Sean & Emma Mahony

If he took the approximate ages of the children from his list and worked out how old they would be at the time of the boating accident and compared that to the very basic list of the ages of the children who drowned, he could just about make them match. If there were 27 children who died, then this list would account for the 10 girls. In addition, the O'Dwyer twins would have been 9 years old, and there were two Domski children both listed as 9 years old, which would infer they were twins. Coincidence it might be, but the numbers almost tallied, especially if a sibling had been a girl, and Alix who had been more than curious was now almost elated, but at the same time extremely concerned he had accidentally stumbled onto a century old murder.

Unfortunately, more proof wasn't going to be found because there were simply no more details of the accident to be found anywhere else in Google, so regretfully Alix gave up this particular search at least for the moment.

He thought briefly about who he could tell, but something told him to just keep it to himself for now.

CHAPTER 19

Despite the possibility that the death of all the children and their parents wasn't an accident, Alix still couldn't get Colonel Peterson out of his mind. As far as coincidences go it was too much to believe that he wasn't in some way tied up with the whole story, and his grandfather Willie McBride. At this point Alix felt he should go and visit Colonel Peterson at the Chateau, and he had a good excuse to do that because the tenancy agreement was still sitting on the table downstairs, unsigned, and almost forgotten about, such had been the distractions of the past couple of weeks.

As it was still the middle of the week, Alix rang Chateau Hugend, spoke to Mary, and asked if he could come and stay on Saturday night. Alix also asked if Colonel Peterson could see him, and to tell him he was bringing the lease, with an apology about the delay.

This didn't appear to be a problem as Saturday is changeover day at the Chateau with one tour group leaving, and another not due until the Sunday.

Early on the Saturday morning, Alix was still debating with himself whether he should ask Colonel Peterson about his family connections with the Petersons who had attended Major and Mrs. Glanville's funeral, as he drove out of the Channel Tunnel towards Ypres and the Chateau.

It was a beautiful late September afternoon as Alix arrived at Chateau Hugend. As happened the last time, Mary organised the transfer of his overnight bag to his room. Unlike the last time Colonel Peterson was sitting in the bar, almost as if he was awaiting Alix's arrival.

He slid off the bar stool and stood up as Alix came in, and gave him the warmest of warm welcomes, with a broad smile, and an outstretched hand.

'Hello Alix, how nice to see you back, we had hoped it wouldn't be too long before we saw you again. What can I get you to drink?'

'A beer would go down very well, John.'

Somehow Alix felt more comfortable on this occasion, calling the Colonel by his first name, and he added, 'I'm really sorry not to have sent the tenancy agreement back, but I've just been snowed under what with school, and the business of trying to find out more about my grandfather.'

'Don't worry, as I'm sure you've found out some interesting things you knew nothing about, if your family is anything like mine.'

Alix continued, 'Yes but there was something very odd, two things. The first was that I had an older brother who died before I was born, and my mother never mentioned him, not ever. The second is I have two photographs of my mother with a different baby in each. One I assumed to be my brother, and the other one was me. The strange thing was the other lady, who looked exactly like the oil painting of my grandmother upstairs in the Dubré room I sleep in, who was in both pictures. I must assume they were taken in England, and obviously that was my Granny Dubré. Now I thought you told me she came back here after the war, and lived here, and Mary told me that as well. So, do you know what actually happened?

Colonel John thought for a moment before replying. 'That's what I thought, and I'm sure Grande Madame Dubré told me that too before she died. Perhaps she was getting forgetful, or we both misheard her.'

That statement seemed to end the conversation and with that Colonel John emptied his glass and got to his feet. 'Look I've got to go and check out the personnel who are arriving tomorrow, and allocate rooms, so will you excuse me for now.'

He walked towards the door, and as a kind of throwaway line 'Help yourself at the bar, owner's privileges what!'

With that he disappeared through the door marked *'Private Staff Only'*

For a moment Alix felt he was being gently rebuffed, almost as if this was a subject that wasn't open for discussion. Perhaps he thought to himself, that his great grandmother Dubré who must have been Colonel John's only source of information had become forgetful at the end of her life.

Obviously, her life had been long and very stressful, because Great Grandmother Dubré had not only dealt with the death of her husband in the Great War, but had also had to cope with a daughter who had disgraced the family name by becoming pregnant without being married. Quite naturally the Dubré family had sent her far away out of sight, and hopefully out of mind. Twenty-two years later a German invasion was followed by occupation, and then finally the ignominy of having to effectively give her precious Chateau away to a British officer who turned it into a hotel. A difficult life that might have meant she chose not to remember the more painful parts.

Alix dismissed these thoughts quickly as he remembered the task he had set himself, which was to find the graves of the other seventeen fallen orphans.

Off he went himself out into the evening sunshine, clutching his little list of names. An hour later he returned across the road to the Chateau, cross with himself for assuming they would all be close to where Willie lay buried. He had found only two, and in the process of searching he realised it was a real needle in a haystack job. The Cemetery was even bigger than he had ever imagined, and his sense of awe at the sheer scale of the carnage at Ypres was reinforced.

Having left his laptop at home he wandered into the bar, where one or two people he assumed to be locals were either standing around or sitting drinking wine. Mary was behind the bar, and she waved him across. 'Alix, the Colonel's apologies but there is a problem with his program for this week, and he must go and sort it out. He had hoped to dine with you, but just can't.'

'Don't worry Mary, I'm happy to eat on my own, as long as you have a decent bottle of wine, I'll be fine.' He hesitated for a second and added 'You couldn't do me a favour?'

'Of course.'

'Do you have a computer with an internet connection, for rather stupidly I've managed to leave my laptop at home.'

Mary nodded with a smile and started walking. 'Just follow me,' and she set off through the *'Private'* door used by Colonel John earlier.

This time it was held open until Alix went through, and he found himself in a corridor with some lovely kitchen smells, and Mary ushered him into a small office on the right, which was furnished with a desk, computer, printer, fax, telephone, and CCTV screen, plus a television in the corner.

Mary sat at the desk, opened the computer, typed in an entry code, and said 'It's all yours, and the password is 'dubre1324'.

Alix found the website for the Commonwealth War Graves Commission, and began keying in names and birthdates. In about 45 minutes he found fifteen graves, and two names who were on the wall at the Menin Gate with no known grave. How sad he thought, it's bad enough to die fighting a war under a pseudonym, with no hope of anyone ever visiting your grave, but to be blown to bits, and not even have a grave is somehow so much worse.

The list now had some degree of completion about it, and Alix was able to fill in the details of where the bodies lay buried on the list he had got out of his pocket.

1. Willie McBride 3rd Sept 1917 Hugend Cemetery
2. Sean O'Dwyer* 1st September 1917 Hugend Cemetery
3. Fergus O'Dwyer* Menin Gate
4. Al Molloy 30th May 1917 Wytschaete Cemetery
5. Mick Moroney 3rd August 1917 Hugend Cemetery
6. Patrick Coglan 3rd October 1917 Hugend Cemetery
7. Eamonn O'Connell 4th October 1916 Hugend Cemetery
8. Sean Stringer 5th September 1916 Guillemont
9. Colme Fitzgerald 10th November 1917 Hugend Cemetery
10. Pat Hayes 5th September 1916 Guillemont
11. Donal Lenihan Menin Gate
12. Phil Kyle 8th November 1917 Hugend Cemetery
13. Peter Patrick 31st October 1917 Hugend Cemetery
14. Alan Smith 31st October 1917 Hugend Cemetery
15. John Smith 1st November 1917 Hugend Cemetery
16. Frank Clinch 18th July 1916 Delville Wood Cemetery
17. James Clinch 8th November 1917 Hugend Cemetery
18. Jack Mahony 18th July 1916 Delville Wood Cemetery

As he completed the list, and rechecked it, Alix realised quite how catastrophic the deaths at Passchendaele were. There had been only five deaths up until then, and then the rest wiped out right here where he sat, or if not right here, then within a couple of miles.

Job done, and the list back in his pocket, Alix returned to the bar, where Mary asked him if he was ready to eat.

'Are you doubling up as a waitress tonight then Mary?'

She smiled, and gestured to the dining room door, 'Yes, we have two waitresses off ill, and another away on holiday, so it is all hands to the pump! Looking round she smiled and said 'the Colonel only trusts me in the dining room when we have an emergency. The seat by the window if that's OK.'

As Alix sat down and surveyed the menu, he noticed there was only one other occupant, a nice-looking lady in a pink jersey, and grey slacks, with quite short hair that had a tinge of grey, and he also noticed the pink lipstick and row of pearls. He smiled, and she smiled back, and Alix went back to trying to concentrate on the menu.

A minute or so later a voice, with a very distinctive Scottish accent said, 'May I ask, are you another early arrival for this week's tour of the 3rd battle of Ypres?'

'No, I'm just visiting my grandfather's grave, and doing a couple of other things, can I assume you are on the tour?'

'Yes, ... sorry I should have introduced myself, with that the lady blushed slightly, 'my name is Jenny, Jenny Andrews, and I've come a day early because I couldn't get my flights to fit.'

'Hello Jenny, I'm Alix McBride, 'Alix stood up as he finished speaking, 'look why don't you join me for dinner, it seems silly to be shouting across an empty dining room.'

'Thank you that would be nice, there's nothing worse than dining alone.' Jenny carrying a bottle of red wine and her napkin, moved across the dining room as Mary came back in again from the kitchen, and seeing them both said, 'That's nice, you'll have plenty to talk about.'

Alix grimaced slightly, then smiled, he hadn't quite seen Mary as a matchmaker, but then again, she was quite right, it was always interesting to meet new people.

Jenny sat down and offered Alix some wine which he readily accepted, followed by an almost embarrassing silence broken by Alix.

'Cheers,' as he raised his glass, and Jenny responded in the same vein.

'So, Jenny, what do you do for a living,' having noticed a lack of a wedding ring, Alix immediately

jumped to the conclusion that Jenny was a career girl, with no assumption she might be divorced.
'I'm in the Queen Alexandria's Royal Army Nursing Corps. We call ourselves QA's and the ignorant call us QARANC's which sounds like a duck quacking!'
This made Alix laugh, 'And what august rank do you hold in this famous organisation?'
'I'm a Major', she replied, blushing slightly, and at the moment I'm at the TPMH RAF Akrotiri in Cyprus, which is why I'm here a day early.
'Major sounds very important to me, what is the TPMH?'
'The Princess Mary's Hospital, and before you ask why I'm not Royal Air Force, there are a good percentage of Army medics and Nurses posted there.'
Their conversation was halted by the arrival of Mary, asking for their menu choices, and they laughed together when Alix chose first, only for Jenny to exactly follow suit. So, it was homemade spiced lentil soup, followed by chicken stuffed with blue cheese in a cream sauce.
Alix also asked Mary for a bottle of the best Chablis in the house, to go with the chicken, and when Jenny remarked that could be very expensive, Mary's reply raised her eyebrows about two feet.
'Yes, it's 86 Euros a bottle but Mr McBride can have anything he wants, he owns the Chateau.'

Talk about a conversation stopper.

As Mary left for the kitchen, there was a prolonged silence as Jenny looked at Alix, 'How come you own this lovely chateau?'

'It was left to me by my grandmother, and it was my grandparent's house on my father's side, and I only found out about it a few weeks ago after my mother's death.'

'Wow what a surprise.'

Alix then found himself telling an almost total stranger the events of the past couple of weeks. He left nothing out from the children's' gravestones, to the Swiss bank account, to the murder.

Jenny proved to be a very good listener, and the two bottles of wine at the table certainly lubricated the conversation, although she had a disconcerting habit of checking her make up with a powder compact after every course.

As he finished Jenny only asked one question, 'So who do you think Willie McBride is, because what a story it would make?'

Alix was about to reply when Mary came through the door to clear away the plates, and Jenny asked her,' So Mary what do you think of your new owner and his mysterious grandfather Willie McBride?'

'As long as Mr McBride leaves things as they are at the Chateau that'll be fine, and I believe he is, so I'm happy. As to poor Willie McBride, I didn't know there was a mystery, but I'm sure with some patient research, there's a lot more to discover about his background. It's a pity all these modern identification techniques can't be used, and then you might know more. Of course, that would mean opening a war grave and you definitely can't do that.'

As Mary said that she clattered all the plates onto a tray, nodded at Alix and left the room.

Alix thought that was a bit abrupt and quite unlike the Mary he had got to know. Jenny's voice on the other side of the table seemed to agree with that sentiment. 'That's you told then,' with more than a hint of mockery in her voice.

Alix felt it was time to go to bed, the chance meeting had been nice, dinner had been fun, but he had no desire to prolong the evening. He stood up about to make his excuses, when Jenny asked to see the list of Orphans who became soldiers.

'You don't mind do you, if I had a quick look at the list you were working on?'

Feeling it was churlish to say no Alix pulled it out of his pocket and sat down again 'No of course not.'

After about a minute and a half Jenny looked up, and bit her lip as she spoke, 'Look Alix I don't know whether this has any significance at all, but ... 'As she said it and hesitated slightly, Jenny pushed the list towards Alix, whilst keeping hold of it so

they could both see. 'Apart from the five men who died before Willie, plus the two who are on the wall at the Menin Gate, and leaving poor Willie out, that means the remaining ten were all killed without exception after Willie was murdered.'
She then added in a conspiratorial whisper, 'Were they murdered too, or was that just a coincidence? What if you could find out that the two for whom there must be no known grave were listed as missing after 2nd September 1917, that would mean twelve men died after Willie.' She kind of gulped, 'Alix there isn't one survivor. Shouldn't you try to find out what happened? There could be a simple explanation, but on the other hand..............', and Jenny's voice trailed off into silence.
Alix wasn't sure he liked the direction this conversation was heading, and he was beginning to feel he had already confided too much to someone who whilst perfectly nice, was in fact a total stranger, so he decided it was time to go. Alix looked at the list which he now held in both hands, pocketed it, and looked at his watch.
'Jenny thank you for that, and for your company this evening, I hope you have a great week, and perhaps we'll meet again.' Alix rose from the table, and with a final 'I really must go to bed, so I'll bid you goodnight.'
He walked out of the dining room and upstairs, completely unaware that by the same time

tomorrow he would find out a whole lot more about the untimely death of his grandfather.

CHAPTER 20

Immediately after leaving Jenny in the dining room, Alix, feeling very uncomfortable, not in the indigestion sense, but the mental sense, had gone straight up to his bedroom.

He really wished that he'd been able to spend more time with Colonel Peterson and found out more about where his Granny McBride had lived after the war. He knew for certain that she had lived in both Cambridge and Ely, where she had bought houses, so that she obviously had money, though from where it had come from, he was still unaware.

As Alix lay in bed unable to sleep, with his mind jumping around trying to come to conclusions that just couldn't be arrived at without more facts. More and more he felt as if there was some dark secret that he was being protected from.

Around two thirty in the morning he finally couldn't stand it anymore, and put the light on, scrambled in his jacket pocket for a pen, sat up in bed and used the paper with the list of names on it, to try to bring some order out of the mental chaos he found himself in by scribbling down a few notes.

Writing down thoughts had always been a way of bringing order when he had studied history as a student, and it was something he had continued to do regularly ever since.

Half an hour later, whilst Alix didn't have any more answers, he at least had a theory, and his theory frightened him enough to make sleep even more difficult, so he was to spend a very restless night. Alix must have drifted off eventually, because the first thing he knew was there was a knock at the door followed by the arrival of Mary with a tray.

'You've slept in and missed breakfast, so I've taken the liberty of bringing you tea and toast with marmalade, because I know what the English are like, so I hope that's OK.' She put the tray down on the bedside table and turned to leave.

'Surely this is way above your role as the Colonel's assistant,' Alex said, and sitting up, thanked her, but she kept on walking towards the door as if she didn't want to chat.

'Mary, can I ask you something?' He said after clearing his throat. 'What did you mean by all these modern identification techniques?'

By this time Mary had got to the door, and still hadn't turned round.

'Mary is there something wrong, have I offended you? '

Whatever it was that was troubling her, Alix felt that breakfast was more important, so rather than chasing after her for an explanation, Alix pulled the tray onto his knee, poured himself some tea, and noticed with pleasure it was Earl Grey, his favourite, and spread a liberal amount of butter and marmalade onto the dark brown surface of his toast. The smell of the slightly burnt toast took him as always back to his childhood, when his mother always burnt the toast before she got a modern popup toaster.

Just as Alix was biting into his first mouthful there was another knock at the door, and back into the room came Mary.

'Alix there is something I need to tell you about my grandfather, Marie, and your grandfather and grandmother.'

'That's OK' Alix said quickly swallowing the toast which rasped down his throat.

'My grandfather Charlie was just a lad of seventeen, and like several of the local boys was entranced by Marie, possibly in love with her. By all accounts and certainly confirmed by my grandfather, Willie McBride and his pals had arrived close to the Chateau, battle weary, muddy, hurt, and terrified.

What they really needed and wanted in many cases was their mother, or at least someone to comfort them. Apparently, they were able to get hot water, soap, their wet uniforms were dried, and the kitchen staff made them a hot meal. They were just lads, but that gave them the ability to bounce back, they soon cheered up, and my grandfather remembered how much like brothers they seemed, much closer than soldiers, and your grandfather Willie was undoubtedly the special one.

Marie soon fell for the boyish charms of Willie, and despite the desperate place they found themselves in, they must have become lovers.' She hesitated at this point, and Alex said, 'please don't worry go on I have a feeling I need to hear this.'

Mary continued very hesitantly. 'To help you understand what it was like, the war seemed to ebb and flow around them. The local lads who in peacetime worked the fields of the chateau spent their lives in hiding from the countless shells that flew overhead. The cellars under the Chateau were where the family and the estate workers hid. They were and are no different today built of the best brick and steel, but unlike others went two levels deep, with an entrance to the lower level carefully disguised.

The reason for the double level cellars is because the Chateau was built in the second half of the eighteenth century for the family Dubré. They had aristocratic friends in France, and when the reign of terror happened after the French revolution in 1789 many of them fled the country, some to Belgium as it is known today. You may not be aware that Revolutionary France went to war with Belgium and invaded, but prior to that, groups of French revolutionaries came looking for the aristocracy.

Cellars were a popular place to hide fugitives from the revolution, and sadly many victims of the guillotine were captured in cellars throughout

France and its near neighbours, but the Dubré's cleverly hidden second level of cellar, which no-one except the immediate family knew about, meant that the lives of several aristocratic families were saved because the searchers never found the second and deeper level.'

Mary once again hesitated, and Alix encouraged her to continue as he suddenly realised where this was all going.

'One hundred and twenty years later the same cellars provided shelter for not only the immediate Dubré family but also the workers on their estate. The depth and the strength of the building meant it survived the worst shelling and fighting of the Great War and proved a great hiding place again.

Although no-one can be certain, that was probably where Marie who would know of its existence and Willie hid together, as he and his comrades returned to the Chateau several times over a period of a few weeks.'

'Go on.'

'When it became obvious that Marie was pregnant, and I believe it was only when Grandmother Dubré found out, and her yelling was loud enough to disturb both Boche and English trenches that Charlie who was my grandfather on my mother's side, realised what had happened. He was in love with Marie, but being the son of a farm worker never really stood a chance with her, but it was all too much for him.'

Once again she stopped, and then very hesitantly continued,

'Charlie, my grandfather, and three friends waited behind the wall and ambushed Willie one night, bound and gagged him, then tied him to the tree outside. After that they hacked at him with knives, and farming pitchforks, and finally....' and at this moment Mary said,' he killed Willie by cutting his throat with a sickle.'

Immediately Mary went into a pocket in her dress and brought out a dog eared, brown, faded photograph, which she handed to Alix. 'This is a photograph of my grandfather, and you'll see he was holding a sickle.'

Alix looked at the faded picture of a young man smiling self-consciously at the camera and holding the sickle. Mary without saying anything else then handed a second photo, wrinkled as well as faded which showed a group of young men, kids really, some in uniform, some not, the ones in uniform had their rifles, and were looking really warlike, and the others were obviously farm workers, or their sons, all again smiling self-consciously as they posed for the unknown photographer, each 'armed' with either a scythe, a sickle, or a shovel.

Mary pointed at one of the lads, and said 'That's my grandfather, and next to him is your grandfather Willie .... well according to Grand Madame Dubré.'
'That still doesn't guarantee it was the weapon that killed Willie.'
'It does, because grandfather made a deathbed confession, He only died 20 years ago at a grand old age, and I was there when he died. There isn't anything in writing, but my sister will support what I've said.' Alix tried to interrupt but Mary getting increasingly emotional continued.
'I remember my grandfather saying that he never stood a chance with Willie because there was something very special about the way the other soldiers behaved towards him. Whether it was the fact he had money, or something, but whatever it was he never stood a chance, and even at the time of his death grandfather was still bitter about it.'

Alix just didn't know what to say, realising that this all took place almost 100 years ago, and quite possibly was the reason he was now the owner of the chateau and had become a very wealthy man.
He suddenly realised that Mary had vanished out the door, without saying anything else at all.
He continued to sit on the edge of the bed, mulling everything he had heard around in his mind.
What worried him far more was the mention by Mary that Willie seemed to be the 'Special One', he

also remembered the conversation with Annie in Belmullet, when she talked about the fact that as a small baby her mother and grandmother had been able to hold him, but after a special day out at the beach, baby boy Willie always seemed to be escorted or even protected by the other children.

Mary's comment about how close the soldiers seemed to be more like brothers, was also understandable bearing in mind what they had been through together.

As that thought passed through his brain, he pulled the list out of his pocket, remembering what Jenny had said last night, and he knew he had to see the second photograph again, if Mary was still around.

Quickly jumping off the bed, he showered and shaved in record time, got dressed, closed his small bag then he positively bounded down the stairs, case in hand, and knocked on the door to the office, where he saw Mary sitting drinking a cup of coffee.

She looked at Alix and said apologetically 'I'm really sorry for all that, it must have come as a shock. I hope you'll forgive me.'

'Mary don't be silly; I am so glad you were able to tell me. 'Before Alix could continue, Mary interrupted in a low voice. 'I'd rather you didn't tell Colonel John or anyone else what I said.'

'Of course not.' Followed quickly by, 'look Mary I know Willie was my grandfather, he's the reason I am the owner of this chateau, and all of that happened a long time ago, but please could I see the photos again?'

Mary pulled them out of her pocket, and a quick look at the second photo showed there were thirteen men holding rifles.

Jenny's comment about 10 deaths after Willie died being too much to be a coincidence really hit him in the face. Two were on the Menin Gate and Willie.

It must have shown because Mary quickly said, 'Are you OK?' Followed by, 'you look as if you've seen a ghost.'

Alix gave her back the photograph, 'No it's just seeing my grandfather again, no more than that.' He turned to go, and then turned back again. Thank you for all your help, I need to get back to my school as I've already made my headmaster angry with the amount of time I've had off.' With that he left walking through the door into the warm sunshine, out to his car and off back to England, with a long glance at the tree stump as he passed.

No sooner had Alix got in the door than the phone rang. It was Ray, saying he had a lot of news on the genealogy front, and could he come round.

Ten minutes later Ray arrived quite out of breath and obviously very pleased with himself.

Whisky poured, bottle on the table Ray went into his briefcase and brought out two A3 sheets of paper, one of which he left folded on the table

'You've certainly got your money's worth here my boy.'

He unfolded his sheet. 'I'm not going to give you your copy until I'm finished with the outline, because knowing you, you'll jump ahead, and you won't listen. There is a big surprise, in fact there are two or three and it'll spoil it if you look.'

He took a sip of his whisky and settled into the chair.

'We'll start at the beginning, which is where you wanted me to start with James Edmundson born in 1797 in Cranleigh in Surrey where his family were considerable landowners. Their money had come from Tea and Tobacco. James and his wife, her name isn't important here, had three children. They had two daughters and a son. Christopher Edmundson, Emma Edmundson, and Jayne Edmundson. As far as I found out, he bought out the O'Donnell family in around 1847, and therefore owned vast tracts of land in County Mayo, but I think you already know that. Anyway, the land sale was almost certainly a consequence of the potato famine

The three children, sorry young adults were sent to Ireland to run the vast estates. The two girls were not alone, Emma was now Emma Tucker having married a William Tucker, and Jayne was now Jayne Glanville having already married a John Glanville.

In 1853 Christopher Edmundson bought a commission in the Army as a Colonel and left for the Crimea with the 8th (The King's Royal Irish) Regiment of (Light) Dragoons (Hussars) who were part of the Light Brigade. He apparently took part in the Charge of the Light Brigade and was one of the only officers captured by the Russians.
As a Colonel, and a senior officer he was treated extremely well, and was even taken to St Petersburg where he was introduced to the Russian Court, almost like a celebrity.
By all accounts the Grand Duchess Freya Nikolaevna daughter of Tsar Nicholas 1st of Russia fell head over heels in love with this handsome English Gentleman, and very surprisingly permission was very willingly given for a marriage, which took place in 1857
She had to renounce her titles, and indeed has all but vanished from the history books, but she returned to County Mayo with Colonel Edmundson and they lived in what had been called Binghamstown House which they developed, extended rebuilt and renamed Edmundson House, and a very grand affair it was too. They had one son William Edmundson who was born in 1860, and he died in India in 1912, although he did have a son James who was born in India, his wife died during childbirth, and there were two daughters Helen Edmundson and Freya Edmundson.

Helen was born in 1858 and Freya was born in 1862, but I'll come back to them in a minute Emma Edmundson and William Tucker had one son John born in 1858, and he in turn had two sons. William Tucker who was born in 1891 who was killed in action in the Great War. The other son James Tucker, married a girl called Margaret Peterson.

Jayne Edmundson and John Glanville had a son Christopher Glanville who married Helen Edmundson daughter of Freya and Christopher Edmundson. That's the one I said I'd come back to, because not only was that a close family marriage in that they were first cousins, but it was to be repeated.

Christopher Glanville and Helen Edmundson had a son James Glanville who married Mary Peterson. He died in the same year as his wife in 1922. Of course that is the other very close family marriage, and it might be significant they had no children. Christopher and Freya Edmundson had a daughter Freya and she was born in 1862. She had married a man called John Peterson.'

At this point Ray could see Alix's eyes beginning to glaze over, so taking a blank bit of paper he drew out everything he had tried to explain. When he had done that Alix said,

'OK I can see that, and also where the Petersons enter the story, but wouldn't it have been easier to just give me my copy to let me see it for myself?' Ray shook his head vigorously 'No I'm not going to do that because as I said before you'll read ahead, and not listen, but let me continue to draw it out,' and he continued where he had left off
They had a son John Peterson, born in the 1890, He married, had three children, but we need only concern ourselves with one, again called John, born in 1923, obviously family names at work here. He in turn married, and in 1945 had a son John Peterson and he is almost certainly the Colonel John Peterson at your chateau.
John Peterson and Freya Edmundson also had a daughter called Emma Peterson. She firstly married a Peter Johnson who was killed in the Great War. She then married Patrick Fitzgerald, and they had one child Gillian Fitzgerald who married William McBride....' At that point Alix interrupted very loudly 'But that's my parents...' without batting an eyelid Ray continued 'and then you Alix McBride were born.'
Ray continued, 'before we chat let me just finish off this tale.' As he said that he handed the second copy to Alix. 'You'll see a few more details scribbled on here. William Tucker who was killed at Ypres was Willie's Platoon Commander, but not only that, James Glanville who went on to win an

MC and DSO was also Willie's Platoon Commander, then Company Commander, then Commanding Officer. John Peterson was also Willie's Platoon Commander. Finally, Peter Johnson was also one of Willie's platoon commanders. That struck me as more than a little strange, that all of them are family.

I think all the names at James and Mary Glanville's funeral have almost all been accounted for, and I'm happy that most of your questions have been answered, apart from Chaesar House. The name was changed after 1901, and I think it is a Gaelic word, and I've taken the liberty of asking a mate in Ireland who knows a fair amount of Gaelic to come up with an answer.

Ray saw Alix's eyebrows raised, 'Don't worry I haven't mentioned anything else, just asked for that to be solved. He did say it rang no bells, but the word might have fallen out of use, so we'll have to wait.' Ray shifted in his chair as if less than comfortable.

'There is one other thing I found out. The John Peterson that Freya Edmundson married may have emigrated to the United States in the early part of the 20th century. John Peterson having been a regular visitor to the USA prior to that and passenger records show at least five passenger lists with his name and Freya as well.

Something dramatically went wrong for the whole family at the time of the depression, because the money source dried up and the lands in the USA had to be sold for almost no money at all, pennies in the pound if you like. The knock-on effect of the money source drying up meant the sale of the vast estates in Ireland, so all we have left today are a few houses owned by descendants of the original Edmundson's.

In other words, the family Edmundson went from serious wealth to poverty in less than 100 years, in fact 90 years to be precise.'

With that Ray sank back in the chair, and Alix leant forwards to look at the map of what was now his family tree, at least on his mother's side.

'I bet you're surprised at all of that, what with your connection to Russian Royalty, but also the fact that you are a relative of the Colonel Peterson you talk about. Do you think he knows?'

It was Alix's turn to shift uncomfortably, 'I just don't know. If he does, why hasn't he told me, unless as I'm beginning to have an awful suspicion there is a dark secret hidden somewhere, and I'm his family competition for whatever it is, and he doesn't want me to know he knows... just hang on', and with that Alix grabbed his copy of the family tree and scanned it closely. Somewhere in the back of his mind was the thought that Colonel John had told him his grandfather was buried at Ypres, but the family tree said he survived. How odd.

'Ray, how complete is this diagram, because if you look at it, just the bit from the marriage of Christopher Edmundson and Freya Nikolaevna, what do you see?'

Ray picked up his copy and looked, and pursed his lips, 'I don't know what you mean!'

'It is staring us in the face,' Alix hissed. 'Colonel John Peterson and Alix McBride are all that's left alive, from that entire family unless there are others that aren't on the list.'

'Look,' brandishing the paper, 'James Glanville and Mary Peterson died in the fire at Termoncarragh, with no children. Margaret Peterson who was married to James Tucker had no children; Peter Johnson was killed in action. My father died young, I have no brothers and sisters, and so far as I know neither has John Peterson. It's almost as if all the family connections to me with one exception have been eliminated.'

Alix's voice was rising, and Ray tried to calm him down. 'Look stop getting in a state for goodness sake, I'm sure there's a perfectly logical explanation for all of this, but I think I should try to put some flesh on the Peterson bones both here and in the USA. I'm sure we'll find there are loads of Petersons all over the place.'

Alix quickly realised he must have sounded almost paranoic, but he really was becoming increasingly concerned, and almost regretted having started this stupid exercise.

'Ray, that would be great' Alix said calming down almost immediately, 'and our local wine merchant will deliver as promised your case of Glenmorangie tomorrow and thank you for all you've done for me. '

A slight hesitation was followed by,

'I'm sorry about the panic but there's something very dark going on, and I'm not sure I want to get to the bottom of it, but I feel I must do for my grandfather's sake.'

At that point Ray left with a promise to investigate the Peterson family in the hope of finding some alive, and Alix went back to his now bulging folder feeling suddenly better than he had felt a few minutes before.

He suddenly realised that Freya Nikolaevna having been a member of the fabulously wealthy Tsars of Russia could well be where his newfound wealth originated. His first thoughts were that the Blumeur Account in Switzerland had to be the source of the money that Madame Dubré had apparently inherited.

It was also perfectly logical to assume that the money dried up after the Russian revolution.

It was only when he looked again at the family tree that Ray had produced that he realised that Willie didn't fit in anywhere. After all he had arrived on the scene at the Chateau, not to put too fine a point on it, impregnated Marie, and was then murdered. The wealth he had inherited couldn't have come from him, or the Dubré's, because there was no connection at all with the sister of the Tsar that Christopher Edmundson had married all these years ago.

In a nutshell that was another avenue closed. Instantly depressed he put the folder down and wandered off into the hall. Suddenly he stopped in his tracks. 'How stupid of me', Alix said out loud. Willie lived in the orphanage firstly with Christopher Glanville and Helen Edmundson, and she was the daughter of Freya Nikolaevna, and the very possible source of the money. Then it was the turn of James Glanville and Mary Peterson, both grandchildren of Freya to look after Willie and the other so-called orphans.

It was therefore more than likely that all the children had money settled on them by Freya, but he'd never be able to find out because they were all dead.

The chill entered Alix again. The word witnesses immediately came to mind. If any of them had lived and had children, then he could have discovered a whole lot more about the money source, and better still found out about Willie, and who he really was. Could it therefore have been the position that it was convenient that all ten survivors died after Willie's murder.

He then asked himself the question about Willie's murder.

Was he killed because he made Marie pregnant and the local lads took revenge, or was he killed because Marie was pregnant and he needed to die to protect a secret, and that was why the others all died as well? Suppose Willie was the secret, but somehow it had been passed on to the pregnant Marie?

She became the secret to be protected in time to be passed on to her son William.

That's fine and good thought Alix, because it should have been passed to him from his father but that hasn't happened.

Then there is his mother, turning out to be a Peterson, and somehow, he had the awful feeling that the Peterson family know something, the secret if that is what it is, but somehow can't access it.

With a jolt Alix suddenly remembered the conversations with Mr. Edwards and the Ypres lawyer about his grandmother specifically instructing them that on no account was she to be told about the briefcase or the inheritance.

He then remembered the School Vicar David Hughes telling him about his father, and the botched suicide attempts. Alix suddenly thought was his father disposed of because he had a son, and had he attempted to kill me to protect me from something.

At this point Alix really began to be really frightened, and it took some minutes for him to calm himself. At least he thought there are no more McBrides, because if there had been an heir, then from what had happened before he could be very dead by now as well.

The next thought that entered his head, was the fact that his older brother was almost illegitimate, in that his mother had married his father in a hurry and very quietly to make the baby legal. Put another way, had she deliberately got pregnant to ensure his father William had an heir.

Alix decided that more Glenmorangie might need to be offered to his friend Ray in the morning, and he went to bed, but sleep just wouldn't come.

At break-time Alix grabbed Ray, 'I need to talk to you urgently.' Ray looked at him frowned and shook his head. 'You look bloody awful; did you finish the whisky after I left?'

'No I bloody didn't, but I need to offer you more whisky to do some more work. Would you check out my mother, her Peterson background, where she went to school, why Cambridge University, and then compare it to my father. I need to know exactly where he lived, went to school etcetera.

'Alix hesitated for a moment, and then continued. 'I think my mother was almost brainwashed by her family to ensnare my father, get herself pregnant by him, and marry him.'

Ray looked at him mouth agape, 'Oh come on you've got paranoia.'

'Ray I haven't got paranoia, but somewhere here there is some kind of secret that has been handed down by my grandfather, through his wife my grandmother, straight to me, deliberately missing out my mother. I am also beginning to think that my father was told by his mother not to tell his wife anything at all to do with it, under any circumstances, because for some reason as his mother she feared for her son if his wife got to know.'

Alix stopped, realising how improbable that sounded, and then gulped as the school bell screeched very briefly, to signify five minutes from the end of break. 'Do you follow me or not.'

Ray shook his head, 'I follow you all right, and you are bats, but he who pays the piper in whisky calls the tune! I'll get on with it, and in all seriousness it's a fascinating tale, and it's lovely to get paid for something as enjoyable as this, so I don't mind at all.

You know perhaps you should take a DNA test, because it's perfectly obvious there is a brick wall when it comes back to your grandfather. There's an increasing use of DNA to try to find long lost relatives, and that might give you the answer you seek

Ray then laughed. 'You know Alix you'll probably end up writing a book about it.'

CHAPTER 21

There were days when Alix lunched at school, the odd day he went for a walk by the River Ouse to look at the boats, when he normally ate a supermarket sandwich, however on this occasion Alix decided to go home.

He looked at the shambles that used to be his dining room table and having poured his 'cuppa soup' and heated his baked beans, liberally spread over the toast, which he placed on his dining room table with a knife and fork. For some reason he then ignored the food and started to reorganise all the information on the table about Willie McBride. Alix was astounded at how much he had accumulated and began sorting the sheets of paper. His brother William's birth certificate was on top of the pile, and he began to read it to see if there was anything he had missed.

At that point his front doorbell rang, and when he answered it he found himself faced by a well-dressed middle aged gentleman, who introduced himself as Mr. Colin Stewart, walking towards him and asking if he might come in.

After producing an official looking card from his inside pocket showing his identity, a somewhat shaken Alix ushered him into his study, well perhaps as he thought later, he hadn't let him, he was more or less pushed aside.

With a dry mouth Alix asked. 'What can I do to help you?'

'You wrote to us' his visitor replied in a flat humourless voice, 'about your father, and we thought a little visit might clear things up. As I hope you might have gathered by now, I'm from the Home Office, in a branch that helps keep the country safe, and I think you'd better take a seat.'

Obviously, this was a man used to giving orders that were obeyed so Alix sat down with a bump.

'Mr McBride, I hope you don't mind if I call you Alix,' a statement more than a polite question thought Alix as he nodded.

'Good Alix; well whilst I am restricted in the things I am at liberty to tell you, there are one or two pieces of information you ought to know about your father.

He was picked out as an uncannily good French speaker but with a Belgian accent when he was at Cambridge in 1942, where he was recruited into the SOE, specifically because he could pass off as a Belgian. In fact, he even had a Belgian passport, and can I assume you know what SOE was?' Alix nodded again.

He was dropped into enemy held Belgium on three different occasions and then brought back safely to England some months later. Additionally, his mother, your grandmother, who was of course Belgian, also accompanied him on each occasion, and returned safely each time to the UK. They organised several important sabotage missions, amongst other things that I am not at liberty to discuss even now.

Your father worked for what became the SIS that you wrote to, from after the war to the early 1960's. William was a brilliant linguist, but very much a behind the scenes man and his extensive knowledge of French, Russian, German, and Eastern European languages made him invaluable to us. He resigned from the service in 1961 when we had a difference of opinion. By 'We', what I mean is SIS and your father, not with myself.' Mr. Stewart's humourless smile reappeared as if enjoying a private joke.

'He was a brave man, and you should be proud to be his son, but you should satisfy yourself with what I have told you. Your father knew some dangerous secrets, best not revealed, perhaps even to this day so my advice is this. You shouldn't shout from the rooftops about who you are, because there are still unpleasant people around who might do you harm.'

As Mr. Stewart stopped talking it allowed Alix the chance to speak.

'Ok I think you've made your point, but I'd like to ask a favour if I may. Do you have such a thing as a photograph of my father, and if so, could I have a copy?'

'No and no.' Was all the reply that Alix was given. This left Alix thinking, this man was just being difficult for the sake of being difficult, and he could make difficulties himself given the chance.

Mr. Stewart, then got up, said goodbye, and as he was leaving, Alix quietly said 'Blunt, Burgess, Maclean, Philby, and perhaps even Blake, that's what this is about isn't it?' As he said it Alix thought the response might be interesting, but it was more than that.

Mr. Stewart stopped, and turned round very quickly to face Alix, and followed up with a very aggressive. 'What did you say?'

'I said, somehow or other my father was either directly or indirectly involved with uncovering, or alternatively covering up the business of Blunt,

Burgess, Maclean, Blake, and Philby. In fact, I might add Hollis as well.'

The SIS man came towards Alix, and stood very close to him, almost eyeball to eyeball. Alix could smell garlic and alcohol on his breath 'I'd be careful you don't say that in public. Your father thought he had connections in high places, only he found he didn't. He found out about things that were best left alone, and perhaps that was why he died when he did. There are things we can protect you from, and things we can't, one of which is yourself.'

He paused, 'Just leave this all alone, and don't concern yourself with matters you don't understand. You may discover you have the same connections as your father, so be very careful Mr. McBride.'

With that he turned on his heel, and walked back to the door, turning once to add.
'You have been warned. We don't want any unpleasantness, or anything to happen to you either.' The last comment was made in a way that expressed concern, and not as a threat which confused Alix slightly.

He was to remember all this conversation with total clarity over the coming weeks, but initially he was shaken primarily by what he viewed as a threat, but even more so by the information about his father and his grandmother. It still left Alix with more questions than answers.

How was his father recruited into the SOE, and his grandmother as well, was the first question?

The second question was where did his father get his expertise in foreign languages?

Thirdly, what happened in the early sixties to cause his father to quit the SIS, and obviously fall out with them, and was his death a consequence of this?

Alix strangely felt more determined, not less, not put off in any way from finding out more about his father and his grandmother.

Where had his father learned and developed his language skills for a start?

Alix suddenly realised he was about to be late for his first class after lunch, so leaving his untouched soup and baked beans he rushed off to school. He was so caught up in his own thoughts he didn't see the car pull out from the kerb behind him and drive past into the town of Ely, or the two passengers get out at the road junction four hundred yards in front of him, and right next to the beginning of the High Street.

It was the second period in the afternoon when Alix was teaching the top set in the Third Form when there was a knock at the door, and in swept the headmaster, Mr. John James, his gown flowing behind him.

Much to the relief of Alix all his young charges leapt to their feet, as did Alix from his customary teaching position which consisted of feet on his desk, seat on the tilt. As he stood waiting for Mr. James to say something to his young charges, Alix noticed the headmaster had company, a young man and his mother, obviously doing the 'tour' of the school. With an inward gasp Alix realised he knew the mother, it was the lady he had spent most of the evening with at the Chateau, just last week. What on earth was she doing here?

Mr. James smiled pleasantly and introduced Alix to the mother. 'Alix I believe you have already met Mrs. Andrews,' then as an afterthought, 'and this is Alfie who may be starting after half term.'

As Alix shook hands with both mother and son, the headmaster continued 'Mrs. Andrews insisted on meeting you Alix, obviously you made a good impression when you met in Belgium at Ypres.'

Alix smiled in an embarrassed sort of way, hearing a couple of sniggering noises from the back of the class. He knew full well the boys wondered about his sexuality, being the only unmarried master in the school. This he thought wryly might put a stop to that.

'How nice to see you again, this is a pleasant surprise; I'll look forward to teaching young Alfie here next term.' Alix thought it strange that in the time they had spent together at the Chateau she had not once mentioned a husband, never mind a son.

As the three of them left the room, and the class returned to a degree of normality, Alix couldn't help grinning, despite his slight misgivings about the sudden appearance of Jenny Andrews. It took him a good five minutes to put a stop to the good-natured ribald comments of his third form pupils.

The rest of the afternoon passed off as most afternoons do, except Alix once again had a feeling that somehow or other he wasn't in control of any of the things that were happening in his life. The reappearance of Jenny Andrews had disturbed him a great deal.

He just kept asking himself why?

Alix really needed a drink, and he soon found himself in the pub, which unusually was deserted.

He had no sooner ordered a beer when who should come ambling in but Tony.

'The very man I need to see,' as Alix turned to the barman, 'that'll be another pint of Adnams please George.'

Tony smiled, 'so what's been happening in my absence. It's great having a wealthy client in the Hebrides, there's some fantastic golf and the whisky is to die for.'

'You look rough, just as if you've had a good try.' Alix grinned replied. 'You asked what's been happening, well a lot, and I need a name from you.'

'So don't spare me, what has been happening?'

Alix took a deep breath and launched himself.

'Not so many days ago I was a schoolteacher with a mother in long term care. Apart from that I didn't really have a care in the world, apart from the fact, as you know I would like to be married but that seems to have passed me by.

Mother dies, and then literally the sh-t hits the fan. I inherit millions through a granny I don't remember and seemingly millions from something called Chaesar which no-one seems to know anything about. Then there is the question of the 17 boys who it appears took the names of some dead children. It is possible they might be children who somehow were the only survivors of a boating accident in Russia.

Tony interrupted 'what do you mean by possible?'

'The slight problem is the Times said there were no survivors.'

Alix quickly responded, 'the Times at that time had a small report and that was what it said. Their exact words were no survivors, and it was from a pleasure boat that sank on a lake near St Petersburg. It appears they were on some kind of reward trip from Vladivostok.'

Tony said that's a bit convenient.'

'What do you mean?'

'Well, it is about six days by train today, so God only knows how long it would have taken over one hundred years ago.'

'How on earth do you know that?'

'Don't forget Alix I did a postgraduate degree in Moscow, and part of that meant I had to travel, and in fact I visited Vladivostok, and frankly never again. The train was unbelievably awful, and by convenient I meant they were a long way from home. Their families aren't going to travel to a funeral, and the Russian government are hardly going to go to the expense of sending all the bodies back. Knowing the Russians it would be a mass grave and be done with it.'

Alix just continued. 'The thing is, I took the list of names of all the children who were reported as drowned. I was then able to extract matching ages with the boys on my list. You see they were not identified in the newspapers as boys and girls there were just names and ages.

On thing that stood out was the fact that amongst the drowned children there were twins of almost the same age as the O'Dwyer twins in the photograph that you saw.

I have a copy of the press cutting at home.' Alix then drew breath and with increasing speed said in all of a rush

'Like Willie they all have graves that match in Ireland so it could well be these children, and I am beginning to think that a whole lot of people had been drowned, but only the boys were rescued……..'

Tony interrupted, 'don't be daft, that kind of thing only happens in novels.'

'When was that report?' Tony asked

'1897 as far as I can remember' Alix responded and then quickly added. 'My grandfather seemed for some reason to be a boy apart, after information an old lady gave me out in the wilds of Ireland. I'm now just wondering, was he someone very rich and special because I am just beginning to think that might be the case.'

'Wow' was Tony's initial response, 'you have found out a lot, and it does sound confusing. What's your plan?'

'Well Ray has done some Family tree stuff, and not just my family, because that grinds to a halt, but of all the other people who Willie had been involved with. They all seem to belong to the one family, as they were all it seems tied up with the same regiment.'

At which point Tony interrupted, 'don't forget that was often the case,…'

'Yes, but not to the extent that Colonel Peterson, who rents the chateau has an ancestor who was with Willie in the Great War, and this kind of thing is repeated. Most amazing of all there is even a marriage after the Crimean war to a Russian princess.'

'Bloody hell that's incredible.'

'I've still got Ray working on all the family trees, and I'm thinking…..'

Tony interrupted, 'why don't you have a DNA test that might….'

'Don't be daft, how could that possibly help,' Alix responded, 'mind you that's exactly what Ray suggested.'

'You might find a DNA match and whilst it is probably a long shot, it's surely worth a try because it could lead you to finding out exactly where you came from.'

'Alix frowned 'where do you go for something like that, because quite frankly I'm fed up with this whole thing, and more than somewhat confused, but I do need answ…..

Tony interrupted, 'We use a chap who is a kind of top-level private investigator in Cambridge with qualifications as long as your arm and a huge reputation. The police and the Home Office use him a lot, so he is extremely busy, and one of the areas he specialises in is paternity cases where he uses DNA to determine the father. His name is Charles Speed and I'll give him a ring. He's quite fussy about the jobs he takes on, so I'll call you back if he is agreeable, and then he will call you. Be warned his fees are on the high side of high.

The next day Alix returned from school to find a message to ring Charles Speed, which he did immediately, and Charles, who seemed very amiable, indeed quite amused that Alix and Tony were long standing friends. He offered to come to the house the following evening, something which surprised Alix, but Charles insisted this was quite normal because client confidentiality was paramount in his line of business.

Charles duly turned up at the house at 5.30pm prompt, in a very flashy Mercedes. He was a big man with a real shock of red hair, and a friendly open face.

CHAPTER 22

The meeting only took a few minutes, during which a scraping of the inside of Alix's cheek was taken. Charles wanted to know if Alix was keen to know about something he called 'nearest common ancestor' which he then explained in pretty simple terms. What he really meant was if he could use worldwide databases of DNA to see what came up as a possible ancestor. Put in a simpler way, as Alix didn't know who Willie was, because he definitely wasn't the child in the grave in Limerick, was there someone in the DNA database that Willie was descended from?

Alix told him that he knew that Willie McBride was in fact his grandfather. It was Willie's family, parents, grandparents that sort of thing that he wanted to know more about.

Costs weren't discussed, and in fact as Alix thought afterwards that it was all painless.

There was little else for Alix to do now until Charles Speed came back to him with whatever he had been able to find out, and he didn't have to wait long for that. He had literally just taken his jacket off on his return from school when the telephone rang. It was Charles Speed.

'Alix I've got the DNA Results, but I'd rather like you to come to the office, so that we can discuss what we've found in more detail.'

A slightly confused Alix replied, 'I thought you preferred to come to the house?'

'You need to see computer generated information and that can only be done in the office I'm afraid', and there was a degree of finality in Charles response.

Alix now in a slightly higher state of anxiety 'It's not bad news is it?'

'No not at all, although it depends on how you look at it, look when do you want to come across to Cambridge?'...........................almost as an afterthought, 'You can come now if you want, the rush hour traffic is disappearing fast, and we're at 15 Parker Terrace above Johnson's the newsagent. The door is to the left, and parking shouldn't be a problem. Shall we say six fifteen, or as near as possible, but if you are a few minutes late, don't worry?' With that the disembodied voice of Charles Speed vanished with a click.

It took Alix about twenty minutes to get to Parker Terrace, and he was able to park his car right outside, and the short flight of stairs took him somewhat surprisingly from a scruffy street, a scruffy door, and well-worn stairs into a pristine, modern well lit, immaculate office.

Charles was sitting at what must have been the receptionist's desk, and he rose to greet Alix. 'Thanks for coming at such short notice, but we've found some things that will interest you. By the way you needn't worry, I use the word 'We' habitually because it sounds more impressive than I. To be honest this is a one-man band mainly because I haven't found anyone I trust enough to work with, and confidentiality is a huge issue as you can imagine........ Come on through.'

Charles ushered Alix into what was another smart office with three computers and space for armchairs and a coffee table. Coffee and biscuits were laid out, and Charles suggested Alix just helped himself as they sat down in the armchairs. 'If we need food later, this street as you'll be aware, has several good restaurants who will deliver food.'

Alix was astonished 'Is this going to take long?' feeling a bit like a patient at the dentist nervously awaiting the drill. 'That depends on how far you want to go with the DNA profile.' As he said that Charles settled himself into an armchair opposite Alix, who suddenly realised what a huge man Charles was. He must have been closer to seven than six feet, and he struck Alix as a man who was also still in a very good physical condition.

Charles continued 'Look it's going to take a little time to explain what is possible, and how it works.'

He settled back in his chair and got out two identical folders. 'I'm going to explain how DNA identification works, and everything I'm going to say can be found in easy-to-follow language in the folder for you to take away with you. Feel free to interrupt if you're confused.'

With that last comment Charles started a monologue, which became a conversation that was to keep them where they were until well after midnight.

Charles launched into his explanation after pouring himself a cup of strong coffee.

'DNA analysis has been around for quite some time, and obviously in my field of forensic pathology we use it most if not all the time. '

Charles leant backwards in the chair visibly relaxing and proceeded to give Alix a basic overview of the processes of DNA.

'As I must assume you know the billions of cells in the human body each contains our entire genetic information, the DNA.

Inside each cell the DNA is found inside the nucleus, and this is the chromosomal DNA which consists of autosomal DNA,

X Chromosomal DNA and Y chromosomal DNA, and then outside the nucleus the mitochondrial DNA.' He stopped, 'OK so far?' Alix just nodded, wondering where all this was leading.

'Our autosomal DNA is inherited from both parents, but the Y-Chromosomal DNA is inherited only from father to son, and mitochondrial DNA inherited only from our mother.'

Charles looked at Alix and continued. 'It's important you understand this basic stuff because it all gets more complicated later.

How all this comes about is that shortly after fertilisation the sperm's mitochondria just dies off and the embryo then only has maternal mitochondria. What this means is that we share the same mitochondrial DNA as our brothers and sisters, but not our fathers. What is important in Genealogy is that the mitochondrial DNA is passed down nearly unchanged through the generations, so we share the same mitochondrial DNA type as our maternal grandmother and so on.

Similarly the Y chromosome is passed down exclusively from father to son, so genealogists use Y Chromosomal testing. This was what I did, with the cheek sample, and found an almost certain direct match.

I repeat what I've already said, and that is this simple Y chromosomal test has luckily come up with a direct match, and seeing Alix on the point of speaking, Charles now leant forward and, in a whisper, almost as if he didn't want to be overheard.

'I did use the information in your DNA to look back to see if I could find an ancestor, which if you remember what I said when we met before, meant who you were descended from. In other words, to see if there was anyone in the European Database.

Look Alix, what I've come up with has shocked me, and that's why I asked you here, because I know this place is swept for bugs and devices, but your house isn't.'

At this point Alix laughed out loud 'Come off it Charles I'm a teacher not some kind of MI6 operative.'

'You may well laugh, but at the least hear me out, because what I'm about to tell you may make you change your mind. But just to be sure, have you had anything strange happen recently at home, to the extent you felt someone had been in the house?'

The look on Alix's face was a complete giveaway, as he remembered his conversation with David Hughes, and the feeling someone had been there. He also remembered David telling him his mother had felt the same thing. 'Don't tell me, because I don't want to know, but when you hear what I've found out in the next few minutes you might understand better why I'm saying that.

What I found was that you have Queen Victoria as an ancestor!!' Charles said it all so calmly, just like it was the sort of thing that happened every day.

'Don't be so daft!!' Alix exclaimed.
'Look Alix, it's very important that you believe me, which is why we're here, because if you doubt the accuracy of what I am telling you the computer screens on the desk,' Charles waved his hand in their direction, 'will confirm it.

What I did was I used the Y Chromosome DNA test, which if you remember what I was saying is that the Y Chromosome DNA is passed down nearly unchanged through the generations, so we share the same Y Chromosomal DNA type as our grandfather and so on.

A test like this coincidentally was the one used to properly identify Tsar Nicholas's murdered family, using DNA from the Duke of Edinburgh.' Charles could see that Alix was sitting with a dumb look on his face and just assumed it was lack of understanding, when in fact Alix was literally struck dumb, and was almost rigid with shock, but still managed to interrupt in a hoarse whisper.
'Queen Victoria, how ridiculous is that.'
Charles with great patience continued. 'Look Alix there's more to come, a lot more, but I do need you

to trust me, to trust my skill, and by the way what we are discussing isn't known by anyone else on the planet.' Charles stopped, and then seeking permission.' Can I carry on?'

Alix nodded, reached for a biscuit and noticed his hands were shaking, as Charles returned to his explanation

'All you need to remember is that the Y Chromosome DNA is contained in the nucleus of the cell. This type of DNA is passed from father to son to son and so on. In that way we can definitely say that your Y Chromosome DNA will be the same as your father, and that of Willie McBride, that much you must surely understand

'Go on. Are you about to tell me who my grandfather's father was?'

Charles smiled, 'That is the $64000 question, and I must admit that without your permission I've already used the DNA we've got, to get a better idea of who you and your grandfather are. As things stand now, your relatives include, Prince Philip, Her Majesty the Queen, King Juan Carlos of Spain, Kaiser Wilhelm, and Tsarina Alexandra of Russia.' He laughed and added 'But to be fair Queen Victoria's descendants must number in the thousands by now so you are only very minor royalty probably, how about 356th in line to the throne.

Tsarina Alexandra was the fourth daughter of Alice, daughter of Queen Victoria, in other words the granddaughter of Queen Victoria. Whichever way you look at it, you could be royalty!!'

'You mean I could be the next King,' Alix giggled. Then they both laughed, and it eased the tension in the room.

Alix then stopped laughing and butted in, 'So who was my great grandfather, because that really is why I am here?'

'I cannot immediately give you a direct answer to that question, but I probably will be able to before you go home tonight, you'll just need to give me a few minutes.'

The thought that Alix was a direct descendent of Queen Victoria astonished him, but as he sat there, he was also wondering how on earth could this be possible through an Irish grandfather. Of course, the man in the military cemetery was now definitely not Willie McBride, but possibly the son of royalty, and therefore very likely not Irish at all. Charles had gone to one of his computers and was bashing a few keys and the screens were breaking down into smaller multiple screens, and the more than one printer was humming away.

'Alix this could take about twenty minutes, how do you fancy good old-fashioned fish and chips? There's a good chip shop about four doors down towards the lights on this side of the road.' He handed Alix a twenty-pound note, 'Just tell them Charles Speed sent you and you'll get everything freshly cooked, and by the time you get back I'll have more answers than questions which will be a pleasant change for both of us.'

Alix realised he was hungry, so without a word went off down the stairs out into the street, to return half an hour later with hot freshly prepared haddock and chips.

'Sorry to be so long there was a queue.'

Alix looked at Charles, and saw a very grave face, the face of a man who has seen something which has shocked him. Alix had only seen a face like that once, when the headmaster came into a classroom to fetch out a boy, and it turned out he had to tell the poor child his parents had been killed in an accident. Consequently, he knew the news wasn't good, and this was confirmed by the lack of a hello, or even acknowledgement of the fish and chips whose wonderful aroma Charles couldn't have missed. Charles shook his head and all he said was,

'Alix, you'd better take a seat.'

He shook his head again, and with a look of real concern said very quietly, almost as if afraid we were being overheard.

'You know we said jokingly that you might be 356th in line to the throne, which means you might be royalty', and at this point there was a dramatic pause............' Well, I think you are, or at least you could be.'

Alix's face must have been a picture, 'You're kidding, aren't you?'

'I wish I was, because it's not that simple.'

Intrigued, in fact compulsively curious Alix said, 'well get on with it, how strong is my claim to be the next King?'

It was obviously meant as a joke, but Charles reply was to stay with him for the rest of his life.

'Not King, but Tsar of Russia.

I think you are a Romanov, possibly the only direct lineage survivor of the family assassinated by the Bolsheviks.' By way of an explanation he added, 'I think the assassinated Alexandra was your great grandmother.'

Alix just stared at him, willing Charles to continue, and he dutifully did, as the beautiful fish and chips began to go cold on the table. 'Let me explain my reasons, that's the least I can do, and we can eat the fish and chips as we go.' As of two minutes ago Alix had lost his appetite completely.

'The Mitochondrial DNA tests and remember a male's Mitochondrial DNA comes only from his mother and is not passed on to his offspring. So, in your case you have your mother's Mitochondrial DNA, it is the Y Chromosome DNA we are interested in here.

The Mitochondrial DNA tests done to identify the remains of the Tsarina and her three daughters confirmed a maternal relationship between HRH Prince Philip, the Duke of Edinburgh, the Tsarina, and her three daughters. That may seem irrelevant, but the principle of this relationship puts a totally different light on Willie, and that's why it makes me think your ancestors were part of the Russian Royal Family, and you are quite probably a Romanov.'

Charles moved to another computer open on his desk 'I'm just going to check on some findings in the identification of the Tsar and his family's remains, to see what comes up, 'and as an afterthought, as he glanced at the fish and chips opened in front of Alix,

'Definitely the best fish and chips in Cambridge don't you think?'

With no appetite at all, even though he knew he'd missed lunch, Alix was just nibbling at the fish through a totally dry and nervous mouth, nodded. This whole thing just seemed utterly ludicrous to him, because he could see no way he could be a Russian, never mind a survivor of the Russian Revolution.

Charles suddenly pressed a button on his computer, and it started printing, and very quickly something Alix noticed was the speed. He thought how much quicker and quieter than the printers at school, and

within a couple of minutes he found himself immersed in Tsar Nicholas the Second, his wife and children. There seemed no doubt at all that all their remains have been positively identified using the same DNA evidence Charles is describing. Nevertheless, their only son Alixei was a haemophiliac, and Alix remembered the weakness of the Romanov male line. Alix knew he wasn't; however one slight nagging thought was at the back of his mind. Why did his older brother William die so young, and the dawning realisation that the heir to Tsar Nicholas was his son Alixei, perhaps that was why he was called Alix. A slight shiver ran down his spine and Alix made a mental note to check his brother's death certificate when he got home, but if he remembered correctly the cause of death was listed as 'Internal Bleeding'. That would be a strong possibility if he were a haemophiliac. Alix continued reading, although to be fair, his mind was more on what Charles was doing at the computer. He kept jumping up from one, and going to another, and in between times devouring the haddock and chips with great relish. Indeed, Alix thought he might offer Charles his hardly eaten supper.
With a satisfied grunt Charles finally stood up and came over and sat down next to Alix.
'Alix, I think I've found the answer, and if it's the truth then it is stranger than fiction.

We were talking about, and hopefully you've been reading about the maternal relationship between the Tsarina her four daughters and the Duke of Edinburgh, although I detect an understandable lack of appetite and an inability to concentrate after what I told you.' Charles nodded at the hardly touched fish and chips that lay in front of Alix.
'Well, there is much more than just that, and if you were somewhat surprised at my previous conclusion, then I have no idea what you'll think now.'
Charles laid out some more printed paper in front of Alix.
'The Princess Alice was Queen Victoria's third child and second daughter, born in 1843 and died in 1878. She was the great grandmother of Prince Philip. In 1862 she married a German Prince Louis of Hesse and the Rhine.
Not many people know but Princess Alice carried the haemophilia gene inherited from her mother Queen Victoria. One of her children Alexandra married Tsar Nicholas 2nd, and she carried the haemophilia gene, and her only son and heir Alixei was a haemophiliac.
Now it all gets a bit technical here.
I talked to you about the Mitochondrial DNA testing which established the common ancestor being Queen Victoria, well there are other vital clues here.

There is something called Nuclear DNA testing, which of course is the DNA in the nucleus of a cell, was done on the Tsarina and three daughter's remains away back in 1991, and the five STR markers confirmed the maternal relationship between the Duke of Edinburgh and the Tsarina. Charles gently pointed at the sheets he had given Alix previously, 'STR as you will remember stands for Short Tandem Repeats. Well Alix, the slight problem we have is who your great grandfather was, because there is now a twist in the tail so to speak because I am also pretty certain that Tsar Nicholas wasn't your great grandfather, nor Willie's father.

Now take this on board if you can, and you don't need to understand any of this, just the results, but I can show you on the screen if you want.' Alix now in too much of a state of shock at the last sentence, just shook his head, 'No you carry on.'

'Well,' warming to his task Charles continued, 'The Tsar's brother Georgij Romanov who died in around 1899 of I believe Tuberculosis, was the link so to speak. Permission was given back in the 1990's to access his skeletal remains to gain further insight into the occurrence and segregation of heteroplasmic Mitochondrial DNA variants in the Tsar's maternal lineage. This was done to make a positive identification of the Romanovs.' He shrugged, 'Sorry, this is real technical speak.'

Alix leaned forward in his chair with a quizzical look. 'Now hang on Charles, you have just told me that mitochondrial DNA is always and only inherited from mother to son.'
'Correct.'
'So, what is the relevance to me, because I can't have any of this DNA because I am a male.
Charles smiled 'I was just coming to that, but now you've obviously taken on board what I have been saying, and if I may say so I am much impressed, we can now move on to the definitive proof. As I said the body of Prince Georgij was exhumed, and we have the Y - STR from him, which is used all the time in modern cases where we need to prove paternity.
In this case the Y- STR, remember the short tandem repeating patterns, well I used them and found enough matches between your good self and Prince Georgij to be certain he was your great grandfather. I then repeated the checks on Tsar Nicholas and you and can be certain he was not your great grandfather.

Alix let out an involuntary gasp.
Charles gave him a sympathetic smile, and added 'I don't know how to put this any other way, but that makes you the Tsar of Russia.' Alix just sat and looked at Charles with his mouth agape.

Charles carried on, 'because until Alixei was born, Georgij Romanov was the heir as the younger brother, a bit like Prince Andrew was to Prince Charles before he married Diana and had Prince William. In this case with all the Romanov's dead, including the son and heir, had your grandfather Willie lived he would have become Tsar on the death of Alixei the only haemophiliac son of Tsar Nicholas. That meant your father William would have become Tsar, and thus automatically you. The fact that the position so to speak doesn't exist is neither here nor there really.'

Suddenly Alix felt a mixture of relief and elation. At last, he had found out who he was, even if the possible consequences of this discovery would be enormous.

All he managed to say was 'Good God!!' This was followed by a long silence as Alix struggled to understand the consequences of everything he had just been told. He finally spoke to break the silence which was becoming quite oppressive

'Russia isn't a monarchy, and never will be, so all of this is strictly irrelevant isn't it.'

Charles looked at him raised his eyebrows, 'I think not, but you'll need to be very careful about how you handle this. There may be people in Russia who would like to see a monarchy returned, but equally there are others who don't, and some of them might be prepared to take extreme measures to make sure you didn't come out of the woodwork. Put another way, they'd like you dead!!'

'That's a bit dramatic isn't it, considering I am technically not directly descended at all from Tsar Nicholas 2nd. After all Willie made Marie pregnant, so William my father was illegitimate, and Willie wasn't even the son of the Tsar, but from what you have said he was the son of his brother Georgij, so Willie, my father and I could never legally be heirs to the throne of Russia.'

Charles looked at Alix 'Would you like to bet money that your grandfather Willie never married Marie, could be one question worth thinking about? Secondly, supposing the Tsar accepted Willie as his child, and even signed a birth certificate to confirm it. Had we not made the advances in DNA identification over the past few years no-one would have been any the wiser. In fact,' and Charles smiled at the thought, 'I wonder how many men would not have inherited titles, land, and even thrones, had their DNA been taken into account. Many wives including Royalty, Duchesses, and Countesses have been guilty of adultery, resulting in a child which has just been innocently accepted by their husband and who has in time inherited either titles, or land, or even a dynasty.'

Charles sat back and then leant forward again speaking as he did so.

'Finally, and on a completely different tack there have been so many rumours over the years about millions if not billions of dollars in gold and diamonds in a Swiss bank that you are now in line to inherit. If that were to be true, and your claim could be....' and his words faded away to nothing, when Charles realised what he was saying.

This gave Alix the opportunity to say what was worrying him the most. 'First things first, have you told anyone; could anyone know about your research?'

Charles coloured slightly, 'No I haven't.' Then by way of explanation,

'Obviously I have had to use one or two old friends in my line of business to access a couple of databases. When they asked me why, I said I was doing some research into heteroplasmy and its uses in criminal investigative DNA. That got me access to the Tsar's family Mitochondrial DNA and the heteroplasmy.

The chances of anyone wanting to, or for that matter being able to trace the records I investigated are at worst extremely unlikely, but essentially very remote indeed. In any case they could have no idea at all why I was taking copies of those particular details. I had your DNA and Willie's DNA on my desk, so they were never put onto the European Database, or any system at all.'

Charles then handed Alix a blue folder.

'Everything I have discovered is in the folder here, and this is the one copy. I won't even keep one myself.

By the way I've also done a bit of reading up about the Romanov's.

Olga the eldest was born on...' Charles stretched across the desk to open the folder, '3rd November 1895. Tatania the second daughter was born on 29th May 1897. Maria 14th June 1899, Anastasia 5th June 1901, and Alexei on August 12th 1904

What I did find however was a stillbirth recorded on 2nd August 1898, although it was very hushed up, and almost airbrushed as if it never happened, and I think that was little Willie McBride. It is just possible that there had been a liaison between the Grand Duke of Russia Georgij Romanov sometime in October 1897, because it would appear the Tsar was in Siberia hunting. I know that for a fact because I can access the Court Records because of my line of work.

What is interesting is that Georgij died of tuberculosis in 1899, and being a naturally suspicious chap, which is a prerequisite for my job, I just wonder if there was no stillbirth; if Willie somehow was spirited away, and then the Tsar had his brother eliminated in an act of revenge, but it was put about as tuberculosis. Incidentally that would also have silenced the only person who knew the truth apart from the Tsar and Tsarina.' As an afterthought he added 'It was also a kind of insurance policy for the Tsar, who needed a son, and of course Alexei wasn't born until 1904. He may have been able to see the storm clouds on the horizon and being unable to admit parentage to the world at large at that time, allowed the child to grow up somewhere else.'

Alix nodded and muttered 'Yes in Ireland.'

Charles was looking justifiably pleased with himself and his homework. Alix was beginning to think Charles was very much a conspiracy theorist. He did however have to admit that there was a huge amount of logic in what Charles had said.

By this stage it was a long way past midnight, and Alix realised he was physically and mentally exhausted. He had wanted to find out exactly who his grandfather Willie McBride was, and he had certainly found that out, but he found himself thinking that he still didn't have the whole picture, and he really needed to go home and think things through.

What was worrying Alix most of all was Charles Speed. Could he trust him to keep his word, and his silence? Alix resisted the temptation to ask him again, because that could be regarded as insulting, so instead he gave his thanks and left. Charles was very quick then to reassure Alix of confidentiality, and of course his account would be in the post.

As he drove back home to Ely with the folder on the front seat beside him Alix idly wondered how much a national newspaper would pay for the story. Not of course for himself, but as a temptation to anyone else. Alix tried to put that kind of thought from his mind, because there were a great many unanswered questions running through his head. Alix realised he was desperate to tell someone. This wasn't the kind of secret you could keep to yourself. There was only one person he could unburden himself to and that was Tony. He reassured himself that they were not only very old friends, but he had also really opened the doors for him to discover his past, and he had always said he wanted to know what was going on.

However it was one thing to ring an old friend in the office, and quite another to ring in the middle of the night, that kind of call only came accompanied by news of a death, or perhaps a lottery win.

Alix looked at his watch, it was just after three o'clock in the morning. He let himself in, switched off the alarm, and then nearly jumped out of his skin.

CHAPTER 23

A voice in the darkness hit him like a tornado, 'Glad to see you safe and sound Mr. McBride or should I say Tsar Alixander?'

The voice stepped out of the shadows and became Mr. Stewart, the man from SIS.

'What do you think you are doing in my house?' Alix's voice was both angry and scared, in fact almost frightened out of his wits, after all his alarm system was designed to keep people out.

The reply was soft, and not unfriendly. 'I'm simply looking after your interests, and I'm sorry to have scared you.'

'Alix, may I call you that, things have obviously moved on since we last met, and we are very worried about your safety, and not a little concerned either for the political and financial situation that our government could find itself in unless we are very careful.'

Mr Stewart stood to one side and ushered Alix into his own sitting room. 'I know how late it is, and equally I know what information you have been given tonight.'

By way of explanation he added, 'We have been able to listen to everything you heard, and intercept all the downloads, plus overhearing everything that goes on here in this house.' With a shrug of the shoulders he added, 'I'm sorry, but when it comes to national security we really have little choice in the matter.' He waved Alix toward a chair, and continued speaking.

'Look you need to sit down and listen. Again, I'm sorry to have scared you like this, but we do believe your life is now in great danger because of the information you have uncovered. Contrary to what you might believe we are in fact your friends, and we are desperate that no harm befalls you.'

Alix sat down open mouthed. 'I really haven't a clue what you're going on about. Alright I have found out about my grandfather, but Russia is no longer a monarchy, so surely, I am just a bit of history, no more, and no less.'

'Were that to be true, but sadly very sadly, sitting in a bank in Switzerland, is a fortune estimated at over 240 billion dollars' worth of gold, perhaps even more than that, and the only person with the key is you!'

Suddenly everything seemed to fall into place for Alix, and not nicely into place either. All the money he had inherited, the ability of his grandmother to buy and sell houses. The strange fact that his grandfather Willie McBride as a private soldier had a last will and testament.

'Blumeur's Bank' he blurted out, 'is that where the Tsar had his fortune, only I definitely don't have the key.'

'Yes, we know that, and it's desperately urgent that we find out where it is.'

'Why?'

Mr Stewart kind of sighed and shrugged his shoulders at the same time. 'Look there are some things you know and lots you don't know, and I'm going to give you a crash course on everything that is important, and then we're going to give you a plan that you'll need to carry out to the letter if we are to save your life, and prevent a massive destabilisation of the world economy, perhaps even prevent a war.'

Alix started, 'This is just ridiculous, look please leave and let me go to bed.'

'OK, but before I go,' and as he said it Mr Stewart stood up as if to leave, 'there is at least 240 billion US dollars in gold, plus God knows what else in that vault in Blumeur's Bank in Switzerland. Some of that you already know, but what you don't know is that now your grandmother has died, only you can access it.

Now you can leave it where it is, and the Russians will undoubtedly eventually get at it, and that amount of gold flooding the world market will cause economic difficulties everywhere. Or you claim what is your birthright after all and put the money to good use in the third world.'

As he walked towards the door he added, 'They, and by they, I mean the Russians, are desperate to get their hands on the gold, and work out for yourself what that could mean. I can tell you they tortured your father, who either didn't know enough or was braver than we can imagine, before they killed him and made it look like a suicide.'

'Wait a minute,' Alix was now wide awake and very scared. Are you telling me that I should somehow know some secret code, or the whereabouts of some key?'

'No and that's the whole point. No-one knows where it is, but you are the only one who can use it. In fact, when you find it, they don't need you anymore.......... if you get my drift.'

'So, if I do nothing, I'm safe.'

'Yes, in a manner of speaking, but like many bank accounts, the gold and whatever money that Blumeur's have which we assume is the Tsar's will have a kind of 'Statute of Limitations 'on it.'

Seeing Alix's frown, Mr. Stewart continued, 'By that I mean, is that 99 years from the deaths of the Tsar and his apparent heirs the money will revert to the Bank unless it is claimed.

By my calculations that is in another 6 years or so. Now whilst your grandmother had the ability to draw money, she was unable to touch the gold itself. The money in the will that you inherited obviously came direct from your grandmother.'

'Yes, I know that.'

Alix weakly waved Mr Stewart to sit down again. 'Does Tony my solicitor know all of this?'

'I'm not sure, but it is very unlikely.'

Mr. Stewart leant back in the chair making himself more comfortable. 'Look Alix, you will need to do some things apparently off your own bat, but we're, or rather I'm going to make a few suggestions to you.'

'OK.' Alix nodded somewhat dumbly, 'But how do I know I can trust you?'

'That's very reasonable, because I could be working for the Russians, and by the way you were quite close to the truth when you talked about Burgess, Maclean, and that bunch of traitors. Your father was key to the investigations, and indeed had he lived, I'm certain from reading the files, Hollis and the man who probably ran the whole show would have been caught as well, but that's another matter altogether.'

Mr Stewart then smiled and added, 'Look, if you really need proof of who I am, please come to our headquarters in London sometime in the next few days, and just ask for me by name.'

Mr. Stewart dug into his pocket and pulled out a card, which he handed over. 'I know you have teaching responsibilities, but on Wednesday your last class finishes at 11am, indeed it is your only class this Wednesday, so shall I send a car, would that help?'

He added, 'When you get to there, just hand the card in at reception, and you'll be escorted to my office.'

'Yes of course.' A weary Alix just sat wondering if there was anything in his life this man didn't know. 'I'll be able to let you see some photographs of your father and grandmother as well, and that's not a bribe either!! I'm going to leave now, and I know you won't sleep, so what I suggest is that you hunt around for anything that might be relevant. What I mean is a document, a false drawer, something that might lead us to the key.'

As Mr Stewart got up to leave, he added one final thing. 'Somehow, I have a feeling the key by itself may not be enough. I know you have the DNA evidence, which of course kind of condemns you. However, you need to bear in mind that Blumeurs are about as old fashioned a bank as you could wish for, and they will want paper evidence in the form of birth and death certificates, wills, wedding certificates, rather than the DNA stuff. Having said that, quite where we get that from, I just don't know, but there's no harm in looking.' With that he was gone, without even a noise from the door closing.

Alix let out a sigh, got up out of the chair, and put the double locks on the front door, thinking they wouldn't be much use if that man wanted to come back again.

He wandered back into the dining room, sat down at the table and burst into tears.

A few people have died gloriously and very many quietly without leaving much behind, but poor Willie, conceived as a mistake, consigned to life in an orphanage without loving parents, to then discover the whole future of the monarchy in Russia sits on your shoulders, and then to perish quite horribly. That is too much for one man to bear he thought, and now that mantle has fallen to me, and it's not what I want.

Well, Alix thought I've not done anything to ensure the continuation of the Romanov line, but here at the end of the tracks so to speak I'm probably going to be held responsible when the Romanov name resurfaces, which could quite possibly be my death sentence. 'At least without the key I am safe, and I can't see where I'll find the key in the house,' came out almost involuntarily, and at that point he must have fallen asleep, thinking that Mr. Stewart would probably have heard every word.

The next thing Alix was aware of was Margaret rattling at the front door, and he realised he'd still not given her a key to let herself in. He must have given Margaret a shock as he let her in, his unshaven wild look contrasting dramatically with his normal well pressed suit freshly shaven with neatly combed hair.

'Come in Margaret, I'm sorry about the mess, I must have fallen asleep at the table'

'Don't worry, but it's ten to nine, and you're going to be late, and you have a class at 9.15 seeing as it's Tuesday.'

With that Alix rushed upstairs and within 10 minutes he was outside and on his way to school, still deep in thought, still not concentrating on where he was going until he heard the shrill ring of a bicycle, the screech of tyres, and a familiar voice shouting 'McBride watch out.'

Looking up Alix saw Tony, complete with bowler hat, college scarf slung round his neck, briefcase in the basket at the front of his 1950's style upright bicycle.

'Alix what are you thinking about, that could have been very nasty. Can I assume you've found out something else from the way you're walking along not concentrating on where you are going?' Before Alix could reply, he took off, shouting over his shoulder, 'See you in the pub at 6.30.'

Alix wasn't sure he wanted to see Tony, but they were old friends, and he desperately needed a confidant and some sensible advice before his visit to Mr. Stewart the following day.

Alix got to the pub early, and had a large glass of orange squash, as he was keen to be sober, and he wanted to ensure Tony was sober too. The Rose and Crown had always been the pub that he and

Tony drank in, so there could be no question of going to the wrong place, but when 6.30 came and went, Alix began to worry, but happily at 6.45 Tony ambled in.

Beers in hand, the usual pleasantries exchanged Alix came straight to the point.

'Tony, ...'

Alix shifted uncomfortably in his seat, looked around the near deserted pub, checked the alcoves on either side were empty. 'What on earth are you doing Alix, we're not in a spy movie.'

'I'm not too sure!!' Then for the next three hours Alix told Tony almost without interruption the whole story, leaving nothing out, the appearance in his life of the terrifying Mr. Stewart, and everything he had learned from Charles Speed. Alix constantly checked the neighbouring alcoves for people and then asked the billion dollar question.

'If you were me, what would you do next?'

'The whole thing is incredible, but you have been led to all of this, I am not in doubt of that. If you think about Granny McBride's instructions that started the quest, then thinking with my lawyer's objective brain, she must have left you something else.' He hesitated for a moment, and then added 'You don't have a safe in the house do you?'

'Not that I'm aware of, but I suppose I've never tried to find a hidden one, because it would certainly be that.' Alix hesitated slightly, 'Do you know David the School Vicar?'

'Yes, of course I know him,' Tony interjected, 'Well oddly enough he told me that shortly after my mother and I moved here to Ely from the Cambridge house after dad died to say with Granny, she, that is Granny Marie felt there had been people in the house, searching. Nothing had been taken but I assumed stuff had been moved. Well, I have had a similar feeling this summer.'

'Why not go to the police, and see if they have any records of a complaint being made in the early 1960's?'

'That is a great idea.'

Tony looked at his watch, and yawned, 'I just had a feeling this conversation would be lengthy, and I don't think it's finished yet. I'm off home, but you go to the police, and go to see Mr. Stewart. You can be sure your secret is safe with me so don't worry.' With a cheery wave he was off, and he remembered to duck too!!

Alix returned home, and wished he'd asked Tony to go with him, because he was terrified that he would find another visitor. To his huge relief the house was as he'd left it that morning although he noticed Margaret had done some tidying in the dining room as well as all his ironing and he blessed her silently.

He felt absolutely exhausted, went straight to bed, and fell into a deep and surprisingly dreamless sleep. There is a saying that if you want your brain to remember something, or you have subconsciously asked it a question and no answer is immediately forthcoming, then just let it run like the computer it is and given time it will come up with the answer.

It did, in the early hours of the morning, when he woke with a start.

His brain had done its job and had woken him up to tell him that the love letter written to the dead Willie McBride had to have some significance. He stumbled downstairs, and sat and read it several times, but could find nothing significant at all. He wondered whether there was a hidden message in invisible ink, he held it up against a strong light, but again there was nothing. It must be his fevered imagination working overtime, and then he realised.

The letter wasn't quite where he had left it.

The awful thought then crossed his mind that someone had been in the house, searching for something, had taken the letter out from the brown envelope and not put it back where they had picked it up from. To be fair Alix wasn't totally sure where it had been left, but it definitely wasn't on the sideboard.

The only person who had been in the house since he left last morning had been Margaret. Surely it couldn't have been Margaret. He remembered her references, but most of all he remembered how she had appeared not long after his mother died.
Alix began to wonder if this was a total coincidence or was there something more sinister. Alix decided to scan and copy the letter to take to Mr. Stewart, but he realised his printer and copier had been moved no more than an inch, and Alix could still see the old outline of it on the desk. When you add to this that it was still switched on, something that would never happen. His mother had always been insistent that everything electrical was always switched off after use to save electricity, so to Alix it was now second nature.
It looked very much as if someone had taken the letter then photocopied it, and Alix also had the chilling thought that if it was true that his life was in danger, then she in some way was involved.
He copied the letter to take with him, and then made a second copy which he stuck in an envelope and addressed it to Tony at his office.
That done Alix looked at his watch, and realised it was almost time to get ready for the school day realising of course he was to be taken to the SIS Headquarters in London.
With his only class due to start shortly after 10 o'clock he had plenty of time to take himself down

to the main police station in Ely. Before leaving the house, he remembered to place the two envelopes in his pocket, and on his way to the Police Station he posted the copy to Tony whilst making certain the one for Mr. Stewart remained in his jacket pocket.

Alix was a well-known figure in the town, so when he asked to see the Inspector about a problem he was having, and gave a brief explanation, the sergeant on the desk who had several years ago briefly been a pupil of his, was happy to usher Alix through.

John Davidson got up from his desk as Alix came through the door.

'Alix good to see you, it's been a while, I gather you might need our help.' John was probably desk bound, around 45 years of age, and a good old-fashioned policeman, who always wanted things done properly, but wise enough to talk first, and not always arrest which might account for a stalled career. For all that, he was a popular, cheerful soul, not averse to the odd pint of bitter.

'John, I'll not take up much of your time, because this is really a historical enquiry. I believe my grandmother filed a report around 40 years ago, when I was a small child and we had only recently moved here from Cambridge. I'm sure you know David, our school vicar, well he was her parish priest at the time, and it was him who recommended she reported the feeling she had that someone had been in the house although nothing was taken. The same thing has happened to me recently, and although I don't want anything done about it, I'd like if possible to see what upset her all these years ago.'

'That could take a few days, and I'm not sure if incidents like this are still kept on file.'

John grinned, 'But it would help if you could give me some idea what it's about.'

Alix grinned back and said, 'Can we just say family inheritance problems.'

Alix got up 'Look I've a class to teach and I'm sure you're busy, so can you give me an idea of how long this will take.'

'If it's on the computer, about 10 minutes – for a pint!!'

True to his word, 10 minutes later John returned with a computer printout, and a bit more besides.

'You are right, your granny McBride did ask for us to investigate a possible intruder back in 1963, but what is even more interesting was when your mother and father got married, and your grandmother bought the house here in Ely she made exactly the same complaint, and that was years before, but there was nothing to find on either occasion.

There is however a note, which said that as your grandmother had some possessions that she valued a great deal that she was worried about then she should buy a safe. That report was dated 26th of September 1945.'

Talk about hitting the jackpot, 'Thank you very much, that is a lot more than I expected, I don't suppose you could tell me if you recommended anyone in particular.'

John grinned, 'No chance, not after 50 odd years, you must be joking.'

With that Alix left, happy in that piece of knowledge, but now the question remained, did his grandmother follow their recommendation, and if so, where was the safe?'

He sped off to his class, and then to the headmaster's office, where a somewhat less than salubrious vehicle lay waiting. It must have been twenty years old if it was a day, with an equally elderly driver, who wasn't to say one word during the entire journey there and back.

CHAPTER 24

Alix was at the SIS headquarters for over twelve hours before he was driven home in the small hours of the morning, exhausted, both physically and mentally.

Of the journey Alix remembered little but the impression that the mausoleum like SIS building made on him was of epic proportions. It's quite one thing to see James Bond under attack in a movie and quite another to cross the threshold. As requested, Alix handed over the card that Mr. Stewart had given him to the attractive young lady in reception. He was then asked to take a seat and wait, and a few minutes later a pleasant young man came to escort him to see Mr. Stewart. Immediately prior to that he was scanned, asked to turn out his pockets, and then given one of these cards you increasingly see that indicate a level of security clearance, to sling round his neck. The lift took him up several floors, very quickly, and then he was ushered into Mr. Stewart's office which had a superb view of the River Thames.

'Thank you for coming Alix, we do appreciate it, I don't think you will have met my colleague Alistair Moses.' A somewhat undistinguished looking gentleman probably in his late thirties stood up as did Mr. Stewart and shook hands with Alix very firmly indeed.

'Alistair will be responsible for your well-being over the next few weeks, although I will always be available.' Was the cheerful opening remark from his host.

Alix hoped that this wasn't the highlight of the day. Mr. Stewart then ushered Alix to a comfortable chair, next to a coffee table which had a seemingly fresh pot of coffee and a mound of biscuits, which indicated to Alix that whatever was going to happen next wasn't going to be quick.

As Alix sat down, Mr. Stewart coughed, and in a quiet voice said, 'Look please call me Colin. I'm really sorry we didn't get off on the right foot so to speak, but please be reassured that we, meaning Her Majesty's Government will do everything in its power to protect you, not least Sir, because in name at least you are the Tsar of Russia.'

Alix looked absolutely horrified at this statement.

'Colin, only my pupils call me Sir, and until we get to the bottom of all of this, I'm just plain Alix, and also don't forget the DNA evidence suggests I'm not the Tsar.'

At which point he remembered the letter, and after a few seconds feeling for it, he pulled it from the inside pocket of his jacket and handed it over to Colin.

'This is a letter from my grandmother Dubré to my grandfather, except it seems to have been written to him after he died. I don't know what it means, but I wondered if you could see what you make of it.'

'Thank you.' Colin opened the letter, studied it for a second. 'I'll give this to our chaps to take a look at it, and if there's anything I'll let you know straight away.'

With that Colin placed the letter on the coffee table and turned round again to face Alix.

'We need to have a recording of this briefing, more of a question-and-answer session really, and he switched on the two tape recorders which seemed to appear from nowhere. 'This interview commenced at 1400 hours with Mr Alix McBride.'

....
....
....
....
.... Some of the information that Alix received during the eight hours he sat in Colin's office staggered him to say the least, but the highlight without any doubt was being able to see some photographs of his father, which he found quite emotionally overwhelming. Colin also explained some more things Alix needed to know, and he would realise the need to follow the instructions he was being given at the right moment, although he wouldn't be drawn as to when that would be, except it would be sooner rather than later.

What impressed Alix the most, even more than Colin's encyclopaedic knowledge of almost everything to do with his situation, was how indebted he must be to Colonel John Peterson, and all those who lived and died to protect the future of the Romanov family. He felt truly humbled that for over 100 years, one family, the Edmundson's, of whom John Peterson was a part, had sacrificed themselves physically and financially so that he Alix McBride could properly identify himself as the Tsar, and in effect finally defeat the Bolsheviks.

It was very late in the evening by the time Alix managed to extricate himself from the SIS building, and sometime after one o'clock before he got home. He decided during the long journey home, that whatever money he inherited, there would be a large portion of it given to John Peterson. Even that could never repay a family who lost everything they owned, going from fabulous wealth to poverty, in the name of protecting the future of the Russian Royal Family.

Alix also rang Tony who was more than happy to get an update the following afternoon, and suggested the office might be a more secure place to chat.

When Alix arrived in Tony's office, for once there wasn't any social chat.

'So, tell me what happened?' Tony leant forward in anticipation. 'Well Tony the best thing about the day was I saw several photographs of my father, and I do look so like him. '
Colin Stewart was totally true to his word, and..,' Tony grinned and interrupted, 'That is so fantastic for you,' adding quickly 'So we're on first name terms now are we?!!'
'Actually, he apologised, and I have no doubt at all he is on my side, and trying very hard to help me find out where this dammed key is.' Alix then continued with what was essentially an afterthought.
'I went to see Inspector John Davidson yesterday morning, and he told me that Granny McBride went to the police because she thought the house was being searched, and whilst no action was taken, they suggested granny install a safe to hide some especially valuable items.' He then added, 'Not only that but I gave Colin Stewart a copy of the letter I copied to you, and he seemed most interested in that.
'So, what else did he tell you?' Tony was leaning well forward in his chair looking intensely at Alix.
'Well, what surprised me most of all was the fact that Colonel Peterson and his forebears, have done an incredible job in protecting the interests of the Romanov family.
To think that I had thought he was, so to speak, not

a friend, well I feel awful about that now. Whilst I knew, thanks to Ray that one of his ancestors had married into the Russian Royal family at the time of the Crimean War, I just didn't connect the dots so to speak. It was logical they would be supportive of the Romanovs, so I feel a bit stupid now.

How it came about was that the Edmundsons were fabulously wealthy and owned most of County Mayo and Colonel Edmundson was captured at the Charge of the Light Brigade. They used to host wealthy young Russians who were taught English, even when it was politically insensitive. When the Tsar needed a bolthole for Willie McBride, and then the group of Russian orphans, it was to the Edmundsons and the Petersons that he turned, which was why the Orphanage was established at Termoncarragh .' Alix leant back and blew his nose. 'Sorry Tony you know most of this already, but it has all fallen into place now, so sorry for repeating myself.'

Tony shrugged his shoulders, 'Don't be silly, I see it all more clearly now, and what a tale to tell one day,' he saw the look on Alix's face, 'Sorry I didn't mean that.'

Alix continued, 'If there is any money at the end of this and Colin Stewart assures me there is not only the gold, but potentially a huge amount of top quality diamonds as well, though quite frankly I find it hard to believe, then I plan to give John

Peterson a serious amount of money as a reward for the efforts of him and his family.

Do you know they went bankrupt in the 1930's because of the money they spent setting up the orphanage and running it. They commemorated many of the dead Irish children with solid gold chalices. They used their own money to give the grieving parents a new start in life, mostly in the United States. Never forget,' Alix emphasised using his hands to reinforce the point, 'that this family sacrificed almost everything for the Tsar, believing they would be rewarded as they were promised, and then lost it all because their financier, the Tsar was dead. The most fantastic thing of all is that they have remained loyal despite everything.'

With that Alix sat back in his chair, 'Oh I nearly forgot that the Chaesar Estate paid my grandmother every year. This allowed her to build up considerable assets, which answers my original question. All of that stopped in the 1930's with the bankrupting of the Chaesers, the Peterson's, the Edmundsons, and the loss of all the lands in the USA and Ireland.'

Tony scratched his head. 'Hang on, it is well known the Tsar spent his personal fortune and had to all intents and purposes almost bankrupted himself during the First World War.'

'The money he used for funding did not come from Blumeurs according to Colin Stewart, but came through another Swiss Bank. It is fair to say that the Blumeur Account was and remains an almost total secret.' Alix replied.

'Oh yes, and I almost forgot, these young orphans as they grew up were trained to protect young Willie. No-one can be sure now, whether they knew who they were protecting, but Colin Stewart is certain they died to protect Willie. It is more than a coincidence that almost all the officers in command of Willie in the Royal Munster Fusiliers were relatives, and it's equally incredible that the young men from the orphanage who enlisted together were kept together no matter what happened around them.'

'Wow.' Was Tony's only response, followed by 'So where do we go from here, and how can I help.'

'I think we both know the answer to that, and it can only be to find the safe if it exists at all.'

Logically that meant a search, so they returned to Alix's house, and checked in every nook and cranny, which kept them up until about two in the morning and was completely fruitless. They lifted carpets, tapped floorboards, looked behind heavy pieces of furniture, all to no avail.

Exhausted the two friends sat on the floor, and discussed where they went from here.

'As I see it,' Alix said 'If there was a safe, then it had to be paid for, and there had to be a point in contacting the bank, but which bank was the question, to see if a cheque was cleared just after the Second World War, to a Safe Manufacturer. 'Do you know if Granny had moved all her accounts from Ireland to England by that time Tony?'
'No I don't but I can almost certainly find that out tomorrow. Look Alix I think we're done here, so I'm off home to bed.'
With that Tony left and Alix went to bed.

In the middle of a Fourth Form history lesson the next morning, Alix was wondering how he was managing to keep things together and achieve what seemed normality to his colleagues and at the same time teach pupils the vagaries of the French Revolution, when Ray burst in. 'Alix wait until you hear what I've discovered, can we meet at lunch, this will blow your socks off.'
Alix after the events of the past few days had completely forgotten he'd asked Ray to do some more genealogical investigating. 'Sure, keep me a seat.'
It was shortly after that his mobile phone vibrated in his jacket pocket indicating a text message had arrived. A quick peep let him see it was from Tony

saying they had drawn a blank insofar as cheques were concerned.

The name Alan O'Farrell suddenly came into his head, thanks to the mobile phone he now held in his hand. He might have some records somewhere, but where on earth was that scribbled note Alan had written to him what seemed like forever ago? Not for the first time in his life Alix wished he was tidier, and now it would have to wait until after school. 'Damn Ray and his genealogy' he almost said out loud.

In fact the meeting with Ray was almost an anticlimax, but then almost anything would have been. There were and are Peterson's scattered all over the United States, with no-one of any note. What was slightly entertaining was when Ray used the word 'Chaesar' stating it is derived from Caesar, as of course is the word Tsar!!

The other thing he found out was that his mother had been born in County Mayo, had followed his father firstly to Dublin, and then to Cambridge University. This reinforced the thought that his father had been targeted and might explain the coolness his grandmother felt towards her.

This school afternoon passed very slowly indeed, and when Alix finally managed to get home, it took him a further twenty minutes of frustrating search before he remembered the folders that Alan O'Farrell had given him. They were lying behind the curtains by the French windows, and Alix had no recollection of leaving them there. He had been certain they were on the dining room table, but looking out of the French windows suddenly made him think of his garden. Why hadn't he thought of it before. The safe could easily have been buried in the garden.

Alan O'Farrell's note lay in his hand

'No details of the Swiss bank available sorry, but £500,000 deposited by them in the Mayo Bank Account of Chaesar, on the 15th of November 1909. If you need to talk some more best ring me out of office hours on 07777665544.'

He rang the number and a distinctly Irish voice answered.

'Hello is that Alan,... Alan O'Farrell?

Alan, it's Alix McBride, you were kind enough to give me your number, and I've got a couple of questions which I hope you might be able to answer.'

'I hope so too, as long as it is totally off the record, because you know my position.'

'Alan, I'm trying to find out if my grandmother either as Mrs. McBride or Madame Dubré kept an account open until after the war.'

'I think you'll find everything pertaining to her in the folder, and as far as I can remember the answer to the question is yes. How are you getting on in your quest?'

'I'm progressing thank you. The next question has probably the same answer I fear, and that is my grandmother received around £500,000 sterling in the early 1930's paid from Blumeurs the Swiss Bank..' Alan cut in, 'Also in the files, and if that's all I'll bid you goodbye.'

As Alix said, 'thanks for your h......' The line went dead.

Alix opened the folder, and within a couple of minutes he found and entry in March 1932 of a payment from Blumeur's of £500,000.

In addition, he found two entries within a week of each other in December 1945.

The first name on the bank statement was Gillett & Hoon, Locksmiths, and was for £525 dated 10th December, and the second was also made out to Gillett & Hoon on the 20th December 1945 for £75. This very much looked like a safe, and the second could only be for installation. That probably ruled out the garden, because you wouldn't pay a firm of locksmiths for installation if you were simply digging a hole in the garden.

'Where on earth is the bloody thing?'

Alix wasn't a man to be easily frustrated, but this was beginning to wear him out. A quick check in the phone book in the Cambridge area gave no mention of Gillett & Hoon, but a search on the internet did reveal the name, but sadly it also showed a company that had gone out of business some years ago.

He then had a brainwave.

He wondered if any of his neighbours had been living there in 1945.

It seemed ridiculous but Alix was only on nodding terms with a couple of them, despite having spent his life in Ely in the same house. He had to be looking for someone in their early seventies who might remember a safe being delivered.

He tried numbers 41, 45, on his side of the road, and he then knocked on number 40, on the other side of the road, and an elderly lady answered.

'Hello, I'm Alix McBride, and I live opposite.' Waving his arms in the general direction of his own house. 'You weren't by any chance living here during and just after the war?'

'Mr. McBride, oh it is you Alix, I remember you as a boy, how sad you had no father, and I'm sorry to hear about your mother. Do come in.' She stepped back to usher Alix in, and it was like going back to Edwardian times. Sitting in a beautiful inlaid mahogany chair was an elderly man who struggled to get to his feet as Alix entered.

'For goodness sake don't get up.'

The old lady said, 'John, do you remember young Alix McBride, and by way of explanation she added 'I'm his sister Jean, and we've lived here all our lives.' In a flash Alix remembered exactly who they were, John and Jean Judd, his mother had always said the Judd's were a strange family who kept themselves to themselves, and they had never married.

'Would you like a cup of tea' Thinking it churlish to refuse Alix accepted and smiled 'That would be nice – thank you.'

As they settled in their chairs, Alix had a good look around the room, it really was beautifully furnished and immaculate.

'What a lovely room you have here, you have very good taste.'

'Oh, not us, that was mum and dad's, we just don't want to change the room, do we John?' and without waiting for an answer Jean continued, 'So what is it we can do for you Alix; my you've become a very good-looking man, considering what a small skinny child you were.'

'Well, I just wondered if you could remember when my granny Madame Dubré lived over the road, just after the War.'

Jean seemed to be answering for both of them 'Yes we do, don't you John?' he just nodded in agreement. 'We were just children then, but we remember her very well. In fact, I had a camera which was something very special then, and she let us take a photo of her one day.'

'You don't remember anything very large being delivered by lorry do you?'

Jean thought for a moment 'No I'm sorry I can't help you there.' At which point John entered the conversation for the first time 'Yes we do, don't you remember Jean that was the day of the big crane, the whole road was blocked, and mummy gave us jam sandwiches and we had Creamola foam to drink for the first time.'

Alix couldn't believe his luck, 'You said a big crane, how was it big then?'

'It was huge, and something it was lifting was covered in a sheet, I think it was a huge sideboard, or chest of drawers, anyway they had to take out the downstairs bay window to get it in. I remember it all quite clearly, for it was a big event. Is that your sitting room as well Alix?'

'No actually it's our dining room, and you've been very helpful indeed. Now I mustn't take up anymore of your time and thank you for the tea.' With that Alix upped and left, and having crossed the road, went straight into the dining room. At least he now knew where it was, and he also knew it was under the floor, because it simply couldn't be anywhere else.

It took Alix two hours to lift the carpet again, and roll it back, and then he spent a further two hours on his hands and knees inspecting every joint in the wooden floor.

There certainly wasn't a trapdoor, so whoever had hidden it was an expert; there was no doubt of that. It was sometime after 10 o'clock when he realised, that what he could see looked like the start of a new piece of floorboard under where the dining table was. With his finger he traced the very faint line across and realised it covered three boards. Having found that he saw the pattern repeated so there was effectively a square, and he noticed the one board in the middle didn't have quite the same appearance at the outside edges as all the other floorboards. Alix realised he was looking at what was potentially one small piece of wood, made up to match the other three.

He fetched a sharp kitchen knife and put it on one of the outside original floorboard edges, and it slid neatly between the boards, and with very little pressure it came upwards, on a hinge, exactly where what had looked like a new floorboard starting. Alix thought this is a real piece of precision engineering.

Opening the hinge, he saw the small door of what he assumed must be a safe. Opening the door, he saw a dial, and he realised there was no way in without the combination.

His grandmother had certainly placed a safe that no-one was meant to find, Alix thought to himself. There had to be something very special indeed inside for it to be this well-hidden. It was little wonder that there had been visitors to the house who were looking but never finding. This is what they must have been after.

What Alix suddenly thought was a safebreaker was what he needed, but in the meantime, he rolled the carpet back, replaced the table, and left the room looking as it was.

Going to bed the intrigue wouldn't leave him alone. This safe looked so secure even an expert couldn't get in. It could only be removed using a road transporter, and taking the window out, not something even the most brazen thief would attempt. His last thoughts before sleep were that whilst he had taught one or two pupils with criminal tendencies there was no-one with that potential, except McGregor in the fourth form perhaps. He fell asleep smiling.

CHAPTER 25

Alix rang Tony on his way to school on his mobile, telling him he had found the safe hidden under the floorboards, and it appeared totally impenetrable. The big question was did Tony know any safebreakers?

His phone rang less than half an hour later, and it was Tony.

'There is a world class safebreaker living in Newmarket. His name is Basil Graham. To warn you he is a recluse, but in his day, he was the absolute best in the country, and as a result spent half his life behind bars. He's about 75 years old, and he lives in a small cottage on the left-hand side, just before the 30 mile an hour sign as you enter Newmarket on the Ely road.

Mention my name if you need to, because we got him out of a spot of neighbour trouble about five years ago.

Basil turned out to be a small, very innocuous man with very little hair, he looked a bit like the popular image of a Swiss Clockmaker. The offer of £100 just to go a few miles up the road, and check out a safe, and give his opinion was too good to refuse. Basil's opinion was that was a very good Mosler safe, probably about 60-70 years old. He said he was unfamiliar with the design, but it looked as if it was a one off. What he did say was that even with all his experience the eight-combination lock is probably unpickable. Unless you have the combination, it is of little use trying to gain entry. In terms of size, he made Alix look closely at the floorboards, it shows the probable outline of the hole that was opened, and that was probably about 36 square feet, which makes it massive.

This makes it impossible to move without a crane, and taking the floorboards up, and the window out, so it is basically burglar proof. The other interesting thing Alix gleaned from Basil was the fact that the storage space inside was almost certainly quite small, the whole point of this safe was to ensure it couldn't be moved, and it probably couldn't be opened even using modern technology. 'You'll need the numbers' was all he said.

Equally he gave the opinion that it must have been put there for a very special reason. In all his years safe breaking, he had only very rarely come upon such a safe that was obviously not designed to be used regularly, but just as a hiding place.

Alix having told Tony all of this was now at somewhat of a loose end. He had heard nothing at all from Colin Stewart, indeed he had this feeling of the calm before the storm. For over a week, there was silence, and then one lunchtime as he was about to enjoy cheese and tomato on toast the doorbell rang, and Alix opened it to the familiar figure of Colin Stewart, standing with a broad grin on his face.

'Hello Alix, may I come in?'

'Yes of course, how are things?' Alix thought how different things have become since their first encounter.

'Can we sit at your dining table because I have something to show you?'

Alix motioned Colin to a chair at the table which was full of books and papers, folders and even a half-eaten plate of Cheese and tomato on toast.

'Sorry about that as he quickly removed the plate and two empty coffee cups to the kitchen, where he put the kettle on.

Colin motioned Alix to sit beside him and brought out of a folder the letter.

'This has proved very interesting indeed. It looks like a letter written in September 1917, but in fact it was probably written in the 1960's after you were born.'

Alix asked, 'Why on earth write a love letter like that when it appears to have been written so long after my grandfather and my father were dead?'

"Well' said Colin, 'It contains a code that was used by some SOE operatives in the last war, and it was written almost like a part of a puzzle for you to solve if that was something you wanted to do.' He nodded, 'quite obviously you have done exactly that, and this is how it works.'

With that he placed a copy of the letter in front of Alix.

'Please just follow what I am saying and keep any questions to the end if you possibly can, as it is somewhat complicated, and that is deliberate, knowing its origins with SOE in France.

The key is the words 'yellow and red', which are opposites

Now you'll need to concentrate here Alix.

Something starting like yellow and red, which are opposites, and that is the key.

Wherever a communication had opposites which could be a colour, or even fat and thin, big or small.'

Alix nodded 'I understand,'

Colin continued, 'which would in this case mean looking for the first word beginning with 'y' following the entry code.'

Let us suppose it is 'you' then the first letter of the message is Y

As you is made up of three letters, you go to the third word along and take the second letter.

Suppose the sequence of words was

'**Yellow and Red Roses from you all bunched together**

Together is the third word and 'O' is the second letter.

What you now have is 'YO'

Together is an eight letter word, so we look next eight words away at the 3rd letter.
Yellow and red roses from you all bunched together just serves to remind me of the countless[8] third letter is U, so we have 'YOU'. There are nine letters in the word countless so we must go to nine words and look at the fourth letter
Yellow and red roses from you all bunched together just serves to remind me of the countless wonderful times we spent together my darling.
Now because of the full stop this means the whole thing starts again with the first word in the next sentence beginning with 'Y'. There is a difference here, because it isn't the first sentence of the communication, so when we see the first word in the sentence beginning with 'Y' we use the number of letters in that word to find the key word again it is a three letter word, so we have to look for the first letter of the third word which is H in heartbroken, which in turn has 11 letters, so I now need to look for the second letter in the eleventh word.
Yellow and red roses from you all bunched together just serves to remind me of the countless wonderful times we spent together my darling.

Now you leave me heartbroken as I am here all alone so why did you have to take your love and go.

The 11th word is '**have**', which has four letters, so we add 'A' and go to the fourth word following which is '**love**', and take the 3rd letter which is 'V'. The second word is HAV, and there is a new sentence, so we need to look for a Y again.

Yellow and red roses from you all bunched together just serves to remind me of the countless wonderful times we spent together my darling. Now you leave me heartbroken as I am here all alone so why did you have to take your love and go. Yesterday we were together and now you are gone everything is lost

The first letter of the 9th word after the nine letter word Yesterday is 'E' in everything.

So the second word must be 'HAVE'

Yellow and red roses from you all bunched together just serves to remind me of the countless wonderful times we spent together my darling Now you leave me heartbroken as I am here all alone so why did you have to take your love and go. Yesterday we were together and now you are gone everything is lost please can I be with you for eternity.

Next letter is the second letter of the 10th word after everything which is and, so the key letter is 'T'.

Full stop new sentence

Yellow and red roses from you all bunched together just serves to remind me of the countless wonderful times we spent together my darling . Now you leave me heartbroken as I am here all alone so why did you have to take your love and go. Yesterday we were together and now you are gone everything is lost please can I be with you for eternity. Yes it does hurt so much just hellishly every minute of every day.

Yes has three letters so the third word first letter of 'hurt' is 'H', hurt has four letters, 'hellishly' is the fourth word with 'E' the second letter.

What I have now is YOUHAVETHE

There will never be another you, so I cherish every single wonderful moment we were together as the best time in my life and I will love you forever.

'Cherish' is the third word after you which starts with a 'Y', so 'C' is the next letter. Cherish has seven letters and the seventh word after cherish is 'together' the second letter is 'O''. 'Together' has eight letters and the eighth word after that is 'and' the third letter is 'D'. 'And' has three letters and the third word after 'and' is 'love' and the fourth letter is 'E'

What you now have is YOUHAVETHECODE

If A = 1, and Z = 26, then the sequence of numbers becomes 25152181225208531545.'

Colin sat back in the chair 'I hope you followed all that, because I didn't when it was explained to me!!'

Alix was quite flabbergasted but had the presence of mind to say, 'I've found the safe, and it appears to need an 8-digit code to unlock it.'

'That's amazing you picked that up so quickly, you wouldn't be looking for a job with us, would you?', said with a grin, 'but there is a slight catch here. This type of coding was used in Belgium by the SOE, and at the end of the day the numbers corresponded to letters of the alphabet, but the variables were changed every week and announced over the radio.

If the variable was 1 then every time the number 1 came up, it was moved one place to the right. If the number 2 came up it was 2 places and so on and so forth.'

Alix grimaced, 'That could give us a problem if she has done that, but we must assume it is now straightforward.' He leant forward and took the letter with the code solved off the table.

'Can you help me move the carpet and the table?' Colin positively leapt out of his chair, 'Absolutely.' Within two minutes the bare floorboards were exposed again, and Alix nodded to Colin 'Find the trapdoor.' Ten minutes later Colin was still struggling, so Alix motioned to him to move aside, and with his kitchen knife clicked the door open exposing the safe door and the 8-combination dial was sitting there.

Colin gave a low whistle 'Your grandmother wasn't in a hurry to have this found.'

Yes, and not only that I've had a top criminal safecracker down here and apparently it's an 8 digit dial, Mosler, plus the fact it is he thinks a one off job, and apparently uncrackable. Also,' and he pointed at the faint lines on the floorboards, 'it's that size so to get it out of here would need a crane.'

'There must be something very special in here,' was the only thing Colin could think of to say.

'Sorry I know that sounds pathetic, but I realise you and I are looking at something which could be more than just of historical importance.'

Alix took the sheet of paper, and slowly dialled the numbers 25152181, and nothing happened.

What an anti-climax. Both Alix and Colin were sweating. 'You don't suppose there's some kind of failsafe device do you Colin?'

'How the hell should I know.' Was the response.

'Well supposing if after three attempts it becomes totally frozen, and can then only be reset by the owner, that would be a very good way ofepreventing unauthorised access. With no granny and no chance of contacting her we lose out in a big way. Look I think we should stop, until I ask my new criminal friend from Newmarket.'

Colin's response was to suggest trying again with every second number.

This time Alix, against his better judgement tried 55112283, and lo and behold there was a click and with a slight tug the door opened.

Alix and Colin looked at each other, and Alix put his hand down into the darkness, and pulled out a small box. He put his hand back in again and there was absolutely nothing else in the safe which now appeared to be empty.

A great sense of disappointment and frustration flooded over him.

'So, after all that, we are left with this box,' Alix groaned.

'Yes, but it's a very nice box,' Colin giggled as he said it, and both began laughing nervously at first, then helpless giggles as the sense of anticlimax took over.

Alix recovered first, 'OK I'm going to open the box.'

There was a small clip at the front, and the box was made of beautifully polished wood. It looked expensive, and then when they opened it, there was what appeared to be an egg.

'My God,' said Alix 'it's a Faberge Egg' It wasn't that Alix knew much about Faberge eggs excepting for the fact that the best ones whilst not priceless nevertheless were fabulously expensive, and of course Faberge had very close connections with the Russian Royal Family.

This egg was a very pale turquoise, and it was almost shimmering. It had a small crown at one of the pointed ends in what looked like gold with tiny inset precious stones, or perhaps inlay.

Holding it in his hand Alix found a small catch, and the two halves came slowly open in his hand, revealing a photograph on the right-hand side of what Alix realised was the Tsar and Tsarina of Russia. On the left-hand side were two small locks of hair, which presumably must have belonged to the Tsar and Tsarina as well. Whilst the insides were beautiful with wonderful enamelling around the margins, Alix had a keen sense of disappointment, because he had fully expected somewhat more, in fact he told himself much later, he thought the egg would contain a key.

'Well that's a bit disappointing,' Alix groaned.

'Wait a minute, the eggs are oval but one of the insides is flat. That means there must be a space behind, the big question is how to find the way in?' was Colin's response.

'I see what you mean, and come to think of it, Faberge Eggs were famous for having hidden openings. Alix grinned at the thought 'The Antiques Roadshow is coming to Ely next week I don't suppose we could ask them ....only kidding!'

The two of them must have tried for nearly an hour to no avail, and it was only when Alix found an old magnifying glass that the way in became clear. Using just a needle in one spot that appeared slightly flawed with the glass, on the outer edge of the right-hand side, the surface picture opened enough to get a finger nail in, and reveal the inner contents.

The whole of the inside was filled with paper which had been folded several times. That was removed without initial examination to reveal the splendour of the wall of this cavity. Colin commented immediately that it was the Romanov crest, but it was the sheer beauty of the workmanship that staggered them. The inset of precious stones mixed with the enamelling just took their breath away, never mind the design. When they opened the very fine paper, what they found firstly was the birth certificate of Prince Alixei Romanov, with the Royal Crest and surprisingly the entry in both Russian and English with the parent's names given as the Tsar and Tsarina. The signature of the Tsar at the bottom was clear to read, as was that of the witness, Georgij Romanov, and the date, the 2nd of August 1898. The whole thing was an echo of history, and Alix was suddenly very aware and somewhat awed. That was the birth certificate of his grandfather, signed by the man now claiming to be his great grandfather, who also just happened to be the Tsar of Russia, and witnessed by Georgij who was actually the child's father. How incredible and horrible that the Tsar made his brother witness the birth, but the act of signature was played out to give little Alixei legality as his son.

The big question remaining had to be, where was the key he had expected to find, because it plainly was not inside the egg.

The second folded sheet of paper had remained untouched such was the beauty of the egg, until Colin exclaimed, 'what about the other paper!' When unfolded it was headed with the Crest of the Romanov family, and the typed letter was signed by the Tsar, and dated 4th July 1910.

I <u>Tsar Nicholas 2nd By the Grace of God, Emperor and Autocrat of All the Russias</u>

DECLARE this to be a First Codicil to my Will dated 23rd January 1908

> **<u>NOW</u> I hereby add to my said Will the following Clause**

> *Alixei Romanov, otherwise now known as Willie McBride, or his male heir, and future male heirs, total access to our deposits in Blumeurs on presentation of his birth certificate, in the event of my death and that of my son Alexei with no male heir.*

IN all other respects I confirm my said Will

IN WITNESS whereof I have to this the First Codicil of my Will dated hereunto set my hand this day 4th July 1910

SIGNED by the said as a First Codicil to his Will dated in our joint presence and then by us in his presence and in the presence of each other: -

The writing was somewhat spidery but the signature 'N' with the Crown imprinted above it was quite clear.
Alix said immediately 'the Tsar must have realised his son Alexei was not at all likely to reach manhood and give him a grandson and heir, so now he was almost covering his bases for the second time.'
Colin just nodded in agreement.
It only lacked one thing, and that was the number of the vault.
Alix and Colin looked at each other, 'Do you think we need the Account Number' Alix asked Colin.
'How the hell do you expect me to know, I suspect the last few numbers are significant, because my people were unable to find anything else in the letter we decoded.'

'I can hardly ring Blumeurs and say I am Tsar Alixei now can I and say I'm coming round to collect my fortune!!'
'Not exactly!!'
'I could find their telephone number, and call them, and ask if I could visit'
'You could, but that might be tricky to arrange.'
I think we need to close the safe, place the egg and paper back inside, put the carpet back, and do this in the morning,' was Alix's opinion, and Colin agreed.
Alix offered Colin a bed for the night but what with his car plus driver waiting somewhere close by, he left to return to London.
Still not totally trusting his new friend, after he had left, Alix rolled back the carpet, reopened the safe, extracted the box, and closed the safe again.
On a whim he then used the combination that opened the safe previously and found it didn't work!! His grandmother was a genius. He then decided to start the combination from the third digit, going once again in two's and sure enough it opened.
The box he took into the sitting room, where there was a large chiffonier, with a kicking board, which slid to the side at one of the corners. It must have been a late Victorian hiding place, which he had known about since he was a child, and he pushed the egg under there and slid the kicking board shut.

He took the letter and the birth certificate out, and they were placed inside 'The Hidden Years' a book about the fall of Hong Kong in 1942, which sat innocuously in the middle of the bookcase. With that he went to bed and tried to sleep.

CHAPTER 26

Sleep under the circumstances proved to be impossible, so Alix went downstairs made himself a cup of coffee, and took it with him to his laptop, and went to Google to do a search for Blumeurs, realising all too well that his previous communication had come up with a flat refusal to give him any information at all.

It didn't matter what search he tried, there was no real information, and certainly no telephone number. Short of turning up at the door, which Alix surmised would be difficult, and probably impossible to gain entry, he was at a loss as to what he could do next.

Perhaps a call to his bank manager might help him to contact Blumeurs, or Tony might be able to use the legal network. He was still mulling these thoughts around in his head as he left the house in the morning, after carefully locking up, pocketing the egg in its case, and slipping the certificate and the letter into the inside pocket of his jacket.

He hoped he might see Tony passing on his way to the office, and he wasn't disappointed. Just as he was about to cross the road, Tony drew up on his bicycle. 'Sorry I haven't been in touch; mother has not been well, so I've spent most of my time at Addenbrookes.' He grinned, 'Thank goodness she seems to be on the mend, it was one of these nasty

D & V attacks that at her age could have been very serious. So, tell me what progress have you made?'
A lot, but I need a bit of help again, Blumeurs the bank in Zurich, I can't find any means of calling them, you couldn't see if you can, could you.'
'I'll try, and I'll give you a call as soon as I know, perhaps we can catch up later.'
'Come round after school I've something very interesting to show you.'
With that Tony took off, Alix crossed the road, and another school day began. He wasn't sure how long he would be able to control his desire to tell the world, but he knew he needed to keep quiet. When the secret came out, which it must, and sooner rather than later. His quiet and peaceful life would change forever.
It was about 10 o'clock when Tony rang 'No joy I'm afraid, but I've been thinking why not go and see Mike MacDonald the manager at Barclays?'
'What a great idea, see you….', and with that the line went dead.
Alix had known Mike McDonald for a long time. He had started as a teller in his local Barclays in Ely and had then gone abroad with what was then Barclays DCO. He used to see Mike in the street when he was home on leave from exotic places like Africa, and Alix believed he had ended up running Barclays in Kenya.
Mike was somewhat of a dinosaur, having so to

speak come up the hard way, and was as far removed from the graduates that banks seem to love employing nowadays, who know everything about money and cashflow and nothing about people.

He was compulsorily retired because he was 55, which was normal for overseas bankers, but had come home not wanting to retire, and Barclays had shown a human touch by returning him to his home branch as branch manager for the last couple of years of his banking life. Alix had always liked the old-fashioned way he conducted the bank's business, which wasn't in front of a computer screen, but rather face to face, and by personal judgement based on his extensive experience.

In fact, Mike wouldn't give Alix an appointment, but insisted on taking him out to lunch at The Old Fire Engine House, a lovely 'olde worlde' restaurant that he hadn't visited in years. Mike was already seated as Alix arrived, having walked from school, and as he rose to greet him, Alix realised how white haired he had become.

They shook hands and Mike said smiling, 'Alix it's great to see you, I've taken the liberty of ordering some of the house red, which is as good as some of the expensive rubbish in the supermarket.'

'Thanks Mike, it's good to see you too, you look well if a little whiter than the last time.'

As Alix sat down Mike looked at him quizzically 'You've suddenly become one of my more affluent clients!' It wasn't said unkindly more as a flippant comment.

'So that's why I get lunch is it?'

'Well, we do like to look after our high value customers, and by the way, I was very sorry to hear about your mother, I didn't really know her, but it's a sad time.'

'Can I assume that is why you wanted to see me, because you think I'm going to need investment advice?' Mike lifted his glass to take a sip as the waiter appeared to take their orders, and Alix used the space to ask, 'What do you know about the bank called Blumeurs in Zurich?'

'That's a curious question, can I assume you are looking to place your worldly goods there, because if you do, you'll be disappointed, I think £100 million is their minimum.'

Alix grimaced slightly 'In a manner of speaking, yes I want to do business with them, so I need to be able to talk to someone at the bank.'

Mike flashed a white grin, and Alix thought that he'd had his teeth veneered.

'You can't do that I'm afraid, they will talk bank to bank or lawyer to bank, and any new customers must be referrals. You need to understand that Blumeurs are one of the oldest Swiss Banks, and their secrecy laws are quite frankly unbelievable.'

Mike thought for a moment. 'To give you an idea of the level they operate at, they were once rumoured to hold the Last Tsar of Russia's entire fortune in gold, which today could be valued as high as $200 billion.'

Alix raised his eyebrows 'I understand, but is there any way you could get in touch with them on my behalf?'

Mike continued to look at Alix very strangely, 'Yes of course, but you'll need to give me a reason.'

'Let's just say I may have an interest in a large sum of money, they are holding on my Granny's behalf that I have only just found out about.'

That seemed to satisfy Mike, and lunch thereafter was a leisurely affair. Mike didn't really press Alix at all on the reason, which was quite surprising really. After paying for lunch Mike took him back to the Branch for coffee.

Immediately after Mike and Alix entered Mike's office he went into his computer, and within a couple of minutes his printer began to gently whine.

On the paper was printed the name of a bank in Zurich called the Georges Blumeur Privatbank AG, Postfach 9133 Zurich, Switzerland. The Postal Account is 85-3154-5 with a Swiss Clearing number of 2515. There was also a telephone number *Tel:* (+41.44) 206 99 00.

Mike said 'Look if you let me have the number of the account, then I can use bank channels to find out if it can be transferred away.'

Alix didn't reply he was fishing around in his jacket for the letter. 'Can I have a pen please?' He then wrote down 25152181225208531545, 'That has to be a coincidence.'

'What is?' Alix pushed over the number and pointed to the 2515, and the 8531545.

'Let's just say my grandmother seems to have set me some kind of puzzle, but I'm getting to the end now. We've got the Postal Account, and the Clearing Number which leaves us,' .... speaking and writing at the same time '218122520' and I bet that is the account number.

'OK let me ring a friend in Switzerland to see what we do next.'

At this point Alix suddenly remembered Mike had worked in Zurich for about eight years.

Nodding, he let Mike get on with making the call, which he did after consulting an address book that would have made a social climber look inferior.

He spoke rapidly in German, something Alix didn't know he could do, scribbled something on his pad, and put down the phone.

'That's a huge bit of luck, I have an old friend who works at Blumeurs, and I have a direct line number.'

With that Mike picked up the phone, and spoke rapidly in German
All Alix understood was the word Helmut, but the conversation was quite brief, and Mike was obviously annoyed.
'Look Alix I don't know what you are playing at, but I have just been told my fortune. Not only is this account very private indeed, but it is also well over 100 years old, and I was told in no uncertain terms I should tell the person who asked me to make the call, that the account is dormant. Additionally, over 20 people like you have tried to access it over the last 85 years, and basically a man who was an old friend has told me firstly, whoever you are, you're an imposter, and secondly not to call again under any circumstances. In fact, he is now so senior in his bank that he has threatened to ensure my employment here is finished. He has friends in very high places in Barclays.

You may not know it, but my wife Mary died a few years ago, I have remarried, and I need this job to pay my kids school fees. We didn't earn much in Africa, and if my two children are to stay at public school, I need this job, and you could just have been the reason for me losing it.'
Mike kind of drew breath, and then almost shouted.
'Alix what the f--ck is going on!!'
He then continued in a calmer voice

'You have been a lot less than frank with me; in fact, you have been completely evasive. I think you should leave, not come back if you ever intend to discuss this again.
So please leave and leave now.' As he said it Mike stood up to dismiss Alix.
'OK, before I go you need to hear what has happened to me in the past few weeks, but' and he put both hands up almost in a gesture of surrender, 'this has to remain in the strictest confidence.'
With that they both sat down, and Alix produced the Faberge Egg, the birth certificate, and the Codicil to the Will, and explained and showed Mike how they all fit together.
'So, you bought this at a car boot sale I suppose!!' Mike's sarcasm was not lost on Alix who retorted.
'No, I have a DNA proven lineage directly back to the Tsar, and that certificate is my grandfather's birth certificate.'
Mike's jaw dropped, and he let out a low whistle.
'Wow, that sounds to me like a novel or a film script, not what happens to real people.
What's amazing is that you can prove all of this.'

'Yes, I've even got the DNA records proving my ancestry and certified by one of the top experts in the UK'
'OK,' Mike said quietly, 'let's see what we can do to uncover the lost Tsar millions.'

He once again picked up the phone, and Alix assumed he was ringing the same number at Blumeurs.

This time the conversation lasted several minutes, and Mike obviously described the Faberge Egg, as he picked it up and turned it in his hands, plus the certificates, and he read out the long number, and the conversation seemed perfectly friendly.

Eventually Mike put his hand over the phone.

'Most interesting, most interesting indeed, they are prepared to see you, so when do you want to make an appointment. It's important enough, obviously,' he said knowingly, 'for them to be available at the weekend, so could you get there for Saturday at 4.30pm, assuming flights can be arranged?'

'I'd have thought so.'

'By the way they want you to be accompanied by a lawyer well versed in banking, banking trusts, and capable of handling large sums of money, so who will you take?'

'Tony Edwards, he's the only lawyer I know, so I hope he's available. I'm pretty sure he can bluff his way.'

'You'll also need all the documentation you have described, the DNA evidence and all that stuff, and,....' Alix interrupted, 'Just say I am absolutely adamant that not one word of this is leaked, and that goes for everyone here as well.'

A few more words were exchanged in German on the phone, and Mike placed the receiver back, and said, 'well that's all arranged'. He replaced the egg in the box with one last loving look, 'I've never seen anything so beautiful in my life Alix and I'd love to own it, but not at the price you're going to have to pay. You must realise that the life of obscurity you have led is almost over, and you are about to become a world figure, like it or not. A lot of people are going to place impossible demands on you, so I think your days of teaching are numbered.'

With that he handed Alix the box, certificate and the letter, and saw him out of the door.

As Alix left the bank and stepped out into the warm sunshine he realised it was 4.30pm and he had missed the lower 6th and 5th form classes. Where had the time gone? There was a message on his ansaphone to ring the 168, so he quickly went into school, as opposed to going home which was his first intention.

Ann the headmaster's secretary greeted him without a smile. 'He's pretty cross, as he's had to take your two classes this afternoon, what on earth have you been up to?' At that moment Mr. James appeared at the door of his office.

'Word please Alix,' crooking his finger as he beckoned Alix into his office. What followed was what the military describe as an interview without coffee, and Alix was hauled over the coals in no uncertain fashion. He took it all in silence, very conscious of the weight of the Faberge Egg in his pocket, but he resolved to say very little.

He was hauled from his reverie by 'So what excuse have you got, I've not been impressed by your attitude since your mother died, and that was a decent excuse for a while but for goodness' sake, it's some time now, whatever is going on?'

Alix looked at him, 'Please give me a couple more days, by Monday I promise you I'll tell you everything that has happened, and the reasons for my careless behaviour,' then under his breath, 'but I doubt you'll believe me anyway.'

With that he was excused, and left, heading rapidly for home, and his meeting with Tony, suddenly realising that as things now stood, he didn't ever need to teach again if he didn't want to, and if there were the billions that Colin described, then he would be able to make a huge donation to the school he loved so much

Tony was waiting at the garden gate as Alix walked down the road, leaning on his bike, head buried deep in a newspaper, reading no doubt the cricket reports in the Times.

'How's mother?' Alix said by way of greeting, 'She's a lot better thank you.'

Alix led the way up the path, realising as he walked, he badly needed to dead head the roses, and remove the weeds that had reappeared between the paving stones.

They walked in companionable silence, until Alix unlocked the door, cut off the alarm, and turned to face Tony who was leaning his bike against the wall of the house.

'I've cracked it!!' Alix exclaimed. 'Not only found the safe but got the combination. That letter that just seemed like a love letter was coded.'

'How was that done?'

'I'll show you later, it was what was in the safe that was mind blowing,' with that Alix went into the side pocket of his jacket, and with a little struggle produced the box. 'You'd better sit at the table, I'm terrified it gets dropped.'

They sat down opposite each other, and Tony opened the box.

His eyes opened wide in astonishment. 'Oh my God!!' As he turned the egg round in his hands. 'Do you know I've read about this, it's one of the fabled Romanov Eggs. It's so beautiful, it almost glows, and the eggshell blue turquoise colours are exquisite. Isn't this the Egg that has been missing since the Tsar was overthrown?' Without waiting for a reply 'Can I open it?'

'Yes of course, just be careful.'

Tony realised right away, that the photograph was Tsar Nicholas, and Tsarina Alexandra, and the locks of hair were theirs as well. 'So do you think that somehow or other this was given to young Willie McBride at some point as a token, and a memory of them?'

'I hadn't thought of that, but it could be right, although I don't know when. Now comes the smart part. It took me ages to realise that there was more than enough room behind the pictures, and locks of hair for there to be other compartments, and even longer to find a way in. Why don't you try?'

Within ten minutes Tony had conceded defeat, so with the fine needle and the magnifying glass Alix opened the right hand side, and Tony literally whistled, 'That is just unbelievable, you do realise that this is absolutely priceless, and moreover it's yours. Then after a moment's hesitation, 'but what did you find inside?'

Going into the inside pocket of his jacket, Alix produced an envelope from which he withdrew two neatly folded sheets of paper. He handed them over to Tony.

'Just Alixei Romanov's original birth certificate witnessed by the Tsar, and a Codicil to the Tsar's Will, which basically confirms that Alixei became Willie McBride and giving his heirs' access to Blumeurs providing the Tsar and Alexei were dead.'

'So effectively you've proved beyond doubt that you are the only surviving Romanov in direct line to the throne, and you are now Tsar Alixander. That is bloody amazing, you couldn't make it up!!'
Alix grinned self-consciously, 'Look Tony there is going to be a lot of money in this for you. Blumeurs are insistent I arrive on Saturday afternoon with my lawyer who needs to be an expert in trust Funds, and all that sort of thing. I told them that you were the very man, and from what Mike MacDonald at Barclays tells me, they will want to deal with my lawyer, and not with me. That seems hard to understand, but I suppose the Tsar wouldn't be ringing his bank manager so to speak to organise a withdrawal.' They both grinned at the thought.
'So my little legal expert, the first thing you need to do is organise us a flight to Zurich, a chauffeur driven car to the bank, and here is the address,' handing Tony the printout from the bank.
'No problem ...Sir, then can I assume you'll want to go to Chateau Hugend to tell Colonel John the good news, assuming you can get into the vault. How do you do that by the way?'
Alix went back into his pocket and produced a photocopy of the original letter from his grandmother Marie to Willie. 'This uses a code that would be familiar to an SOE veteran. It is all to do with numbers of letters in words, and the key is

also the opposites,' and he pointed to the words yellow and red.

For the next twenty minutes Alix showed Tony how it worked, and how the letters turned into numbers, and the numerical sequence of 8 numbers opened the safe and were also the sort codes for Blumeurs.

'I expect you'll want to see the safe.'

'Absolutely dear boy,' so the two of them rolled back the carpet, and Tony also failed to find the hinged door. Alix also showed Tony the larger lines on the wooden floor, where the safe had been installed.

As they rolled the carpet back into place Alix said, 'I think I'd like to go to Chateau Hugend on Saturday night if possible.' Then with a broad grin 'Just book us on a private jet, will you,................... there's a good chap!!'

'I see it's master and servant now, is it?'

With that Alix gave Tony a playful punch, 'Don't be such a prat. But whilst I'm thinking of it, you'd better organise a flight to Brussels afterwards, and then a car to the Chateau, and I'll phone John with the good news.'

'OK McBride I'm off home.'

Tony moved towards the door, and suddenly stopped.

'Using my somewhat aged brain for once, I can just see two problems, or at least potential problems, and I should have thought of it earlier.'
'Go on'
'Well,' Tony continued slowly and deliberately, 'You don't really want to be showing the bank your DNA evidence, because it kind of gives them an excuse not to recognise you.'
Alix shook his head, 'Yes I had been wondering about that.'
Tony warming to his subject, 'You see there is no way your grandmother knew anything about DNA testing, and certainly Tsar Nicholas wouldn't have either. What would have been important was the birth certificate signed by the Tsar, and that would be their proof.
However', and Tony shook his head and grimaced, 'Blumeur's will point to a lack of a wedding certificate, and if they want to wriggle on the hook, which let's face it Blumeur's will, then they have the excuse that your father was born out of wedlock, was illegitimate, and therefore is not legally the heir. Put another way for them that will be game, set, and match. There won't be a lot anyone can do about that, and let's face it the DNA just confirms their case'
With that he came back, and sat down.
'There is one thing that I have always thought slightly strange, and that is how your grandmother

was sometimes known as Dubré, and at other times McBride.' With a puzzled look on his face he added, 'I wonder is it possible they were married, and it was kept secret. Look at all the information we now have, the birth certificate and the Codicil to the Will, from the Faberge Egg, the bank account details, the egg itself, the access codes to the safe and then the vault. I just can't believe between the Tsar, Willie, and your grandmother, that they would have missed the obvious, and that was the need for Willie to have married Marie to make the whole thing legitimate, and watertight as well.'

Alix interrupted, 'Just exactly what do you mean Tony, what are you trying to say?'

'What I'm trying to say is that somewhere there has to be proof that Willie married Marie, although that proof may well be hidden somewhere so safe, yet again so findable.'

'So' Alix said, 'Any bright ideas?'

Tony looked down at the floor, 'I'm just wondering if there is another door to the safe. When you think about it, the whole thing is so enormous that you'd think there would be another chamber.'

With that the two men got back on to their hands and knees, but despite their best efforts, there was no sign of a further trapdoor.

'The only other thing might be a trapdoor in the side of the chamber where I found the egg.'

Tony looked at Alix, 'Genius.'

Alix remembered his grandmother's system of changing the numbers, and opened the door again with a satisfying click, but again, despite both men running their fingers around the cavity, pressing, pushing, looking for joints, levers anything, the result was zero.

'You don't think our Basil Graham would be able to throw some light on this, or perhaps the whole thing is a wild goose chase?'

Tony got to his feet, 'I'm going home,' looking at his watch, 'It's two in the morning, and we can't ring Basil now,' and with that he walked out.

It was to be the following evening before Alix was able to speak to Basil. After telling him he had got into the safe with the 8-digit code, he then asked about the possibility of a hidden chamber off the original chamber. No immediate answer was forthcoming, but 2 hours later Basil rang, suggesting that if there were more digits Alix should close the safe and lock it, then enter the access code, only one digit later, and then adding the next digit. The sombre warning was that get it wrong, and the safe could be sealed.

Heart in his mouth Alix, remembering to start the code another digit later, added the next number, and with heart beating he heard the familiar click. On opening the safe, he immediately noticed a chamber off to the left. Slipping his hand in, he came out with a folded sheet of paper.

Hands shaking, he unfolded the paper, and found himself looking at what he assumed was a wedding certificate, all handwritten.

Marriage solemnised at Hugend Chateau on this day the 31st of August 1917, between Willie McBride [minor] from Belmullet, County Mayo, Ireland[Orphan] and Marie Dubré[minor] from Chateau Hugend. Daughter of Monsieur Pierre Dubré[landowner] and Madame Marie Dubré
Witnessed by Madame Marie Dubré[mother][Marie Jane Dubré
Donal Lenihan[friend] [Donal Lenihan]
Signed [Willie Mcbride] Willie McBride and [Marie Dubré] Marie Dubré
I Father Georges Berthoin, Priest of this parish do declare this wedding to have been solemnised under the rites of the Holy Catholic Church.
[Georges Berthoin]

Alix was absolutely staggered. Here was his grandfather's signature, to his wedding document, hidden after all these years, and in an instant he knew that this was the time when Marie his grandmother was given the Faberge Egg by Willie, containing his birth certificate and the Codicil to the will.

All this happened just days before Willie was murdered. Was this perhaps the reason, because the

farm lads discovered what had happened, and perhaps not because she was pregnant.
The fact that Alix now had the definitive proof he sought, didn't seem to register, all he could think of, was the wedding being conducted with the sounds of gunfire dominating the proceedings, and how frightened they must have been.

CHAPTER 27

Alix kept putting his hand to his jacket pocket, and to his inside pocket, feeling the reassuring lump of the box, and the wadding of the envelope every five minutes throughout the flight. He had also taken the DNA reports, and Tony had brought his mother's will, and Grandmother McBride's instructions.

The car brought them quickly to Blumeurs, and if Alix had been expecting some grand building, he would have been very disappointed. Blumeurs was situated almost in a back street, and the frontage looked anonymous. Tony sensing Alix's disbelief said, 'Don't worry, some of the oldest and most famous private banks hide their incredible wealth under this cloak of anonymity.'

No sooner had they rung the bell at 4.30pm prompt than it was answered by a small lady, with grey hair tied back in a severe bun. Alix thought she looked as grey and nondescript as the bank.

'Mr. McBride, and Mr Edwards?' it was more a question than a statement.

'Yes', they both replied in unison. Alix thought to himself he hadn't seen Tony this smart in his pinstripe suit, white shirt and highly polished shoes in a very long time.

'On behalf of Blumeurs may I welcome you to Zurich.' The accent was almost flawless English,

'If you would please follow me,' with that she walked towards an archway, and down a small corridor which had doors on either side. Alix felt he had entered the Tardis with Dr. Who beside him, because it was massively bigger than it looked.
The unknown, unnamed lady who Alix assumed must be some kind of secretary knocked on a door and ushered the two Englishmen in.
The room was well furnished with a huge partner's desk behind which sat two men, who smiled as Alix and Tony entered. Alix walking slightly ahead, and Tony, almost deferentially a step or two behind.
'Hello, I'm Alix McBride, and this is my lawyer, Tony Edwards. The two grey haired tall gentlemen who were dressed in charcoal suits, white shirts and reddish ties stood up and introduced themselves as Herr Bucher, and Herr Kutz.
They motioned to Alix and Tony to sit down, and without any preliminary pleasantries they began what was to be the Swiss version of the Spanish Inquisition.
The man Alix assumed to be Herr Bucher spoke first 'I hope you realise Mr. McBride that you are the latest in a long line of imposters who have attempted to pass themselves off as Romanovs. We have only agreed to see you because Mr. Macdonald has good friends here in Zurich and he told us you have a very pressing claim.'

Alix nodded 'Yes anyway I think so.'
'You must understand that not only will we require original birth and marriage certificates, but we will also require compelling proof of your right to access the vault, and of course the key.'
Alix and Tony looked at each other, 'So you don't have the key?' It was now the bankers turn to look at each other, and Herr Bucher continued.
'Perhaps we had better start at the beginning. Can we see evidence of this man you call Willie McBride's birth certificate?' Herr Kutz put his hand out, palm open to receive it. Alix fumbled in his pocket, extracted the certificate from the envelope and handed it over the table.
'But this isn't the birth certificate of Willie McBride, it is Alixei Romanov.' The two bankers again shook their heads and looked at each other. 'Herr McBride this is not an auspicious beginning.' Both bankers again shook their heads, and Herr Kutz again put out his hand. 'I trust you have more.'
Alix handed over the Codicil to the Tsar's Will, and both bankers peered at it, opened a drawer in the desk, and pulled out a document. 'We have seen this before, and it was a proven forgery, and so you will have to do better.'
Alix, who in his heart of hearts had thought that all he had to do was turn up with the documents and the bankers would literally throw themselves at

him, was not only disappointed but concerned that after all the research, they had been on a wild goose chase.

His silent thoughts were broken by 'Where is the Egg?'

'I have it here in my pocket.'

'Well, we need to see it.'

Alix struggled to get the box out of his pocket, unfastened it, and handed over the egg.

'We must now take it to another part of the bank to have it verified,' said Herr Bucher.

At this point Tony stood up obviously quite angry. 'You two gentlemen, need to start to show some respect. Mr. McBride here is without any doubt at all the only surviving Romanov, there is more than enough proof. I have even more documents in my briefcase to confirm his claim. I can also tell you this, whatever you intend to do with that beautiful egg you will do it in front of the Tsar, and you will do it with respect.' He sat down as abruptly as he had stood up.

The two bankers talked behind their hands in German, and eventually both stood up, and left the room without a word.

Neither Alix or Tony spoke in the silence that followed, both uncomfortably aware of the two security cameras scrutinising them.

As dramatically as they had left the two bankers returned, carrying what looked like a small black block about two inches square.

'Sir, if we could please have the Egg' Herr Kuts asked Alix politely.

He took the egg and inserted the crown on top of the egg into one side of the block. As far as Alix and Tony could see the four spokes in the corner of the crown fitted exactly into four small holes in the block. The tension in the room suddenly dramatically increased.

The banker then turned the egg in a clockwise direction, and out of the block came a key, like a Yale, but smaller.

'Herr Edwards I must ask you to remain here, and Herr McBride, I must ask you to accompany me. You should have a sequence of numbers that we will need, which I feel certain you will have in your pocket. Some of the digits will be the bank's code, but the other numbers you will need to key in alternately with my colleague here.

Please let me apologise for our behaviour, but we as a bank never thought such a day would come.'

Alix realised now the significance of the code he got from Colin, and dumbly followed Herr Kutz and Herr Bucher out of the room.

'See you, Alix.' Tony grinned and then laughed. 'Out of the door as a commoner, you will return as royalty I expect!!'

About 10 paces from the door, the bankers turned left and entered a small lift followed by Alix.
The lift descended slowly giving Alix no real idea of how far underground they were. Suddenly the lift stopped, the door opened, and Alix and the two bankers were in a well-lit room, silent apart from the humming of a generator. As far as he could see there were four doors leading off, one to each wall, and a desk with three chairs in the middle.
'Now Sir, what will happen next is that my colleague will key in a number on the keyboard set into the desk here, and you must key in the next number in your sequence. There is a total of 18 numbers, and get one wrong, you won't get in.'
Herr Kutz having finished speaking, then sat down Herr Bucher added 'Firstly I must ask you, have you got the 9 number code.?'
Licking his lips nervously Alix nodded, if the numbers left when he crossed out the bank codes were indeed the numbers. He looked around the room and thought how like a cell it looked with at least four visible cameras, no windows, he suddenly felt very claustrophobic.
The banker appeared not to notice Alix, and continued, 'It will be my job to key in the numbers, and there will always be at least two people from the bank before we can open the vault. Each of us has a code unknown to the other, and it changes

daily.' He smiled at the thought, 'Our security is very correct!!'

Alix had a sudden thought, 'but what if I lose the numbers, or someone steals them?'

'We use iris recognition technique, and you won't be aware but that has already been done to you and your colleague. Future access will use this, so numbers are obsolete, apart from this moment.'

'But surely that means Tony my lawyer could, although it wouldn't ever happen, come in here and remove everything.'

'No, only you can do that, but as you will see shortly, removal would be impossible. To prevent possible fraud, you will be asked to nominate a bank account, and then any transactions that take place will have to be by that route.

Your lawyer will instigate the transaction, but you will have to approve it. I will answer your unspoken question about force or coercion to make you do someone else's wishes. As you can see, no-one else apart from you and Herr Edwards can enter the bank. Herr Edwards has serious restrictions on the amount of money and frequency of withdrawal. He can only use your nominated account. Secondly, we will give you a telephone number to ring which will freeze your deposits until you attend personally and unfreeze them. Finally, once a month we will contact you and ask that you respond to confirm all is well. If you don't respond, then again, the account will be frozen until you do. When you ring the number just ask for either Herr Kutz or Herr Bucher.'

Herr Bucher then pointed to the keypad and said 'Shall we begin.

Alix slowly followed the banker as he keyed in his nine numbers, and then when the final zero was keyed, there was a clunking sound, and the door immediately in front of Alix opened very slightly with a slight additional plopping sound.

'Don't worry, that is the vacuum seal. We will now leave, and you lock the door from the inside. When you are finished, just ring the bell by the door, after closing the door to your vault, and it will automatically lock, and we can then come in.'

He then added almost as an afterthought. 'May I say on behalf of both of us and Blumeurs Bank how pleased we are to see Your Majesty.' At which point both bowed and left the room.

Alix walked slowly towards the door as if in a trance. He pulled it open, and what he was confronted with was a windowless room, with three doors leading off on each of the walls. He surmised this was probably a steel box, and more besides, situated a good 100 feet underground, probably surrounded by bedrock.

There were what appeared to be wine racks, although they were obviously not, and each rack was literally stacked with small gold bars, giving the well-lit room a greenish gold tinge. The effect was truly remarkable, and then he noticed on the floor several small boxes, each measuring probably 12 inches long about 9 inches wide, and six inches deep. He lifted the lid off the top box and opened it. He couldn't believe his eyes, the whole box was full of diamonds, all cut, and although he knew very little about diamonds, he did recognise that some were very large indeed. If each one of the twelve boxes contained the same, then the value was unbelievable.

To one side of the stack of diamond filled boxes was a smallwooden open topped crate, containing some boxes identical to the one in his pocket containing the Faberge Egg. He opened the one on the top, and it was even more beautiful than the one in his possession.

Alix stood in stunned silence, what on earth had he done.

He knew he needed fresh air, and quickly, so he closed the door to the vault, rang the bell, and the two bankers reappeared within a few seconds.

'Is everything in order Your Majesty?'

Yes, absolutely and thank you.'

He remembered about the emergency number, and Herr Kutz, said 'All you do is ring +41.44 206 99 00 and ask for extension T. You should remember that as T is short for Tsar. That will automatically seal the vault until you attend in person and unseal it, which of course you can do with our Iris recognition. One final word of warning do not on any account tell even Herr Edwards your lawyer of this number.'

With that they were in and out of the lift, and back with Tony who was drinking coffee and schnapps, looking pleased with himself.

A few minutes later sitting in the back of their chauffeur driven car Tony looked at Alix 'Are you all right?'

'No..........', a slight hesitation from Alix, 'Why?'

'You look as if you have seen a ghost.'

'So would you. I've just seen gold bars stacked almost from floor to ceiling and not in a small vault either. Add to that several boxes of loose diamonds and Faberge Eggs, there must be billions of pounds in value there. What on earth am I going to do Tony?' There was despair in his voice.

Tony put his fingers to his lips. 'Keep your voice down, walls and chauffeur's have ears.' He then continued.' 'I gather from the man who brought me in the coffee, that as your lawyer I supervise the account, and my firm gets a retainer from you of one million pounds sterling a year. That should keep my partners, not to mention my ex-wife very happy indeed!!'

He then added 'We will get a letter confirming this from the bank, and then we can proceed. Have you got any thoughts?'

'Yes, I need a drink!!'

Tony smiled 'So do I, but I'm sure there'll be plenty on the Lear jet, and' looking at his watch, 'we'll be in the air in about twenty minutes, then you can relax and drink away to your liver's content.' He laughed at his poor joke.

The fact was Alix just felt totally depressed, never really having given much thought to what opening the vault would mean. It was also hearing the words 'Your Majesty,' that had really hit him hard. The two of them continued their journey in silence, both deep in thought, and in fact nothing was said between them until they were strapped into the luxurious seats of their private jet.

For the second time in one day Tony said, 'I could get used to this.' This at least brought a smile from Alix, but it was somewhat wan, and not even convincing at that.

'Come on Alix, cheer up, you're incredibly rich, and about to be famous.'

Alix grimaced, 'That's the problem. I almost wish I'd never started this stupid game. I have no desire to be a Tsar, a King, or an Emperor, I'm happy just being me.'

Alix leant forward, 'Do you know the bankers told me there was over 240 billion dollars' worth of gold, never mind the rest. What on earth am I going to do Tony?'

'How about me, I'm a good cause!!' Tony leant back and took another sip from his drink, 'Actually to be serious, why not discuss it with John Peterson. After all, without him, you would either be dead, or never have been. I think his family deserves a say in what should happen next.'

Alix nodded imperceptibly, 'I suppose you are right, and then again it could go to the Third World, where it could make a huge difference. Mind you what with the global banking crisis, and the UK debt, I could make a big hole in that couldn't I.'

Alix seemed to relax a little. 'I'm happy to keep a little, but what a difference I could make. ...'

Tony cut in, 'Mind you technically when this all comes out a lot of people will feel you are Russian, and I don't think Russia will be best pleased if you diverted vast sums of money away somewhere else. They will feel it is theirs, and with a lot of justification too.'

Their conversation was interrupted by the pilot coming through saying they would be on the ground in five minutes.

The two friends remained silent, each with their own thoughts, until they were safely ensconced in the chauffeured car that was to take them to Chateau Hugend.

Alix then suddenly turned to Tony. 'Have you told Colonel John what's happened?'

'Considering that we've never even met, no!!'
Tony put his hand reassuringly on Alix's arm, and in any case whatever information you or Blumeur's give me is kept in the strictest confidence. Look you have friends around you who will never reveal confidences, and it is more than Blumeur's reputation is worth for these two haughty bastards to talk, so relax.' He then added as an afterthought with quite brilliant timing 'Trust me I am a politician!!'
That seemed to break the tension, and both men laughed hilariously.

CHAPTER 28

Alix and Tony arrived at the Chateau just before dusk. The leaves were just beginning to turn on the trees, and the lights were shining through the windows. Alix was completely unaware of the scene, because his eyes were firmly glued to the tree where his grandfather had perished so horribly all those years ago. He would never be able to come here for any length of time, without being completely overcome by emotion for a wasted life. At the same time he also knew he could never stay away, so like it or not he was tied to this place by history.

Alix suddenly realised that Tony was talking. 'McBride we're here, let's get inside and talk to Colonel John.' Followed quickly by, 'Is that him waiting at the door?'

Alix slowly got out of the car, feeling as if he had aged by 20 years, and the two of them walked towards John standing in the brightly lit entrance hall. He stepped forward hand outstretched.

'Alix how good to see you, come in.'

Alix shook John's hand and held his other hand out open towards Tony. 'I don't think you've met my lawyer, Tony Edwards. Tony this is John Peterson, the man I've been telling you about.'

Introductions effected they moved to the bar, where Mary stood waiting with a broad smile on her face.

'Good evening gentlemen, what can I get you to drink?'

Large whiskies poured, the three of them sat down by the roaring fire. It may still be late September, but there was a certain chill in the air, so the warmth of the fire was very welcoming.

'So, Alix, tell me about what you have found out about your grandfather?'

Alix looked at Colonel John and smiled. 'Before I do that, I just wanted to say thank you. Firstly, I had no idea we were related, I think we're something like second cousins, but more importantly thank you for what you have done for my family to keep them safe and well for the last hundred and ten years or so. The only question I have is why didn't you tell me?'

Before the Colonel had the chance to answer, Mary appeared as if by magic. 'Gentlemen dinner is served, so perhaps you'd go through to the dining room. Has the Colonel told you, you will be dining alone, as he has granted us all a week's holiday starting tomorrow, so no happy campers, no military bores, just feet up time to look forward to.' She made a face as if realising she might have gone too far, but Colonel John just laughed as the three of them got up and emptied their glasses before walking into the empty dining room.

Unlike the last time they had dined together Colonel John seemed very relaxed, and very quickly responded to Alix's question about probably being second cousins.

'Alix it is a long story, but perhaps now would be a good time for you to hear it. Before I go any further however, may I be presumptuous enough to ask if you got the proof you were seeking of your family tree?'

At this point Tony interrupted, 'John, you are looking at the man who would be King.... Alix is the undisputed Tsar of Russia, as he is the only surviving Romanov in the blood line with the most amazing collection of birth certificates, codicils to a will, and marriage certificates to prove it.'

At that moment, to the utter amazement of Alix, Colonel John rose from his chair, and firstly bowed, and then went on his knees. 'Your Majesty you have no idea what this means to me and my family, or for that matter Mother Russia. We have waited in silence for many years for this moment.'

Alix looked at the top of Colonel John's head, 'For goodness sake please get up John, and stop all this pratting about. We both know there is no royalty in Russia, and so please continue to call me Alix.'

'I can't do that Sir.'

'Well, you must........ And that's an order.' The grin on Alix's face did much to reduce the tension around the table, and Colonel John got to his feet but not before Mary entered with the menus looking somewhat quizzically at her boss.

This gesture of Colonel John's pretty well reduced the three men to silence until Alix raising his glass of his preferred white wine. 'Here's to you John, and your family, all the generations who have served my family so well.' All three clinked glasses and drank.

'OK, now I want to know how all of this came about John, every last bit, and whilst that's not a direct order,' Alix grinned and swallowed more wine, 'I really need to hear it all, and leave nothing out.

Colonel John started to say Sir, stopped in mid 'S'....

'Let's get the food out of the way first.'

Dinner over, Colonel John nodded to his two guests 'This is going to take some time, so shall I tell Mary to bring in the biscuits and cheese, coffee, and we can help ourselves to liqueurs?'

Alix asked as Mary withdrew, 'why is she waitressing, I thought she was essentially your manager?'

'Very much, but the three girls who normally rotate in the restaurant all have a tummy bug, I think they eat the leftovers, and something had gone off, so Mary volunteered to cover.'

After an understanding nodding of heads, Colonel John disappeared, returning with a tray of liqueurs, and a decanter of port. Mary followed seconds later with a superb and huge cheese platter, biscuits and butter, plus a large coffee pot, with three cups and saucers.

As John sat down and Mary placed her tray on the table, John smiled and gently dismissed her. 'OK Mary, off you go, enjoy your time off, and thank you very much for covering for the girls so well,' joined quickly by Alix and Tony.

'Where were we? It's now helping yourself time.' John swept his arm over the cheese platter, and drinks.

He settled back in his chair, poured some coffee and a large glass of port.

'You may not be totally aware, but James Edmundson was the beginning of the events that have led us here today. He was born at the end of the 18th Century and his family were very wealthy indeed

He bought the lands and properties in County Mayo in the 1840's and sent his three children out to run the vast estates.

His son Christopher Edmundson eventually bought a commission in the army at the time of the Crimean war, and in fact rode and survived the infamous Charge of the Light Brigade. Not only that, he was captured by the Russians, which began the connections between his family and Russia which remained incredibly strong until the assassination of the Tsar and the Russian Royal Family in 1918.

The cause of this was Christopher's marriage to Princess Freya Nikolaevna the sister of Tsar Alexander 2nd, who was by all accounts a very beautiful woman. Christopher brought her back to County Mayo as his bride, and she renounced all her titles, but fortunately for the Edmundson family not all her money.

Tsar Alexander 2nd was very keen that the young men of the aristocracy in Russia became proficient in English. As you can imagine relationships between Great Britain and Russia in the years following the Crimean war were not particularly amicable, so social interaction between the two countries was almost impossible. The Edmundson's ensconced in their little corner of Ireland, with almost limitless coastline, few people, and pretty inaccessible by road made it an ideal spot to deposit young Russians for periods of a few months, to sometimes several years, during which time the governesses and tutors employed by the Edmundson family taught them the English Language, English grammar, and usage, but their presence was never really noticed.

It was logical when young Alixei was born, and of course you will be aware he wasn't the son of the Tsar, but his brother George, and the Tsarina, after an illicit affair. You will also realise that the Tsar who was beginning to worry about his family's future, signed the birth certificate as the father, and had it witnessed by his brother Georgij, thus ensuring the lineage,' whilst nodding at Alix. 'Alixei, who was now Willie McBride made the journey to County Mayo accompanied only by a nanny and a wet nurse. Again as you will be aware he was brought up in an orphanage that had been the house that the Edmundson Family established in Termoncarragh, and which had been used to educate the young men from Russia .

You may not be aware that the journey was made by sea in a ship of the Russian navy specially selected for the task. This allowed the young Willie to be brought ashore under circumstances of great secrecy.

The orphanage at Termoncarragh eventually housed a further 17 boys. They had become orphans after a very sad sinking of a pleasure boat near St Petersburg.

In about 1908 just after a Russian Royal visit to Osborne House on the Isle of Wight, where the Tsar and Tsarina spent time with the British King and Queen, that the Russian Royal yacht the Standart, returned home to St. Petersburg via the southwest coast of Ireland. Here the children of the orphanage were brought aboard, and their future duties made clear. What is meant by this, is unquestionably that they were told, we must assume by the Tsar, who Willie was, and made to swear they would protect and defend Willie with their lives, and they must never reveal the truth about Willie.

I am certain the Tsar knew that Alexei his haemophiliac son was unlikely to survive to adulthood, therefore there would be no official male heir through him. He also knew in his heart of hearts that the Bolsheviks were gaining in popularity, and with no children to be a future Tsar, the future of the Romanovs was pretty grim, and of course how right he was to be.

Thanks to young Willie he had an heir, and with him the possibility of a continuation of his line.

It was because of the visit of the Tsar and Tsarina that Termoncarragh was rechristened the Chaesar Orphanage, and here the children remained as they grew into adults, and until they all volunteered to fight against Germany.'

At this point Alix interrupted, 'but some of them were surely too old to still be children in an orphanage.'

John said, 'I agree, but times were very different then. They were always the only occupants of the house, and it is quiet enough around there now, but what with the potato famine and the numbers emigrating to the USA it was empty then, so there was not really anyone to notice, and having been so protected they were really very immature anyway.'

John returned to his story.

'It would also appear that at about this point in time the Faberge Egg along with the key codes to the Romanov vault at Blumeurs, were given to Chris and Helen Glanville who were running the orphanage. Chris Glanville being the son of John Glanville who married Jayne Edmundson, one of the three previously mentioned children of James Edmundson who bought all the estates. It appears from banking records that the egg and the codes were deposited with the Bank of Mayo, which today is part of the Bank of Ireland.

At that stage Willie wasn't old enough to appreciate the significance of the egg, and in any case his father the Tsar was alive, as was Alexei the ill-fated haemophiliac son.

When it became even more obvious that Alexei wasn't ever likely to produce an heir, and the Bolsheviks were gaining in strength, the Tsar altered his will with a Codicil, which again was smuggled out of Russia and in all probability ended up in the same bank vaults, although its whereabouts wasn't known until you Alix,' nodding in his direction, 'amazingly found the Codicil and the birth certificate . The wording was careful to ensure that Willie became heir to all the Tsar's lands, and possessions, and when the Tsar abdicated in early 1917 this meant that Willie knew who he was.

Quite how this information was sent to Willie isn't known, but the will written by Willie on the battlefield leaving all his assets to Marie, would certainly indicate he knew who he was and what his responsibilities were. By that you can take it he knew he needed to secure the succession and have a child preferably a son.'

At this point Tony suddenly interrupted, 'But where do you fit into all of this?'

'A good question.' The Colonel reached for another glass of port.

'My great grandfather John married Freya Edmundson the daughter of the Tsar's sister Freya who was now Edmundson. This brought us into the Edmundson family, and I believe there was a family meeting around 1898/99 time where my great grandparents along with the other brothers and sister Edmundson's met and discussed what was to happen with young Alixei Romanov and the 17 orphans.

My great grandmother's sister Helen, who had married a man called Christopher Glanville agreed to open and run the house in Termoncarragh for the orphans, including Willie and to bring them up as Irishmen. Not only that, but to give them new identities as you discovered Alix during your amazing investigations.'

Again, Alix interrupted, 'but how did the egg come back to my grandmother?'

'Are you also telling me that the children, the survivors of the sinking, first came to Termoncarragh, sorry Chaesar House, and were then given Irish names after they had arrived?'

'As far as the children are concerned, I just don't know the answer to that.' John replied, 'or the egg, I haven't a clue. You must remember all this took place over a hundred years ago.'

As he said the last sentence, Colonel John looked at Alix , as he mopped his brow. Alix who wasn't a great liqueur drinker asked him what he would recommend.

'Have you ever tried Sloe Gin?' asked the Colonel

'Yes, I have on one occasion, it was rather nice as I remember,' Alix reached forward and poured himself a glass. 'Tony, aren't you having a liqueur?'

'Thank you No, I'll stick to port,' grinning at Colonel John, 'I'm assuming there is more?'

'Hmphph' was John's disgusted response, 'Do birds fly on one wing?'

'No'

'Exactly, and you'll never see me with just one bottle of port!!'

After a minute of childish sniggering, Alix tried his sloe gin, and turned up his nose. 'Now that is nothing like as good as the stuff I had in England.' The Colonel shook his head, 'Of course you probably had civilian sloe gin, with sugar- Yuk!! I don't know whether I told you, but I was in the Micks, who would be known to you as the Irish Guards, and our regimental officer's stick was the blackthorn. Well, you get sloes and therefore sloe gin from the blackthorn bush, and proper military sloe gin is made with very little sugar and it includes almond flakes. I guarantee you'll like it better the more you drink.'

With that Colonel John sat back in his chair.

'To continue with the story of the Edmundson family, it was also agreed at that family meeting that we would protect young Willie McBride's welfare with our lives if necessary, and that is how the pact we all have began.'

Alix leaned forward, 'I'm getting a taste for this sloe gin,' as he poured a generous measure into his glass, and Tony and John grinned at each other.

'Anyway, as I was saying,' said John, 'we came to an agreement that we would protect young Willie with our lives if necessary.'

Once again, the Colonel topped up his glass and Tony's glass of port.

'To return to Willie and Marie, I think, in fact I'm certain that when they met, and I would have to say became sexually involved, Willie knew he could be killed at any time, although you will see how we as a family tried to protect him. The important thing to remember here is that he now knew his destiny, so he had to leave an heir.

This more than any other reason was why Willie used Marie and made her pregnant to ensure his line didn't die out, and the Romanov's would continue. What no-one bargained for was that Willie and Marie would fall in love, and unbeknown to his murderers they were married. This of course totally legitimised William's claim to the Russian throne. Again, the wedding certificate was in all probability taken abroad by Marie.'

'Hang on John, 'a slightly slurred Tony interrupted again, 'Willie didn't need to fight, the risks were enormous, surely you as a family could have hidden him?'

'Willie volunteered to go,' with that unexpected statement Alix and Tony sat bolt upright. 'Why, when Willie knew who he was, and how important it was for him to stay alive?' They both said in unison.

John replied in such a quiet voice you could almost hear a pin drop. 'Newspapers of that time indicate that volunteers were being sought before conscription became compulsory. Volunteers would be allowed to serve together, but conscripted recruits would be scattered between regiments. Willie's pals by now sworn to defend him to the death, therefore all volunteered, so they could protect him with their lives, because if they had failed to volunteer they would have been conscripted and separated. Part of it might also have been the childlike enthusiasm to fight the Germans and be closer to their homeland. Perhaps they felt if the Germans could be pushed back far enough, they might even be able to walk to Russia, without ever understanding what terrible consequences it would have for them.

Of course, not one of them survived the war, and it might be important to note that it was after Willie's death that the death toll of his friends took a dramatic increase. All the dead were accounted for, apart from two whose names are on the Menin Gate which means they have no known grave, so were more than likely blown to bits. It's quite possible that the despair they must have felt, and the sense of failure at not protecting Willie just made them careless, almost like a death wish.

As a family we are proud to be able to say that James Glanville descended from James Edmundson and married to Mary Peterson, was one of Willie's officers, John Peterson, my grandfather was also, as was William Tucker who was descended from the Edmundson line and was killed in action, saving Willie's life by throwing himself onto a hand grenade. Even odder was Peter Johnson who had married Emma Peterson who was another of Willie's officers, and he too was killed in action. Marie went to County Mayo in Ireland, possibly to the orphanage to give birth to William in

Belmullet, and around this time she was able to get her hands on the Egg and the Codes, using the will written by Willie after they got married. I'm fairly certain she knew the hidden secret of the Faberge Egg. At any rate it is likely they had been placed in a vault in the Mayo Bank.

Alix who was beginning to feel quite lightheaded tried to interrupt.

'Just hang on Alix, have some more sloe gin,' and Tony this time filled up his glass which he slurped at noisily. John meanwhile continued his story.

'During the 1920's Marie received regular amounts of money from the Chaesar estate through the Mayo Bank.' John took another glass of port which he drained in one large sip, seemingly unaffected by the alcohol.

My family and the Edmundson's had been in receipt of funds from the Romanovs for keeping Willie secure. This plus our fabulous fortune through Freya Nicolaevna, enabled us to buy a great deal of farming land in the USA, and we also used this money, in fact almost all of it, to help the grieving parents emigrate, and to set them up on farms all over the vast tracts of land in huge country. Sadly, Ireland isn't the place to make money off the land what with potato famines and republican strife.

Our money completely dried up from the Romanovs during the Great War, and after his abdication and death, there was no more money. This loss was made worse by the stock market crash in the USA, and the great depression that followed so by the mid 1930's we were effectively bankrupted, having lost the land, apart from a few houses in Ireland and then the forced sale of our farms in the USA.

Remembering our vow made to the Tsar, the family then decided our role in life would continue to be the protection of the heir to Willie McBride, young William, plus any future heirs. This meant we had to continue to protect the Tsar, and future descendants.

At this point John looked towards Alix who seemed to be struggling to stay awake. 'Alix, waken up this is important.' Alix shook himself, mumbling 'Sorry,' And poured himself a cup of black coffee, which seemed to revive him.

John continued 'Alix you need to hear this. This is where Gillian McBride entered the story. She was the daughter of an Emma Johnson who was born Emma Peterson, daughter of John Peterson and Freya Edmundson. The task of protection of William which was the reason she married him, went on regardless, and she gave birth to you Alix, so no-one could be in a better position to make certain you were going to be safe.

Sadly she couldn't save your father's life when he was was murdered by the Bolsheviks. They tried in vain to get the bank details for Blumeurs from him, despite severe torture and physical violence he took the secret to his grave.'

Alix started to reply, 'I thought he committed sui….' And then his eyes closed.

Alix had heard everything right up until then. He had been feeling very strange since he finished his pheasant, then increasingly drowsy and quite honestly drunk. This was probably no surprise considering the day he had just spent in Zurich. Suddenly he tried to get up from the table, but his legs simply didn't work, and he fell over.

CHAPTER 29

Alix knew one thing for certain, and that was he had the mother and father of all hangovers. He could hardly bear to open his eyes, and in fact he realised how little he remembered of the previous evening apart from the sloe gin, and that was reinforced by the awful taste in his mouth.
He slowly opened his eyes, not sure what to expect, but what he saw was a light recessed into what appeared to be a steel roof, with bars over the bulb. For a moment Alix thought he was in a prison cell and wondered what on earth he had done after dinner. He then heard snoring to his right, and realised he wasn't alone. Lying in a bed next to him was Tony, to all intents and purposes dead to the world.
Looking around Alix realised they were in a small but functional room, some metal furniture, but no windows. He gingerly got out of bed, and instinctively felt for his watch, but it wasn't there. His trousers and jacket were hung neatly on a clothes hangar but when he went through the pockets there was no sign of his mobile phone, and his shoes appeared to be missing as well.
The door to the room was slightly ajar, and as Alix walked tentatively towards it, he heard a slight groan from behind him, and heard Tony moan,' God I feel awful.'

'Me too, but where on earth are we?'

At that point as if on cue the door opened and Colonel John entered, with two other men a step or so behind him. They were both young, shaved heads, and their khaki vests did little to hide a mass of tattoos on their arms, and chests, and the muscles that positively rippled in a way that only highly trained physically fit men could look. At a quick guess the men were military.

'Ah you're awake at last,' was John's opening greeting.

Tony looked at him without getting out from under the blankets. 'John, where exactly are we, because this isn't the chateau, and I don't remember getting here at all.'

'Neither do I,' added Alix, 'and who are your friends,' nodding at the two men who remained unsmiling, and Alix thought somewhat threatening as they stood just behind John.

'Well, there has been a change of plan I'm afraid. You remain of course my guests, but as of now we will I'm afraid have to confine you to the cellar, which you will have gathered by now is right here. I should add this is the lower floor, which I do remember telling you about when we first met, and we are about 50 feet underground.'

John smiled, 'But I digress. There is the small problem of the vault and the gold it contains. I have some powerful friends who are very interested in the gold, and in fact need it rather urgently, so I must ask you Alix to allow me to accompany you to Blumeur's where you can arrange for its transfer to a safer place.'

'Excuse me,' the shock must have shown on Alix's face. 'I thought we were all in this together, you and your forebears have been defending the Tsar's interests for over a hundred years.'

'Well that just got discontinued.' John cleared his throat

'As I was saying we, that is my new friends you can see are here with me and I need you to come with us.' John looked at Tony 'Whilst he remains here as an insurance policy that you will behave.'

'You have no chance.'

John shook his head rather sadly, 'Don't worry my friends won't beat you into submission to make you do as we would like, but we do have rather a delicate situation here, so in both our interests I'll tell you what I know, and then explain what will happen.

With that John drew up a chair, turned it round and sat on it back to front leaning both his elbows on it to support his chin.

'Ok I know it will take Iris recognition to gain entry to the vault, and I also have all the codes. In addition, don't even think about asking me to phone extension 'T', because I know that will lock the vault until you can get there to unlock it.'

He shifted slightly in the chair and then continued. 'I'm going to give you 24 hours to think this over. If you haven't agreed to come willingly to the bank and gain entry for us, then we will be forced to take some extreme measures to get you to do what we want.'

'And that is?'

'I hate to say this, but we will take your friend,' looking directly at Tony, 'outside and kill him!' This was said without any change in John's facial expression, and obviously not in jest.

At this point he was interrupted by a sharp gasp from the lawyer.

'Oh, don't worry Tony it will be quick and painless, but I don't think Alix will allow that to happen.' After a short pause to let that unpleasant prospect sink in John continued, 'As I've just said, that when you accompany us to the bank, Tony remains here as insurance.' John grinned as he stood up leaving the chair where it was, and his two escorts turned and stared as they walked towards the door.

He turned and added, 'We are not uncivilised, and there is plenty of food and drink in the kitchen but sadly no phones, or watches, or television, and certainly no chance of escape. In any case my friends who are here on a Battlefield Tour wouldn't want their vacation interrupted, so if you did, and they had to come looking for you then they could be extremely cross.'

With that that throwaway threat the door was closed, and Alix could hear footsteps across the floor, then a door banging followed by the sound of keys turning in a lock and bolts being secured.

Alix looked at Tony, and neither said a word.

Tony was the first to speak, 'What have we done to find ourselves in this mess?'

He then added very quickly 'I'm sorry now I encouraged you to check out your family.'

'It's not your fault, if anyone is to blame it is me. I didn't have to set off on such a wild goose chase, but let's not get into recriminations or a pity party, and I'm actually very willing to do as Colonel John asks.'

He then added, I'm seriously dull because that man,' waving his arm disgustedly towards the door, 'lied to me the first time we met, and I missed it completely.'

'How do you mean missed it?'

'Well, he told me his grandfather was buried over the road in the cemetery, and when Ray gave me the family tree, it showed his grandfather survived the war and had a son who was that bastard's grandfather, and I didn't pay close enough attention. There has been more than one inconsistency in his stories, and I just assumed, well actually looking at it now, I don't know what I assumed.'

Alix got to his feet, 'Anyway I'm perfectly happy to do as he says.'

Tony looked at him and shook his head, 'Oh the innocence of those who work in ivory towers. Haven't you been reading the papers recently?' Then without waiting for an answer, 'You know the world economy is in turmoil, well just imagine what the sudden appearance of all that gold is going to do?

We're not talking about a piddling little amount, what was it again, around 200 billion US Dollars, why that's almost as much as it costs to run the NHS.' Tony's attempt at humour fell flat which wasn't very surprising given the circumstances, but he pressed ahead anyway.

'Apart from anything else, do you think they'll let us live after you go through with their plan. I'm certain we'll be quietly disposed of, because they can't run the risk at point future of us telling the world.

Let's face facts, Colonel John suddenly isn't your charming old school army officer, he's almost certainly a bloody Russian agent, probably working under cover for decades, waiting for this moment.'

Alix started to respond, 'Look T...' and then suddenly thought the better of it. After a moment's hesitation he started up again.

'Tony I can't run any risk of you being killed, so I'll do as they ask. After all I'm a long way from poor now, so I can live without the Billions.' Alix tried to smile but with a dry mouth and his tongue sticking to his teeth it proved impossible.

'Look Alix I don't think you realise quite how serious the repercussions could be politically and financially for countries like the UK. If all that gold suddenly swamped the markets, the price of gold would plummet and with it the economic prospects for millions of people.

Don't you remember how the Chancellor Gordon Brown sold off some of the UK's gold reserves in 1999. Well before the sale we had 715 tonnes, about 23 million fine troy ounces, valued at only 6.5 billion dollars. The USA has over 8000 tonnes, and that is probably worth around 75 Billion Dollars, and these are the biggest known gold reserves in the world.

If I didn't know better, I'd say the figures for the gold in Blumeur's is probably wildly optimistic and must take up seriously more than one vault. What we are talking about here is over 45,000 tonnes of gold.

Did you see more than one vault?'

'No, I didn't but there were doors in each of the three walls, and the vault I was in was at least as large as this room with gold stacked floor to ceiling, so I suppose it is possible.'

'It's just that with the wealthiest man in the world, and I can't remember his name, but he's pushed Bill Gates out of top spot, is only worth some 55 billion dollars, and that does make the bank's figure in excess of 240 billion seem unreal.'

Alix looked at Tony, 'Yes it does seem excessive, but again Russia was a vast country, the Tsars down through the generations must have acquired huge wealth. As far as I can remember, although I can't be certain, Russia has mined, and panned for gold for over two hundred years. It is conceivable that the Romanov's and their predecessors slowly built a fortune in gold, unbeknown to the world at large.

Looked at over 200 years that would mean over 20 tonnes of gold a year, so looked at that way it must be possible.'

At this point the conversation dried up leaving both men with their own thoughts.

Thus began the worst 24 hours of Alix's life.

CHAPTER 30

What began as a firm commitment to be going to the bank with Colonel Peterson, and Alix found it difficult to think of him in first name terms anymore, began slowly but surely to weaken.

He began to think about his father and how it appeared he had died protecting the secret. Alix had to assume now that his father had uncovered the banking details, the egg and its contents, perhaps even his parent's marriage document, and had been able to prove he was the rightful heir to the Tsar.
The more he thought about it the more he realised that in the early 1960's there would be no such thing as Iris recognition, so entry to the bank would be very much by ID and passwords.

Alix also remembered what Colin Stewart had said about the code in the love letter. If that had been used by SOE agents during the Second World War, then his father would have worked out the codes.

The whole thing got more horrible by the minute. His father must have discovered the safe, although quite how he did it without his wife, Alix's mother, finding out no-one would ever know.

He would have opened the safe, found the egg, found the birth certificate, and closed it all up again, and had then been tortured to death to get him to reveal where it was, and the codes to unlock it.

All these thoughts were now rushing through Alix's head time after time, after time, indeed they wouldn't go away.

In the early 1960's there was no DNA evidence usage, because it was at that time an undeveloped science, so anyone armed with the birth certificate plus authentication from the Tsar would be accepted as the legal heir to the gold.

Suppose that person also possessed Tsar Nicholas's Codicil to the Will, then that would be compelling evidence. The more Alix thought the more he was convinced that somehow or other the Peterson family had it in their possession, but by itself that wasn't enough.

DNA testing and Iris recognition had made things a lot tougher for anyone wanting access to the fortune in Blumeurs. In fact, the more Alix thought about it, the more he realised it was impossible for Colonel Peterson and his friends. They were now totally reliant on him as the only one who could get them into the vault, and well they knew it.

Conversation between the two men had pretty well dried up after the first few minutes, as they both sat alone with their thoughts. Tony had wandered off, and Alix assumed he was looking for a way out, but he returned looking morose. 'It's completely sealed, and unless there is a secret door, there's no way out.'

Alix just sat on his bed, face impassive, but his brain working overtime. Whatever way he tried to look at it, he kept coming back to his father's bravery, and the terrible and very short life his grandfather Willie McBride had led. Abandoned by his parents, brought up in an orphanage, sent to war, and then brutally and slowly tortured and murdered, in a kind of revenge frenzy.

Finally, Alix realised he had no choice. He would not, indeed could not disgrace his father and grandfather. There was no other choice open to him, so he had to refuse to go to the bank even if it meant the death of his old friend. How could he live with himself if he let Colonel Peterson into the vault, but on the other hand how could he live with himself if he let Tony die.
At this point the silent tears began to flow, and Tony looking anxiously towards him must have realised the decision Alix had come to.

'Alix, you mustn't reproach yourself, you are a Romanov, and you have no choice, I understand that. You are very brave, and your father would be immensely proud of you.'

Alix just shrugged his shoulders.

Before Alix could say anything, they heard the key in the lock, the bolts being pulled back, and once again Colonel Peterson was at the door with his two best friends.

'Well Alix it's decision time.'

'Don't you dare call me Alix, I am your Tsar and you will address me as Your Majesty or Sir.'

'We have no Tsar in modern Russia, but enough of this time wasting, we must go now to Blumeur's.

'No, I've made the decision that my father made. I won't go.'

'You leave me no choice, 'and with that the two bodyguards grabbed Tony and dragged him out of the room followed by Colonel Peterson, who said over his shoulder 'You can still change your mind you know, but you have less than one minute.'

Alix shouted after Tony, and his eyes filled with tears. 'I'm sorry.'

Through the door all Alix heard was Tony's voice, 'At least have the decency to let me walk. I know what you must do, just get on with it.' This was followed by,

'No I will not get on my knees.'

Suddenly two deafening shots rang out in rapid succession, and this was followed by the Colonel reappearing through the door.

'Follow me' As the stunned Alix stood up, the Colonel grabbed his arm firmly and walked him towards the open door with the locks, and through there he could see Tony's body on the ground with a rapidly growing pool of blood around him on the floor, and blood spatters on the wall of what seemed like a small hallway.

'We carry out our threats, be in no doubt of that.'

With that Colonel Peterson walked out the door, which was promptly locked and bolted.

Alix was too stunned to cry, he just felt totally burdened by responsibility. It was only in the past hours that he had experienced a dawning acceptance of who he was, who he had become, and the centuries of tradition to which he was now inextricably linked. He began to think of his great grandmother Tsarina Alexandra and the horrible suffering and death her whole family had to endure, and in an odd sort of way it made him feel stronger.

His thoughts were interrupted by the return of Colonel Peterson.

Once again he had two bodyguards, this time different men, but very much the same in terms of muscles, tattoos, and a general air of unpleasantness. The Colonel seemed very cheerful considering he had just ordered the murder of a perfectly innocent human being.

He looked at Alix and bowed very deferentially.

'I'd like to apologise for my behaviour earlier Your Majesty,' said without a trace of sarcasm, 'but sometimes deaths no matter how unpleasant are necessary to achieve an important result.'

Alix stared at him, more in defiance than anything, but he noticed the Colonel wouldn't meet his eye.
'You can just dismiss the death of my friend as necessary, when you know and I know you could have let him go. He wasn't doing any harm to anyone.'

'I understand, if it is any consolation he was a very brave man, as you are sir. It takes a very special kind of courage to send a man to his death for a principle.'
He smiled almost sympathetically, 'May I sit down?'

Alix nodded stiffly.

The Colonel sat down in the same chair as yesterday, and at the same time Alix thought he heard a faint noise outside.

'Your Majesty I am afraid we have to move this process on, and in fact we need to accelerate it, so there's a couple of people I want you to meet.' With that he clicked his fingers, and through the door came a man and a woman, both of whom Alix recognised.

When you see your double, and you are not a twin, it is a terrible shock.

Standing right in front of him was his twin. Alix stared in disbelief; his jaw must have dropped.

'This is Alix, the Colonel waved towards the man at the door. 'Alix, there's a good chap, Say hello Sir to your Tsar.'

The man he called Alix bowed and said
'Hello Sir, I feel very privileged to have been presented to you.'

Alix was totally stunned. He had on many occasions heard a recording of his voice and this was exactly how this man sounded. It was just like listening to himself.

As to the woman next to him, she was the lady Jenny Andrews he had met here at the Chateau. The one he had shown the list to, who arrived at school with a boy purported to be her son, who had told him she was an army nurse with the rank of Major.

'I think you've met Tanya before.'

'Yes, but who exactly is she?' Alix trying terribly hard to pretend she wasn't there at all.

'Ah Tanya is probably the top plastic surgeon in Russia. She has rebuilt faces of wounded soldiers so incredibly well their families went from non-recognition to being unable to see any evidence of trauma. She is a truly remarkable lady, because of the techniques she uses which seem to give almost instantaneous results without scars that take time to fade. I'm sure you'd want to know why you were able to meet her in the restaurant.' The colonel smiled softly at the memory.

'You'll remember how I was unable to meet you for dinner, well it was so easy to organise after that. By the way Tanya was able to take some good close-up photos of you at the table and record your voice when she visited you at school. That is how we have been able to make Alix the perfect match to Alix,' and he laughed out loud at his joke, and Tanya smiled without her eyes ever meeting those of Alix.

'Do you remember the powder compact Tanya used, well it is a very sophisticated camera, and the voice recording was of course very simple indeed. Another of Tanya's skills is voice box alteration using lasers so a voice can be duplicated. '

The Colonel clicked his fingers again to dismiss the two, and they walked quickly out of the door and out of sight.

'It's time we got down to the nitty gritty. You must have worked it out for yourself, that we plan to substitute our Alix for you.'

Alix immediately cut him off, 'You can't do that, because he won't pass the Iris test!!

'He would if he had your eyes.'

With that the Colonel got to his feet and walked out the door. 'We can't give you 24 hours to decide, whether you cooperate or are blinded, but rest assured we'll be back, and as you have already witnessed, we don't make idle threats.'

Once again Alix was left alone with his thoughts.

The strange thing was that now he knew he was going to die; he had lost all sense of fear. He had a kind of adrenaline that was keeping him going, and he felt neither tired nor hungry. In fact, he felt totally alive, and somehow he felt almost in control.

As the hours passed his ongoing thoughts simply confirmed that there was no decision to make. Alix had already allowed his friend Tony to die, so he was perfectly prepared to die too. One thing he wouldn't do was to give in to their threats. After all there was only himself to worry about, as he had no family to involve.

Alix also consoled himself with the knowledge that if whatever they were going to do to his eyes, and it failed, then Peterson and his gang of thugs had nowhere left to go. He would be blind, and so would their substitute, and so the vaults would remain sealed.

In fact, Alix told himself it seems the Colonel has inadvertently lost the advantage, so the question was how he could best use that situation, and he smiled inwardly at the thought.

Alix eventually fell asleep and was woken by the sound of the keys and the bolts.

He opened his eyes to see the Colonel at the door, this time with three guards, none of whom were familiar.

'Sir, it is decision time. Are you going to help us access the vault or not?'

'No, and that is my final decision.' In a vain attempt at humour Alix followed this with 'I don't wish to phone a friend, or ask the audience, and I've already used my 50:50!!'

There was just the slightest flash of what might have been irritation that crossed the Colonel's face. 'That's a great shame.'

He turned to the three men 'Fetch the chair.' One of them went outside and pushed in an old-fashioned wheelchair. Please Your Majesty get into the chair, I don't want to have you manhandled, so show some pride, you are after all a Romanov.'

Alix refused to get off the bed, and looking the Colonel straight in the eye began to speak.

'Just before we leave, perhaps you might just think about some things.

What happens if this eye, or iris transplant fails, then you have nowhere to go.'

'Sorry sir, it's not an iris transplant, they are too risky because the iris can be altered by the operation. What we plan to do is to take your whole eye. We have teams of surgeons upstairs who specialise in this kind of thing, and they have a 100% success rate. For several months now they have been practising to make sure.'

Alix grimaced, 'Doubtless on innocent people.'

'No..... criminals' the Colonel smiled.

'You can't have a perfect tissue match, without which it will fail, and I repeat you will have lost everything.'

'Absolutely not,' and the Colonel positively beamed. 'We were able to obtain exact cross matching from Charles Speed, when he scraped the inside of your cheek, and took some blood. This means the Alix we selected from literally thousands of candidates is as close in tissue match as a twin.'

Alix inwardly groaned. 'It still could fail, so shouldn't that be your last resort?' He stood up and walked towards the wheelchair, 'OK let's do it.'

At this the Colonel appeared to take step back, almost as if to say that was the last thing he expected, and Alix knew he had gained a measure of control. He realised that he had called his bluff.

'You are a very brave man, even when it comes to your friend's life, and even more so your own, but we shall see how strong you are when it is children who are dependent on your cooperation.

'Well, that's OK by me, because I don't have any living relatives unless I count you, Colonel Peterson, and I don't classify you as living.'
Alix grinned at his own joke, but the smile froze on his lips, as there was an almighty commotion, some grunting and muffled yelling, as four figures were dragged into his line of vision. He saw the terror in their eyes, and realised it was four of his favourite fifth formers, David Gray, Stuart Grimes, Ken Smith, and Terry Old, all bound and gagged.

'You bastard.' Looking straight at Colonel Peterson. 'Using children is as low as it gets.'

'It's decision time,' John said, completely ignoring Alix's comments.

'We will give you 24 hours to agree to accompanying us to Blumeur's. When you do, one of my men will stay with the boys, and one squeak from you and they die. In fact, one comment from you at any point in the future and we will get to them and kill them, and you as well.' Colonel Peterson moved towards the door. 'I'll let you sleep on it,' he added,

'But at this time tomorrow we will unlock the door, and if you have not agreed to our demands to go to Blumeur's, then we will draw lots and kill one of the children, and this will be repeated every 24 hours. On the fifth day you Alix as the only survivor will go under the surgeon's knife and be blinded for the rest of your life.'

With that bombshell Colonel Peterson walked out of the door, followed by his associates' one of them pushing an empty wheelchair. The door clanged shut, the bolts could be heard sliding into position, and suddenly everything was quiet.

Alix turned to the boys and undid their bonds, removed their gags, and the ear plugs which had meant they would not have been able to hear the threats of their kidnappers. He was instantly impressed by their demeanour, and even now there were no tears, no panic, no yelling at all.

'OK gentlemen, I think I owe you an explanation, but first of all what happened to you?'

At this point they all spoke at once, until Alix put one finger up to his lips.
'One…………at…………a…………time…………please.
David Gray was the first to speak.

'Please sir, what is going on, and what is going to happen to us?'
Alix could see that despite his bravado that tears were not far away.

'Oh, you have nothing to worry about; it's me with the dreadful secret. You see I have just inherited an awful lot of money, and these men want to convince me I should hand it over to them. When I have agreed to do that, we all go home.'

To keep the initiative Alix having convincingly lied to them repeated the question.

'Well sir, you know we are trying for the Coxless 4's on the river. We were training by ourselves when we saw this boat seemingly stuck in the middle with thick black smoke coming from the stern like the engine had blown up. The people on board were shouting for help, saying they had no life jackets or even a dingy, but when we got alongside, we were grabbed and pulled aboard, and they sank our boat. After that they put, I think something like chloroform over our faces, and that's about all we remember until we woke up somewhere outside this room. We were gagged and bound, then brought in before the four men and you. We do remember one other thing which is the men were speaking in a language that sounded like Russian.'

Alix grimaced, that merely confirmed what Tony, poor Tony had concluded and that was that Colonel John Peterson the classic loyal army officer was in fact on another and more sinister payroll.

There seemed little point in discussing their predicament, and Alix anyway had made up his mind that he would offer himself to have the surgery, and lose his sight, rather than run any risks to his boys. He also decided that he would insist on seeing evidence on television that they had been returned home safe and well before the surgery took place.

Having made the decision, Alix was very much at peace with himself, almost resigned to his fate. He knew however that it was important to keep the boys occupied, so he set them the task of checking all the outside walls for any signs of ancient doors or even escape tunnels. After all a 200-year-old structure built to hide fugitives must have had more than one entry and exit. In his heart of hearts, he was fairly sure any escape routes would have been found by the Colonel and probably blown up, but he certainly wasn't about to tell the boys.

It must have been about six hours into their ordeal, that one of the boys came running into Alix's room to say a cupboard was moving.

CHAPTER 31

Alix rushed along the short corridor into the next room, and sure enough the cupboard in the corner which must have been there forever seemed to be sliding along the floor.

Alix motioned the boys to be quiet as the floor where the cupboard had been lifted like a hatch, and up popped the head of Alain Nallen the cemetery gardener Alix had met on his first visit to the Chateau. He had a broad grin on his face, with one finger up to his lips indicating silence. He pulled himself out of the trapdoor, and then helped Alix and the boys to slide the cupboard back into place.

Alix whispered, 'What on earth are you doing here?'

'I've come to help you get away, and I'll tell you all about it when we are safe. Now what we must do is to ensure these awful people don't know how you got away, so just let me show you what we will do.'

The cupboard was back in place, and Alain pressed a catch at the back of one of the drawers which was quite invisible unless you knew where it was, and the cupboard slid out to the side again. He then pressed a spot in the middle of the wooden floor, and a trapdoor dutifully opened so almost anyone could enter the hole in the floor providing they went in backwards and felt for the steps with their feet.

Alain looked at the boys and gave them a reassuring smile. 'Isn't this an amazing piece of engineering boys, and precision engineering at that. All it uses are springs and levers, and to think this was designed before the French Revolution, and it has saved a lot of lives since then.'

Alix went first followed by the four boys who all kept completely silent as they were told to do. Alain then went down the steps and pressed a button on the wall, and the trapdoor closed behind him, followed by a second button which he explained would make the cupboard slide back into place.

Alain then reassured Alix that there wouldn't be any sign of the entry or exit. The tunnel emerged some 400 yards from the house in the side of the steep riverbank and was a comfortable and dry if stooped uphill walk, and well-lit by Alain's torch. Alix could see the tunnel was steel lined all the way and he wondered if this was a Great War construction or from earlier times.

As they reached the entrance to the tunnel, Alain motioned them all to be quiet. He half opened a small oak door with vertical and horizontal banding on it, and immediately closed it again.

'I think we have a problem,' he whispered. 'It is almost dusk, and I should have come later. The Chateau and the Cemetery are absolutely crawling with Russians who are all pretending to be students of the Battle of Passchendaele, when in fact they are here in the main as security as far as we can see.'

Alain shrugged his shoulders, 'but we felt that waiting until nightfall might be too late.'

He motioned towards the door, 'There are two of them chatting by the river not 50 yards away, and whilst that doesn't stop me getting in and out, because the long grass beside the path acts as a shield. I can't risk it with the four youngsters.'

Alix turned to the four boys and said in a whisper. 'This is exciting, but silence is required, so be completely quiet until I tell you, OK?'

The four boys nodded.

Alain sat down and opened a small haversack that appeared on the ground next to him as if by magic.

'Hands up who wants some Pepsi,' he whispered, and four youthful hands shot up.

'I've also got some ham rolls,' and four hands shot up again.

Alain continued whispering.

'Look gentlemen we have got to be patient and sit it out, we have no choice. Don't worry that entrance in the cellar, and this entrance have remained hidden for over 200 years, so some stupid Russians will never find them now.'

Everything changed very shortly after they had finished eating and drinking and had packed the rubbish away. Even through the door, the small party could hear shouting in Russian, and even the sound of men running along the path right outside.

'I think they've discovered that we are missing,' Alix whispered, as he said that Alain had opened the door just far enough to see outside. The Russians by the river had gone, and as far as Alain could see, everything looked clear. He turned to the five escapees

'When we go out the door, we must go right and crawl for about 50 yards, by then we will hidden by some bushes. They have red berries, so when you get there, crouch by the path and wait until we are all together.'

In less than two minutes they had all reached the bushes, which marked the start of a small wood.

After half an hour of very brisk walking and crawling, Alain led the small party into another wood, and shortly through the front door of a house. This entire journey was conducted in absolute silence until they arrived indoors.

There were soon steaming mugs of tea, big thick sandwiches which the boys ate hungrily, suggesting that Alain had prepared accordingly. Seeing how tired the boys were, Alain suggested it was time for bed, telling them all, they would be totally safe as this was his house. Alix felt uncomfortably close to the Chateau, but Alain assured him that he was sure the Colonel didn't really know where he lived, or even if he existed for that matter, and that if he did, he was a simple Belgian of no consequence.

Just after the boys had bedded down in the loft, and had fallen asleep almost immediately there was a tap at the door and Mary came in. She gave Alain a hug, and kissed Alix on both cheeks.

Alain smiled at her and looked across at Alix 'You owe your life to my niece. She just knew by the preparations that had been made what was about to happen. Indeed, as part of her cover she added the hypnotic to your wine and all the liqueurs.'

'What do you mean as part of her cover?'

Alain said 'It's a long story, but sufficient to say Mary and I are all that is left from the eighteen orphans. My father was Donal Lenihan, and as I think you know Mary is my niece'

Alix interrupted, 'Donal Lenihan was one of the orphans whose name is on the Menin Gate, because his body was never discovered. He was also the only one of Willie's friends to witness the wedding between Willie and Marie.'

'Ah, well as you can see Donal didn't die. You see Donal saw the systematic killing of the remaining ten boys by Major Peterson after Willie was murdered, and eventually deserted. You must understand that the survivors were given futile tasks which had the biggest risks attached. They were forced on night fighting patrols, being one example, and carrying up supplies in broad daylight being another. At least two were seen to be shot in the back with the excuse they were cowards by not leaving the muddy shell hole they were sheltering in, when to do so meant certain death.

My Father hid in such a shell hole until after dark, and then apparently crawled on his hands and knees for over a mile until he reached the chateau.

Willie had told him about the secret entrance to the cellar, because that was where he and Marie carried on their relationship, and incidentally where they got married. The war had moved away a bit, so the cellar was hardly used, and my father hid down there for nearly two years, coming out at nights to scavenge food. Madame Dubré eventually found out, and he told her why he was hiding, and she never uttered one word to anyone about him.

Indeed, I think she washed his clothes, and fed him amongst other things after she found him hiding and knew what had happened.

After the Armistice, what with all the displaced people and refugees, it was simple for my father to get papers, and he decided to adopt a new name, so the Nallen is the Nal from Donal, and the Len is from Lenihan, out of respect for the name.

Alain then knelt and bowed his head. 'My father would be so happy to see you. I have dedicated my whole life to this day Sir.'

Mary who had watched all of this, put up her hands in front of her. 'Alain we're not out of the woods yet, even although our house is right at the edge of the estate, we must be very careful.

I've just been back to the house, and the guests this week are a bit different to the usual crowd. The Colonel has them listed as Russian academics, but I'll bet you a great deal of money they aren't who they appear to be. We've everything from men who look like the Mafia, to others who could be SAS except they are Russian. When I was leaving a few minutes ago more of them were arriving. This new lot came in very sophisticated looking people carriers and one of these massive American Winnebagos, plus one very large lorry and two huge vans with what looked like aerials sprouting from it. If I hadn't known or suspected they were up to no good, they almost looked like a television outside broadcasting crew and equipment.'

Alix interrupted, 'If I said they were a medical team, would that be a possibility?'

Alain looked at her the shock clearly showing on his face. 'I thought you were dismissed after dinner last night, and told to come home to have a week's holiday?'

Mary just looked at him with love on her face, and stroked his cheek 'We were Uncle Alain, and now I know why!!'

'Hang on Mary, how long ago was it that Tony and I arrived at the Chateau.'

Mary looked quite shocked, 'Yesterday evening of course, how long did you think you'd been in the cellar?

'Two days!' Mary looked at him a bit oddly, 'Am I right in that you have had your watches and phones taken, and that you were told by Colonel Peterson that they would be back in 24 hours?'

'Yes.'

'Was the cellar silent, and did you sleep some of the time?

'Yes.'

'It's a form of sensory deprivation which makes you lose track of time very quickly, so when you're told it will be 24 hours, and someone comes in before that, then you believe 24 hours has passed.

'I stayed because I wanted to be certain that the original plan to put you in the lower cellar was happening, so I hid until they dragged you,' looking at Alix as she said it, 'down the stairs. I then crept outside and saw two vehicles arrive, the first unloaded four stretchers, and that was obviously the boys, and then a Chrysler Voyager arrived, and you got out along with that lady you had dinner with not so long ago,' looking once again at Alix.

'That did confuse me, but then I realised they must be about to attempt to replace you with someone who looked like you.'

'If I may butt in Mary,' Alix interjected. 'They planned to remove my eyes and transplant them into that plastic surgery freak, and if I wouldn't cooperate then they planned to kill my young lads one at a time, every 24 hours.' By way of explanation he added, 'They are fifth formers at my school, and they were kidnapped yesterday.'

Alix rubbed his head with both hands, 'What I don't understand however, is why did they murder Tony?' Before any more could be said, there was a loud knocking at the door.

Mary looked at her uncle, and shrugged her shoulders 'I'm so sorry Alain, but I had little choice, because they were going to get away.' Gesturing towards Alix, 'and I couldn't let that happen. I told Colonel Peterson where he could find you.'

Just for a moment there was silence followed by the sound of smashing glass and splintering wood, as the men that Mary had just described crashed in the door, followed by a grim looking Colonel Peterson, and an equally unamused Tony Edwards.

'I'm so sorry uncle, that I've not been totally honest with you.' Mary was close to tears.

Alix looked at Tony, 'You're supposed to be dead!!' He almost yelled,' I heard you shot, and I saw your body. Just what the hell is going on?'

'Shut up' was Tony's only response.

Mary looked at Colonel Peterson 'John, I think you at least owe all of them a full explanation. The children can be released somewhere in the middle of Brussels we have no need for them after this.'

'That's fine, but this man' pointing at Alain, we have no need for him, and the Tsar can live until we have used his eyes,' The word Tsar was almost spat with venom by Tony.

Colonel Peterson put his hands up for silence.

'In about half an hour the man who believes he is Tsar will go under the surgeon's knife, and his eyes will be used to enable Russia to stabilise her economy by allowing us to reclaim what is rightfully ours. The gold never belonged to the Tsar it belongs to the people.'

He turned to look at Alix who was looking around in undisguised horror. Firstly Tony, and then Mary, both working with Colonel Peterson was just too much. It was hard to believe, but had he been taken for a sucker.

He realised the Colonel was addressing his remarks at him, and he appeared to be encouraged by Mary of all people to almost gloat.

'Alix, you'll never be the Tsar. You will be history soon, as has everyone who has been part of the Romanov family.

Let me explain in some detail to you, so you finally understand why we must finish this ridiculous business once and for all.'

As he said that Alix just knew he was about to get the whole story once again, probably with justification thrown in. It's strange how the triumphant often need to tell the vanquished why they are so great, and the losers so poor. That was exactly what Colonel Peterson launched into as if he could read Alix's mind

'When young Alixei was born in 1898, the Tsar knew full well he wasn't the father, but he put his signature to the birth for the sake of the continuation of his line, he certainly didn't do it for Russia. To humiliate his brother Georgij he made him witness, and then had him murdered, but had it put about he died of tuberculosis the next year 1899.

The doctor and midwife who attended the birth were murdered and their bodies disposed of. The wet nurse, the nanny and the military escort who took Alixei to Ireland were also murdered.

The 17 children who joined the boy who was now Willie McBride in the orphanage became orphans because of the sinking of a pleasure boat near St Petersburg. The press were kept in the dark, and it was assumed there were 144 passengers including 27 children.

The stopcocks were removed from the boat by the crew who escaped in the only lifeboat along with 27 children. Sadly, none of the girls on board the lifeboat, and there were ten of them, survived.' At this point the Colonel paused almost for dramatic effect.

'There was in fact one survivor from the ship itself, who made it to shore, and he lived only fifteen minutes, because the men on the bank kept throwing him back in the lake again until he too drowned. The publicity was almost zero.'

Alix couldn't help interrupting as it was the final confirmation of his theory that that was the source of the seventeen orphans. He had kind of worked out this was where the orphans came from, but at least he knew he had been right.

'You bastard.'

The Colonel flicked his wrist as if swatting a fly.

'Don't interrupt.

The Glanville's who originally owned the Orphanage had an unfortunate boating accident in 1913, and their son and his wife were murdered in 1922 and it was made to look like suicide.

A couple of the parents of the dead children refused to emigrate, so they met with very regrettable fatal accidents.

It was tragically necessary to make sure none of the orphans survived for long after Willie died, because dead men tell no tales as the popular story goes.

I'm very much afraid that your father William,' the colonel looked directly at Alix, died under torture. He knew exactly how to access the vault in the wonderful days before DNA and Iris tests. What was even sadder was the fact that the clumsy people who interrogated him wanted to know how much he knew about the person you call the 'Fifth Man', and they didn't realise he was so important to us as the man who could lead us to the gold.

Their enthusiasm killed him, and we had to make it look like suicide.'

At this moment Alain spoke up. 'Your people failed in one thing Colonel,' his voice cracking with emotion. 'Donal Lenihan survived the war. He was my father, and he witnessed your grandfather's crimes, and everything is written down from that day to this, including my suspicions about you. If I go missing, Mary knows where my notes are, and ....' Alain suddenly tailed off in mid-sentence, realising that Mary, his beloved niece was in fact working for the Russians.

'That doesn't worry us,' said Tony, 'Mary, John and I, we'll be long gone.'

At this moment, a whistle blew outside, and suddenly a voice spoke from somewhere close by. The voice became a man, and that man was Colin Stewart. He came out from the kitchen where he must have been hiding for some time.

He nodded towards the Colonel and his companions. 'Your game is over, that single blow on a whistle was a signal that your escorts, and your medical team, plus all the vehicles have been neutralised by my friends.' Smiling he added, 'So don't get clever, if you have any weapons lay them on the floor and step back.'

Then as if seeing Colonel Peterson for the first time 'Hello John, long time no see.' At this the Colonel went very white. 'You thought we'd never meet again, but I'm glad to say we have. If my memory serves me right when we knew each other in the Regiment, you were less than honest, and you let your friends down. We have suspected you of disloyalty for several years, without being able to prove anything, but now we have finally caught up with you, and you have confirmed the traitor that you are by what you have just said.

You know what your failure will mean, and that is the certain death you were going to inflict upon these lovely people, because you and I both know your master's do not tolerate failure.'

At this point there was the very loud detonation, followed immediately by a scream of pain from Colonel Peterson, as he fell to the ground with blood streaming through a hole in his left trouser leg at knee level.

Colin looked up and smiled, 'Mary that looked like a classic kneecap job, I'm glad you haven't forgotten all the things we taught you when you were in Belfast.' Although his comment was almost drowned out by the screaming noises from the Colonel.

The hate in Mary's eyes was intense, but the suddenness of what followed was both unexpected and startling. Colin drew a small pistol from his pocket, knelt, and said in a loud voice, 'This is from the Regiment,' and promptly shot the Colonel through the other knee.

Then totally ignoring the screams from the wounded man, Colin turned to, and gestured towards Alain, Mary and Alix, at the same time as he beckoned to the man Alix recognised as Alistair Moses from his visit to the SIS building, who was standing in the door. He also pointed at Tony and the prostrate form of Colonel Peterson, and to all five gave the same well-worn phrase.
'You are all under arrest for attempting to obtain property by deception, and acts involving aiding a foreign power against the interests of the United Kingdom under the Official Secrets Act. You do not have to say anything but anything you do say will be taken down and may be given in evidence.'
With that and before Alain, Mary, or Alix could say a word they were handcuffed, and coats thrown over their heads. Alix was almost frog marched out of the building. then felt himself pushed into the back seat of a car, which sped off. He assumed the others were treated in much the same way.
The coat was soon removed from Alix's head, and he found himself sitting next to a man dressed in plain clothes who had a certain military bearing to him, and he assumed to be a police officer, and a driver dressed pretty much the same.
Attempts to engage in conversation, or ask questions proved futile. The car journey was short, probably about 20 minutes, and spent in silence, then Alix found himself on a small aircraft with

Alain, Mary, Tony, and the whimpering Colonel Peterson. All were escorted, and kept well apart, so there was no chance of eye contact. The thing that also struck Alix as odd, was the fact that this was an aircraft with no windows

He felt utterly confused, even demoralised. To have seen his friend Tony apparently die, only to discover that he was involved in what now appeared to be a gigantic fraud, and perhaps even espionage. To have been threatened with blindness, probably death, and the murder of four of his pupils was almost more than he could take. He began to doubt if he was the Tsar, and the more he thought about everything he had found out, the more he began to believe that he could have been the subject of an elaborate con trick.

The one constant in all of this had been Colin Stewart, who had told him what would happen at the Chateau, and by and large he had been right. The bluster and threats from Colonel Peterson would have seemed real enough had Alix not been forewarned. However, the faked murder of Tony was not part of the information Colin Stewart had given him during the afternoon and evening at the SIS headquarters, although he had never thought that his friend Tony could possibly be an accomplice.

So why had Colin not told him about the children, or the fact that Tony was obviously a crook, but then again, he surmised how could he have behaved normally with Tony, having been told the truth about him, and would he have believed Colin Stewart anyway.

All these jumbled up thoughts were bouncing around in Alix's head as the aircraft landed, he assumed in England, although there were no windows to see through to confirm this.

Before disembarking the coat was once again slung over his head, and Alix assumed the same applied to the others, and he was guided down some very short steps, and walked for possibly twenty yards before being helped into the back seat of a car.

All he was conscious of was the clicking of what sounded like a thousand cameras, and a noisy babble of voices asking unanswered, even unintelligible questions.

After what seemed like only minutes in the car, and another walk of perhaps fifty yards, Alix heard a door opening, and he was pushed into a room and the coat removed from his head. He blinked, and realised he was in a prison cell. Looking round, again the absence of a window, and a door which he assumed would soon be locked. The mute escort removed his handcuffs and spoke for the first time.

'You are to remain here in custody, although you have your own clothes, plus there is a television as you can see, newspapers, and basic tea making facilities. You will remain here as our guest, until

Colonel Stewart decides what is to happen to you next. The Colonel suggests you read the newspapers, and' looking at his watch, 'the News is on the television in ten minutes. I'll switch the TV on, because the Colonel wishes you to see exactly what it is you have become involved in. With that he switched the TV on and left.

Alix noted there were sandwiches wrapped in cling film, which he ate hungrily, the kettle had been boiled prior to his arrival, so he had a steaming hot mug of tea as well, and then his eyes fell on the newspaper on the table.

The headline in the Times hit him like a hammer.

CHAPTER 32

'Police & Intelligence Services Foil Multi Billion Pound Fraud '

'Police aided by the Intelligence Services intercepted and detained four men and a woman, all but one believed to be British nationals, at a Chateau in Ypres in Belgium. They are said to have been involved in a conspiracy to obtain the fortune in gold that was linked to the assassinated Tsar Nicholas 2nd of Russia, and are the latest in a long line of fraudsters and imposters beginning with Anna Anderson who claimed she was Anastasia Romanov over 50 years ago.
Unconfirmed rumours claim the Britons arrested are a solicitor, a schoolmaster, a Catering Manager, and a retired Army Officer. One foreign national is also suspected of being involved, but as yet no further details are available.
Police sources would not enlarge on this information, but a press conference will be held later today.'

There had to be a mistake, Alix just couldn't believe what he was he was seeing. Surely Colin Stewart wouldn't allow such rubbish to appear in the national press. He banged on the door, but there was no response.

He went back to the table, picked up The Times, and to his horror the paper underneath was the Eastern Daily Press. The front-page headline was a disaster for him personally, in a newspaper well known and well circulated in Norfolk and Suffolk, and very widely read by many of his schoolteacher friends in Ely.

'Ely Schoolmaster Implicated in Multi Billion Pound Fraud '

Police aided by the Intelligence Services have prevented a massive $200 billion fraud, and arrested four men and a woman after a long investigation culminating in a shoot-out in a Belgian farmhouse. Although unconfirmed by the police, our sources state that one of the men arrested is a schoolmaster from King's School Ely who may also face charges under the Official Secrets Act.

It is believed but not yet confirmed that the group had planned to use false identities to gain entrance to a Swiss Bank, and remove the huge fortune believed to have been stored there by the Romanov Family, murdered during the Russian revolution in 1918.

The headmaster of King's Ely, Mr John James was unavailable for comment.

More news is expected within the next 24 hours

What on earth would Ray be thinking now, and for how long would his garrulous Welsh friend resist the temptation to go to the press. Never mind Ray, what about his headmaster was Alix's next thought, knowing he had promised to have the whole business settled, and now this, which must have finished any chance of staying at King's.

As Alix was reading the front page of the newspaper, the BBC news programme came on the air. The newsreader, Fiona Bruce opened with

'Breaking news tonight Wednesday...... More arrests in the Tsar's Gold Fraud.'
She mentioned a couple more news headlines involving politicians, and an oil spillage before returning to the breaking news.
'It is understood from sources in Whitehall that there have been more arrests in the Tsar Gold Fraud case, where a gang came very close to stealing over $200 billion in gold, and diamonds from a Swiss bank. It is understood, but not yet confirmed, that the gold has lain undisturbed and unclaimed for over 95 years. The Gold may have been held there possibly for over two hundred years, but finally in the name of Tsar Nicholas 2nd who of course along with his family perished at the hands of the Bolsheviks in 1918. The gold has long been the target for fraudsters and imposters, but little has been heard about it since the discovery of the Romanov bodies almost 20 years ago.
Now it appears there has been a fresh attempt to access the fortune in gold, and it has only been thanks to some very impressive detective work by the Home Office that this very clever attempt failed.
The gang were very close to their target; indeed, it is believed that one of their number managed to penetrate the bank's failsafe security system by using falsified DNA evidence to support his claim

to be the Great Grandson of the last Tsar, claimed reliable sources inside the Home Office

Initially arrested were three UK nationals, a Colonel John Peterson MC who was the tenant of Chateau Hugend at Ypres in Belgium, where he has been running a Battlefield Tours Company for over thirty years. A Norfolk lawyer Tony Edwards from Ely who it is understood used his legal knowledge to falsify several legal documents. A schoolteacher named as Alix McBride from King's School Ely who was playing the role of the great Grandson of Tsar Nicholas 2nd.

In addition two Belgian nationals Mary Nallen, and her uncle Alain Nallen who both worked at the Chateau. Mary Nallen who also holds a British passport is thought to have worked with Colonel Peterson for thirty years or more. Alain Nallen has worked for the Chateau Hotel and the War Graves Commission since World War 2

At this point the newsreader was handed a sheet of paper. 'Within the past few minutes, a Forensics Expert from Cambridge named Charles Speed has also been detained, and a Simon and Betty Edwards also from Ely. It is understood that Mr Speed has been charged with conspiring to obtain property under false pretences, and Mr. and Mrs. Edwards who are the parents of Tony Edwards have been detained under the Official Secrets Act.'

Another sheet of paper pushed in by an unknown hand appeared on the newsreader's desk.

'A press conference is now under way at the Home Office, and we are going over there right away.'

Alix groaned with his head in his hands. How stupid he had been made to look, and then suddenly he realised that insofar as the world at large was concerned, he was as guilty as the rest of them.

In fact, it was slowly dawning on him that he was probably facing a long prison sentence for fraud and something to do with official secrets, which means spying.

The inherited money was no consolation, and then the horrendous thought dawned on him. Did the millions that he had inherited even exist at all?

He suddenly realised he hadn't seen any copies of the legal documents he had signed in Tony's outer office transferring the money.

Alix groaned inwardly again, nearly in tears. All he wanted was to go back to teaching at King's, and of course with all this publicity, and the likelihood of prison that wasn't going to be possible, and he was most probably as poor as he had ever been

He was distracted from his thoughts by the picture on the screen, which showed a desk with several microphones, and there sitting at the desk was Colin Stewart, and someone whose name he didn't quite catch, but who was obviously a home office minister.

The Minister was introducing Colonel Colin Stewart as 'The man who headed up a multi disciplined team who have spent several months collating evidence against this tight knit group of fraudsters and imposters, on behalf of the Home Office. Finally, after a small exchange of fire they captured the team intact, although Colonel Peterson was slightly wounded in both legs as he tried to escape and is now being treated in a secure hospital.' The minister nodded at Colin Stewart. 'Colonel Stewart will now make a short statement, and then will take questions, but the gentlemen of the press must realise he will be unable to give you answers where this country's national security is involved.'

Alix barely focused in on what was being said, but when his photograph was shown he began to listen to Colonel Stewart very intently indeed.

'Mr. Alix McBride along with Colonel John Peterson, and Mr Tony Edwards have been at the heart of this attempt to rob Blumeur's bank in Zurich of over $243 billion dollars.' By now the photographs of all three men were on the television screen.

'These three very cleverly along with the help of a Mr. Charles Speed an expert in DNA Forensic evidence. They dishonoured the memory of a brave man, inventing a completely fictitious background.

Mr. Speed then faked the DNA connection with the Romanov's.

Miss Mary Nallen and her uncle Alain Nallen were heavily involved in maintaining an apparently genuine battlefield tours company and were complicit in that they aided and abetted Peterson and Edwards in setting up and running said company. The code illegally obtained by Mr Edwards, along with the DNA evidence was enough to convince Blumeur's that Mr. Alix McBride was in fact a direct descendent of the last Tsar Nicholas the 2nd.'

At that point Colin Stewart paused to sip some water from a glass in front of him.

'Whilst there is a great deal more evidence to be examined, and this will come out in the future, all I want to add now is the fact that we have irrefutable evidence that the vault in Blumeur's is in fact empty.

There is no gold, and it has been common knowledge in government circles for many years that Tsar Nicholas 2nd spent his entire fortune keeping his army fighting during the Great War.'

As he closed the folder in front of him with a degree of finality Colonel Stewart added,

'In closing this statement, I will not take questions because of the extreme sensitivity of our continuing investigations, which involve the security of this

country. We have come close to great harm, and the perpetrators will in due course be punished.'
With that, and to the obvious surprise of the Minister, Colin Stewart rose from the table, nodded to the assembled press and cameras. He then walked back through the door he had entered some minutes ago.
The television screen continued to show the empty seat, and then the Minister made for the exit door as well, obviously not happy with his subordinate, but still not as angry as the press ensemble that were almost baying for blood, having been denied their promised pound of flesh.

Alix switched off the television, and lay down on the basic iron bedstead, covered by rough brown blankets, thinking these are real prison issue, and I'm going to have to get used to them.
He had been very surprised to see Colin Stewart on the television, and the fact that he held a senior Army rank. Alix was even more surprised at his version of events. In fact, he told himself they weren't even truthful. The whole DNA issue, plus the photographs linking Willie to the orphans from Russia could not have been faked.
The headstones in the cemeteries all over Southern Ireland, the gold presented to the churches, and the mass emigration of the parents of the dead children. There was no way he could miss out the Faberge

egg either. All these things were fact, and he had seen the evidence with his own eyes

Ray had studiously done the family tree, everything, absolutely everything pointed to the fact that this whole thing wasn't the invention of crooked minds. The final clincher was the absolute lie that the vault was empty. He had seen the gold with his own eyes, so what on earth was Colonel Colin Stewart playing at.

Alix didn't have to wait long to find out.

CHAPTER 33

There was the sound of keys in the lock, and bolts being withdrawn, and the noise immediately took Alix back to the cellar at the Chateau, and he shivered at the memory.
A large grey-haired man, looking like a very fit ex rugby player, appeared in the door.
'The Colonel will see you now, just follow me please.'
The politeness encouraged Alix who had half expected to be handcuffed and a coat thrown over his head. He was also surprised by his surroundings after he left his cell. What he found wasn't the drab grey paint of a prison. There were no barred gates to negotiate, and amazingly he was quickly into a beautiful wood panelled corridor, with lovely views of the countryside out of the windows to his right, and several doors leading off to the left. Alix concluded they were in the wing of a large country house, and he wondered idly if this was one of the 'safe houses' he had heard of in the press, and on television.
He followed his escort into a large hallway with the stairs rising on either side to a large landing in the middle, the walls all the way up the stairs hung with what seemed like family portraits. They didn't however climb the stairs, instead walked beneath the landing and after a double knock on the door in

front it was opened from within by Colonel Colin Stewart himself.

He put out his hand, a gesture which Alix brushed away.

'Alix I'm glad to see you, please come in and take a seat, there are some explanations you need to hear.' He stood back to let Alix enter the room, and as soon as he did, two familiar figures rose to greet him. It was Mary and Alain, both smiling.

Alix, both shocked and angry turned to Colin Stewart,

'I've about had enough of this, so you need to do some serious explaining about what the hell is going on. Where are we, why have you treated me like this?'

Looking at Mary directly 'You lied to me, and then at Alain, 'You as well, all that rubbish about Mary being your niece, when she is your daughter isn't she?

Alix continued scarcely drawing breath, turning to Colin

'I....

'Calm down Alix' he interrupted quickly, 'I'm really sorry about what you've been put through, and the fibs we've told you, but if you remember our conversation in my office, you must realise by now what has been going on.' Colin motioned Alix to take a seat, which he did on a settee opposite

Mary and Alain, still viewing them with a cross between outright hostility and suspicion.

'I want to set the record straight, and hope you'll understand what an incredibly valuable job you have done for this country.'

'Go on.'

Colin took a sip of his coffee, as Mary poured a cup for Alix.

'What this has all been about isn't just the vault full of gold, nor is it the fact that you are the only direct blood line survivor of the Romanovs.' Colin opened his hands palm side slightly upwards. 'You must have seen the press conference.' Alix nodded dumbly. 'Well, a lot of that was simply untrue, but done deliberately to protect you.

You see, and this may sound somewhat complicated, there have been a lot of people, mostly Russians, but in some cases their agents who have been working for many years to get their hands on the contents of the vault. Inevitably the Security Services have a lot more than a passing interest in this prodigious amount of money. I am sure you understand were the gold to be released on the open market, having got into the wrong hands, it would seriously destabilise many country's economies, including our own, even perhaps lead to conflict.

However, in this case that is almost a side issue, because we have been looking for a very deep-seated Russian agent who has been acting as a kind of post office, somewhere in the UK. Thanks to your efforts we have been able to unmask them both, because there is two of them.

Firstly, we have believed for a long time, but lacked the proof that Colonel John Peterson was in some way involved with the Russians.' Colin smiled at the memory, 'Poor man will never walk again without crutches, what a shame!!'

He nodded towards Mary, and then looked back at Alix. 'Alix, you owe your life to Mary and Alain, and I hope you realise that. Just to let you understand why Mary shot the Colonel in the knee. We recruited her into the Service when she was a student in Belfast, and that was where John Peterson was doing an Intelligence Staff job in the army. She believed he betrayed her fiancée at the time, who was subsequently tortured and shot by the IRA, so what you saw was a small act of revenge.'

Mary then eased herself into the conversation, 'I'm sorry about the uncle and niece bit, but we felt the last thing you needed was a father daughter complication. We tried to stimulate enough interest for you to go and dig around about your grandfather. Thank goodness you did; we all owe you a great deal.'

Looking at Alain Colin added, 'Alain was the only connection we have to the young orphans, in that his father was the only one to survive Ypres. He has his father's diaries and helped us concentrate on Colonel Peterson when he arrived to run the Chateau. It was no coincidence that this happened. You see for most of his later years his sole efforts have been towards being in the right place at the right time, with a working plan when you or an heir of the Romanovs worked out how to get into the vault.'

After another sip of coffee, and a nibble at a biscuit Colin continued, 'Are you still following me Alix?' Alix nodded.

'Well we in the SIS are certain John Peterson was onside with the Russians all his life, but we only had that confirmed by the family tree your colleague Ray worked out for you. Anyway, to return to Alain, who has worked with us since he was a young man, complete with Belgian nationality who did an incredibly brave job during the 2nd World War with the SOE. He organised the visits to Belgium made by your father and grandmother, who were able to hide in the lower cellar, where you were held, on many occasions keeping them safe. You too have cause to be grateful for Alain's encyclopaedic knowledge, because that undoubtedly kept them alive during these terrifyingly difficult times.'

Colin Stewart's voice was almost emotional by this time. 'Mary and Alain have been our eyes and ears

at Chateau Hugend for over 30 years. Mary in fact had become the confidant of Colonel Peterson, so much so she even helped him to drug you', nodding towards Alix, 'and in fact so convinced her employer of her support that she became remarkably well informed about exactly what was going on. Never forget your debt to these two.'
Alix shifted slightly in his seat, 'OK I can accept that, but why all the lies in front of the watching millions on television. My headmaster isn't exactly going to welcome me back with open arms after that lot. I'm either a criminal, an enemy agent, a spy, or I look like a total fool having been supposedly taken in by these villains.' Alix suddenly changed tack. 'Talking of villains, please tell me about my lawyer Tony.'
Colin Stewart grimaced, 'Well that one took us a bit by surprise really. He appears to have become part of the family firm so to speak. He was very easy to talk to, and full of interesting information when we asked him nicely,' grinning at the memory.
'In the beginning he was just an interested party, acting we think as your friend, and genuinely interested in helping you.
It would however appear that after you went to his parent's house for supper that Tony became privy to the bigger picture. By that I mean the consequences of the gold in the vault, and the

potential dominance it could give Russia. What he found out was that his father, and to a lesser extent his mother had been working for the Russians for over fifty years.

We have been looking for fifty years now for other men who could have become involved in the world of espionage at Cambridge University at the time of Burgess, Maclean, Philby and Blunt. Do you remember Alix when we were having a tense little conversation about the death of your father, and you mentioned these names and that of Hollis. Well, you were largely quite right, because your father was working on his exposure, and was sadly discovered. What kept him alive was the fact that the Russian authorities who were running their British agents, also knew that your father was the key to the fortune in the vaults in Switzerland. They were unwilling to kill him, but we believe they attempted to get him to talk about what he had found out about Hollis, as well as give up the key codes for Blumeur's but your very brave father refused to talk. We believe his death was accidental because in the very real sense of the word he was too invaluable to them to lose. His death was then made to look like a suicide.'

There then was a deathly hush in the room, Alix almost said something, but before he had the chance Colin Stewart continued. 'What we now know, after a few very interesting conversations with Mr. and Mrs. Edwards is that Mr. Edwards was responsible for the death of your father, and he ran Hollis, or someone similarly senior in the Intelligence world, and was if you like their conduit, their safe post office. After all, who would ever suspect a lawyer practising in a family firm that had been established for years in a provincial city, of ever being a Russian Agent?

That is, 'and Colin's eyes twinkled, 'until you find out his father Tommy held extremely left-wing views, and indeed went to fight with the Bolsheviks in 1918.'

Alix held up his hand to silence Colin.

'OK, I accept all of that, and obviously I'm very grateful to Alain, and Mary.' He looked at Alain, 'If it would be something you wanted, I can almost certainly put you in touch with your family in Russia.' Alain looked confused. 'Look I have a list of names of the dead children from the boat that sank, and the ages of the boys coincided with the age of the orphans. I thought that the coincidence was too much to ignore, but I couldn't fathom out about the girls, until that bloody man Peterson filled us in on the gory details. Now I am certain I know who your father really was, and sadly your grandparents who drowned, but hopefully there will still be some family alive and traceable in Vladivostok. In fact, assuming I do still have some money,' as Alix said that he looked at Colin

Stewart who nodded, 'Well in that case I'd love to come too and help you if that would be OK. I feel that's the very least I can do.'

Turning to Mary he added, 'As far as Chateau Hugend is concerned, I will make the deeds over to you, on the one condition you continue to run it as a Battlefields Tour Centre, and I can come and visit. I'm sure between the two of you, there is more than enough knowledge to be successful, and the notoriety will ensure you a steady stream of visitors.' At this Mary smiled, and nodded at Alix 'Thank you, thank you very much.'

'That Colin assumes you can extract us from this horrendous publicity, but before I forget I'm intrigued to know about Charles Speed.'

'He was essentially just corrupt and was bought by Tony and his father. A prison sentence will literally shut him up for a while. Colin then stood up and moved to the door. 'There is one other person you need to thank,' and opening the door said, 'Come in Margaret.'

Margaret the cleaner from Alix's house in Ely walked in with a smile on her face.

Colin following her caught the look of astonishment on Alix's face. 'Margaret has been in our employ for several years and is an expert in electronic eavesdropping devices. She quite frankly bugged your house so we knew everything that was going on, and we could see all your visitors and hear what they had to say. She also placed tracking devices in the soles of your shoes, which sadly were removed when you were detained in the cellar, so we had to rely on Mary to find you and bring the opposition to us so to speak.

He grinned, 'Alix you need to be more careful about whom you employ without checking more than one reference, although I thought ours were rather good. Had you checked them all, you would only have spoken to one of our friends anyway!!

'Margaret, 'Alix asked 'Did you scan and print the letter? You were almost sacked because you moved the printer, rearranged some of the briefcase contents and left the printer on, because I did work out that it had to be you, but thank you anyway.

As Margaret was allowed to leave, Alix added 'I'll be needing a new cleaner I suppose, which is a pity because you are very good.' She smiled and left.

'Before you give me any other surprises, what about Jenny the nurse I met at the Chateau, who turned up at school, and then reappeared with Colonel Peterson, and my double?'

'That's an interesting one,' Colin replied, 'What I can tell you is the eye transplant thing was rubbish. Even the iris transplant was almost certainly fiction because even a partial failure would have doomed them. As to the woman herself, she has disappeared off our radar, but I can tell you there is no such QARANC officer. We do have a very good view of

her in the Chateau, from one of our cameras, and as far as I'm aware her identity is being worked on as we speak. Your double was a bit scary, but we've found out it was cleverly done using a new type of latex, which our scientists have now got their sticky hands on, so they are grateful to you for that.'
Turning to the pile of papers on the coffee table Colin handed one sheet to each of the three guests. 'Please sign where I have marked,' by way of explanation, 'this just says you'll be strung up if you ever reveal anything you've heard or seen here.' He smiled 'It's just an official secrets thing, Mary and Alain are familiar with it, Alix, you just sign it, and remember not to sell your story to the newspapers, or we will be forced to kill you.'
He smiled and added to a shocked looking Alix, 'Only kidding!!'
'Now let me tell you how things are, as we sit here. I will announce to the press that all three of you are being released on police bail pending further investigations. You have not yet been charged, but we will infer that at worst it will be under 'Conspiracy to defraud.'
This will allow you to return to your lives, although Alix you will have to expect that things will never be the same again.'
Colin then suggested that Mary and Alain should leave. There was an awkward moment as they left, with Alix promising he would come over to see

them within a few days, although, and it brought a smile to their faces, he would be bringing a new lawyer, if he could find one.
After they had gone, Colin asked Alix to sit himself down again.
'I'm sure you have more questions?'
'Well yes' he asked 'How do I get my hands on all the documents that Tony Edwards held for me?'
'Already sorted, we've taken the liberty of finding you a new law firm in Cambridge, called,' with that he rummaged in the inside pocket of his jacket and brought out a business card. 'Wilson and Gromoff.' Colin studied the card for a moment.
'Alan Wilson has handled some delicate matters for us in the past, so you can trust him, and better still you'll like him too, in fact I think he's an old boy of your school. He already has everything that was on file in Ely so all you need to do is make a phone call.'
Colin then added 'Look we know there will be a problem on your return to School. Your headmaster isn't an easy man, and I can't just say you've been released without a stain on your character, because that will still leave doubts about your right to be the Tsar, and the gold that may or may not be in the vault.' As Alix tried to interrupt Colin held up his hand.
'I know, and you know what is in there, but the world must not find out. You will undoubtedly

come to some decision at some point in the future about what is to be done with it but be warned if the Russians and others think the gold is in the vault and you don't have an heir, your life is safe. You and your eyes are the only means of access, so don't forget that. Right now, they aren't at all sure, so let's keep it that way.

Look' he added, 'what is going to happen is that in a couple of weeks we will make a press release absolving you of all blame, saying that you were perfectly innocent of everything you were accused of. We will have to add that you were both naive and very foolish but nothing more.'

Alix shook his head, 'Is that the best you can do, because that isn't going to help me get me with my headmaster. I'm certain it's the sack for bringing the school into disrepute.'

'Well Alix there are a couple of things that might help..'

CHAPTER 34

Two hours later Alix left the safety of the house the way he had arrived, in the back of a chauffeured vehicle with a blanket over his head. He realised this was so he couldn't ever compromise the safe house in which he had been an unwilling guest. Duly on the lunchtime news complete with photographs came the announcement that all three of them had been released on police bail pending further enquiries but they could expect to be charged with conspiracy to defraud.

He then spent a busy couple of days tying up loose ends, and sorting his finances out, when he heard on the 6 o' clock news the short announcement that Alix McBride, Mary Nallen and Alain Nallen were not to be charged.

The local Eastern Daily Press the next morning had a photograph of Alix on the front page, which must have been taken at a School Christmas Party. He had a silly hat on his head, and the headline in the paper said

Schoolteacher Taken for a Fool

King's School Ely teacher Alix McBride has been released from Police bail without charge after his alleged involvement in a multi-billion pound fraud. Police and Home Office sources said Mr. McBride had been very naive and stupid, and they

felt they would be unable to get enough evidence to bring a prosecution in a Court of Law, but the file would remain open.

It is understood the King's School Ely Board of Governors will meet shortly to discuss Mr. McBride's future at the school. One governor, who didn't wish to be named, was quoted as saying 'His position is absolutely untenable. He has brought the school into disrepute through his greed and stupidity, and that is unforgiveable

This was followed almost immediately by a phone call from the headmaster's secretary, telling him the School Governors and the headmaster wanted to see him at 12 noon prompt. He was to report initially to the headmaster's office, and she stated the Secretary to the Governors had recommended he bring a lawyer.

Alix in his best dark suit, and carrying his grandmother's briefcase, as if it weighed a ton, crept unnoticed into the headmaster's office at 11.55 am prompt, to be asked to take a seat, by a very unsmiling secretary.

At twelve on the dot, the door to the left of the headmaster's office opened, revealing George Kirby who had been secretary to the Governors as long as Alix could remember. Normally a cheerful soul he had a look of thunder, and there wasn't even a greeting, just 'Come this way.'

The Governors were drawn up and down sides of a long, beautiful mahogany table. At the top sat the Chairman of the Governors Sir Geoffrey Dawson, with the headmaster to his left, and the Secretary to his right. Alix saw not one friendly face.

He noticed there were two seats at his end of the table, and the secretary motioned to him to sit down saying 'No lawyer Mr. McBride?'

'No, and I'll not take a seat if you don't mind, because I suspect this will not take long.'

He placed the briefcase on the end of the table, and before the Chairman of the Governors had a chance to say anything Alix commenced speaking in a low but perfectly steady voice.

'I have not come here to defend myself. That would quite obviously be a waste of effort on my part. I am certain you feel I have in some way brought the school into disrepute, and four of our pupils into great danger.' At this there were almost growls, certainly more than mutterings down the length of the table.

'All I will say is this. If any of you never knew your father, and discovered the grave of a grandfather you knew nothing about, there isn't one of you who wouldn't want to know more, even at the cost of finding the proverbial skeletons in the cupboard. That is all that I've done. The fact that I could be the great grandson of Tsar Nicholas the 2nd is either fortunate or unfortunate, and the fact that I may or may not have inherited incredible wealth is neither here nor there. The kidnapping of the boys was certainly not my fault.'

At that point a very red-faced man in the middle on the left hand side of the table shouted an interruption. 'This Tsar business is just a load of poppycock. You've been caught attempting to steal a huge amount of money and got off because of some legal technicalities, so don't try to give us all these lies and excuses.'

At this point there were mutterings of approvals, and more growls around the table.

Alix then quite calmly opened his briefcase, and brought out a crisp cream linen envelope, and a small heavy oblong parcel, lifted up out of the briefcase by its two handles. He felt the four governors closest to him pull back almost as if he was producing a bomb, and he smiled.

'Gentlemen I can see your minds are completely closed, and suspect you came to a decision to insist I resign from the staff here, before I ever entered the room.

Well, I'm not prepared to argue with you, even though you all know where my loyalties lie. After all, as you are well aware I have spent most of my life here man and boy. Even to infer I would do anything deliberately to bring this school into disrepute is laughable.'

As he was talking Alix moved down the table and handed what to all intents and purposes was his resignation letter over to the Chairman.
'Please read this aloud to your colleagues.'
The chairman sliced open the letter with what looked like a mother of pearl fruit knife taken from his waistcoat pocket and began to read.
As he read his eyebrows almost disappeared into his hairline.
'From the Office of the Prime Minister.
This country owes a debt of gratitude to Mr. Alix McBride who at all times in the past few days has acted with immense courage in the face of great personal threats. He has played a large part in the apprehending of Agents of a foreign power and ensuring the future stability of the world's gold reserves. You should accept as the truth the information he has given you, and I would like to think you will be able to find a way to allow him to return to do a job he loves without a stain on his character.'
The Chairman then almost gasped.
'Dictated by and signed personally by the Prime Minister.'

To say there was a shocked and stunned silence in the room was an understatement.

Alix by this time had taken his place at the end of the table nearest the door where he had left the small oblong box with two carrying handles.

'If I may wait outside whilst you all have a chat. I'm advised by the authorities in London, that I should not answer any questions, nor will I, but trust the letter will do all my answering for me.'

With that Alix left the room, and sat in the small chair outside the door, noticing the school secretary's reluctance to catch his eye.

In less than two minutes he was ushered back into the hallowed presence of the Governors.

The atmosphere was totally different from a few minutes ago, indeed he was greeted by friendly smiles, but he still refused to take the seat offered. The Chairman rose to his feet. 'Look Alix on behalf of all the Governors I'd like to apologise for our hastiness. We really had no idea what you have been through, and what you have done for us all. I only hope we can return to the good relationship we all had with you before.

Alix looked at the Chairman with a lot less than respect in his eyes.

'I don't think that will ever be possible, having had some time to gather my thoughts outside. However, you all know the very high regard in which I hold this school. It is only because of that regard will I return, and there is one essential condition I must have accepted by the Governing Body without reservation before I return to the classroom.'

With that Alix walked back up the table to the headmaster carrying his small but obviously heavy parcel by the two handles.

Handing it over to him he said, 'Headmaster please open this up, but I think you need to place it on the table first, because it is very heavy.'

It took about half a minute for the headmaster to unwrap the parcel, and when he did there was an involuntary gasp from all the Governors.

Alix smiled. 'Yes, gentleman that is a gold bar, a 400 troy ounce gold bar to be precise, and worth at today's prices in excess of £300,000.'

Alix looked at the headmaster 'Mr. James I know you have several language degrees, are you able to decipher the writing on the gold bullion bar.'

'Yes, it's Russian.'

Alix smiled 'Perhaps any last doubts you have about my honesty will now disappear.'

He looked at the Governors, 'Here is my one condition.

I am prepared to finance the school to the tune of 40 million pounds sterling, on the condition it is used to build and maintain a new house, which I wish to be named 'Chaesar House' in memory of my grandfather's orphanage.

Having said that I see the Bishop's House is on the market, and I'm sure it could be easily modified.

Also, there are to be 17 Chaesar Scholars, with 100% funding of school fees for children from married families whose father or mother has died, and who lack the income for this kind of privileged education.'

By way of explanation Alix added 'This is by way of a memorial to the 17 children who died under false names in a war that was not of their choosing, having been brought up in an orphanage far from their home, after their parents, and in some cases their sisters were cold bloodedly drowned probably in front of them. I intend to give each scholarship the Christian and Surname of the innocent Russian who died, because without them I wouldn't be here today. I hope that in the future, the pupils of this School will keep their memory alive. '

The silence that greeted this announcement was total.

'Finally, before I go home and let you discuss this, there is one more condition, which I forgot to mention. This donation is anonymous, and difficult as this might be, I don't want one word of this discussed outside these four walls.' Then pointing at the Governor's Secretary,

'I suggest that you burn your notes.'

With that Alix turned and left the room, sweeping up his briefcase as he left silently thanking Colin Stewart again for his timely and accurate advice.

POSTSCRIPT

Alix gave himself until the following Monday to get his life back in order. He made an early decision to talk to the dozens of press and television cameras gathered outside his door, whilst refusing to answer any questions about the supposed vast fortune, he nevertheless felt they had gone away happy with the story he told.

Once again Alix had cause to be grateful to Colin for the misinformation he had spread about the vault in Blumeur's Bank, because many of the questions he answered had been about his disappointment on finding the vault empty.

Also, much of the attention left Alix when it was announced that Mr. And Mrs. Edwards, plus Tony, and Charles Speed had all been charged under the Official Secrets Act of Passing Information to a foreign power. In addition, several middle and high ranking civil servants had been hauled in for questioning, so the heat was definitely off.

His return to teaching went relatively quietly and he reconciled himself to the fact that his pupils would never again refer to him as 'Sir'.

He was now very firmly 'Tsar', although they did in fairness make it sound more like a parade ground sergeant major shouting at an officer cadet, than deliberate cheek. Alix by and large let it pass.

It was however about a month back into teaching, just when Alix felt the storm clouds were beginning to pass, when there was a ring on his front doorbell early one Sunday Morning.

A little bleary eyed, but thankfully dressed and shaved, he answered the door.

A woman was standing a few yards back from the door, who must have been in her middle forties, and looked vaguely familiar.

'Hello Alix.'

He looked at her again, and it must have been the blank look on his face.

'You don't remember me, do you?' and she turned her lips down and frowned in a kind of pout. He looked at her again, she was certainly attractive, and she was definitely familiar.

'I'm really sad, for I'm Anna, don't you remember me from University?'

In a flash he was a student again, as he remembered a fun girl his mother really approved of, who vanished back to Ireland at the end of their first year and never returned. He was heartbroken because he had been in love for the only time in his life, and in fact the speed his heart was beating told him he still felt the same.

A moment of awkwardness.

In a slightly hesitant voice Alix said, 'Do come in, and I'll put the kettle on.'

At that moment Anna stepped to the left, and a young man came out from the right side of the door where he had been standing hidden from view. Anna smiled self-consciously.
'Willie, I don't think you've met your father. Alix you won't know our son, born after I left Cambridge and named Willie Peterson McBride.

Printed in Great Britain
by Amazon